D0965833

WHEN A CHILD IS BORN

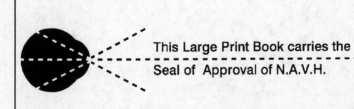

This Large Print Book carries the
Seal of Approval of N.A.V.H.

WHEN A CHILD IS BORN

A REGENCY YULETIDE COLLECTION

VIRGINIA BROWN,
JO ANN FERGUSON,
KAREN FRISCH
AND SHARON SOBEL

THORNDIKE PRESS

A part of Gale, Cengage Learning

GALE
CENGAGE Learning·

Farmington Hills, Mich • San Francisco • New York • Waterville, Maine
Meriden, Conn • Mason, Ohio • Chicago

GALE
CENGAGE Learning®

LIBRARY OF CONGRESS CATALOGING-IN-PUBLICATION DATA

Names: Brown, Virginia, 1947– Child of mine. | Ferguson, Jo Ann. What child is this. | Frisch, Karen, 1955— Through the eyes of a child. | Sobel, Sharon. Baby's first Christmas.
Title: When a child is born : a regency yuletide collection / by Virginia Brown, Jo Ann Ferguson, Karen Frisch, Sharon Sobel.
Description: Large Print edition. | Waterville, Maine : Thorndike Press Large Print, 2016. | Series: Thorndike Press large print clean reads
Identifiers: LCCN 2016030523| ISBN 9781410494238 (hardback) | ISBN 1410494233 (hardcover)
Subjects: LCSH: Christmas stories, American. | Large type books. | BISAC: FICTION / Historical. | GSAFD: Regency fiction.
Classification: LCC PS648.C45 W47 2016 | DDC 813/.0108334—dc23
LC record available at https://lccn.loc.gov/2016030523

Published in 2016 by arrangement with BelleBooks, Inc.

Printed in Mexico
1 2 3 4 5 6 7 20 19 18 17 16

TABLE OF CONTENTS

■ ■ ■ ■

CHILD OF MINE?

BY VIRGINIA BROWN

■ ■ ■ ■

In memory of my son Michael

CHAPTER ONE

Hampshire England, 1812

The Honorable Robert Bray, now Baron Braxton, stepped out of The White Hart Inn on the Exeter Road, tugged on his leather gloves, and pulled his greatcoat more closely around him. It was bitterly cold. Christmas was three weeks away, and he was travelling home to Wiltshire to spend it with his mother, sisters, and brother. A daunting thought.

They would smother him with memories and expectations, something he had successfully avoided until the past year. Even before his father's death, he had not felt at home in the ancestral manor, not felt at home with his family. Nothing had happened to change them, yet he felt as if he had changed in some inexplicable way that he could not undo. Perhaps war did that to a man. He felt aimless, at home now only on the battlefield, yet he'd had to relinquish his commission to return to an England he no longer knew. Now he would endure weeks of family celebrations, all because he had yielded to his youngest sister's heartfelt pleas to come be with them in their first Christmas season without their father. It was going to be difficult.

"If there is any justice in this world, they'll be distracted from maudlin lamentations by a comet or the latest London gossip," he muttered as he neared his coach. He dreaded emotional scenes. There had been more than enough of them in the past twelve months.

Henry, his coachman, scolded a young woman with a bundle of flowers in her arms, chasing her away from the carriage. "Go on with you, girl. His lordship doesn't need any flowers."

Casting a quick glance in Braxton's direction, the girl ran across cobbled stones toward the rear of the inn, her hooded cloak flapping around her thin body. Ferris, his footman, opened the door for him, and he stepped up into the coach and settled back against plush velvet squabs. On the opposite seat, boxes and baskets and tins of biscuits were stacked neatly. Peace offerings, perhaps. Gifts to salve his conscience for staying away from his well-meaning but often

12

overwhelming family.

Well-oiled springs eased the forward lurch of the coach as it pulled away from the yard and moved out onto the Exeter Road. Warmth emanated from hot bricks placed in a tin box at his feet, and small lanterns illuminated the interior. He put his head back against the velvet, and thought about going to sleep but knew he could not. In only a few hours, he would be at his ancestral home, and any hope of having time to himself would vanish until he left again for London.

Propping his booted feet upon the seat opposite him, he stretched his long legs out and tried to get comfortable. Glass windows reflected his face, and he saw a man he didn't recognize anymore. The years of fighting on the Continent had aged him. He no longer looked as young and naïve as he'd once been, though he was still only in his mid-twenties. He'd seen things that no man should see, heard things no human being should have to hear, and done things he didn't want to remember. It was said war was hell, and he knew it to be true.

The man staring back at him was vaguely familiar: gray eyes, dark hair in need of a trim, clean-shaven, but the mouth rarely smiled lately. A scar cut over one thick brow, dissecting the arch, giving him a sardonic appearance he rather liked. It reflected how he viewed the world these days. Gone were his once-foolish expectations of fair play, justice, and the proper order of things. He had gained a more jaded perception of reality now, one that had been earned on the battlefield and in war council rooms.

A faint mewling sound interrupted his musings, and he glanced out the other window to see the source. Nothing but dark gray skies and shop lights met his gaze. It didn't occur again, and he laid his head back against the cushion. Mud smeared his jackboots, and he stared at them idly. He noticed a faint blot of muck on the pale material of his breeches as well, and he rubbed at it. Winston, his valet, would be disconsolate if he wasn't properly turned out at every moment. He found that amusing, if often annoying. Obviously, his valet needed an education in the military college of survival. Clean breeches were not high on the list of priorities.

The mewling sound was louder this time, jerking his attention to the boxes and baskets on the opposite seat. Curse it all, Henry must have left the coach door open and an expectant cat had got in. It'd be all he'd need if the animal gave birth on the

Kashmir scarf he'd bought for his mother.

Leaning forward, he peered into the open basket that held bread, cheeses, some excellent port, and two boxes of comfits for his sisters. No cat or kittens. A quick search of the wooden box holding wine gave up no stowaways, and he began to wonder if he was hearing things when he reached for a basket he didn't recall seeing before. It held a plaid blanket, and a motion beneath the wool left him in no doubt that the cat had chosen this spot for her hiding place.

When he drew back the wool, he half-expected a feline to leap out at him, or at least hiss, but what he found was even more unexpected and shocking. A cherubic face gazed back at him, wide blue eyes regarding him solemnly, dark curls framing a tiny head. The baby seemed just as surprised as he was. Then a smile curved the rosebud mouth and it made the mewling noise again, this time sounding more like a soft coo.

Stunned, Robert didn't move. Couldn't move. All he could do was stare. A thousand thoughts went through his head in the space of a few moments, and as the carriage rocked faster through the village, it occurred to him that someone must have put their child in the wrong coach. No doubt, at this very moment, they were calling the King's

15

Guard to report an abduction, or at the very least, sending out searchers for the coach that held their unfortunate baby.

He rapped sharply on the roof to alert Henry, and a small door slid open for Ferris, the footman, to peer inside.

"Yes, my lord?"

"Ask Henry to stop the coach immediately. We must go back to the inn at once."

"Yes, my lord."

The door shut, and Robert looked back at the baby. A tiny fist waved in the air, then the smile started to tremble, and the baby began to wail. He banged again on the roof, harshly this time, and when the door once more slid open, he ordered the footman to come at once.

If Henry wondered why his lordship was behaving strangely, he was too well-trained to show it. The coach stopped, and Robert had a glimpse of closed shops and a church steeple as the door opened and Ferris appeared in the opening.

"Yes, my lord?"

"Do you know anything about babies?"

Alerted by the now loud wails of a child, Ferris leaned into the coach, his eyes widening with surprise. "Not much, my lord. I do have younger brothers, but don't see them much."

"Come up. See what you can do for this child, while we go back to the inn and find its mother. This is intolerable. People shouldn't misplace their children."

"Yes, my lord."

But an hour later, Robert realized that returning to the inn had been pointless. No one knew the child, no one claimed a child missing, no one would take the child. The portly innkeeper gave him a look of mild reproach when Robert suggested he should keep it, since the child had been abandoned in the inn yard.

"It is not my responsibility, my lord. Take it to the vicarage. They'll no doubt look after it 'til its mam can be found."

Robert thought that sounded like an excellent idea. He had Ferris tote the child and basket back out to the coach, and they went immediately to All Hallow's Church on the edge of the village. A knock at the vicarage door was answered by a woman with a kind face and curious brown eyes when she saw the baron and his footman.

"Are you leaving a charity basket, my lord?" she inquired with a smile. "It is very kind of you."

"Yes. Well, er, no, not exactly. That is, I am leaving the basket, but it is not for charity. May I speak with the vicar?"

17

"Yes, my lord. Do come in. Would you like some refreshment, my lord?"

He politely refused and went to stand by the fireplace, removing his gloves and hat as he waited for the vicar to arrive. The woman he assumed to be the vicar's wife shooed a small child away from the basket the footman had set upon the floor near the door, and the little girl looked up at her from beneath a mop of burnished brown curls.

"But I want to see the baby."

"A baby? Why, there's no such thing, Prudence. What would his lordship be doing with a baby?"

Just as Robert opened his mouth to verify that he'd indeed brought a baby, the child announced its own presence with a loud screech like a cat whose tail had been caught in the door. He winced. The vicar's wife stared with an open mouth and went immediately to the basket. She knelt beside it and pulled back the plaid wool blanket. She gave a small start and turned to look at him.

"Why, it is a baby. My lord?"

He felt suddenly like a callow youth trying to explain a misdeed. "It was abandoned. It was suggested I bring it to you, so here I am. Is the vicar available?"

Desperation began to turn into annoy-

18

ance. He had no idea who or why someone had thought it appropriate to abandon their child in his coach, but now he wanted only to safely place the baby and be gone.

The vicar's wife nodded. "I sent Tommy to fetch him, so he will be here soon. May I see the wee one?"

"Of course. Maybe you can get it to stop crying. We've done all we can."

It was true. Ferris had jostled the infant, patted it, even sang a little song to it. And while the footman's ministrations had helped for a few moments, the instant he stopped, the child cried again. In only a short space of time, Robert was at his wits' end.

Apparently the vicar's wife had far more experience in that area. She picked up the baby and unwrapped it, and when something fell out of the blanket, she picked it up. As she rocked the child, and cooed to it, the baby stopped crying. Sliding an expert hand between the folds swaddling it, she announced it needed a clean clout. Then she handed Robert the folded, sealed sheet of cheap vellum she'd found with the child.

"I'll go put a dry clout on the wee one. Is this addressed to you, my lord?"

Puzzled, he took it. *Lord Braxton* was scrawled across it in an inelegant but quite

19

legible style. He nodded. "Yes. Where did you get it?"

"It was in the baby's blanket. Let me see what I can find to make it happy and I will be back, if you do not mind waiting here. My husband should be home very shortly."

Nodding, he unfolded the vellum and read the contents scribbled on the inside. A cold chill that had nothing to do with the weather went through him. He reread the note again, just to be certain he understood.

Lord Braxton, I can no longer care for your child. Please see to her welfare. She is a good baby, and I know you will be a good father to her.

That was it. No name for the little girl, no signature, no hint of who might have written it — just the news that he was a father blazing out at him from the ink that was slightly smudged. Paralyzed by amazement mixed with consternation, he searched his memory for any possible clue as to who might be the mother. He'd not been back from the Continent long enough for it to be recent, and if his calculations were close, it would have had to occur during his bereavement furlough when his father had died. That had happened right after Christmas, so the baby would have to be, what — at least two months old? No wait — there was his return well before Christmas, when his father had first fallen ill, and he'd come at his behest to help tend to legal affairs that still needed attention.

So who was the mother? It wasn't as if he made a habit of tumbling innocent girls or naïve milkmaids, and he had a strict policy of meeting his basic needs with those who knew how to take care of such matters with no cumulative complications — like infants. There was the actress, but as far as he knew, she'd shown no sign of increasing, and that was over with before . . . Was it Susannah? No, it couldn't be her. The widow had recently married again and they'd had such a brief fling between husbands, he didn't think he could be responsible for a baby. Besides, she was up in Scotland now with her new husband, not in Hampshire or even in Wiltshire.

"My lord? May I help you?" a masculine voice inquired, and he looked up to see a man who must be the vicar approach him with a faint smile. "I do hope I'm not intruding on bad news?" When Robert didn't reply, the vicar gestured to the letter. "You seem to be distraught."

"Oh. Yes. Well — it is bad news of a sort, I suppose." He frowned. How did he explain this now? It was one thing to leave a nameless child at a vicarage, but quite another to abandon a child someone claimed he'd fathered.

"I am sorry to hear it, my lord." The vicar chose a chair close to the fire and sank down into it. "Please sit down, if you will. There's a chair here by the fire. My son tells me that you've requested my presence. Does it have to do with your bad news, my lord?"

"Well, yes. A child was abandoned in my coach this afternoon. I am bringing it to you."

The vicar's brow rose, and the man regarded him over the tips of his fingers as he pressed his palms together and placed his hands against his chin. "Indeed? And does that letter relate to the child?"

He wanted to say no. It would have been easier. No blame would be attached to him and he wouldn't be expected to do anything other than leave the child in the care of people who would tend her needs. But honesty forbade that. He would not lie, and truth be told, he could not duck any obligations he may have incurred, knowingly or not.

"Yes, it does. Your wife found this letter in the blankets. It claims that the child is mine. I do not, however, know that to be true."

"Ah." The vicar gazed at him a moment longer, and said, "How long have you known the mother?"

"I have no idea who gave birth to this child. However, in the interest of fairness, I will be most happy to leave a donation for its welfare."

"That is most generous of you, my lord."

Relief eased his tension, and Robert nodded, but before he could suggest a suitable amount, the vicar continued, "But we cannot keep the child. We are a poor parish and have far too many needy widows and orphans as it is. While you honor us with your faith that we would give the child a good upbringing, it may be best if you care for your baby in your own way."

Shock was swiftly followed by irritation. "I am not unaware of my duty, but I have no assurance that this child is mine. Nor do I wish to care for a child."

"I understand, my lord. Perhaps we do not always do what we should, but then we must accept the consequences of our actions as best we can."

Heat flooded his face as Robert realized he was being schooled in moral conscience by the vicar. It was not completely undeserved.

Whatever he might have responded went

23

unsaid as the vicar's wife came back to the parlor, announcing that the little girl was now in better humor. In a very short time, Robert found himself back in his coach with the baby, a supply of clean clouts, some toys, and a jug of goat's milk.

It was the longest journey he could ever recall taking. He and Ferris dealt with the fussy infant who didn't like goat's milk and wailed the rest of the way through Hampshire. She didn't like being in the basket, didn't like being held, and didn't like anything but chewing on a toy lamb or staring out the window. Neither man could manage to arrange a clean clout that would stay on the child, and he thought that he'd had less trouble learning how to harness a horse to a cannon than he had putting a square of linen on a baby's bottom. It was humbling.

By the time the coach stopped in front of Heath Hall, he had smears of sour milk mixed with the noxious contents of the clout on his breeches, boots, and coat sleeve. His white cravat had been pulled loose and hung like a flag of surrender from his neck, two of his buttons were torn free — one having caused panic when it was thought the little girl had ingested it — and most of the gilt braid on Ferris's footman's uniform had been unraveled and dangled in strings. The baby, however, survived it all in what seemed to be an excellent humor, and fell asleep just as the coach turned into the long, curving carriageway leading up to the house.

Robert and Ferris eyed one another across the sleeping child as the door opened, both of them hissing, "Shush!" at the same time to the startled footman who had come to greet them. Ferris watched glumly as Robert descended from the coach, leaving him instructions to take the baby to the servants' quarters when she woke and not before, and he would decide what must be done the next day.

"Under no circumstances are you to inform my mother or sisters of this child's existence," he added, fixing Ferris with a fierce glare that earned a nod. Once Robert was certain his directions would be followed, he pulled his greatcoat around him to hide the damage done by the tiny terror, and went into the hall.

CHAPTER TWO

Miss Clare Seaton perched on the piano bench next to her best friend Emma Bray as she attempted to play a Christmas carol in an entirely new key so that Clare could sing. Emma's efforts were highly commendable, but less than successful. Both laughed at the discordant sounds produced, while Emma's brother Charles and his twin sister Catherine listened with pained faces reflecting their dismay.

It was a familiar reaction. Clare and Emma had been best friends since girlhood, and their escapades as children had frequently summoned pained, dismayed reactions from their families and friends. Sir Ralph Seaton, Clare's father, had been a schoolboy at Eton with the late baron, Lord Braxton, and their families had remained close over the years. It had made for some lively holidays.

Clare exchanged a mirthful glance with

Emma when Charles complained, "Must we sing deadly dull carols?" She lifted her eyebrows and Emma immediately struck up a funereal dirge.

Charles groaned. "You've made your point. Dash it, Clare, don't encourage her."

"I wouldn't dream of it," Clare replied demurely, and he snorted disbelief.

"Emma dear," said Lady Braxton, as she sat before the cheery fire with a counterpane of needlework. "Play something more sprightly. You know how Robert detests melancholy music."

Emma tilted her blond head, looking prim and proper in her mourning clothes, but Clare knew better. She needed little encouragement to be sprightly, a fact Clare greatly appreciated.

"Robert isn't here yet," Emma argued. "And we must remember to call him by his proper title now, Braxton, instead of his Christian name as we have always done."

"Well, it is correct, although such a bother," her mother replied serenely. "I cannot help but think of him as Robert. It takes such getting accustomed to, doesn't it? I mean, the changes one must accommodate when there's been a death."

Clare sympathized. She'd lost her mother several years before, and was well-acquainted with the customs of grief and ravages of loss. Now that Papa was off in the Army again, with the fighting on the Peninsula having escalated, her household consisted of herself, several servants, a boorish cousin, and a widowed sister who had come home with three small children after her husband's unexpected death two years before. Clare would have stayed home for the holidays to be with her two nieces and young nephew, but Sarah had taken it into her head to take them to her late husband's parents instead. Left with only Marcus, an arrogant cousin far too accustomed to being held in high regard he did not deserve, she had defected to the Bray family home for the holidays. With their period of mourning almost at an end, she looked forward to the season.

And if the truth be told, she highly anticipated Robert's return. Emma's oldest brother had been the bane of their existence when they had been children, but she viewed him in a quite different light since she had seen him for the first time in years at his father's wake. The changes in his manner and appearance had intrigued her. He was no longer the pesky older brother, but a handsome man with a somewhat grave countenance and haunted eyes. Something

28

made her want to erase those shadows, replace them with laughter.

"He's here," Charles announced from the front window, and Emma let out a squeal of delight and raced for the entrance hall. Clare waited in the parlor, not wanting to intrude on a family reunion. Lord Braxton had been gone for ten months this time before giving up his commission to return home and take his place as the new baron.

Even Lady Braxton looked excited as she cast aside her needlework and stood, one hand trembling slightly as she held to the back of her chair and waited for her eldest son to come to her. She stood with back straight, chin lifted, black-and-gray-threaded hair austerely arranged beneath a widow's cap, and her black silk mourning gown fitting her still-slender figure.

Chaos attended the baron's progress from the entrance hall as Emma, four of her dogs, and Catherine fussed over him, the girls chattering away and the dogs barking until he uttered a short, "Hush." The dogs quieted, though they did not stop bounding around his feet. Emma clung to his arm, and Catherine brushed her hand over his coat as they escorted him into the parlor.

Snow dusted the shoulders of his caped greatcoat and frosted the sable strands of hair that tumbled over his forehead. If not for that touch of boyishness and a faint curve of his mouth that indicated amusement, he would have looked quite stark and forbidding.

"You were expected hours ago, you know," Emma chided, and he lifted a dark brow.

"I was unaware I had given an hour for my arrival," he said dryly.

He was even more handsome than Clare remembered, and her heart gave an odd lurch. *None of that,* she silently admonished herself. Childhood attachments should remain in the past.

"Oh, you did not," Emma replied. "I just worked out the time myself from previous trips. Were the roads beastly?"

"Not yet, but they soon will be. Here, do give me room to walk. Why are so many dogs in the house when they should all be out in the kennels?"

As he waded through a pack of furry pets that had swelled to six from what Clare could see, Emma made excuses for her menagerie and Catherine shooed a cat from atop the settee to give her brother a place to sit. He gave the spot a brief glance before his gaze found Charles, and he paused.

Leaning against the fireplace mantel, Charles teased lightly, "Ah, the prodigal son returns to a hero's welcome. All we need are flowers strewn at his feet."

Robert's glance at his brother was full of humor. "Did you set these creatures on me? Call them off."

"Oh, no. I rather enjoy you being the focus of their attention instead of me. It grows a bit tiresome after a while."

"We never fuss over you, Charles," said Emma indignantly. "You're always here."

Emma's pale blond hair and fair skin were a striking contrast to Robert's dark hair and complexion, and she was petite where he was tall and lean. Catherine was medium height, willowy of form with a creamy complexion and fine, dark eyes like her mother; she was on the serious side, bookish but not a bluestocking. Her twin Charles was tall like his brother, although with a sturdier build, and saved from homeliness by a charming smile, beautiful blue eyes, and sunny disposition. Clare had always felt very comfortable with all of them, yet waited rather nervously for Robert to take notice of her.

Braxton crossed to his mother, and Lady Braxton presented her cheek for his kiss, her eyes glowing as he bent to press his lips against her cheek. "You're home," she said softly, and he nodded.

31

"Against all odds. I made you a promise I would return, and I have kept it."

"You always keep your promises." She patted his hand, and then her nose crinkled slightly. "Have you been ill, dear?"

"No. Just cramped in a coach for hours — Emma, what are you doing?"

Emma had waylaid a footman entering the house with his arms full of boxes, and gleefully snatched at several packages.

Clare laughed at her obvious delight as she found one in particular. However, Braxton walked over to her and took it from her hands. "These are gifts, and you must wait until they're offered."

"But it's for me, I know it is." Emma paused, leaned forward, then sniffed. "Mama is right. You smell as if you've been ill. Do you still get sick riding in a coach?"

"I outgrew that years ago. Give me back the box."

Pouting, she returned the beribboned parcel and he turned, catching sight of Clare. He paused, his brow lifted. She had stood to one side of the piano, but now that he'd seen her, she stepped forward to drop a small curtsey.

"Clare has come at my invitation to spend the holidays with us. You do recall Miss Seaton?" Emma asked.

The baron's gray eyes lingered on her a moment. "Of course. How could I ever forget? I still have the small scar on my arm from a rabid dog she insisted upon trying to rescue as a reminder of her."

"He wasn't rabid, my lord," Clare said cheerfully. "Just hungry and angry. I warned you not to frighten him."

"So you did. He did a fine job of protecting you from my efforts at playing the white knight."

"Your valiance was not ignored, my lord," Clare replied with a sweet smile. "We named him after you."

His silver eyes gleamed with amusement. She noticed that a scar now bisected his left brow and gave him a rather dangerous look that she wasn't at all certain he deserved. His tone was slightly reproachful. "I remember Bobby quite well. It took me several years to recover from the embarrassment of having a scruffy mutt named for me."

"You seem to be well-recovered," she observed, and he grinned.

"I hide my deepest wounds well."

"Oh pother," scoffed Emma. "Don't lie to Clare. Bobby followed you everywhere. I do believe he missed you more than he did any of us when you went back to school. You're staying until Twelfth Night, aren't you? We have a cracking good masquerade planned."

Lady Braxton gave a sigh. "Emma, your language. Where do you learn these dreadful phrases? They are most unbecoming."

As she spied two more footmen laden with packages, Emma started toward the entrance hall, saying over her shoulder, "Clare gave me a book on how to speak thieves' cant."

While Lady Braxton looked horrified, Charles laughed. Clare hastened to explain. "It is actually a dictionary of sorts on how to understand tradesmen if in London, not a tutorial."

Fanning herself rapidly with a spray of beaded feathers artfully arranged on a jet handle, the baroness remarked that ladies had servants to speak to tradesmen for them, so Clare did not mention that they also intended to use the book for a play they were writing for the Twelfth Night celebrations. Perhaps it was best to save that news for later.

She felt Lord Braxton's gaze narrow on her, and knew that he suspected there was a more detailed explanation, so she refused to look at him, instead watching Emma accost a footman who staggered under the weight of a heavy basket.

"Do take off your greatcoat, Robert," said

34

Lady Braxton. "You must be roasting in here."

"No, I must go to my chambers and clean up. Winston will be aghast if I leave my coat down here."

A faint stench drifted to Clare as she stood close to the baron, and her nose wrinkled slightly. There was a most peculiar scent emanating from his coat — as if milk had gone sour.

Braxton turned abruptly when a thin wail was echoed by Emma's delighted squeal. It was disconcerting, and she looked past him to see her friend reach into a huge wicker basket held by one of the footman. It appeared as if the poor fellow had been in some sort of scuffle, as his uniform was untidy and his expression harried. He stood stock-still and wild-eyed as Emma opened the basket's coverings.

"Did you bring me more kittens, Robert — Oh my heavens! Whatever is this?"

Drawn as much by curiosity as by the sudden arrest of the baron's forward movement, Clare joined Emma, and was quite startled to see her lift a baby from the basket. The child's face was knit in a frown, its lower lip thrust out, with silvery tears clinging to long black lashes. They all turned as if coordinated to stare at Braxton.

He stood in the middle of the room, a most peculiar look on his handsome face. "I'm done up now."

Robert winced when Emma cried, "But wherever did this baby come from?" Matters had just taken a turn for the worse, and he sighed.

"Pixies brought it," Charles suggested. "Or it rode in on dragonfly wings. Unless it was found under a cabbage leaf in the garden. But I admit to curiosity as to why Braxton had it brought inside in a basket."

"Yes, dear," said Lady Braxton, turning to look at her eldest son. "This is most irregular."

Braxton gave Ferris a severe look before saying, "It is a foundling. I attempted to find the mother, to no avail."

"Oh, how delightful," said Emma, and even Catherine, usually self-possessed, cooed at the baby as she bent to touch it lightly on the head. Clare had immediately rescued the baby from Emma's inexpert hands, and showed her the proper way to hold the infant. Robert, however, had the opinion that the child was much sturdier than Clare seemed to think as he recalled the harrowing carriage ride from Hampshire to Heath Hall.

Emma glanced at the baroness as she positioned the baby's head in the crook of her arm. "We can keep it, can we not, Mama? I've never had a baby before."

Charles started laughing, then went into a coughing fit at his mother's quelling glance, while Robert stood silently cursing the fates that had brought him to this juncture. It was an impossible situation.

"You already have ten dogs and probably twenty cats by now" — he said to Emma — "and I am sure you are driving the cook mad filching extra food for them all the time. You do not need anything else that others have to care for, Emma."

"Why, that is a mean thing to say," she retorted indignantly. "I take very good care of all my pets."

"This is a baby, not a dog or cat. No, you cannot keep it."

"I know this may be inconvenient to ask —" said Charles, "But why do you have it?"

"It was left in my coach while I stopped at the White Hart. I came out and didn't know it was in the basket until we were nearly through the village. We returned to the inn, but no one has any idea who the child belongs to. The local vicar would not take it, so I had no choice but to bring it here. It has thrown up on me, my boots, and my coach, so if you will all excuse me, I am going up to my chambers and clean up. Ferris, take the child to Mrs. Seyler. Do not — I repeat, do *not* — allow my sister to keep the baby."

"Mrs. Seyler has gone to her sister's until tomorrow night, dear," said his mother. "Perhaps one of the kitchen maids, or even Mr. Drew, can take it."

He had a brief vision of Mr. Drew, the dignified butler, with the baby's fingers pulling at his nose, and smiled. "No. Let Drew remain inviolate. One of the kitchen maids will suffice."

Escaping upstairs before they could ask any more questions, he allowed Winston to take off his greatcoat and help him out of his jacket, boots, and vest. While Winston went to prepare his bath — a necessity if he was ever to be rid of the smell of clabbered goat's milk — he removed his shirt and breeches. No doubt, they were fit only for burning.

As baron for nearly a year now, he expected his wishes to be at least considered, if not granted. But upon his return downstairs in clean garments, he found his two sisters and Clare playing with the baby on a blanket spread upon the parlor floor. Charles sat nearby, an assessing glitter in his eyes as he regarded his older brother with an odd smile. It was annoying.

His gaze shifted between his sisters and Clare Seaton, and lingered. The awkward child had somehow become a graceful young woman, her fiery hair neatly contained with ribbons and pins instead of flyaway, her bony arms and legs now softly rounded like the rest of her body. He shouldn't dwell too long on that thought, he supposed, and was about to look away when she glanced up at him. Troubled lights gleamed in her fine eyes. Her gaze dropped, and there was an air of disappointment about her that he found puzzling.

"Did I not tell you to leave the baby alone, Emma?" he demanded.

"You said nothing about me taking the baby, however," Clare added calmly, and his jaw clenched in irritation.

"Mere semantics and you know it. Why is the baby here, may I ask?"

"We've named her Guinevere," Emma replied, not at all rattled by his obvious annoyance. "Is she really yours?"

Stunned, he stared at his sisters, grateful his mother had retired to dress for supper. He sought for an answer that wouldn't be a lie but would skirt the truth. Then Emma held up the open letter with his name written on the front, and he sighed. He must have left it in the basket. Careless of him. That explained Clare's air of disappointment and his brother's grim amusement.

"As I have no idea who her mother is, that remains a mystery," he replied shortly.

Emma looked perplexed. "How does that happen? Don't you have to at least be somewhat acquainted with the mother to produce a baby?"

Charles gave a snort of laughter, but he ignored him. His brother was obviously going to be of little help. Still, he had no idea how to broach the subject of babies with Emma. He found himself at a complete loss as to what to say, and was grateful for any intervention.

Clare looked up at him, her deep green eyes carefully empty of emotion as she said, "Perhaps you should inquire again at the White Hart."

He regarded her thoughtfully. Clare and Emma had been the bane of his existence when he'd been a boy. They had played more tricks on him than he cared to remember, and their escapades had often ended with him either unwillingly involved or blamed, so he was rightfully suspicious of her motives. But he had to admit, he'd also contemplated making further inquiries at the inn as soon as possible.

"Yes, Robert," said Lady Braxton as she sailed into the room. "You must make all the inquiries to find the baby's mother. I am quite put out with you, you know. A gentleman does not go 'round making babies."

When Charles gurgled with laughter, Lady Braxton added, "I meant, of course, that a gentleman takes care of his obligations. He does not wag them about in baskets and misplace their mother."

Once more, he ignored Charles, who gasped with the effort to contain his amusement. "I quite agree. I would honor my obligation if it is proven to be mine, but as of yet, I have no idea where the child belongs."

"Guinevere can stay right here with us, do you not agree, Clare?" Emma announced, and her friend pressed her lips together without committing to a reply. But when she looked up, her eyes brimmed with laughter. He found that really irritating.

"That is a ridiculous name, Emma," he said sharply. "You have a dog named Guinevere."

"It's a fine old name. I suppose you can think of a better one?"

"We could call her Emma Clare," he said

scathingly, and to his disgust, neither his sister nor Clare objected.

"Excellent," Emma said, and made the baby laugh by teasing her with the toy lamb tickling her nose. "Emma Clare, you may call me Aunt Emma, and this can be your Cousin Clare. We are so glad to have you as our St. Nicholas Day gift."

"That is not until tomorrow," Charles added. "And if today is any indication, there's no telling what he may gift us with next." Robert shot him a crushing glance. It didn't seem to faze him at all. Draped casually in an overstuffed chair, his brother grinned impudently. "I'm looking forward to playing Hunt the Slipper with our little niece. We can hide it in her cap if the hunter gets too close."

"That'd be cheating," Emma said virtuously.

"Robert," his mother said, and beckoned him to her chair by the fire, "I daresay this will cause scandal. I had begun to think I would never be a grandmother, but now that you've proven yourself capable, I would much prefer you marry and provide a legitimate heir."

Heat scoured him, not from the fire but from discomfiture. "My lady," he said formally, incensed at her doubt he could provide an heir, "this is hardly suitable parlor conversation."

"Well," she said as Mr. Drew came to the door to announce supper, "we can discuss this later, I suppose."

He had no intention of discussing it with her later if at all possible, and wanted only to find the child's mother. Barring that, he wished he could deliver little Emma Clare to a Foundling Home where she could be properly cared for and he could enjoy his Christmas holiday. Well, he thought ruefully, he had hoped for his family to have a distraction from what he'd feared would be overly maudlin emotions, and they certainly did. Yet he now found himself wishing he was back on the battlefield instead of in the awkward situation that confronted him. It would be much more preferable than dealing with the uncertainty of the baby's origins and his possible part in them.

CHAPTER THREE

"Oh, do not glare at me so, Braxton."

Clare bit her lip to stifle a chuckle at her friend's cheeky comment. Emma had plopped the baby into the baron's lap without asking permission, and he gave her an appalled look that fully indicated his emotions. "Take the child," he said curtly, but his sister shook her head.

"No, you hold her while Clare and I bring in our gifts. Don't be churlish. It's St. Nicholas Day and you should be pleasant."

"Why is this child here instead of with the wet nurse I hired?" the baron asked no one in particular. Little Emma Clare stared up at him with an unwinking gaze that he avoided. When she put a small hand on a bright waistcoat button, he shifted her quickly, chiding, "No no, little one. Buttons are inedible. Emma! Come take this child at once."

Instead, Emma grabbed Clare by the hand

and tugged her toward the door, ignoring him as the baron sat bouncing the baby on his knee, looking uncomfortable.

"Are you sure that is wise?" Clare whispered to Emma as they left Braxton in the small drawing room with the baby. "He doesn't look at all pleased."

"Well, if it's his baby, he should learn to be pleased," Emma said practically. "He will be in her life a long time."

That made sense, and Clare sighed. Though it was accepted that gentlemen had liaisons with unchaste women that on occasion produced children, she had been hugely disappointed that Robert would be one of them. His obvious resistance to the baby was understandable under the awkward circumstances, yet she had never considered him to be cruel. And it would be cruel indeed were he to reject his own child.

Troubled, she followed Emma to the library to fetch the gaily festooned packages and gift boxes. Lady Braxton entered with some parcels of her own, and the three of them went back into to the parlor, their arms full. By the time they returned, Robert was pacing the room with the baby in his arms, jiggling her about and pointing out the window as she fussed. Emma paused in the open door, giggling as her brother informed the child, "My mad sister is going to try to keep you but I'll save you from such a fate. She'll have you tricked out in lace collars and sleeping in a basket beside her bed like one of the dogs. Look out there. Your mother is out there waiting for us to find her."

The baby smiled at him and patted his face with a chubby hand, and for a moment, he let her explore his mouth and jawline with tiny fingers. "You needn't think being cute will get you far in life," he said to her as she poked him in the eye and laughed when he winced. "Although you do seem to be quite good at that."

Clare thought it a sweet moment. Despite his obvious reluctance, the baron could not deny a more gentle emotion, and it touched her. She nudged Emma, and they stepped back and then started talking as if they'd just arrived. By the time they entered the parlor, Robert had set the baby down on a blanket and stood with his back to her, looking out the window.

"We brought Emma Clare some gifts, too," Emma said as Clare went straight to the baby and lifted her into her arms. "I have two lace caps, a rattle that Mama said used to be yours, and a little gown that I found packed away in a trunk upstairs.

There are more that we'll have to go through later."

"There's a stuffed horse she can ride when she's older," Clare added as she checked the baby's clout for dampness. "And a lovely old pram for outings."

Robert turned to stare at them as if they'd gone moon-mad. His eyes narrowed and he shook his head. "The child's mother will be found and the infant will be swiftly returned."

Emma looked at the baby in Clare's arms and then looked up at him. "Even if she is a Bray? Will you truly allow a child of your blood to be reared without knowing her family?"

"It's done all the time, Emma," he said brusquely, although a flicker in his eyes gave away his uncertainty.

"That does not make it right. Do you have any idea what happens to children taken to Foundling Homes? Most die before their second birthday. Those who survive are doomed to a life of hard labor and low wages, struggling just to survive."

Clare fully supported Emma's humanitarian causes. Her friend espoused better care for animals, children, and the lower classes that lived in abject poverty. It was an unusual frame of mind for one of Emma's birth, but she seemed to have been born with an over-active conscience, which was one of her most endearing traits, in Clare's opinion. There were so few young women who cared about more than finding a husband or the latest gossip from Almack's.

Lord Braxton regarded his sister with the air of a man who has heard the same speech many times, and she hid a smile at his long-suffering sigh. "But we cannot change the world, Emma. There is a need for chimney sweeps and scullery maids."

"Certainly. There is also a need for better working conditions and higher wages."

The baron glanced at Clare, who couldn't help a smile. Taking pity on him, she set the baby back on her blanket. "It is quite fortunate that there are organizations working to effect just such goals. I am acquainted with a Miss Purslane who has done great work in promoting the well-being of foundlings, and has helped bring about the changes that stopped the Coram Men from their dreadful practices."

"Miss Purslane is connected with the Foundling Hospital, I take it?" the baron asked, and she nodded.

"Yes. If you are familiar with the terrible practice of poor girls paying men to take their babies to the London Foundling

Hospital for them, and how cruelly those babies were disposed of instead, I am certain you will agree that those depredations were best ended. Captain Coram never meant for the hospital he founded to be profitable for ruthless murderers of innocents."

Braxton looked troubled, and glanced at little Emma Clare where she sat on the blanket brandishing a silver rattle. "I had heard of such evils, but thought them just lurid tales."

Clare followed his glance toward the baby. As if sensing their regard, the cherubic face creased in a toothless smile and she gave the rattle a brisk shake. While Clare was no expert, she thought the baby must be nearly six months old, for she could sit up and had some control over her limbs. After making a few discreet inquiries of Emma, Clare had begun to think that perhaps the baron might be innocent of the child's parentage due to his frequent long absences from England. Of course, it was still possible.

At the baffled gloom evident in Braxton's face, she felt compelled to offer her assistance. "Whether it was your intention or not, you have most likely saved this baby from a desperate situation, my lord. I am more than willing to accompany you back to the White Hart to try again to find her mother, if you wish."

"No! If the mother gave her away once, she might do so again," Emma said sharply. "She is best here with us, where we can look after her. Oh, do say you agree, Robert — I mean Braxton. Please, do not be cruel enough to say no."

Lord Braxton stared at his youngest sister with an expression caught between chagrin and dismay. Clare remained silent. The matter had to be settled between the two of them as to the baby's eventual fate, although she suspected that Robert had not changed so greatly that he would ignore the child's plight. She fondly recalled the boy who had forgiven the dog that bit him.

So she wasn't at all surprised at Lord Braxton's reply. "Think of the child's mother, Emma. Should she not be given the chance to reunite with her daughter? Perhaps there are circumstances we can relieve for her. Few mothers really want to give up their children."

He had an excellent point, and Clare saw, from Emma's crestfallen expression, that her sweet-natured friend agreed.

"Very well," said Emma with a sigh. "First thing tomorrow we shall go back to the White Hart and search for her. Although, you must promise me that if we cannot find her, you will not do anything drastic. Please? If she is your child, she must be properly reared, and if her mother is incapable, we must see to it."

A faint smile touched the baron's mouth. "Whether she is my child or not, we will be certain she is properly reared. Does that make you feel better?"

Emma brightened. "Oh, rather! I knew you would not be so mean as to send her away."

"Emma, I never said —"

Bubbling over with enthusiasm, Emma was no longer listening. She scooped up the baby and buried her face in the folds between her neck and shoulder, making the child giggle. Clare tilted her head to watch Robert as he surrendered to the inevitable, no doubt marshaling his forces for another skirmish at a later time.

Then his gaze found hers, and he gave the barest shake of his head, as if to say he yielded to a temporary truce. Clare smiled, and he smiled in return. Emma was a force of nature at times, her good heart often overriding common sense, but Robert had rarely been able to resist his sister's pleas. When they'd all been children, that trait had often gotten him into trouble.

Now that they were adults, it only re-affirmed Clare's good opinion of him.

St Nicholas Day supper and gift exchanges were made merrier by the lovely things Lord Braxton had brought from London. A Kashmir scarf for his mother, ribbons and yards of silk for Emma and Catherine, and leather gloves for Charles, as well as comfits for all, even a box he declared just for Clare. Since he had not known she'd be present, she was quite certain he had intended it for another, but she accepted it graciously. As her own gifts for the family were oranges, lemons, nuts, sticks of peppermint, and other edibles, it was easy enough to recipro-cate with the delicious treats. It also made for a delightful gathering.

Catherine held up several square enve-lopes, her tone triumphant. "An invitation for all to a soirée at the Earl of Brundage's estate, two country balls, and a reminder of the mummer's play to be held in the village next week. If we were completely out of mourning, we could hold a card party or fête here. I fear it would cause talk if we did, though."

"How unfortunate," Lord Braxton com-mented, but his expression reflected relief at the restriction, and Clare stifled a smile.

The baby crawled across her blanket toward him, and using his legs as support, pulled herself to a wobbly standing position. Before Clare could get to her, she collapsed onto her bottom, lower lip poking out as she looked up at Robert.

His immediate reaction was to scoop her up, telling her she was all right and far too young to try anything so audacious as walking. Then he glanced up to see them all watching him and paused, looking embarrassed. Clare went to his rescue and took Emma Clare and put her back on her blanket, sitting beside her with the silver rattle as a distraction.

Charles groaned at the news of all the soirées, balls, and fêtes. "Is there not an alternative to dances? I had hoped for hunting parties instead," he said to his brother. Braxton agreed.

"I am quite certain we can get up a small party to ride to the hounds, as we usually do on Boxing Day."

Charles looked much relieved, and the glance he exchanged with Robert was rife with humor. "If we could arrange it to coincide with the Brundage ball, it would be most convenient."

"Rarely is anything deemed socially acceptable very convenient," Braxton replied dryly, and knew his younger brother understood his reluctance to join in the festivities. Since he'd inherited the title and estates, matchmaking mamas had thrown their daughters at his head with unrelenting hope and determination. It was his duty to wed and provide heirs, but he was in no hurry. And now that this complication had interrupted what he'd begun to think of as a much calmer time in his life, he feared even further disruption.

He gazed at the baby being cuddled by Clare. It was a striking scene. Clare's brilliant red-gold hair made a lovely foil for the baby's dark curls. An artist would love to paint their portrait. He mulled over the chance of commissioning a painting by Lawrence of the two of them, then wryly realized that he was putting the cart well ahead of the horse. Not only did he fully intend to reunite baby and mother as soon as possible, but what possible reason could he give Clare for even suggesting such a thing? Yet the sweetness of her holding the child banished some of the bitter memories that haunted him.

Clare handled the baby as if she were accustomed to it, and he wondered if she helped with her widowed sister's children. It seemed such a natural thing for her to care for the child. And despite himself, he couldn't help thinking that the baby was a pretty little thing, winsome with her infectious laugh and sweet nature. While he knew well that a baby, especially one that might be illegitimate, would not enhance his social standing, he wouldn't mind keeping the child at all. That silent admission was surprising. But he knew that he could not blindly accept responsibility for her, either. He must find out the truth. If the baby was his, he would meet his responsibilities. If not, he wanted to know who had put her upon him, as well as the reasons why. It was a mystery he intended to solve.

It was cold early in the morn after St. Nicholas Day. Pale steam blew from the horses' nostrils as they got into the carriage for the trip to the White Hart. Robert sat across from Emma and Clare, who tended the baby as she wiggled in their laps. The wet nurse rode silently at his side, and he found the entire situation so awkward, he had little to say on the journey. It was embarrassing to think he might have created this debacle and an innocent child might suffer for it, and even more embarrassing that he had no idea who the mother might be.

Cooing at the baby Clare held in her lap,

Emma looked over at him. "You needn't be so grim, Braxton. We may well find the mother after all."

"That would be most beneficial for all concerned, I daresay." He regarded his sister for a moment. "Although you may be disappointed. It truly would be for the best, you know. A child needs its mother."

"And its father," she said pertly. Then she bit her lower lip and pressed her face into the curve of the baby's neck and shoulder. "I do so miss Papa. I wonder what he would say about the baby."

Robert didn't want to think about what his father might have said. It would not be very complimentary, he was quite certain of that. Lord Braxton had not viewed the escapades of some gentlemen with tolerance. He would think even less of his own son for siring a child without the benefit of marriage.

"Whatever the outcome," said Clare calmly, "I think it is commendable to go to such lengths to protect her. Emma Clare could not have been left with a more generous family."

Emma gave her a fond glance. "You are very kind to say so, Clare."

Robert lifted an ironic brow. It was easy to make such comments when not faced with the consequences of one's actions, he supposed. But he found it deuced difficult to consider it a generous thing to hunt down the mother who must have abandoned her child to his care without thought of what it would do to the child or to him. He intended she be made to accept her responsibility. If she was indeed someone with whom he'd had a tryst, he would see to their welfare — after a stern dressing-down for her temerity. A letter or private word with him would have been much more the thing. After all, he wasn't that dour a fellow that his former lovers would fear him, he hoped.

Frosted tree branches reflected brittle winter sunlight as they traveled the Exeter Road toward Whitchurch. Heat from hot bricks warmed the coach, but a chill still necessitated gloves, lap robes, and greatcoats. By the time they reached the White Hart, it had grown quite cold in the coach and they were all glad to go inside to warm themselves by the huge fireplace. A cheery blaze lit the common room and lent heat, and they were fortunate enough to find a place in the inglenook.

Clare untied the baby's warm fur-lined bonnet, laughing when the child grabbed the ribbons and immediately tried to eat them. "I think she must be hungry," she said as she successfully removed the ties from the baby's fingers.

"Shall you bespeak a room where the wet nurse can feed her, Robert?" Emma suggested.

Somewhat taken aback, for he hadn't considered all the details inherent in the rearing of children, he procured a small private room. Emma and Clare remained in the inglenook while he sought out the innkeeper. The bluff, pleasant-speaking man smiled broadly at first. Then he shook his head, his smile fading as Robert broached the subject of the baby.

"My lord, as I told you before, I cannot fathom who might have left a child in your coach, but ye must surely know 'tis none of my doing," he protested. "I've no ale-maids here with children. Be ye certain 'tis not a jest at your expense?"

"If so, it is not amusing," Robert retorted. "I would like to speak with your ostlers and any workers who may shed light on this mystery."

The innkeeper's eyes narrowed and he shook his head. "They be busy with the Christmas season travelers, milord," he protested, but stopped suddenly at the baron's intimidating stare.

Robert felt a hand on his arm and half

turned, as Clare smiled at the innkeeper. "It is very kind of you to help us, sir," she said, ignoring his obvious intention to refuse. "I am sure you agree that a child should be with her mother, especially at this time of year. Perhaps someone here saw the child before the mother put her in the wrong coach."

After a brief pause, the innkeeper blew out a gusty sigh and gave his rather ungracious permission to make inquiries of his staff. "Don't be keeping them from their duties long," he admonished them.

Robert slanted a glance at Clare, lifting his brow. "It is amazing what a beautiful woman can accomplish with a smile," he observed when the innkeeper left them. "I had absolutely no luck gaining his permission last time."

A dimple flashed in her cheek, and thick lashes lowered over green eyes gleaming with good humor. "It is much more likely he rethought the risk of offending you."

"He seemed to have little regret on that score. Perhaps you will be so good as to join me in my questioning of the ostlers? I've a notion that you will get much more information from them than I could."

"Indeed, my lord. Shall I fetch Emma and the baby? It may help if they see her."

He thought it an excellent notion, and sent a lad to fetch his sister and the child. As they walked toward the stables in the thin winter light, he found it difficult to keep his gaze from Clare. The bonnet brim hid her glorious hair and shaded her face as he studied the sweet curve of her cheek. He might have been tempted to flirt, if not for the grave nature of their mission. It hardly seemed appropriate in light of the fact he searched for the mother of a child claimed to be his, so he held his tongue. What a deuced awkward situation this had become.

Despite it all, he found himself inexorably drawn to Clare Seaton. Memories of childhood pranks aside, he'd not often thought of her in the intervening years between adolescence and adulthood, but the re-acquaintance opened an entirely new world of possibilities. Yet if he made his interest known, how would she receive him in light of the current situation? Especially when the issue of the baby's paternity might yet undo him.

The innkeeper had not exaggerated about the busy season. Travelers on the road created a steady stream of carriages large and small, and weary horsemen paused to warm themselves by the inn fire while their horses were tended or exchanged. It took some time, but they questioned three employees before they learned that a young woman had been seen with a baby the morning of Braxton's presence at the inn, and that she had attempted to gain employment.

"Is she working here now?" Clare asked the youthful ostler.

"No, ma'am. Ole Coop — beggin' your pardon, ma'am — Master Cooper, he don't hire maids what have family. Says they take off work too much," the young ostler said. His admiring gaze lingered on Emma and Clare, and Braxton hid his annoyance.

"So the young woman had this baby with her?" he asked, and the ostler nodded.

"She did, milord."

Clare, cradling the baby in her arms, spoke up. "Are you certain it was this baby?"

The young man studied the rosy-cheeked infant, then nodded. "As certain as I can be, Miss. It's the eyes. Striking, they be."

Robert glanced at the baby and had to agree. Her long-lashed eyes were big, round, and of an unusually bright blue. He thanked the lad, and gave him a half crown for his troubles.

It was the only information they managed to learn, and, after another fruitless hour, turned up no one else who could remember a girl with a baby two days before, so they returned to their coach. As they started home, only Emma seemed pleased.

"Apparently the mother is unable to provide and has given her up," she said calmly. "Now we can make plans for the baby's future."

"I hardly agree," Braxton said. He eyed his sister for a moment, recognizing the mutinous glint in her eyes. "The mother must still be found, Emma."

"But what if she's dead?"

He blew out a harsh sigh. "What if she isn't?" he countered. "You cannot keep that child, despite what you obviously think. Don't be silly." He immediately regretted his impatience.

Emma lifted doleful eyes to him, her lower lip quivering slightly, and he fought the urge to give in to her. At this point, anything he said would sound overly harsh, so he hesitated before speaking again. Then Clare spoke up.

"I daresay we will all deal much better once we know for a certainty about the mother," she said briskly, and after a moment, Emma relented, nodding.

"Yes, I see the sense in that, I suppose." Emma buried her nose in the baby's neck, making her giggle. Her voice was muffled by the fur bonnet and baby's blanket as she added, "I suppose I just fear she'll want her back."

Braxton thought that would be the best thing for baby and his family, but held his tongue. Truly, he'd have to know more about the mother and her situation before he took action. It was a tangle he'd never considered, and he wondered just how young mothers coped with the awful consequences of such things when they were unmarried or unexpectedly widowed. How did one care for their children with no position or money?

As if knowing the direction of his thoughts, Clare said, "We must be certain to add extra warm clothes and mittens for the poor boxes this year, don't you think, Emma? There was no summer at all and the weather is so dreadfully cold already, I am certain the rest of winter will be bitter. The harvest was slim this year, and I think of all the children who are without proper coats as well as enough food. It's especially hard on the tenants of landholders who do not provide properly. If it was left to me, I would have such wretched men flogged."

Surprised by her uncharacteristic vehemence, Robert said, "I think that rather harsh, Clare. What landholders do you know who do not provide well for their tenants?"

63

"Lord Woodruff comes to mind," Clare replied immediately. "I know he is your neighbor and you went to Eton with his youngest son, but he has a reputation as a lord who puts profits above the welfare of his tenants."

"Rumors can be wrong," he said, frowning, and she shook her head.

"I heard how he treats those he is supposed to maintain directly from a former ladies' maid who left his employ. His household staff is frequently abused, and his tenants live in squalor. I am sorry if it distresses you, but I have no respect for such a person."

"It does distress me, but not for the reason you may think. I consider it detestable to take advantage of one's rank in such a manner. It is ill-bred."

Something flickered in Clare's eyes, and her tension eased as she let out a soft breath. "It relieves me that you feel the same way, Robert — I mean, Lord Braxton."

He smiled. "I have been Robert for most of our lives. I see no reason to change that now, Clare. I may still call you Clare, I hope?"

"Of course. As you say, we've been Robert, Clare, and Emma far too long to stand on ceremony among ourselves. In public, we can maintain the fiction that we are proper."

He laughed, appreciating her wit, and remembering a dozen different things he liked about her. Why hadn't he recalled them earlier?

"So," Emma said, rubbing her gloved hands together, "we are going to provide clothes and food for the children. You know it won't be a proper Christmas celebration without fruit and sweets too. Oh, I know — we could have Father Christmas come to pass out gifts."

"Who would play Father Christmas?" Clare asked, and when they both looked at Robert, he shook his head.

"Not under any circumstances."

"Very well," Emma said with a sigh, and lapsed into silence.

After a moment, Clare suggested, "What of Charles? Could he be persuaded?"

"I doubt it," Emma said.

Clare smiled mischievously. "Perhaps we could try bribery."

Emma clapped her hands together. "Brilliant! I think I know just the thing, too. I happen to know a certain lady who has taken his fancy, and I promised him I would invite her to join us at a quiet dinner one evening. Befitting those still in half-mourning, of course."

She said the last with a glance toward Robert, and he inclined his head in her direction. He had little regard for the mourning rituals, but it would never do to say that anywhere it might be repeated to his mother. The baroness would be aghast at the impropriety.

"I think I saw a velvet robe in the attic when we went up to search for some clothes for Emma Clare," said Clare, her green eyes sparkling with enthusiasm. "And we can make a wreath of ivy for his head, and fashion a sack of some kind so he can carry the gifts. Are you certain you can coax him into agreeing?"

"Quite certain. He has been most insistent I invite Miss Delaney, which I fully intended to do, of course. But now, I have another, better reason."

Clare smiled broadly. "What else do we need done that he can help us accomplish, I wonder?" Emma laughed and clapped her hands in glee.

As they began a lively conspiracy against Charles, Braxton crossed his arms over his chest and leaned back against the squabs, envisioning his younger brother dressed in dark green robes with a ridiculous wreath of ribbons and greenery perched on his

66

head. Charles would be most annoyed. Perhaps the season might yet be bearable.

CHAPTER FOUR

Two weeks after their visit to the White Hart, Robert stepped into the morning parlor to find Emma and Clare with their heads together near the fire. More Christmas secrets, he assumed, a faint smile touching his mouth as he crossed to give the baroness a kiss on her cheek.

"Are you feeling better?" he asked, referring to the previous night when she had grown quite melancholy while observing Emma and the baby.

"Indeed," she said with a brisk smile. "Forgive my megrims of last night, if you will. It just seems that everything has changed so much. I suddenly remembered how your father always enjoyed Christmas with all of you at the table."

"Especially the Christmas Pudding," he reminded her, and they both laughed. The late baron had been most gleeful if he received the piece with the coin, and Robert suspected his mother had a hand in arranging his frequent successes with Mrs. Seyler. The cook had no compunction in making certain that it appeared on his plate every year.

Still smiling, Braxton glanced up in time to see his youngest sister scurry toward a rather shabby young lad waiting in the hallway. When Clare Seaton glanced up and saw him watching, her face flushed quite rosy. He found that intriguing. And slightly suspicious.

After a swift glance at Emma, who had disappeared down the hallway, she turned to smile at him. "My lord, I hoped you would see fit to accompany me on a walk in the fresh air this morning."

Taken aback, he glanced out the window. The sun gleamed on leaded glass panes, but a brisk wind promised a distinct chill in the air. "You must be quite hardy, Miss Seaton. It is near freezing, I understand."

"My father always said a brisk walk did a person good, and I thought the baby might also benefit from an outing. She will be wrapped up well, of course, and in the pram, but it might be just the thing."

"Oh, do go, dear," his mother said. "I used to walk you in that very pram, although I must admit, it was usually a bit warmer.

69

Young people today have so much more stamina, I suppose."

"Never let it be said that I have no stamina," he said dryly, and soon found himself at Clare's side, rolling a rather cumbersome pram down the frozen carriageway with the baby bundled up so that only her eyes were visible beneath folds of wool blankets. He wore his gloves and greatcoat as well as a hat, and Clare wore a heavily lined pelisse, scarf, hat, and gloves, her hand resting lightly on his arm as he pushed the wicker pram's huge wheels over the uneven ruts. He expected the baby to bounce out at any moment, but other than offering a few sounds reminiscent of a lamb bleating, she gave no sign of discomfort.

Remnants of snow lingered along the carriageway and under bushes, while the rest had been scraped away by footmen. Hills beyond the house glistened with crystallized snow turned blue and sparkly beneath the brittle sunlight.

"Why did you feel it necessary to lure me from the house, may I ask?" he inquired, and was gratified by the flush that stained Clare's cheeks. "Does it have anything to do with the rather unsuitable young man I saw in the hallway?"

"Dash it all, Robert. I've never been able

to hide anything from you. You do realize that's the reason you ended up entangled in some of our worst mishaps, don't you?"

"I have no idea why I always felt compelled to save you and Emma from your foolish schemes," he replied calmly. "It always ended badly for me."

Laughter edged her tone. "Yet it rarely stopped you from trying again."

He inhaled deeply of cold air that smelled fresh and spiced with anticipation. "What plot have you concocted now, may I be so bold as to inquire? And do not bother telling me that there is none or that you are not involved. You were usually the leader in most of the madness, if I recall correctly."

"If you are referring to last week's incident with the snowballs knocking your hat into the ditch, I plead innocence. It was the butcher's boy who managed that feat."

Snorting his disbelief, Robert studied her profile for a moment. "It wasn't the butcher's boy who first pelted me with snowballs. He just had the best aim."

"Alas, I am out of practice," she lamented, sliding him a mischievous glance from under her lashes. "I used to be much better."

"Perhaps it was the excitement from the mummer's depiction of Saint George slaying the dragon that hampered your ability," he suggested, watching her mobile face, enjoying her reactions to his teasing.

"More like, it was the extra cup of cider punch," she retorted, and he laughed.

"Charles may have overdone the spirits," he admitted. "He becomes very generous this time of year."

"I cannot imagine what Lady Braxton would say if we had returned from the village in our cups."

"It would not have been pleasant. Not that your distraction from the topic of the young lad in the hallway hasn't been entertaining, but you still have not answered my question. What do you and Emma have planned that is likely to be outrageous?"

"Must it be outrageous?" she asked pertly.

"Why change now?"

After a short hesitation, she said, "Emma and I have planned a mummer's play for New Year's Day. Would you care to join our troupe?"

"I would not," he said immediately. "I have no desire to end up like Charles, festooned in ivy and holly and wearing a dress."

"Robes," she corrected. "And that's as Father Christmas. Very well, if you don't wish to be Saint George or the dragon, we could disappoint your valet and let you play the part of Doctor Quack."

"Winston has agreed to be a part of the play? Perhaps I should rethink his employment. He is obviously a man of little wit."

Laughing, Clare put a hand atop his arm again, her touch light but searing into him as if she'd branded him with a hot iron. It wasn't as if he could actually feel her skin through gloves, a shirt, jacket, and greatcoat, so it was a novel reaction and he wondered at it. Conflicting emotions battled within, and he took several moments to regain his mental balance. Could it be possible that he was attracted to her as more than just a lovely friend? He'd never thought of her that way until recently, but then, except for a few brief moments at his father's wake, he hadn't seen her since they were children. She was definitely a woman now, and a most lovely and fascinating one at that.

He managed to cover his inner turmoil as Clare turned the conversation to the Brundage ball that had been held the week before, the growing pile of cards left for Emma and Catherine, and his brother's friends who called on them with alarming frequency.

"One would think the country to be more quiet, yet I find my hall often littered with young men these days," he remarked, and glanced down at her as a capricious gust of wind tugged her green satin bonnet ribbons loose.

Quickly grabbing them, she retied the sash, her laugh soft. "Young men must always be lured by beautiful young women like your sisters, my lord."

"And what of you, Clare? Are you not also a lure for young men?"

Tilting her head, she glanced up at him. "That question invites me to sound vain or plain, so I shall pretend you did not ask it."

He laughed at her impudent reply. "You are quite modest, I see."

"Oh, quite," she agreed demurely.

Intrigued, he found himself smiling down at her, enjoying even this frigid walk. Frost clouds formed in front of his face, and the chill did not abate in the brittle sunlight. When the baby whimpered, he turned the pram and they went back to the house. Holly and ivy and cedar boughs festooned the outside lamps, but the inside would not be decorated until Christmas Eve for good luck. Mr. Drew opened the door for them, his austere expression softening as Emma Clare cooed beneath the mounds of wool blankets. The wet nurse came to lift her from the pram, and the baby smiled and reached for Robert. He was somewhat taken aback.

"She seems a hardy child, my lord," Drew said, and Braxton nodded.

"Yes, she is — what on earth?" he said, startled by the sight of his youngest sister running toward him with her coat hanging off one shoulder.

Emma flew at him across the entrance hall, lavender skirts clutched high in both hands, showing her ankles. Her eyes were wide. "Robert! Quickly, we must go at once."

"What madness have you concocted now, may I ask? No, do not pull on me, Emma."

Impatiently, she tugged at his sleeve, her coat only half on as she glanced at Clare. "It is true. She is not far from here. We cannot delay. Oh, do cooperate, dear brother."

Braxton stood still, shaking his head. "I have no idea what you're talking about, so you can hardly expect me to fly out of here not knowing where I am going or why. What bee do you have in your bonnet now?"

"No bee. Just the baby's mother."

That snared his immediate attention. "You know her?"

Emma nodded. "I do now. A young man just informed me of her name and location. We must hurry though, for she is intent

75

upon leaving soon."

"How did he know we've been searching for her?" Braxton asked with a frown.

"After church last Sunday, Clare put a notice in the parish hall that we were seeking a wet nurse for a baby who was abandoned, and asked that if anyone knew of a young mother who recently lost her child, to please contact us."

Robert looked at Clare. "That was quite clever of you. No blame to place, just a plea for assistance, which is much more likely to be effective. Well then. Let us go and find this young woman and see if she's the baby's mother."

Emma sighed. "I truly think she must be. The description of the baby she supposedly lost is very similar." After a brief hesitation, she added, "There's something you should know as well, Braxton."

It was her tone of voice more than her averted eyes and flushed face that warned him the news would not be welcome. He nodded tersely. "Go on."

"Franny once worked here as an upstairs maid. She left us last year to work in the manor of the Viscount Woodruff. It is reported that her baby is yours."

"Franny?" He gave her a blank look, trying to place the girl with no success. "Why would someone think her baby is mine?"

Emma hesitated, glanced again toward Clare, and then blurted, "Because you were seen with her in the village when you came home to help Papa with his business affairs. Not long afterward, she left Heath Hall."

It still took a moment, but then he recalled a slight, rather mousy maid whom he'd helped pick up a spilled bag of vegetables in the street outside the market. He stared incredulously at his sister. "You cannot be serious."

"Of course not, Braxton, but there was talk in the village of the girl carrying on with her employer's heir and . . . and well, that would be you."

He was aghast but managed to contain his chagrin. "I look forward to speaking with her."

That grim pronouncement spurred him into having his carriage brought 'round front in a very short time. Within a half hour of learning about Franny, they were on the road to a nearby village. This time Robert, Emma, Clare, and the baby were accompanied by the young boy he'd seen earlier in the hall, a thin, rather nervous lad who seemed awed to be taken up in the huge coach.

Arms crossed over his chest, Robert

leaned into the corner of the carriage to contemplate the events that had brought them to this moment. And he found, to his surprise, that he wasn't very eager to be rid of Emma Clare. Somehow, the sweet little girl had grown on him despite his efforts to hold her at arm's length. No doubt, Emma's insistence that he play with the child had a lot to do with it. She'd used the same tactics with her kittens and puppies when they were younger, piling them in his lap so that he had to pet them until he found he enjoyed it.

But Emma Clare wasn't a puppy or kitten; she was a child, and he could not risk her being left in a situation that would endanger her. Franny had already left her once. She might well do so again, depending upon the circumstances. He fully intended to learn from her why she had lied about the baby's paternity, then demand she do the right thing by her child.

That was his intention.

Sitting across from him, Clare Seaton recognized grim determination in the baron's face and wondered as to his intentions. She did not believe he had seduced a maid, so the mother must have lied. But what was the reason for it? If she was employed by the Woodruff family, she could not be destitute. Still, women with children rarely worked in domestic employment unless they left their child at a Foundling Home where they could visit them once a month, or if lucky, once a week. Would Lord Braxton understand the mother's dilemma? In her experience, men of the upper classes rarely did.

When the coach stopped in front of a small thatched-roof cottage on the outskirts of the village, Clare took a deep breath. She hoped the imminent confrontation would not be too painful for Emma or the baron — or for the mother, for that matter. Surely, only a desperate woman would abandon her child.

Ferris opened the coach door and put down the steps. The baron, followed by Emma, Clare, and the baby emerged into the icy wind while another footman rapped on the front door. The boy who had directed them hung back, as if afraid of recriminations, but Braxton put a gentle hand on his shoulder and told him not to fear. "I will not allow anything terrible to happen."

Clare hoped he meant that, and glanced at Emma. She had a pinched, worried expression as she looked at the baby held tightly in Clare's arms, and she knew that the tender-hearted young woman dreaded the possibility of relinquishing the child.

When the cottage door opened a crack, Ferris announced the baron, and a soft cry was heard, then the door slowly opened wider. The footman stepped back and the baron went in, followed by Emma and Clare. It was a tiny room, scrupulously clean, but bare of any but the most basic necessities. No fire burned in the grate, and a wooden table held no hint of food. A kettle sat upon the hob in the fireplace, but with no wood or coal to heat it, it was useless. The tall, plain woman who let them in was wrapped in several layers of clothing to stay warm.

"My lord," she said flatly, "I know why you are here. She's in t'other room." A tilt of her head indicated a section of the cottage that had been separated with a flimsy wall of blankets hanging from the low-beamed ceiling.

Lord Braxton indicated Emma and Clare should precede him, and they stepped around the tattered blankets to see a woman lying on a straw-stuffed mattress placed on the floor. Clare's throat tightened. Dank, damp air permeated the room. The woman lying on the mattress must have been pretty once, but now looked gray-skinned and emaciated. The poverty was so evident, the air of hopelessness so rife, that Clare found it difficult to hold back tears.

Breath frosted in front of his face as the baron asked, "Are you Franny?"

The tiny figure wrapped in scraps of material and blanket nodded, then burst into tears. "Oh my lord Braxton, please forgive me," she gasped between sobs. "I didn't know what else to do. No one would hire me after I was turned off by the viscount, nor would he admit to the baby. I was desperate."

Her sobs grew louder and Braxton stood rigidly, seeming unaffected unless one looked at his eyes. After a moment, he asked gently, "Why did you leave your child in my coach?"

Wiping at her wet cheeks with the edge of blanket, Franny mumbled, "I know 'twas wrong, my lord. But I'd prayed, you see, that God would send someone to help my baby. Then I looked up and there you were." Her drenched eyes shifted to Clare, and her lips trembled as the sleeping baby stirred in her arms. "It seemed an answer to my prayers. You were such a kind family. Oh, if I had not met Lord Woodruff's footman and gone to work there, I would have been happier staying at Heath Hall. So I — oh, I know 'twas wicked, but I wrote that note, hoping you would think it was some other woman, and put my baby's basket in your carriage when the coachman looked the other way."

"The flower girl," he said suddenly. "Henry shooed you away because he thought you were selling flowers."

She nodded woefully, tears streaming down thin cheeks. "Yes, my lord."

"Franny, I don't quite understand," said Braxton. "Are you telling me that the footman is the father of your child? If that is so, we can rectify this situation quite easily. He will be brought up to snuff immediately."

Franny bent her head, shaking it slightly, and her voice was so low Clare had to lean in to hear. "It were not Sherman, my lord. I caught the fancy of Lord Woodruff's son, and he spoke so sweet and so nice and I thought . . . oh, I knew he'd never marry me, but I thought he would do right by me. But when I told him about the baby, he . . . he had me turned off. Said I stole gold cufflinks, but I swear I did not, my lord! I have never stolen."

"Don't fret," said the baron. "I believe you. So, without a letter, you have been unable to find other employment."

"It's . . . it's not just that, my lord." Staring at her fingers clenching the blanket, she said softly, "I've been sick. The doctor said I have the consumption and need to go to the hospital in London. But I would have to leave Annie at a Foundling Home."

For a moment, no one spoke. The frigid air in the room seemed to grow colder, if that were possible. Emma made a soft sound of distress, and Clare must have squeezed the baby because she woke, and reached up a chubby little hand to touch her cheek. Cooing, the baby patted a single tear that slid down Clare's face, and she found it difficult not to openly weep. Her throat ached with suppressed emotions; anger, grief, and sympathy mingled painfully.

The yearning expression on Franny's face as she watched her baby was nearly enough to undo her. Clare had to look away.

"I see," said the baron finally, and then added briskly, "It is an impossible situation. You simply cannot leave your child with strangers, no matter how willing they may be to take her."

Clare could hardly believe her ears. Surely he could not be so cruel? Had she misjudged him that greatly? Emma's gasp went ignored as Lord Braxton looked around the tiny cubicle, then back at the woman lying on the thin mattress. Franny had gone even paler beneath her gray pallor and nodded woodenly. Her voice was a mere wisp of sound.

"Yes, my lord. I understand."

"No, I don't think you do, Franny."

Turning, Lord Braxton called for Ferris, and when the footman stepped into the cottage, he said, "Help this young lady pack up any belongings she wishes to take with her, Ferris. She will be coming with us to Heath Hall."

Ferris nodded, and when Franny looked up with wide eyes, the footman said, "I should have known the child was yours right off, you know. She has your eyes."

It was true. Franny's eyes were the same deep blue as her daughter's, though filled now with silvery tears. Clare looked at Lord Braxton, and though his expression was solemn, a hint of emotion glistened in his eyes too. Emma openly sobbed with relief, and impulsively took the baby from Clare and knelt by the bed so she could see her mother.

For an instant, the child sat motionless, then let out a squeal and began to buck in Emma's lap, little arms held out to Franny. The sick woman took her and held her close against her thin chest as the baby babbled happily. Franny managed a tremulous smile of relief.

Looking up at her brother, Emma held his gaze for a long moment, then said simply, "Thank you."

Braxton merely nodded. Clare felt as if she had witnessed an especially tender moment between the siblings.

The woman who had answered the cottage door stepped around the blanket wall and put her hands on her hips, her gaze taking in the crowded area. "Well, I see that you're going to do your duty by the girl, milord, and I'm glad for that. I told Franny not to worry, that it would all get sorted out."

With a straight face, Lord Braxton said, "Your faith in me is most commendable."

It was, Clare thought, an unexpected solution, but one she heartily approved.

CHAPTER FIVE

Lush pine and cedar boughs draped over doorways and on fireplace mantels lent a spicy fragrance to the rooms. Charles had tied a sprig of mistletoe with red satin ribbon and was teasing his sisters with the possibilities of dangling it over the heads of guests. The house had been busy all day, visitors arriving for cake and tea, and much merriment rang in the parlor when Charles brandished the mistletoe. Squeals and laughter greeted his attempts to kiss pretty girls.

The baroness wore her best mourning gown of black bombazine silk, as was appropriate, with jet jewelry and a brooch fashioned from the late baron's hair. Clare thought she looked quite regal, sitting in the parlor, presiding over the festivities with a somber air of enjoyment. It had not yet been one year and a day since her husband's death and she observed the customs precisely.

Emma and Catherine were in half-mourning, with Emma wearing a gown of lavender silk and Catherine in a white gown with a deep purple shawl. They wore subdued garments and cameo jewelry yet managed to be quite lovely, while so different in coloring. Clare wore dark green, her gown caught beneath her breasts with glittering silver braid, and a light shawl around her shoulders.

Christmas Eve promised to be festive, with a huge Yule log burning in the fireplace and a second round of carolers from the village crowded into the entrance hall for hot punch. Laughter filled the house, as did the rich fragrances of food mixed with the sharp scent of greenery and brisk air every time the front door opened to allow in new visitors.

Lord Braxton did his duty by the carolers, expressing his appreciation for their songs and well-wishes, and Emma and Catherine crowded close to exclaim over how much children had grown since the year before. It was their custom to offer tables of food and drink to their tenants who came caroling, a nod to former times when the wassail bowl was passed and coins distributed.

"We're about to play Snapdragon," Emma said to Mr. Lindsay, a friend of Charles's.

"You must join us."

The quite dashing Mr. Lindsay grinned down at Emma. "If I burn my fingers, you must promise to make a fuss over me, Miss Bray."

Emma pretended to consider it, her blue eyes sparkling, then she nodded. "Very well, I shall be quite sympathetic that you are not quick enough to snatch your raisins from the fire."

While Catherine flirted with a military officer Lord Braxton had invited to join them, much to the delight of his sisters, Charles mooned over a pretty girl from nearby Swindon, Miss Thea Delaney. Clare was coaxed into playing the piano before she relinquished it gratefully to Miss Delaney, who played beautifully and had a lovely singing voice. Charles immediately draped himself over the side of the piano to give her his undivided attention.

In the crush of revelers, Clare managed to escape to a quiet corner. She and Emma had put up silver and gold paper stars and decorations in the rooms, mingling them with the greenery, and a huge ball of mistletoe gilded with gold and scarlet red ribbons hung prominently in the front parlor. She watched, smiling, as Emma gathered people to participate in Snapdragon.

"Don't you care to play?" came the question from right behind her, and she turned to see Robert smiling at her.

Her heart skipped a beat. The baron looked very handsome in his dark blue jacket, white breeches, and an elegant cravat of snowy linen that set off his strong features to great advantage. Gray eyes crinkled slightly at the corners as he gazed down at her, and she found her voice before he could think her mooning over him.

"I'm not at all certain I want to be in that mad throng at the same time as flaming brandy and hot raisins contained in only a shallow dish," she said with a laugh.

"I thought you more daring, Miss Seaton."

"Then I fear you are to be disappointed, my lord. I harbor a peculiar desire for uncharred fingers."

"An affliction my sister will be most happy to cure if she learns of it, I am certain."

"Oh, I beg of you not to share it with Emma, or I will find myself seized up and forced to join in the madness."

"As I am much of the same frame of mind, I yield to your pretty plea. I was about to go visit with Franny. Would you like to join me?"

She laid her hand on the arm he offered her, nodding. "I would like that very much.

Is she feeling better?"

"Mrs. Seyler assures me that she is, although the poor girl looked quite wretched after the doctor left."

Clare was quiet for a moment. The doctor had grave reservations as to Franny's future. "It seems a shame," she said at last, as they progressed through the house to the servants' quarters. "She's scarcely old enough to be a mother, and now she's so dreadfully ill."

"All we can do is see she's fed well and kept warm and comfortable for now. The doctor said there's no harm in allowing her to see the baby as often as she likes, and Emma has been faithful about the visits," he said, putting a light hand on the small of her back to guide her. His hand felt so warm, so comforting, making her wonder what he would do if she turned into his arms.

"Emma is one of the kindest souls I have ever known," she said instead, banishing the thought from her mind.

"I agree, but if you tell her I said that, I shall insist you misheard me. She's already far too adept at getting her way. If she knew I thought her kind, she would soon have twice as many dogs underfoot, and no doubt, half the parish poor installed in the parlor."

"I shudder to think it, but I am sure you are right."

Braxton reached around her to open a door, waited for her to step ahead, then closed it behind them as they mounted a narrow staircase. The sound of laughter and music was muted now, a blur of muffled noise. This section of the house belonged to the servants, and it was kept segregated as to male and female by a door between the corridors. The baron knocked, and was admitted by one of the kitchen maids, who smiled shyly as she led them to Franny's room.

Emma had decorated the room with some of the silver and gold stars strung like bunting over the window, and the narrow iron bed bore a rope of cedar boughs across the foot rails. It was a small room, but clean, and a bright rug on the floor held a pair of soft slippers no doubt donated by Emma. Franny wore a white nightgown with a high collar, and her hair had been brushed and lay in two plaits over her shoulders. Blankets covered the bed, and pillows piled behind her back as she sat up as if to rise.

"Please stay abed," Lord Braxton said with a smile. "I don't wish to burden you with our presence, but I received a reply to my message to Viscount Woodruff."

When Franny blanched, he hastened to add, "There is no concern that the viscount will ever attempt to lay claim to your daughter. I have his written repudiation of the possibility his son is the sire. I am sorry to say, that is probably in your best interests."

Looking down at the blanket, Franny nodded. "I did not think he would acknowledge her, but I did worry he might make trouble one day if he chose. He said some dreadful things before he turned me off."

"No doubt. You need not worry about Woodruff any longer. You are safe here, and may stay as long as you wish." He hesitated, then said, "I asked Miss Seaton to accompany me so that you may feel free to speak frankly. If you wish for me to wait in the hallway, I am more than glad to do so, but in light of your illness, I must know your wishes regarding Emma Clare. Or Annie, as you named her."

After a brief silence, Franny said softly, "She's not been christened, and Emma Clare is a lovely name, my lord." She lifted her eyes to gaze up at him. "You have been so kind, and I do not deserve it after the trick I played on you, but I know that whatever you decide for her will be the best thing. I place her in your hands, my lord."

"I will honor your trust, Franny."

Clare drew in a deep breath. Her first thought had been that it was a discussion that could have waited until after Christmas Eve, but then she realized that Lord Braxton had just relieved Franny of any uncertainty regarding her daughter's future. It was a gift that had to be the most precious she had ever received.

"Your instincts are reassuring, my lord," Clare said on their way back down the narrow staircase. "I believe she is resting much easier now."

"I hope so." He glanced down at her, cupping her elbow in his palm to steady her as the stair board creaked beneath their feet. He paused, and waited until they reached the bottom of the stairs to say, "It is not often easy to know what to do in these situations. I've no training in such matters. I am much more competent at battle strategy or even animal husbandry than I am at the disposition of children."

"But you are not disposing of a child, my lord. On the contrary, you have given her a future."

"If I can keep my sister from planning her Court presentation by the time she's five, I will have accomplished a miracle," he said dryly, and she couldn't help a laugh.

"Emma often seems to succeed in her efforts, so I do not envy you the attempt."

"Our father once refused to allow her to bring a puppy into the house, insisting that dogs belong in the kennels or stables. By the week's end, she had two puppies and a litter of kittens sleeping in her doll beds in the nursery. My father was bemused at how it came about, but we all knew Emma had cozened him into giving his permission. However, we never quite figured out how she managed it."

"Persistence and charm," Clare replied promptly, and he nodded thoughtfully.

"You may be right. Charles used to claim it was witchcraft."

"Rather shortsighted of him, I think."

"That describes my brother perfectly. Did you notice that he seems quite smitten with Miss Delaney?"

"I did. Catherine is smitten with Captain Moore, and Emma is taken with Mr. Lindsay. Love is in the air, my lord."

Robert stopped just before they reached the entrance hall, startling her by taking her hand in his and holding it. To her astonishment, he produced a sprig of mistletoe and held it above her head.

"It seems to be the season for love, Clare."

Heart pounding, Clare looked up into his eyes, the gray depths alight with laughter and some other emotion. Did she imagine it? Perhaps it was just the reflection of wall sconces, or even some of the rum punch the gentlemen drank earlier. But she was not imagining the brief pressure of his hand squeezing hers or the silent invitation of the mistletoe dangled above her head.

"Christmas is indeed a season for love, peace, and joy," she managed to say much more calmly than she felt.

"I've not felt free to say anything until the baby's parentage was resolved, but now that we know the truth, I must ask how you would feel about marrying a man with a child."

Startled, she searched his face, noting that the shadows in his eyes were gone, replaced by the glow of some other emotion. Could he mean — but what else would he mean, if not that? So she said carefully, "That would depend upon the man and the child, I suppose."

"I see that I must be more specific," he said dryly, and pulled her toward him, his hands tender and yet possessive as he held her close. "How would you feel if I asked you to marry me?"

"Are you asking me?"

"Oh Clare, sweet, tempting, outrageous Clare — yes, I am asking if you would do me the honor of becoming my wife."

"You realize that I would drive you mad, don't you? I am not at all biddable, and I would expect you to forgive me when I do something you consider outrageous. Also —"

Then there was no time to say anything else, for he bent his head and kissed her, his mouth moving on hers with infinite tenderness. She closed her eyes, and he deepened the kiss until she felt lightheaded and had to curl her fingers into his waistcoat to keep from swaying.

"Am I to understand that you feel some affection for me, Robert?" she asked when he lifted his head at last, daring to hope it might be true.

"Indeed." He pulled her closer, his voice rasping as he said, "This has been a season of surprises. I never expected to find my heart snared by two bewitching females."

Clare's head swam, and she tilted her chin to look up at him. "May I be so bold as to ask to whom you refer, my lord?"

"You and Emma Clare, of course. Ah, you must know that I find you irresistible, Clare. I think I fell in love with you when I was twelve and you put salt in the sugar bowl just before afternoon tea. No, don't deny it. It was worth being put to bed without supper to see the look on Miss Whittington's face when she took her first sip. She was a dreadful nanny."

Biting her lower lip, Clare admitted, "It was worth it, wasn't it? So, are you saying that you are in love with me, Robert?"

He looked struck by the question, then grinned and nodded. "I suppose I am."

"Thank God. I thought I would have to declare myself first."

Laughing, he asked, "So you love me?"

"Since I was eight years old and you tried to save me from a not-very-rabid dog."

He kissed her again, passionately this time, so that her toes curled and she could hardly breathe when he released her. "I love you, Clare Seaton," he said against her ear, and she drew back to look into his handsome face, her heart swelling with emotion.

"And I love you, Robert, Lord Braxton."

He smiled. "I plan to spend the rest of our lives together, you know."

"That's very daring of you. Think of what life with me might be like."

"Oh, I have, believe me. My memory is perfectly clear, and I shudder to think what you may do next. Yet I find the possibilities exciting as well as frightening. Do you think you can share my attentions with another young female?"

"That would depend on the nature of your attentions, of course," she replied with a smile. "I do not wish to be jostled on your knee or sent off with a nurse if I grow irritable."

"Do you not? I shall keep that in mind. Of course, you realize I must also ask Emma Clare of her wishes concerning this matter before we make any future plans."

"Perhaps we should consult her together. Although it must wait, I fear, as her bedtime was much earlier."

"I think it safe to say she will approve." He lowered his head to kiss her again, this time letting his mouth linger on hers before he pulled back and drew in a deep breath. "We should join the others before I compromise you right here in my mother's hall."

"I should rather enjoy that, I think," she said as she allowed him to take her hand.

"So would I, my dearest. So would I."

Just before they reached the parlor, he paused again. "I would like to apply to your father for permission to court you properly, Clare. I understand that he is with his regiment at this time and it may take quite a while for the wedding arrangements to be made. Do you object?"

"While my heart says I would rather not wait so long, I daresay Emma will keep me so busy with plans, the time will pass quickly."

He groaned. "*Emma.* Of course, she will have us all running to and fro like March hares. Perhaps we should elope after all. Gretna Green is not so very far."

"And deprive your mother and sister of their participation? I am not at all certain I want to live the rest of my life with their recriminations ringing in my ears."

He sighed. "Your good sense carries the day. Shall we join the rabble? I hear shouts of pain and can only imagine the charred fingers that await us in the parlor."

It was, Clare decided, the happiest moment of her life.

Christmas Day was both familiar and much different than he had envisioned it when he had reluctantly set out for home, Robert thought as he sat at the head of the dining table. After a year fraught with death and disappointments, he had somehow managed to find happiness — and a woman he wanted to spend the rest of his life loving.

Services at the village church had been both solemn and joyous, and he had been glad to see that, despite hard times, his tenants had warm clothes and enough food. He gave all the credit for that to Clare, for she had enlisted Catherine and Emma in her efforts to be certain the parish poor had their needs met even before Boxing Day. The vicar had been quite overwhelmed, and his sermon had reflected the joy of giving and blessings on those who shared their gifts.

On the carriage ride home from church, they had passed children pelting one another with snowballs as the church bells rang with celebration. Somehow, it eased the anger and bitterness that had been with him for so long, the horrors of war that were always a reminder that there was a steep price for peace, but that it was not in vain.

Now, sitting at the family dining table laden with glittering china, elegant silver, crystal, and flowers, he thought of a much brighter future. Tempting scents from roast goose, steamed trout, vegetables, and puddings filled the air, mingling with laughter from his family.

Mrs. Seyler stood next to Mr. Drew, and Robert caught Clare's eye and smiled. It was family custom to express thanks to those who prepared the holiday dinner every year, and kitchen maids smoothed their aprons as they flanked the cook and butler. The dining room grew quite crowded. Trays of sherry in small crystal glasses were offered, and as the staff each took one, he stood.

Thinking of his father's annual tributes to those who made their lives easier, Robert cleared his throat. "As you know, it is the Bray family custom to convey our gratitude to all of you who see to our daily comforts with such efficiency and kindness. On behalf of Lady Braxton and my brother and sisters, I would like to propose a toast. To a year of good health and prosperity for us all. May all your hopes for the future come to pass."

While he did not have the eloquence of his father, it was a heartfelt expression and the staff beamed with appreciation. Then Mr. Drew directed the footmen to bring in the platters of food to the sideboard, while Ferris and two other footmen offered trays to the family and guests seated at the table.

Clare, seated at his right side, leaned forward to say softly, "You did very well, my lord."

"Not, I fear, as elaborate as my father's toasts. He had the gift of making every person here feel as if they were special."

"And you have the gift of making us all feel safe."

"Safe?"

"Indeed. You could always have left Emma Clare at a Foundling Home, you know, and abandoned Franny to her fate. But you chose to bring them under your protection. Everyone here, family and staff, knows that you are a man worthy of their loyalty and respect."

"And you, Clare? Do I have your loyalty and respect as well?"

"You have my heart," she said simply. And Robert knew that, at last, he had truly come home.

WHAT CHILD IS THIS?

BY JO ANN FERGUSON

CHAPTER ONE

It smelled as if it would snow at any moment. Cold and damp, the whole countryside held its breath, waiting for the first storm of the winter season.

Adelaide Rowland looked from the lighted windows of the church in the middle of the small village to the basket she carried. A church was supposed to provide sanctuary for anyone who needed it, and she couldn't think of anyone who needed it more than she did. She had done as her lady had asked, riding as far as the few coins she had would carry her, walking and begging rides farther south and east, getting as far from Layden Mote as possible. Along the way, she had endeavored to hide what she carried in the basket. As soon as anyone suspected, she slipped away, taking her precious cargo with her.

Why had Lady Norah been so tightlipped when she had told Adelaide to take Lily, the lady's baby, and leave the manor? Her lady asked her to vow not to speak Lily's true name or say anything that might connect her with her parents and Layden Mote. Nobody else, including the staff, must know Adelaide had taken Lily. That could endanger the baby. The lady had not explained how or why, but Adelaide had promised to reveal nothing.

Did the request have anything to do with the messages and guests arriving and leaving at odd times of the day and night from Layden Mote when the family was at the country estate? Adelaide had hoped, when her lady woke her in the middle of the night and gave her such a peculiar set of orders, that Adelaide — at last — would know what was going on.

Instead, Lady Norah told her only to travel to a village named Stonehall-on-Sea, east of Brighton along the southern coast. Lady Norah had insisted on giving Adelaide some of her own clothes to keep her warm. She had pressed a few coins into Adelaide's hand and promised her more, but in the rush to leave, the extra money had been forgotten. Maybe it was because her lady had risen from her sickbed where she had spent the last two days. As she gave Adelaide orders and obtained her vow to hide the truth, Lady Norah had sneezed and coughed until Adelaide struggled to understand her words.

One thing had been clear. Adelaide needed to leave without delay. She had, and now Adelaide's shoes were worn through from days of walking through the countryside. She had stopped only to buy food with the few pennies she had left. She was now near where she was supposed to meet Lady Norah and her husband. But where were they?

How often had her mother warned Adelaide it was dangerous to be curious about one's employers when she was only a maid in their household? Adelaide's job, her mother had repeated, was to do as ordered and never to speak of what she saw or heard. Doing anything to jeopardize her position at Layden Mote could lead to tragedy, because her parents depended on her small income to pay for their food and shelter.

Her stomach rumbled, a reminder she had not eaten in more than two days, although she had been able to obtain milk for Lily. She had saved her last few coins for buying milk. The baby could not go without food, but Adelaide was not sure how much longer she herself could keep going. Finding a few windfall apples had done little to ease her hunger pangs. Before she left Layden Mote, she had placed some of her healing herbs in a pocket beneath her apron. She should have put food in as well. She was thirsty and exhausted, but nothing dimmed her curiosity. Why had the lord and his lady sent away their only child, who was barely three months old, with a household maid?

Adelaide would not get an answer standing on a deserted village green. She slipped into the church's porch. The small vestibule was empty except for a pair of empty vases. The cold wind off the sea had stripped away any color.

The inner door creaked as she lifted the latch. She froze. Lady Norah had urged her to remain out of sight as much as possible until they met again. If someone heard the door and came to investigate, she might have to find another hiding place for the night. She did not know where. She could sleep in the cold, but Lily must be kept warm.

The door swung open, and Adelaide peered past it. Two lamps were lit near the altar and the pulpit, but no one was there. She glanced toward another lamp on the table behind the pews. Paperwork was scattered on the table, and the poor box was visible. Nobody there, either.

Easing inside, she shut the door. She stiffened, but the hinges were silent.

The church was like other country ones she had seen. The center aisle with wooden pews on either side was divided by round columns. A few windows had stained glass, but most were plain. Doors flanked the altar. One, she guessed, was to the parson's office. The other might lead outside or to another room. The unadorned pulpit sat beneath a square sounding board, and the altar was as simple as the rest of the sanctuary.

It was warmer in the church than it had been outside, where the wind had cut through her pelisse and made her teeth chatter. She loosened the coat's buttons to let warmth past the thick wool. When one sleeve slipped over her hand, she ignored it. She did not want to risk disturbing the baby.

Leaving the pool of light from the table lamp, she slipped into the shadows. She ached from lack of sleep, but focused on putting the basket on a pew where it would not tip over.

She drew aside the blanket covering the baby's face. Sweet Lily, with her soft red curls, was asleep. She seemed to be surviving on goat's milk mixed with the porridge

Adelaide was able to purchase or trade for. Like the money, anything she had to barter with was gone.

Adelaide touched a chain around her neck. The locket on it was finer than anything she owned, and her lady had told her *not* to sell it. In fact, Lady Norah had emphasized that at least a half dozen times while Adelaide dressed and got the baby from the nursery. It was not the most valuable piece the lady owned, but it must mean a lot to her.

But surely, her daughter must mean more.

Not that it mattered. There would not be anyone in such a small village who would pay her a fair price for the chain and locket. She must devise another way to get milk for the baby. She had enough for tonight's feeding. Tomorrow, she would have to beg or steal what the baby needed and food for herself.

The door to the porch opened with a creak. Adelaide ducked between the pews as she heard the distinctive sound of a boot with a single hobnail in the left heel. She had heard that footstep often in the past week. The click of the nail head tapped against the ground or a stone, then silence, followed by another click moments later. She held her breath, praying Lily would not make a peep as she drew the basket to the floor with her. A man was following her and the baby. Why?

The air in her lungs grew stale, but she did not release the breath. That slight sound might betray her. Thus far, she had eluded him in a cat-and-mouse game she didn't understand. From where she kneeled, she could not see him, and hoped he could not see her. She pressed her hand over her mouth as she heard him snarl a word that had no place in a church. Beside her, on the floor, the baby stirred. If Lily cried, they would be discovered.

Suddenly, the man rushed past her pew. She saw a dark cloak, a dark hat on dark hair, dark pantaloons, and dark sleeves of a heavy coat, but nothing else. A door opened and closed not far from the altar. He had run through the church and left.

Why?

Sitting on her heels, Adelaide wrapped her arms around herself and struggled to breathe. Her shoulders sagged, aching when released from the tension holding them taut. She could not guess why the man and his hobnail boot appeared whenever she and Lily were alone.

"Do you need help?"

Her head jerked up at the question in an

111

accent that was definitely not British. Her eyes widened as they locked with ones the color of lilac buds. The man's elegant beaver hat perched on blond hair. His mouth, though in a straight line, was edged by faint lines that suggested he smiled easily. He was dressed with casual elegance. Buckskin breeches vanished into his knee-boots. His heels, as he walked closer, struck the tiles with the authority of a man accustomed to being obeyed.

There was no click of a hobnail.

Her heart halted in mid-beat. What if more than one man was following her? *Don't panic,* she warned herself.

Slowly, she stood. The blond man scanned her from head to foot. She knew how disheveled she must appear after days of traveling from the fells near Ullswater among the northwestern lakes.

"I'm fine," she said, almost choking on the commonplace words.

His brows, a few shades darker than his hair, lowered as he glanced from her to Lily.

Oh, sweet heavens! She had been so amazed at the unique color of his eyes that she had not kept Lily hidden.

Forgive me, my lady.

"I am pleased to hear that," the blond man said in the accent unlike any she had ever heard. Where was he from? Not France. One of the German states, perhaps? She forgot her curiosity when he demanded, "You're not planning on abandoning that child, are you?"

Theodore West — at long last, he was becoming accustomed to the name — watched the young woman's face lose its faint color. Her large brown eyes widened farther. They were almost the same shade of caramel as her hair. He guessed her cheeks usually were a soft rose like her full lips. She was not tall. He could have rested his chin on top of her dusty bonnet.

Dried mud clung to the hem of her simple light blue gown. Her black pelisse was too big, and she had rolled up the sleeves. If her shoes once had been polished, there was no sign of it. The toes were scuffed and dirt edged the soles.

She swayed, and he put out a hand to steady her. She edged away.

"Why don't you sit, miss?"

When she glanced toward the door, he prepared to halt her. Or should he let her go? He had business to tend to, and he could not be distracted. The smugglers along the southern coast were adding to their illegal trade by not only bringing untaxed cargo into England, but carrying important secrets out to the king's enemies. A courier was supposed to have met them near here several days ago with information gathered by associates.

He swallowed his frustration. When he had embarked on this life — defying his father's edict that he learn his duties at home — he had seen it as the chance to have the adventures he had craved since he was a child. His life now was great fun, but not at times like this when none of the puzzle pieces would come together to create a picture. Patience was what he needed, but patience was a virtue he did not have.

The baby gurgled. As the woman bent to check it, Theo realized he had misread the situation. She was gentle as she picked up the child. However, he had not mistaken the exhaustion painting dark circles under her fearful eyes. What was frightening her?

"You should sit before you fall over," he said, putting a bit more sternness in his voice.

She nodded and lowered herself to the pew. She resembled a scared rabbit trying to hide in a hedgerow.

"Thank you," she whispered. "I'd like to be alone now."

"I'm sorry if I intruded on your prayers."

"You don't need to apologize." She looked everywhere but at him. Was she trying to avoid his eyes or looking for whoever caused the fear in her eyes?

Before he could ask, doors opened at either end of the church. The one beyond the pulpit was silent, but the one from the porch screeched, the noise resonating to the high ceiling.

Its sound vanished beneath the cry from the woman beside him. She jumped to her feet, holding the baby and clutching the handles of the basket. She pushed past him. He reached for her, but she slipped out from between the pews.

The motion seemed too much for her. He grasped her arm as she wobbled. It was not her forward motion that had tripped her. It was fear. Her gaze was focused on the man entering from the porch.

"No!" she shrieked. "Stop following us!"

Theo felt tremors race along her skin, but he forced his voice to remain calm as he asked, "Who is following you, miss?"

"He is!" She hunched over the baby, half-turning away to protect it. "The man with a single hobnail in his left boot's heel."

Looking from her to his partner who appeared as puzzled as he was, he wondered what was going on. Who was threatening this pretty young woman and her baby?

CHAPTER TWO

Adelaide stared at the two men entering the sanctuary, one at either end of the church's center aisle. The two men could not be less alike. One, though he did not wear his clerical clothing, must be the parson, because he appeared at home in the church. The other, who now stood beside Mr. West, resembled the devil himself. He was dressed in black like the man who stalked her.

"Hathaway isn't following you, miss," Mr. West said calmly.

She edged in the direction of the altar. She might be able to slip past the parson and elude them in the darkness. Lily must have sensed her fear because the baby began to cry so loudly, the noise echoed off the walls. A hand settled on her arm, and she flinched.

"You're safe here," said the man she guessed was the parson.

"Am I? How do you know that?" she

cried. The men stared in shock at her outburst. Bother! She needed to guard her tongue better. It had often gotten her into trouble with the housekeeper at Layden Mote. "Pardon me. I should have said thank you. Are you . . . ?"

"I'm Dr. Lazarus Flanders, the vicar of this church." His gentle smile soothed her panic. "That baby sounds hungry."

"She just awoke."

"If you wish to feed her, you may use my office. I'm sure these gentlemen would . . ." His voice trailed off as he looked past her. "Neville Hathaway, is that you?" He walked past her, extending his hand in a greeting to the dark-haired man who, she now noticed, wore tan breeches instead of black pantaloons. "It's been a long time since you last paid us a visit."

She bounced the baby, quieting her, as she watched the vicar shake the hand of the man in the black greatcoat.

"This is my — friend, Theodore West," Mr. Hathaway said. "We saw the light on and decided to stop by to see how you and your family fare, Lazarus."

"How kind of you!"

As the vicar went on, Adelaide glanced from him to the other two men. Had Dr. Flanders failed to notice Mr. Hathaway's hesitation on the word "friend?" It had been momentary, but her senses, heightened by fear, had caught it. What were these men up to? Was it as innocent as Mr. Hathaway paying an old friend a call, or was there a more sinister reason for them coming into the church?

Stop it! she ordered herself. If she started seeing bugaboos everywhere, she would fret herself into doing something stupid.

As the other two men talked, Mr. West turned to her. "I believe I owe you an apology." Again, she tried to guess where his faint accent had originated, but she could not. "I shouldn't have accused you of a crime as heinous as abandoning a baby. Anyone can see you care about the child."

"I do." Until Lady Norah sent the baby with her, Adelaide had seen Lily only from a distance. Days of traveling together had allowed the baby to slip into her heart. It would not be easy to return Lily to her mother, knowing Adelaide would never have time with her again.

He brushed his fingers across the top of Lily's head, then yanked them back as Lily let out another hungry squawk.

"I didn't mean to — That is —" Mr. West stammered, looking abashed. "I'm sorry I woke her."

"You did nothing wrong," she said, hurriedly. "She's hungry, and she wants everyone to know it."

Dr. Flanders turned to her. "Forgive old friends for taking time to reminisce when we should be helping you . . . ?"

She considered giving him a false name, but nobody here knew who Adelaide Rowland was. Why would anyone recognize the name of a housemaid from a distant estate?

"Miss Adelaide Rowland," she said. She could not use the baby's real name, so she added, as the baby's crying eased to a gurgling sound, "This is Beatrix, my niece."

"A dear little mite." His smile broadened. "Why don't you all come with me to Mermaid Cottage?"

"Mermaid Cottage?" she asked at the same time Mr. West did.

"It's where my family lives. You know Priscilla and Daphne will be eager to see you, Neville. Miss Rowland, you two will be comfortable there."

Tears, unbidden and unwelcome, billowed into Adelaide's eyes. She did not want to display weaknesses in front of these men, but the vicar's generosity was beyond anything she could have dared to dream for. To be able to sleep in a place that did not reek of livestock droppings seemed as grand as being invited to King George's fanciest palace.

Another cry from Lily settled the matter. Thanking Dr. Flanders, Adelaide put the protesting baby into the basket and wrapped the blanket around her to protect her from the cold.

Mr. West picked up the basket and the baby. When she opened her mouth to protest, he said, "You'll want to button your pelisse, Miss Rowland. The wind is getting stronger."

She did, then took the basket back without saying anything. She was unsure what she *could* say that would not sound silly.

"One of the costs of living by the sea," the vicar said with a smile as he turned to the porch door. "In the summer, it's beautiful in Stonehall-on-Sea."

Adelaide stopped, and Mr. West bumped into her. She ignored him as she asked, "*This* is Stonehall-on-Sea?"

"I assumed you knew," Dr. Flanders said, his hand on the door's latch.

She shook her head. How would she have known? There were no signs to tell her the name of the village, and there had been at least a half dozen villages between this one and Brighton.

Mr. West stepped around her. "Is

Stonehall-on-Sea your intended destination, Miss Rowland?"

"Of course not!" she said with a taut laugh. Would he believe her lies? He had been kind to her and Lily, but her lady's orders not to trust anyone until they met again rang through her head. "If it was my destination, do you think I would have sought shelter in a church rather than in the place I was bound?"

"Where is that?"

Her answer had to sound sincere, so she picked the first town that came to mind. "Dover. I'm meeting family there. Is there anything else you need to know before I feed this hungry child?"

As if she understood the words, Lily let out another cry.

Mr. West stepped aside, but curiosity never left his gaze. She would have to be cautious. Avoiding him at the vicarage might not be easy, but it was one night. Tomorrow, she must try to find Lady Norah and Lord Layden. With luck, they would have already heard of her arrival.

She was definitely due some luck.

She was lying.

Theo knew that as well as he knew his own name. Adelaide Rowland was not headed for Dover. He was unsure where she was bound or why, but he recognized someone else who was skilled at spinning just enough truth into an answer to make it palatable. In his work to try to keep the uneasy peace on the Continent, he had learned to tell such tales and to know when others did.

He watched as wind buffeted Miss Rowland when they emerged from the church. She was a slight thing, but reminded him of the story of the mouse who belled the cat. She was frightened, yet she gave answers as if she did not have a care in the world beyond making sure the baby was fed.

Who was she?

He glanced at Hathaway who shrugged. They had enough problems with the smugglers along the southern coast. He must not let the puzzle of a spirited young woman distract him.

Even as he thought that, he could not keep from looking at her. She was making herself small against the cold. Pulling off his greatcoat, he settled it on her shoulders.

"To keep the baby out of the wind," he said, wondering if she were as adept at identifying a half-truth as speaking them.

Either she was not or she wanted the thick wool's protection around the baby because she whispered, "Thank you, Mr. West."

Theo was relieved the walk to the vicar's house was short. It was dashed cold! When they were ushered inside by a footman, he was astonished. A vicar with a footman? The house was of generous proportions and well-furnished. The entry hall was divided by an elegant staircase with a parlor on one side and a dining room on the other.

Two women and a little girl came toward them. The silver-haired woman wore a simple gray gown identifying her as a servant. The pregnant younger woman had blue eyes and blond curls piled atop her head. The child, who looked to be about five or six, was a younger version of her pretty mother.

"Baby?" the child asked.

"It would seem so, Daphne, by those cries," the younger woman said.

Dr. Flanders held out his hand to her. "My darling, you remember Neville, of course."

"Of course." The younger woman smiled. "Welcome, Neville."

"Allow me to introduce my friend, Theodore West, from the Continent," said Hathaway. "West, this is Priscilla Flanders, our host's wife and daughter of the earl of Emberson."

Beside him, Miss Rowland gasped. He understood her astonishment. He shared it. A lady of noble birth married to a vicar in a small, out-of-the-way village? How had *that* happened?

Bowing his head, he said as if nothing in the introduction surprised him, "Good evening, my lady."

"No need for formality," Lady Priscilla answered. "Here, I'm Priscilla, wife of the Reverend Dr. Flanders. You, Mr. West, are far from your homeland."

He was not surprised at her comment. Each time he opened his mouth, he reminded everyone around him that he was not English. "True, but the ties between England and Hanover are strong and deep." He smiled as he spoke *a* truth, not *the* truth. Even Hathaway did not know he was from a small country named Westenwald rather than the nation of Hanover where the British royal family once had lived. Only his superiors had that information.

Priscilla nodded, then glanced at Miss Rowland. "And who do we have here?"

With a kind smile for the little girl peeking into the basket to see the baby, Miss Rowland gave her name before adding, "I'm sorry for the hubbub."

"No need to apologize," Priscilla replied.

"It sounds as if your baby is tired of waiting for her supper. If you wish to come with me . . ."

She turned and gave a series of orders to the older woman whom she called Mrs. Moore. The housekeeper took the child by the hand and headed toward the rear of the house. Priscilla motioned for Miss Rowland to follow her.

Miss Rowland took a step, then tried to shrug off his greatcoat without letting it fall to the floor.

"Allow me," he said as he lifted it off with a flourish. He gave her a smile and a half bow.

As he straightened, he caught a flurry of emotions in her eyes. All were quickly hidden, impressing him, while at the same time warning that she might be even more skilled than he had guessed at concealing the truth.

The question was: What was *she* hiding?

CHAPTER THREE

Lazarus stood as his wife came into the small parlor at the back of the house. It was a comfortable room and one they preferred over the elegant chamber off the entry hall. He watched her with a faint smile. Even now, after years of marriage, he wondered why an amazing woman like his Priscilla had married him. Then he told himself not to question the blessing she was in so many ways.

"Everyone is settled for the night." Priscilla sat and put her hand on her distended belly. "What do you think of our guests?"

While he sat, he considered her question. "For a while now, I've suspected Neville works for the government. He gave up the stage several months after we first met at that lecture."

"Mr. West appears to be an involved partner in whatever he's doing, too." She laced her fingers together over their unborn child. "I must admit, I'm most troubled by Miss Rowland."

"Why?"

"She's as frightened as a kitten in a kennel, and she isn't being honest."

"The baby —"

"Is her sister's, according to her. I've arranged for a young mother, Ida Croft, to come to nurse the baby tonight. I'll make arrangements in the morning for the rest of Miss Rowland's stay."

He put his hand atop hers. "You think she'll remain here?"

"I don't think she has a place to go. She mentioned Dover, but her claim of meeting family there doesn't ring true."

He smiled. "Priscilla, you know I trust your intuition. What do you propose?"

"We can't turn them out. Why don't we invite them to stay through Christmas?" She patted her belly. "I could use some assistance with the pageant at the church, and Miss Rowland might be willing."

"And, by Christmas Day, the problem may have resolved itself."

She nodded. "My thoughts exactly."

Adelaide spent an uneasy morning at Mermaid Cottage. She had to find a way to remain in Stonehall-on-Sea and learn if the

Laydens had arrived. She had no money for an inn, even if there was one in the village. She considered asking if the household needed help, but the staff already had the house well taken care of. She had spoken to the cook, Mrs. Dunham, when she took Lily to the kitchen for her feeding. If Mrs. Dunham had understood her oblique hints about being trained in a stillroom, the cook gave no sign of it. Adelaide hoped she would not need to use the stillroom. She had brought caraway with her in case Lily had colic. So far, she had not needed it nor any of the other herbs she carried.

Instead, her own stomach tightened with stress. She had told more lies, including the big one that Lily was her sister's child. If someone asked her to explain why her sister had not taken the child with her to Dover, she had no idea what she would say. So far, her lies had been accepted at face value, making her feel even more guilty.

Discovering Mr. West had left with Mr. Hathaway should have relieved her stomach somewhat, yet she could not help wishing she had had more time to talk with him. She appreciated his kindness at the church and afterward, and she would have liked to learn more about him. She had never met anyone from one of the German states.

What was his life like in his homeland of Hanover, and why was he in Stonehall-on-Sea with the mysterious Mr. Hathaway?

You're too curious, her mother's words reminded her again. *Do your duties and be grateful you have a position.*

Her mother's lectures about not trying to make oneself better than one's beginnings had started when she had discovered Adelaide was sneaking into the book room at Layden Mote to read late at night. But Adelaide knew her mother was right. She and her parents would starve if Adelaide was dismissed.

She worried about her family as well, so she fought the urge to return to the shadowed shelves where only a candle witnessed her delight with what she read. A housemaid never would travel to the exotic and exciting places she read about, but she could take those images with her into her dreams. Still, Adelaide was tired of being frightened by what *could* happen if she said the wrong thing or did the improper thing, so frightened she suspected she was letting life pass her by.

Was it wrong to want to be more than she was? She longed to know about the world around her. Curiosity might have killed the cat, but it was thriving within her.

Adelaide heard a clock chime. She was late for the midday meal. She had enjoyed a hearty breakfast, but had endured too many days with too little food. With Lily having another feeding in the kitchen where the volunteers who came to share their milk felt most comfortable, Adelaide could eat her fill in the dining room.

Dr. Flanders and Lady Priscilla were by the table when Adelaide came into the comfortable room. The lady had asked her to use her Christian name, but Adelaide could not bring herself to.

"Ah, there you are," Dr. Flanders said, motioning to the chair on his left. "I hope you like beef stew, Adelaide."

"It sounds wonderful." She smiled at her hosts. "You have a lovely home."

"Thank you," Lady Priscilla said. "We enjoy it. I hope you will."

Adelaide hesitated, then dared to say, "I see you have many books here."

"Do you like to read?" Dr. Flanders asked as the footman came into the dining room with a large pot holding the steaming stew.

"Yes!"

He chuckled at her enthusiasm. "Do you have any favorite author or subject?"

"No. I simply like books."

"I understand." As he took the ladle to

131

serve himself, he added, "Please avail yourself of our library. There are several hundred texts here and more at the church. I find I can't resist buying a book that interests me. I'm sure you know the feeling."

Adelaide nodded, then wished she did not have to lie to such a nice man. She had no idea how wonderful it would be to own a book, though she had imagined often, while standing in the book room at Layden Mote, that those beautiful volumes were hers.

"Ah," said Lady Priscilla, "I was wondering when you would join us." She held out her hands as Daphne bounced into the room.

The little girl climbed into a chair beside her mother, chattering nonstop about seeing Lily in the kitchen. "I like babies," she announced as seriously as a judge handing down a sentence. "Can I play with Beatrix after we eat?"

Adelaide looked down at the table. Disgust filled her as she heard Daphne innocently use Lily's fake name. How could she lie to these people who had opened their home to her and the baby? She promised herself that she would apologize once she had returned Lily to the Laydens.

"Beatrix needs to take a nap," Lady Priscilla said with a chuckle, "and so do you."

"Mama —"

A glance from her father silenced Daphne, and she put her hands together on the table.

Adelaide bowed her own head as grace was spoken by the vicar, then prayed she would be forgiven for her lies.

While they dined on the delicious stew and fresh bread, Lady Priscilla spoke about plans for upcoming Christmas events. Daphne added excited comments. Adelaide was not surprised Mermaid Cottage hosted a party for the whole parish on Christmas Day, but there would be other celebrations before then.

"In fact," the lady said, "I was hoping you would stay here with us long enough, Adelaide, to help with the children's Christmas pageant at the church."

"Page-ant? A bug?" asked Daphne.

As Lady Priscilla explained to the little girl, Adelaide grinned. Not just at the child's questions, but because the lady was asking her to remain at Mermaid Cottage. Adelaide wanted to hug her.

"Of course," she said, "I would be delighted to help." What a perfect solution to her need to stay in the village and get to know the parishioners! Someone surely could help her find the Laydens.

"Our first practice is tomorrow afternoon," Lady Priscilla said. "If we go to the church after lunch, we'll be back in time for a tea."

"Excellent," Dr. Flanders said. "I'm glad that's taken care of. Now I have another parish matter . . ."

Adelaide listened with only half an ear as the vicar and his wife spoke about arranging for pies to be delivered to those who needed help with their Boxing Day meals. She could not have arranged the situation better if she had planned it herself.

Theo walked soundlessly through the trees, taking extra care because the afternoon sun, heading toward the western horizon, cast long shadows ahead of him. The trees overlooked the beach where, as soon as the moon rose, smugglers would be plying their dirty trade once again. He did not care how many bottles of brandy or how many rolls of lace were brought into England without being taxed. What concerned him were the smugglers taking important items out of the country. Documents, letters filled with information helpful to the French, maps. Those smugglers must be stopped before they sold out England and its allies for a few guineas.

When he edged by a spruce, the smell and the touch brought forth memories of trees decorated with candles for Christmas until they looked like stars fallen to the earth. The English did not share that custom, and he missed it.

Something to the right caught his eye. A movement. His hand tightened on his gun, then, realizing it was Hathaway, he relaxed. Or relaxed as much as he could when he and Hathaway were reconnoitering the shore about a mile from the vicar's house.

He wondered how Miss Rowland was settling in there. Or had she turned down the generous offer from the vicar's family to remain through the holidays? He had not been surprised at the Flanders' generosity when the vicar mentioned the invitation before Theo and Hathaway took their leave. Then again, why would she stay when she was on her way to meet family in Dover?

Because that's a lie, he reminded himself. The vicar must have sensed that as well. Why was a young woman, who dressed in ill-fitting clothing suitable for the upper classes, traveling unchaperoned with a baby not her own?

Even more puzzling, why did his mind keep returning to Adelaide Rowland? But he knew. He was fascinated with the young woman. Not because she was baffling or because she was pretty. No, she possessed an inner light. She tried to hide it, but it flared whenever she spoke without thinking. Her cheeks then turned a brighter pink, as if she had come to life instead of hiding the real Adelaide Rowland behind the façade of falsehoods she had woven for a reason he could not guess.

A rustle pulled him from his wayward thoughts again. What was wrong with *him*? He needed to concentrate on his task. He had refused to be the son his father expected — and had broken his mother's heart in the process — in order to have this life of espionage. He should —

Shouts erupted from Hathaway's location. Theo swore under his breath. A man with a scarf over his face was taking aim at Hathaway. Theo shot first. As the man fell, fire sliced through Theo's left shoulder.

Theo collapsed to his knees. Blood rushed down his chest. Pain exploded through him when he tried to draw in a breath.

Sounds burst from among the trees. A fist striking flesh. Two. Another pistol fired. People running away.

Silence.

Not even the sound of his own breathing.

He pitched forward onto his face, his last

sight that of Hathaway's horrified expression.

CHAPTER FOUR

Adelaide was stepping onto the stairs when the front door slammed open. She rushed down as two men entered. Mr. West leaned heavily on Mr. Hathaway, who sported a swollen eye. Mr. West pressed his hand to his left shoulder. Blood seeped between his fingers.

"What happened?" she asked.

Before either man could answer, household servants appeared from every direction. Dr. Flanders pushed past them and stared at his erstwhile guests.

The vicar had the same question she did. "What happened, Neville?"

"Ambush." The dark-haired man assisted Mr. West to a wooden chair in the dining room and helped him sit. "Someone didn't want us near the beach."

"Smugglers?" Adelaide asked before she could help herself.

Mr. West's eyes narrowed. "What do you

know about smugglers?"

"You're all right!" she gasped.

"What makes you think that?"

"You're talking."

He glanced at Mr. Hathaway with an expression she could not decipher. "Will you answer the question, Miss Rowland? What do you know about smugglers?" the dark-haired man asked.

"Only stories I've heard." She frowned. "Questions must wait. Mr. West needs to be tended to."

Dr. Flanders stepped forward. "She's right." He motioned to the footman. "Assist Mr. West to the room he used last night."

"I don't want to bleed on your carpets," Mr. West protested, but his voice was weak. Was he hurt worse than he wished them to guess?

Neither the footman nor Mr. Hathaway paid him any attention. Putting their arms around him, they assisted him up the stairs.

"Mrs. Moore," Dr. Flanders asked, "do you have anything to staunch bleeding?"

Adelaide did not give the housekeeper a chance to answer. "I have plantain with me. It'll stop bleeding." When the vicar and his housekeeper looked at her in surprise, she added, "I never travel without my healing herbs. I learned that from a wise old woman."

"A very wise woman," he said. "Do you know how to apply it?"

She nodded. Minnie, who had been in charge of Layden Mote's stillroom, had taught her well.

"Good! Mrs. Moore will be available for whatever help you need. Meanwhile, I'll let my wife know so she isn't disturbed by the noise and voices."

Adelaide nodded. The local midwife had called earlier and insisted Lady Priscilla go to bed and stay there until she returned to check her.

Mrs. Moore led her up the stairs, to a door across the hall from where Adelaide had slept last night. Knocking, she asked, "May we come in?"

"We?" called Mr. Hathaway.

"Miss Rowland and me."

When the door opened, Adelaide walked in and discovered it was a twin to the room she and Lily used, except the walls were painted a delicate blue instead of green. She glanced toward the large half-tester bed, but it was empty. Mr. West was perched on a chaise longue, a towel held to his left shoulder.

Dismay lengthened his face. "You shouldn't be here."

"Miss Rowland knows about taking care of wounds," Mrs. Moore said. "If you're half as smart as I suspect you are, Mr. West, you'll let her tend it."

Adelaide heard a snort behind her and saw Mr. Hathaway trying to smother a laugh. Relief surged through her. His amusement was a good sign his friend was not hurt as badly as she feared.

"You heard Mrs. Moore, West," Mr. Hathaway said. "Follow your own advice and take advantage of the skills of those around you."

Mr. West nodded, then closed his eyes as if the simple motion had hurt. "Miss Rowland, do your worst."

"I'd as lief do my best, sir," she retorted. "I'd never do less."

This time, as Adelaide's face grew warm at her brash words, Mr. Hathaway's guffaw escaped. He took his leave when Mrs. Moore sent him and the footman away.

"What do you need, Miss Rowland?" asked the housekeeper.

"To see what we're dealing with."

"If you wish to know the truth, Miss Rowland, my pride is hurt far more than my arm."

"I doubt that." She walked over to where Mr. West sat. "Will you remove your coat?"

He tried, but needed her help and Mrs. Moore's. His face grew more ashen as he moved his left arm. A crimson blotch oozed along the front of his white shirt. Above that was a round hole. He had not just been ambushed — he had been shot!

Her stomach threatened to erupt, but she focused on what Minnie had taught her. She breathed in and out through her nose. Her stomach began to settle as she moved to view his back. As she had hoped, a matching hole was visible there, though the blood was less. She guessed he had hunched over in pain, sending the blood forward.

"Good news," she said, trying to make her voice sound cheerful. "The ball went through your shoulder."

"Huzzah!" he said with a wry grin. "We should have a party to celebrate."

"Let's get you bandaged before you begin the guest list."

He arched a tawny brow, and she guessed he had not expected such an answer. It was a habit she needed to break. If she spoke in such a manner to Lady Norah or the housekeeper at Layden Mote, she would be dismissed.

A weak smile tipped his mouth, and she felt her own twitching in response. What was it about Mr. West that was so appealing, daring her to be herself? No one else had ever made her feel like that. With him, at moments like this, she did not have to pretend to be something she was not. She could be a person, a real person with thoughts and opinions she did not have to hide. She did not have to pour the real Adelaide into a mold of the perfect maid.

Had she lost her mind? She must do as she should in order to take care of her family. Their needs were more important than her own. Yet, as Mr. West looked at her with a twinkle in his amazing eyes, she dared to believe she could be more.

A pulse of some strange emotion that was a mixture of nostalgia and dismay rippled along her spine. She missed Layden Mote and her familiar world there, but she dreaded returning to her position as a maid who might as well be invisible. She had experienced more than she ever expected on her journey, and she was no longer the person she had been when she left Ullswater. Somehow, however, when she returned home, she would have to become the maid she was again, because her family depended on her.

To cover her shock at her thoughts, she said, "Mrs. Moore, in my room you'll find a packet labeled 'plantain' on the dressing table. Mix it with paraffin. I'll need fresh water and bandages. If the cook has comfrey in the stillroom, have it mixed as well. Some people respond better to one than the other." She gave the housekeeper a few more instructions, lowering her voice so Mr. West could not hear.

Adelaide's concern for Mr. West's condition returned twofold when he did not make any further remarks while she tore his shirt away from his injured shoulder. He remained silent when she used fresh water to clean the wounds, dabbed both of them with the plantain ointment Mrs. Moore had prepared, and wrapped strips of linen around his shoulder.

She washed blood from her hands and wiped them dry on her apron. "I'm done for now. You were lucky the ball missed your bones."

"Thank you." His accent seemed stronger when his voice was hushed. "I appreciate your efforts, Miss Rowland."

She had Gilbert come in and assist him in removing his boots. The footman helped Mr. West to bed, then waited in case she needed him further.

"Drink this," she said as she held out the cup of tea Mrs. Moore had laced with valerian. The housekeeper had made the tea extra strong to hide the herb's bitter taste. "It'll ease the pain." She did not add that the valerian would help him sleep in spite of the pain. When Mr. West took the cup and balanced it on his knee, she went to a nearby lamp and blew out the flame. What he needed was sleep, which was the best healer. "You could have been killed in the ambush."

He made a snort like his friend's, but there was no amusement in it. "Hathaway is wrong. It wasn't an ambush. We startled those men, and they panicked. I was shot because all my attention was on the man who was about to shoot Hathaway in the back." His lips pulled back. "Fortunately, *my* shot guaranteed he didn't have the chance."

She stared, astonished at the change in the gentleman who had given her his coat to protect her from the cold. His expression was savage, and she wondered how thin the veneer of civilization was around him. Somehow, she managed to stutter that he should drink his tea and rest.

"If you need anything," she said, "Gilbert will be right outside your door."

"You mean you're not going to tuck me in?"

Heat flashed through her, inundating her

with images of him on the bed and her leaning over him to make sure he was comfortable, his arm curving around her as he drew her lips toward his.

With a gasp, she said, "Mr. West, you shouldn't say such things."

"Why not?" He took a sip of the tea, but his gaze never left her. It teased her to speak her mind, to give him full access to every thought.

She resisted. "It isn't proper."

"What isn't proper is you looking as gray as death. At least now, you have some color in your cheeks. It is much better, if you wish to know the truth."

The truth? Adelaide recalled how many lies she had told since her arrival in Stonehall-on-Sea.

"The truth is you need to sleep, Mr. West. If you require anything further . . ." She glanced at where Gilbert stood, staring straight ahead as if oblivious to everything in the room. "Gilbert will assist you."

"Thank you again, Miss Rowland, for your ministrations. May I ask you one more question?"

"Certainly," she replied, though she was far from certain about what he might ask.

"What *do* you know about smugglers?"

Startled, she blurted, "Nothing! I told Mr.

Hathaway that downstairs."

"Did you?" He touched his forehead and grimaced. "I must have missed that. Forgive me. I don't mean to harass a woman who has seen to my care with such skill. I'll see you at breakfast, as I trust I'll survive until the morning."

"I trust you will." Bidding him a good night and reminding him to finish the tea, she left the room.

Adelaide went across the hall to her room. Closing the door, she was pleased to see Lily sleeping in the cradle Dr. Flanders had brought up to the room.

She let her shoulders sag, surprised how stiff they felt. Seeing Mr. West with his lifeblood draining from him had been more horrible than she could have guessed. She sank down onto the bed and hid her face in her hands. He could have died. He still could. Wounds festered and people died. First thing in the morning, she must explore Mermaid Cottage's stillroom to make sure it had the basic herbs she needed. It was too late in the year to harvest any now.

She shifted and bumped into the baby's basket. She should take advantage of this time to air out the blankets that had been wrapped around Lily. Since their arrival at Mermaid Cottage, she had not had a chance to do so between caring for the baby and for Mr. West.

She lifted them out and gasped when something hard struck the floor. Scooping it up, she saw it was a small book, no bigger than her palm. It must have been hidden in the basket.

Sitting, she opened it. The handwriting belonged to her lady's husband, Lord Layden. She began reading, then quickly closed the book. It was a love sonnet written by the viscount to his wife. No one, save for Lady Norah, should read what her husband had written. Why had the lady stuffed the book in the basket with the baby?

Another question to confound her. The rendezvous with her lady and Lord Layden could not come soon enough.

CHAPTER FIVE

"I have to go, West."

Theo hated to agree, but Hathaway was correct. Right now, Theo would be a liability in their work. Just as important, Hathaway was showing definite promise, exactly as Theo had guessed when first seeing him on stage in a London theater and with his adoring fans afterward. A few questions whispered in the appropriate ears, and Theo had gotten the information he needed to approach Hathaway and invite him to become his protégé. A past littered with experiences, legal and not quite legal, made the young man perfect for the role of a lifetime, serving the Crown without letting anyone know he was doing it.

"Where are you going?" Theo asked. "And for how long?"

"To find the courier from up north. I'll be gone as long as that takes."

"No longer than a fortnight."

"West —"

"No longer than a fortnight," he repeated. "By then I should be healed enough to go with you. Report to me each week. Where are you heading first?"

Hathaway paced the bedroom. "We know he set off from the northern lakes. Can we send a message to our contacts at the Mote to obtain more information about their courier?"

"No. It's as if they've disappeared off the face of the earth." Theo sighed. "You've heard the rumors the same as I have."

"That their estate was overrun and ransacked? That our agents there were alerted and were able to slip away?"

He nodded.

"Do you believe that?" It was clear Hathaway was having a hard time swallowing the tale.

"It wouldn't be the first time something like that has happened." Theo had an irritating itch on his left side, but resisted scratching. That would jar his bandaged shoulder. "Probably not the last either."

"So where are they now?"

"I'd guess they're searching for their courier, as we are. If he has been captured or killed, their work and plenty of ours was for nothing." He held his right hand out to

Hathaway. "Good hunting, my friend."

Hathaway shook it. "Watch over these people here, West. They're good folks, but ill-prepared to protect themselves if those who shot you decide to avenge their cohort's death on our allies."

"Allies?" he asked, puzzled. "What do the vicar and his wife know of our work?"

"Nothing for certain, but I can guarantee they suspect quite a bit. Lazarus has proved to be an excellent source of information without ever asking why I might want it. As for his wife . . . she's very sharp, and she has great instincts about people." He paused, then added, "In addition, they are my friends. They welcomed me into their lives. Watch over them."

"I will." Theo sank into the pillows as Hathaway left. If something did not turn in their favor soon, valuable information might end up in the wrong hands. It was a failure he did not want to face.

How did Miss Rowland fit into this? Her arrival in Stonehall-on-Sea could be a co-incidence, but Theo didn't believe in them. She had been quick to disavow any connection with the smugglers. Almost too quick.

He frowned, recalling how, when they first met in the church, she had feared a man was following her. How could he have forgotten that? Was that a tale she had spun? She had not been honest about other matters, including the baby's identity. What else had she been false about? The smugglers?

Being suspicious of everyone means you can't even trust yourself. His father's advice vexed him as much now as it had when he had first heard it. His father had explained that at some point, a man had to trust his instincts to tell him if someone was loyal.

At what point? he remembered asking.

That, my son, is what you must learn.

He wanted to believe Adelaide Rowland was uninvolved with the smugglers. Yet, his instincts warned him she was a part of the whole jumble. Had she layered more lies upon the ones he already knew were false? He could not ignore the truth just because he was drawn to the warm-hearted woman with the surprising wit which delighted him when it poked past her proper behavior. He had to find answers and fast! While Hathaway was away, he would keep an eye on the vicar's family to make sure they remained safe, and he would do the same with Miss Rowland.

Just in case. . . .

Adelaide shifted Lily's basket when she heard excited voices as soon as she reached the church's porch. There was no reason to try to stay out of sight any longer, because word had spread through the village that she and Lily were the vicar's guests along with Mr. West. Nobody had questioned her tale that Lily was her niece. She hoped nobody would guess the truth about her and the baby.

Beside them, Daphne was jumping up and down with excitement. The children inside must be eager to get started on the Christmas pageant.

"You may need more than a one-armed man to maintain some sort of order." Mr. West smiled as he opened the door, taking care not to move the sling supporting his left arm.

His color was much better after five days of bed rest. When Adelaide had changed the bandages after breakfast, she had seen his wound was closing well with no signs of infection. Even so, he had several weeks to go before he could expect to be free of pain.

One thing had not changed. He wanted to return to his work. That Mr. Hathaway had left already had not helped curb his impatience. She was unsure what they did, but half-finished sentences and sudden silences at Mermaid Cottage warned her that they had many secrets.

Or was she looking for trouble where there was none?

She did not have the chance to answer her own question because, as soon as Mr. West opened the door, a half dozen children sprinted out. Like Daphne, they seemed to talk without taking a breath. Again, she wished Lady Priscilla had been able to join them. The midwife had insisted she remain in bed until the early contractions stopped.

The only way the children would go inside was if she did. Adelaide walked inside, taking care not to brush against Mr. West's sling or tilt the basket. Several women sat at the front of the church. The mothers of the children, she guessed.

Adelaide set the basket on a pew. She clapped her hands together. Hard. The noise was sharp against the roof, and the children stopped and stared at her in amazement.

With Mr. West's help, she herded the boys and girls to the altar rail where she had them stand in a row. She guessed they ranged in age from nine to a tot barely three years old. There were ten, enough for a Christmas pageant, similar to the one that had been acted out in her local parish church when she was little.

She stood there, looking at the children. Assigning roles should be next, but she did not know them and was unsure which would do well in a specific part.

Mr. West seemed to have no such concerns. Charming the children, not to mention their mothers, he soon had them all sitting in a circle while he read the Christmas story from the book of Luke. They listened, rapt, while he changed his voice to portray each character.

She listened, too. She never had heard the story told in quite the same way. Not only did he change voices for each character, but he also made the sounds for each of the animals as well as singing the angel's message. Laughter greeted that because he had difficulty — or pretended he did — staying on key.

"Now you know the parts you'll need to play," he said, closing the Bible.

"That's our baby Jesus." A little boy pointed to Lily, who was asleep in the basket in spite of the children's laughter.

"That's a *girl*," chided another child. "Baby Jesus was a *boy*."

Adelaide smiled while Mr. West grinned. "True. However, you must remember that you each will pretend to be something or someone you aren't. Some of you aren't really lambs or angels, are you?"

"That's for certain," came a mutter from

155

where the mothers sat.

Everyone laughed again, and Mr. West put the Bible on the lectern. "I think that's a good way to end the day. Come . . ." He glanced at Adelaide.

"Tomorrow at the same time," she said.

"Come tomorrow at the same time, and Miss Rowland will help you pick your parts."

The children cheered, excited. They left after their mothers thanked Mr. West for his kindness toward them.

Adelaide walked to the porch door with the mothers. Her hopes that one of them might have information on the Laydens were dashed when, one after another, the women shook their heads. No newcomers had arrived in the village in recent weeks, other than her and Mr. West.

She smiled her thanks, but her stomach roiled. Where were Lady Norah and her husband? She could no longer ignore the facts. Something had gone wrong. Otherwise, they would have reached Stonehall-on-Sea by now. Had Lady Norah's health taken a turn for the worse? Should Adelaide retrace her steps to Layden Mote?

A shudder raced through her at the thought of the long journey . . . and the man with the single hobnail in his boot. She had not seen or heard him since she moved into Mermaid Cottage, but she could not believe he was gone for good. Had *he* done something to her employers? No, she did not want to think of that.

But she must. She had been invited to stay with the vicar's family until after the holidays. But what then? She needed a plan for what she would do if the Laydens did not arrive.

Perhaps she was simply getting ahead of herself. Maybe her mistress and her husband had stopped at a friend's house. The lord and his lady had many friends. The manor often had visitors. Many were brought to Lord Layden's private office and the door closed. No servants were allowed to linger nearby or even walk past until those guests took their leave.

Adelaide had tried to ignore those visits, telling herself they might not be strange. Maybe all the peerage acted so. Not that it mattered now. She had never learned the name of any of those callers, so she could not turn to them for help. Lady Norah had once told her that her family had an estate north of London. Surely they would welcome Lily there and perhaps even know why the Laydens had not come to Stonehall-on-Sea as they planned.

"You're deep in thought," said Mr. West. Though he was smiling, the twinkles she had seen in his eyes were missing. Was he concerned about her? He gazed at her as if willing to shoulder her burdens if she would share them.

She shifted her eyes away, reminding herself how he had charmed the children. Letting him do the same to her would be foolish. She had no idea what he might be, but from the way he spoke and acted, his class was far above her true one.

"We should go," he said when she did not answer. "You know how tongues will wag if someone catches you unchaperoned except by a little girl and a baby."

She almost laughed out loud. She was no young miss who needed to worry about her reputation so she could marry well. She would never wed. Servants had no time for courting or family life. But . . . if she were to have a husband, she would want it to be a man like Mr. West. A man who made her smile and dared her to be her true self. Letting him draw her into his arms, she —

She silenced that thought.

"You're right," she said. "Let me get Daphne and Beatrix." She had learned to speak the fake name with ease.

He stepped aside as she went up the aisle.

When she heard him behind her, she said, "You're good with children."

"It comes from having a surplus of siblings."

"How many?"

"Eleven."

"Really?"

He nodded. "Now you know why I give myself a hearty portion whenever food is offered. I learned only fools expect there to be second servings."

She laughed with him. As he began to regale her with stories of his many brothers and sisters, he picked up a drowsy Daphne in one arm. Grimacing slightly, he leaned the little girl's head against his shoulder while Adelaide drew on her pelisse and lifted the basket off the pew. They walked out together.

Again, rebellious thoughts filled her head as she imagined them as a real family. He had given her an astounding gift. He allowed her to believe — even for a few minutes — that the impossible was possible.

"How are you faring?"

Looking up from the pages he was studying, Theo watched his host walk into the front parlor. Theo folded the pages and, careful that he did not put pressure on his stiff shoulder, put them beneath his coat.

"Much better," he replied.

"Glad to hear that." If Flanders was curious about what Theo had been reading, no sign of it showed on his face. Instead, it was long with obvious dismay.

"What's wrong?"

If the men whom he and Hathaway sought had returned, trouble would come with them. It might only be stolen food or livestock, but it could also mean real danger for unsuspecting villagers. He wondered, as he had before, if the seaside village was as innocent as it appeared. The criminals he and Hathaway pursued might have allies here.

The vicar sat. "To own the truth, I'm facing three dilemmas."

"*Three?* Can I be of help?" The words came without bidding. How many times had he told new agents never to become involved in matters beyond their mission? Often enough that he should heed the advice himself, yet, it was difficult to turn down the man who had opened his house to him without a single question.

"With one, no." His mouth quirked. "My wife's aunt is coming to call later this afternoon. She has strong opinions about Priscilla marrying me."

"After so many years?"

"Priscilla's aunt doesn't forget or forgive."

"She sounds like a termagant."

Flanders's smile burst forth. "Your words, not mine."

"But you aren't going to argue with me."

"It isn't a host's place to disagree with his guests."

Theo laughed, then wished he had not because the movement made his shoulder ache worse. He must be cautious, especially since he had discarded his sling after the second practice at the church. Hadn't he learned his lesson when Miss Rowland made him laugh?

Miss Rowland. . . . She was a puzzle. He enjoyed watching her with the children as they practiced for the Christmas Eve play. She was gentle with them, but encouraging. She could appear as prim as his grandmother one minute and make an outrageous comment the next. He found himself thinking of things to say to bring forth her intriguing side again. Who was she, and why was she in Stonehall-on-Sea? He was no closer to answering those questions than he had been a week ago.

"My second dilemma is far more important." Flanders folded his hands between his knees and leaned toward Theo. "Before he left, Neville told me more about what happened on the shore the day you were shot. It disturbs me that the smugglers were so close. Until now, they've remained east of here, mainly because we have no caves to stash their goods away from excise officers."

"Or where village leaders are willing to look the other way in exchange for gold to line their purses."

"I don't know which of the two is a worse threat to our young men: the lure of easy riches if they become smugglers, or a life in the Royal Navy if they have the misfortune to run into a press gang."

"Press gangs have been here?" The navy did not have enough volunteers, so they sent out gangs to "recruit" hapless men who fell for their traps baited with plenty of free rum.

"Not recently. I wasn't cordial to the last group that tried to spirit away some of our boys." His smile, drawing aside his lips and showing his teeth, made him look more like a predator than a parson. "That was almost six months ago, and they haven't returned."

"Well done!" Theo was more careful as he laughed this time, and pain did not rivet his shoulder. He hoped it was a good sign. Later, he would put on some of the salve Miss Rowland had given him to ease the discomfort. "It would appear you're well on

162

your way to solving that dilemma. What about your third one?"

"Ah, that's the one where you may be able to help, West."

"What do you need?" He had been foolish to offer his assistance, but he could not take back his words. That had been one of the earliest lessons his father had insisted he learn. A man charged with the responsibility of those around him did not have the luxury of changing his mind.

"Each year on Christmas Eve, the village enjoys an ancient tradition. A wooden horse called the Hooden Horse is led through the streets, while people ring bells and sing carols around it. It goes from house to house, asking for donations to the poor."

"I don't understand why such a tradition is a dilemma."

"The man who usually serves at the back has been called away from Stonehall-on-Sea."

"He's the rider?"

"No, he's the actual back half. The horse is a wooden structure carried by two men. One at the head and the other at the tail."

Theo stared at the parson, wondering if he had misheard him. "Let me understand what you're saying. You want me to be the horse's rear end?"

Flanders chuckled. "When you put it that way, I daresay I've given you every reason to decline." He grew serious. "I'm asking because I know you and Neville are here looking for someone. Someone you believe to be in Stonehall-on-Sea. What better chance will you have to visit the cottages in the village than by being part of our Hooden Horse merriment in a couple of weeks?"

"Hathaway told me you were a valuable ally." He offered his hand. "You have your horse's backside, Dr. Flanders."

As the parson explained more about the tradition, Theo could not stop smiling. His chances of catching the prey who had eluded him too long had just improved.

A lot.

CHAPTER SIX

A maid held out a basket filled with clean baby clothes. Adelaide took it and pushed aside guilt that she had let the girl launder them on such a rainy day. How quickly she was becoming accustomed to being waited on! Not knowing what to say, she settled on, "Thank you."

"I'd be glad to take it upstairs, Miss Rowland." The maid looked nonplused.

"I'm happy to do it. It's like playing with doll clothes." She turned away, but saw disagreement on the maid's face. For those in service, no task was a game. A single mistake could mean being given one's *congé* without a recommendation, making it impossible to find another position.

A shiver cut through her. If her employers had vanished and were never found, what would that mean for her and the rest of the staff? She had no idea if Lily was the heir to Layden Mote or if it went, at Lord Layden's death, along with his title, to some male relative. What would happen then? Would they continue to work at the manor, or would the house be closed and the servants sent on their way with a quick letter of recommendation from someone who had no idea of their skills? Not that it would do her any good, because, for someone like her, the Mote was the *only* employer in the area.

Stop it! There were dozens of reasons she could think of — and there must be more she could not imagine — why the Laydens had not come for their child. Deciding to spend time with the baby and then maybe read a little before supper, she walked toward the stairs.

The door opened. Adelaide stepped aside when a dripping umbrella entered, followed by Mr. West. He started to shake it and himself, but halted when he saw her.

"I didn't get you wet, did I?" he asked as he leaned the umbrella against the wall.

"I'm quicker than that. How is your shoulder?"

"A bit tired." He gave her an impudent grin. "You needn't worry about me being more foolish than usual. I don't want you fretting."

"Fretting is a waste of time. I try to avoid it." *What a lie!* She was worried every waking second about Lily and her parents.

"A good way to live your life. Wish I could do the same." His expression grew introspective before his smile returned. "My shoulder won't let me overdo it. Stretching, even slightly, is painful."

"I'm glad you're being careful."

He wagged a finger at her. "Don't put words in my mouth, Miss Rowland. I never said I was being careful."

"I suspect, Mr. West, you're always careful." *Oh, my!* She had spoken again without thinking. The familiar heat slapped her cheeks, and she guessed they were flushed.

He laughed. "Quite to the contrary, and I can prove it. Dr. Flanders invited me to participate in one of Stonehall-on-Sea's beloved yuletide traditions. The village's Hooden Horse."

She shifted the basket of laundry to her other arm. "What's that?"

"A wooden horse, adorned with ribbons for a mane, is toted about the village with great ceremony."

"It sounds like fun."

His tone became disconsolate. "If one is the head, perhaps. But when one isn't . . ."

"Dr. Flanders asked you to be —"

"The horse's ass? Yes." He raised a single finger. "Choose your next words with care,

Miss Rowland. I'd advise you not to say you believe I'm well-suited for the role."

She laughed, and was delighted how his eyes sparkled in response. They teased her to move closer. She took a single step forward, unable to halt herself.

Suddenly, the entry hall became busy as the Flanders family, including a very pale Lady Priscilla and every servant rushed in. Adelaide gasped. She realized everyone was arranging themselves to greet an important guest.

Mr. West snatched the laundry basket from her. Going into the dining room, he slid it under a chair by the serving buffet where it would not be visible. He drew her hand onto his arm and whispered, "You can collect it once her ladyship has received her proper amount of pomp."

Or that was what she thought he said, for the brush of his warm breath against her ear made her pulse thunder. He placed his hand over hers to keep her from stepping away. He need not have. Her knees were so unstable, she doubted she could have moved. The roughness of his palm sent heated shivers up her arm and into her brain where they exploded like a sky filled with fireworks.

The door opened, and a woman entered.

Adelaide had not guessed Lady Priscilla's aunt, for it must be she, would appear so youthful. No gray marred her black hair which was arranged in an intricate style. When she removed her pelisse, her stylish gown was a sedate purple, suggesting she had recently emerged from mourning. Her gaze swept over each of them, and Adelaide was sure the woman saw through the thin fabric of her lies.

"You have a houseful of company," the woman said, "but I suppose a parson's door is always open." There was a definite sniff in her words.

Adelaide dampened her urge to leap to the defense of Dr. Flanders and his wife. They should be commended, not derided. She glanced at Mr. West and saw his eyes narrow.

Lady Priscilla smiled. "Welcome to Mermaid Cottage, Aunt Cordelia. Allow me to introduce Theodore West. Mr. West, this is —"

"I am Lady Cordelia Emberley Smith Gray Dexter." Her aunt spoke each surname as if it were more important than the previous one.

Lady Cordelia smiled as Mr. West bowed over her hand with the polish gained through long hours of practice. He had not told Adelaide much about himself, other than stories of his siblings, but she was certain he had told her at least one lie.

He should be addressed with a far more prestigious title than just "Mister."

Hearing women's voices from the small parlor, Theo turned and went in the opposite direction. He had been able to avoid Lady Cordelia most of the day, and he hoped to continue until dinner was served in a couple of hours. He had not guessed one woman could turn a comfortable home inside out. Lady Cordelia was as powerful as a hurricane. He had faced criminals and turncoats and those who would see him dead because of his loyalties, and none of them had unnerved him as much as Lady Priscilla's aunt did. He wondered how Flanders endured having his wife's aunt as a guest when she judged him unworthy of her niece. Her comments were not overtly condescending, yet the meaning was clear. Perhaps the family was accustomed to the faultfinding lady, but he was not.

He let a sigh slide between his lips. His own aunt, Alfreda, was like Lady Cordelia, assured her opinion was the sole one, and slicing anyone who suggested otherwise to pieces with the sharp edge of her tongue.

He had learned to give her a quick hug upon her arrival and her departure and otherwise stay out of her sight.

As Theo entered the entry hall, two men stepped out of the front parlor. He recognized Flanders, but the other man was a stranger.

The vicar motioned for Theo to join them. "Theodore West, allow me to introduce you to Malcolm Kingsley, who will be the head of our Hooden Horse. Malcolm, this is our guest whom I was telling you about."

Theo shook the man's hand. Kingsley was bald, though he could not have been over thirty years old. His dark brown eyes were, Theo noted, assessing him. Two could play at that sport, and he took note of the fine cut of the man's coat. It did not match his threadbare black breeches, which appeared to be sewn by a ham-handed tailor. His boots had been patched multiple times. Had he dressed himself from the church's donation box? Theo would never hold poverty against a man, because he had met many honest people among the poor and many dishonest ones among those who deemed themselves nobility.

"Pleasure to meet you," he said to the bald man.

"And you, West."

"I appreciate both of you stepping in," Flanders said, "to save our tradition."

"You aren't the usual horse's head?" Theo asked, sure he recalled the vicar mentioning the man carrying the horse's head had done so many years.

"My uncle has taken ill. I offered to fill in." Kingsley shrugged and gave a sigh that suggested he would have preferred that someone else had taken over the duty. "One never can guess what one will end up doing to help family, can one?"

"True." Theo watched Kingsley as he turned to talk with Flanders.

His gut told him something was not as it should be, but he was having a difficult time heeding those hunches since he had met Miss Rowland. Besides, he could not put his finger on what might be amiss. He understood the man's reluctance. If he had not been looking for suspicious activity in town, he would have gladly handed over the role, as well.

Soft footfalls came from the stairs, and Theo glanced, as the other men did, toward them. Miss Rowland's caramel-colored hair was in a neat chignon, and she wore a pale pink dress that gave a rosy warmth to her cheeks. He had to exert his willpower *not* to cross the entry hall and offer his hand to assist her on the last few steps.

"I hope I'm not interrupting," she said with a smile that seemed a bit warmer when her gaze alighted on him.

"Of course not." The vicar gestured toward Kingsley. "This is Miss Adelaide Rowland, another guest at Mermaid Cottage. This is Malcolm Kingsley."

With a nod, Kingsley acknowledged the introduction, then began to talk with the vicar about people whose names Theo did not recognize. He assumed they were villagers. When Theo asked the other men to excuse him and Miss Rowland, Flanders nodded but kept talking about a family in need and how he hoped the pennies tossed at the Hooden Horse would be enough to assist with buying them food through the winter.

Theo took her arm, but she started to pull away and murmured, "I need to get something in the parlor."

"What?"

"The baby's basket. I left it there after we went to pageant practice today."

"Get it later." He did not like how Kingsley stared at her when the bald man thought no one was looking.

"But —" She must have seen his determination on his face, because she nodded. As they walked along the hallway, Theo could feel Kingsley watching them.

Don't look for trouble where there may not be any, he warned his instincts, which had set off an alarm as if something wase very wrong. *You have enough already.*

CHAPTER SEVEN

Theo pulled on his greatcoat in his bedroom the next morning, wanting to head outside to get some fresh air. He would take a walk before midday, and then go with Miss Rowland to watch the children practice their pageant. Perhaps some of them had learned their lines instead of spending their time playing hide-and-seek among the pews.

As he stepped out of his room, he glanced across the hallway. The door to Miss Rowland's room was wide open. He should not look in, but he could not keep himself from doing so.

He could not look away. Miss Rowland sat on the chaise longue beside Daphne who was holding the baby in her pudgy arms. The little girl was looking down at the baby with delight, and Miss Rowland kept a steadying arm behind the child along with a hand beneath Lily in case Daphne's hold faltered. An expression of love warmed Miss

Rowland's face when she gazed at the children.

He could no longer trust his instincts where Miss Rowland was concerned. Had he made a mistake? Was her claim that the baby belonged to her sister true? He shook his head as if to clear away the mesmerism of the scene. He could not let himself be waylaid by appearances. He must stick to facts.

He smiled as he admitted that one fact was how Miss Rowland's inner light seemed to glow more brightly as she laughed at something Daphne said and gave the little girl's shoulders a squeeze. She was a woman who deserved to have a home and a family and the love both would bring her.

He walked along the hallway, knowing those were things he could not offer her now. He had vowed his work would come first. He had set aside his own family to have his great adventure. To walk away now endangered England and the whole Continent.

Meeting Adelaide had clouded what was once a clear decision. His life had become one grave and desperate chase after another. In spite of that, she brought laughter up from a place deep within him. Not polite amusement, but genuine laughter. He had not guessed how much he missed that until he met her.

"Mr. West, were you looking for us?" Miss Rowland asked.

He made sure his smile was innocuous when he faced her and the children. She cradled Beatrix in one arm and held Daphne's hand. It was a compelling domestic scene, but not, he reminded himself, one meant for him.

"I was about to take the air." Inspiration struck, and he added, "Why don't you join me? We could collect holiday greens for the house."

She smiled, and something peculiar quivered in his middle. No, it was no longer peculiar. It happened each time she let some of her light shine in his direction. Whether when she changed his bandages or when her eyes glittered with amusement as she gave him a sassy response to his teasing, having her focus her warm smile in his direction was the cause of the intriguing frisson.

"Go! Go!" shouted Daphne, jumping up and down in her excitement.

"Why don't I ask Dr. Flanders for his permission to take one young assistant?" he asked.

"Good," Miss Rowland replied. "Perhaps

you could do that while we take Beatrix downstairs for her feeding. Shall we meet you in the entry hall?"

He started to nod, then heard Lady Cordelia's voice come from the other end of the upper hallway. "I'll meet you outside."

"I understand." She turned to go down the back staircase.

Minutes later, Theo waited on the walk outside Mermaid Cottage. The day was crisp, but not as damp and cold as previous days had been. The fresh air and light breeze were invigorating. He glanced along the road to where a small wood flanked it. While they were finding greens, he would keep an eye out for any clues to the men who had attacked him and Hathaway.

The door opened, and he was not surprised when Miss Rowland and Daphne emerged with a footman in tow. Gilbert carried a saw and pulled a small cart where they could transport any greens they chose. No doubt Dr. Flanders felt it vital Miss Rowland not be alone with him. Or was the vicar more worried about another attack among the trees? The wood where Theo had been shot was farther to the east, but a worried father might not want to take any chances. Nor did he. Not with Miss Rowland, or the child.

The footman stayed behind them as they walked. Close enough to keep them in sight, but far enough away so they might talk without him overhearing.

"You escaped just in time," Miss Rowland said as they walked toward the wood with Daphne running about in excitement. "Lady Cordelia asked me if you were in the house, and I could honestly tell her no."

He chuckled, and his shoulder twinged. He should carry the pain salve with him . . . just in case. "Am I that transparent?"

"About Lady Cordelia? Yes." She pointed to the first trees. "Shall we begin here?"

When he agreed, they walked into the wood. The bare branches on the trees whispered in the gentle breeze, and the evergreens danced. For a moment, he felt as if he was home and a boy again, wandering through the forest and pretending he was a knight of yore, hunting a great, fierce dragon.

They laughed and teased Daphne and each other as they gathered holly and spruce branches. Gilbert cut the pieces, because Theo discovered his shoulder was not yet fit for the task. The footman stacked the cuttings as best he could in the small wagon, unbending just enough to smile when the little girl brought him a single soggy leaf she thought was perfect for decorating.

As they wandered through the wood, they reached a stream. When Daphne announced her desire for some fir branches from the far side, Theo carried the child across, using the stones sticking up from the water, and made her promise to wait while he assisted Miss Rowland.

"Hurry!" Daphne sat on a boulder and rocked her feet against it.

"You heard the boss," he said with a smile when he returned to where Miss Rowland stood. "Ready?"

"I think so. Are those stones slippery?"

"Not bad. I'll help you." He took her hand. Her fingers stiffened, then gentled within his. Her skin was soft against his callused palm, and she stood close enough so wisps of her hair, caught in the breeze, stroked his face as lightly as he wanted to caress hers. The thought astonished him, and he almost stumbled as he stepped onto the first stone. He caught himself and reassured her that he was fine. How could he explain he had been tripped up by his longing to draw her into his arms, an idea he had to banish from his mind? Being shot had already made a bumble-bath of his plans. He could not be distracted further by Miss Rowland.

Neither of them spoke when they reached the far side of the stream. He did not want to release her hand, but was aware of the footman chaperoning them. He placed her hand on his sleeve and contented himself with the chaste touch.

"Thank you, Mr. West," she said as she reached to take Daphne's hand.

He halted and brought her to face him. "I think we've endured enough challenges to allow us to dispense with such formality."

"Challenges?"

He counted on his fingers. "You returning me to health, trying to be good guests in a busy house . . . and, most challenging, an opinionated Lady Cordelia."

When she grinned, he smiled. She was a treat for his eyes. He had encountered many lovely women in his travels, but none of them had ever made him long to see her smile as Miss Rowland did. Whenever he won one from her, it seemed like a great victory to be celebrated in the grandest way he could imagine.

With a kiss.

Disturbed by his own thoughts and knowing how much he wanted to put them into action, he stepped away. He walked toward a tree where Daphne was pointing at a squirrel. He needed to put some space between them so he could think. He had, somehow, misplaced his mind. The first lesson he had learned, and the first he had impressed on Hathaway, was not to let a woman captivate him while on a mission. His focus must never waver, not for a second, because that could lead to disaster and death if war began anew on the Continent.

Never forget that. Not ever. Not for anyone.

Advice that had been easy to follow . . . until he met Adelaide.

Why was he acting so strangely?

Nothing had made sense since Lady Norah woke Adelaide and sent her away with Lily, including Mr. West asking her permission for the intimacy of using her given name. Laughter battered her lips, but it was filled with as much sorrow as amusement. If he had met her at Layden Mote, he would have used her first name without a second thought, assuming he even noticed her.

Now was the time to tell the truth. She remained silent. Until she completed her task, she must do as she promised Lady Norah and say nothing. Did that pledge hold if the lady and her husband were missing? Was she imperiling *their* lives by keeping the truth to herself? She had no idea, and, until she did, she had to hold onto her pledge of silence.

Mr. West returned to where she stood. Determination hardened his face. She could not guess why.

"What do you say?" he asked, as if there had been no break in their conversation. "Will you call me 'Theo' and give me permission to use 'Adelaide' when I speak to you? I can't see any reason why it would upset the rest of the world."

Baffled by his choice of words, she said, "If that is what you wish."

"No, it must be as *you* wish. I wouldn't impose my feelings upon you."

Her traitorous heart beat with joy. She tried to keep it under control so her voice remained calm. "I can't imagine you imposing your feelings on me."

"Theo." His expression became the teasing grin she adored.

"All right, Theo," she said, lowering her eyes as she spoke his name. It tasted wondrous. She was sure his lips on hers would be more delicious.

Enough! she told her heart, hoping it would understand why she could not fall in love with him. He was a gentleman. Every motion he made displayed that, even when he offered his arm to her as if she were a lady. To own the truth, when she put her fingers on his sleeve, and he patted her fingers before letting his hand linger atop hers, she had felt like one.

When Daphne called to them, she went with Theo to where the little girl stood. They laughed together as they found more pretty branches to put in the cart Gilbert had not brought across the creek. Theo kept the little girl giggling with stories of how he and his many siblings collected greenery years ago. When he began to tell them about something he called a *Tannenbaum*, Adelaide was as fascinated as Daphne at the idea of a tree lit with candles on Christmas Eve.

Adelaide's happiness collapsed when she heard the soft sound that had haunted her. The sound of a single hobnail against stone. Here? It had to be just the clicking of a pebble against the stones in the stream. It *had to be.*

It came again.

She whirled. She saw the three of them and Gilbert, who now stood on the other bank. No one else.

"Is something wrong?" Theo asked.

She did not answer. Instead, she strained her ears and gasped when she heard the sound again. For her to be able to hear a single hobnail striking a stone must mean the man in the black cloak was close. She caught sight of what might have been a shadow farther along the stream.

What if it was not a shadow? What if the man was close by? She was safe with Theo and Gilbert . . . or was she? Theo was recovering from being shot, and she had no idea if the footman could protect them.

"Adelaide, what is it?"

She squinted, trying to pierce the shadows beneath the trees. Could she see him from here? Was her pursuer there, or were her fears making her see and hear things?

Strong hands framed her face and tilted it toward Theo. Dismay burned in his eyes, and his lips were taut, but his hands were as gentle as if he cupped a newborn chick. She knew, in that instant, she would always be safe with him. Though he had no idea what upset her, he was ready to jump to her defense. She had not guessed how wonderful it would be to have a man stand between her and the darkness. She had fallen in love with him, a man far above her station.

To her heart, that no longer mattered. It wanted to pour out its fear and have him hold her close, keeping terror at bay. She wanted to confide in him how much she wished to know where the Laydens were. Lady Norah had been specific about Adelaide going to Stonehall-on-Sea, but they had not come. The Laydens might be dead. The thought gnawed at her bones, and she shivered.

"You're getting cold," Theo said, drawing her close again. "We should head back. We can talk where it's warm."

She nodded, desperate to flee, even though it was unlikely she would ever have another chance to be within his arms.

Theo found a note waiting for him when he returned with Adelaide and Daphne to Mermaid Cottage. He left Gilbert to unload the greenery while he read the short message from Hathaway. It had been sent from Dover where Hathaway had met with the two people who had sent the courier from their estate near Ullswater, with orders to come toward Stonehall-on-Sea. Unfortunately, Hathaway did not include their names in case the note went astray. Like Theo and Hathaway, the husband and wife were also involved in the effort to stop vital information from leaving the country. Hathaway reported the wife had been ill. Both expected to return to work by week's end.

Which meant Theo needed to be ready to leave by then. He tested his shoulder. Stiff and painful. He could not even manage to use a handsaw to cut thin twigs. How could he be expected to handle a gun or protect himself in a fistfight? Until he was healed, he would present more of a danger than a help to his fellow agents.

"Good news, I hope," Adelaide said as she walked down the stairs.

"Yes." It *was* good that Hathaway had made contact. He had to remind himself of that. "Hathaway is staying with some mutual friends. He informed me that they're doing well, though the wife has been ill."

"I'm sorry to hear that."

He needed to change the subject before he said something he should not. "Where are you bound?"

"This way." When Adelaide took his arm, she opened a door he had not noticed before. A stairwell was inside, one he guessed led to the kitchen. He went with her, not bothering to ask why she was going.

He winced when his shoulder brushed the wall. Once his father learned of this wound — and he would, because he had an efficient network of spies — the pressure on Theo to give up this life would increase.

Adelaide opened the door at the base of the stairs, and splendid scents assaulted him. Those aromas of roasting meat and baking bread lured him into the kitchen. The large, hot room became silent as he entered. A trio of maids stared at him, their mouths agape. An older woman, obviously the cook, snapped orders with the speed and efficiency of a general. The maids hurried to obey.

The cook, wiping her hands on her apron, came over to greet them. "Miss Rowland, Mr. West, this is indeed a surprise."

"We don't mean to intrude on you at this busy time," Adelaide said. Glancing over her shoulder, she asked, "Theo, have you met Mrs. Dunham?"

"I've met her amazing masterpieces at every meal." He bowed his head to the cook who dimpled. "It's a pleasure to meet the woman behind such artistry."

The cook asked him about particular dishes he had enjoyed, and he was able to give her several examples. He did not realize Adelaide had moved away until he heard her talking to someone in a room opening off the main kitchen.

"Ida is almost finished feeding sweet Beatrix," Mrs. Dunham said, as proud as if the babe were her own. "Would you like a piece of cake, Mr. West, while you wait for Miss Rowland to return?"

"How could I say no to such an offer?"

The cook brought him a generous-sized slab of cake. The frosting was orange-flavored, and he caught a hint of lemon in the cake. He smiled his thanks when she put a cup of tea next to the plate. He enjoyed the treat as he watched the maids work under Mrs. Dunham's eagle eyes. One of the maids smiled at him, but hastily looked away when the cook called to her. He turned his attention to the cake.

A few minutes later, Adelaide stepped from the other room to find Theo in casual conversation with the cook. The man could enchant anyone with his smile and obvious interest in what they had to say. She looked at the baby in her arms.

"He has bewitched me," she whispered, knowing the baby would keep her secret.

After Theo rose and thanked the cook, he followed Adelaide up the stairs. She was glad he remained silent. On the ground floor, she walked toward the parlor. He stood in the doorway as she went to collect the basket she had left there.

"It's an elegant solution to carrying the baby," Theo said, pointing at the basket on a chair not far from the hearth.

"It is, but I prefer to carry Beatrix in my arms in the house."

"I'd stick with the basket myself."

"Why?" She faced him, curious.

"With me, a baby is safer in the basket."

Understanding dawned. "You've never held a baby before? You said you had eleven brothers and sisters. You never held any of them?"

He shook his head. "My mother worried I'd drop one of them. I was young and impatient." He gave her a wry smile. "The latter may not be a surprise for you."

"You're right, but don't you think it's long past time for you to learn how to hold a baby?"

"I assumed I'd learn if I ever had any of my own."

"Your poor wife! Having to take care of a baby and watch over her husband, too." The familiar blush heated her face. Why couldn't she guard her tongue around Theo? Every day, she grew more certain he was of the nobility, and, at the same time, she found herself treating him with the familiarity of friendship.

Friendship was not what she longed to share with him. No other man had delighted her with a touch or had thrilled her soul by allowing her to be herself, even when, at times like this, her own thoughts made her blush. A few men had tried to woo her at Layden Mote. Marriage might not be in the future of a servant, but affairs were as rampant belowstairs as above. The careless maid who found herself pregnant was dismissed. It was a risk she had never been willing to take, even if one of the men who approached her appealed to her. None had . . . until Theo West walked into the church and everything changed.

To hide her embarrassment, she said, "Sit down."

"What?"

"Sit anywhere. You're long past due discovering the joy of holding a baby."

He complied with a smile, choosing the settee. "You make me feel as young as Daphne."

"She has more experience than you do in this area."

"After what I saw upstairs, I know that's true."

Her shoulder grazed his uninjured one as she placed Lily in his waiting arms. She tried to ignore the ripple of warmth from what should have been only a casual contact. It was no longer possible. Theodore West affected her as no other man had.

Nothing she tried had put a stop to her reactions to him. His smile made her feel happier. When he laughed, she wanted to sing. The moment his eyes locked with hers, she pushed aside everything else in the world to focus on the connection between them.

Tenderness and awe spread across his face as he shifted his arms, bringing Lily closer to his chest. Her own heart danced within her at the sight of the strong man cradling the baby.

Her heart was doomed to be broken when they parted ways, but that did not seem too much to pay for the joy of sitting beside him as he cooed to the child. She pushed thoughts of the future from her mind and savored the perfect moment, knowing, like so many other ones they had shared, it might never happen again.

CHAPTER EIGHT

Rain pelted the windows, tracing irregular paths along the glass. The sea and sky had melded into one gray mass. Mermaid Cottage had regained a bit of its serenity with Lady Cordelia's departure yesterday. She was visiting friends at an estate a half-day's journey west. She intended to return on Christmas Eve to celebrate with her niece's family.

However, the day had begun with a screech because Lily woke crying and had not let up. Adelaide had paced her room, trying to comfort the baby. Lily's tiny abdomen was hard with air she pulled in as she shrieked. When walking her failed to help, Adelaide had sat, letting the baby lean against her left forearm as she stroked Lily's back with her fingertips. That and a dosing with caraway seemed to ease the baby's discomfort enough, so by the time of her midday feeding, she had become less fussy.

Lily refused to sleep. The baby could not understand the events that sent her away from her home, but she could miss Lady Norah's familiar arms. In the past few days, Adelaide had allowed people and events to keep her from the baby too often. To own the truth, she missed the quiet moments when she held Lily. The baby was beginning to coo and make other sounds. With many different women coming to nurse the baby, Adelaide wanted Lily to know there was someone who was with her every day.

Collecting Lily after her last feeding of the day, Adelaide decided to cuddle her. It might help. She needed a quiet place where the baby could doze off.

She came up the kitchen stairs. Nobody was in the smaller parlor. Dr. Flanders was working after the evening meal. Lady Priscilla was with Daphne, telling her a story before bedtime and listening to her prayers. What Theo was up to, she could not guess, though he had mentioned meeting Mr. Kingsley at the local public house, the Dog and Crown, to discuss their duties as the Hooden Horse.

Adelaide walked into the parlor. It was quiet and cozy. A fire crackled on the hearth, warming the room. The wood paneling reflected the light. An overstuffed chair upholstered in gold fabric invited her to sit and watch the flames.

She did, putting her feet on a small stool. Leaning back in the chair, she wondered what it would be like to have a beautiful baby like Lily for her own, then halted when she imagined how much Lady Norah must miss her daughter. At Layden Mote, the lady had a nurse, a wet-nurse, and two assistants to take care of Lily, but she had spent several hours each day with her baby.

Why hadn't Lady Norah come to collect her daughter? What had gone wrong with the Laydens' plans?

Those questions haunted her. She had no idea how to uncover the answers.

Theo . . .

His name whispered in her head, and she guessed he could be a great help in discovering what was keeping her lord and lady from claiming their daughter. He and Mr. Hathaway clearly knew the area well. Maybe someone they knew had seen the Laydens or knew what had happened to them.

Tell no one Lily's true name. Don't allow anyone to learn you're connected to us or Layden Mote. Lady Norah's instructions had been clear in spite of her coughing. *Promise me, Adelaide. You must promise me.*

The memory of making that vow was as

unambiguous as the lady's words. How could she have known then what that pledge would entail? She had not considered for an instant that Lady Norah would fail to meet her. After all, she had her child.

After the holidays. . . . She would keep her promise until then. After that, she would have to seek help. Lady Norah could not have intended her to keep her promise into the new year.

In her arms, Lily's breathing slowed as she fell asleep. Not wanting to rouse her, Adelaide gazed out the window and watched the bare trees rock in the wind.

"Ah, here you are," said Lady Priscilla as she entered the small parlor.

"How are you feeling?" Adelaide asked, resisting the urge to come to her feet in the presence of an earl's daughter. To do so might endanger the fragile web of lies she had spun.

"Much better. I have permission to get up a few hours each day as long as the contractions don't begin again."

When the lady sat, she picked up her sewing from a basket by her chair. She was making another small nightgown. Were the ones Lily wore supposed to have been for Lady Priscilla's baby? If so, the lady's generosity was boundless. They had been at the house for more than a fortnight, and the vicar and his wife treated her as if she were as much a part of the family as their daughter.

Another wave of guilt, as high as the storm-swept waves, washed over Adelaide. If she admitted her deception, would the lady forgive her or toss her out of her home? She could not imagine Lady Priscilla doing the latter, but telling the truth threatened more than losing the roof over her head. She risked losing any more time with Theo, who wore his aristocratic mien with the ease of a man born to nobility. It was a part of him, like the color of his hair and his eyes. Something he had inherited by the circumstances of his birth.

And she was naught but a household maid.

What a mess she had made of everything!

"I'm glad we have a chance to chat like this, Adelaide," Lady Priscilla said, not looking up from her sewing. "I thought you might be interested to know most people were sure my marriage to Lazarus wouldn't last more than a few days, a month at the most."

"Why?" she asked, startled at the lady's words. Anyone looking at the couple could see how much in love they were.

"No one believed the daughter of an earl would be content being married to a country parson." She smiled, her gaze turned inward. "I have to admit, they're right. I'm not content. I'm happy."

"Even though Society turned its back on you?"

"That means nothing to me. However, though the *ton* was aghast at first, they've seen the underpinnings of England weren't toppled by our marriage. I suspect most have forgotten about us while they concentrate on more recent intrigues. The few times we've gone up to London, no doors were closed to us."

Before Adelaide could respond, Mrs. Moore came to the door. "Pardon me, my lady, but I need a few minutes of your time to settle next week's menus."

"Of course." Putting her sewing into the basket, Lady Priscilla rose with care. "Excuse me, Adelaide. I'm sorry to cut our conversation short." The lady left with her housekeeper.

The baby stirred in Adelaide's arms, but did not wake. Deciding to risk putting Lily in the cradle in her room, she stood and walked upstairs. Placing the baby into the cradle, she held her breath. Lily shifted once, then was still.

Adelaide moved away one step, then another until her legs touched the chaise longue. She sat, closed her eyes, and sighed. Not for the first time, she wondered why Lady Norah hadn't sent a nursery maid with Lily instead of her. She had teased Theo about not holding a baby before, but, until her lady placed little Lily in her arms, she could have counted on one hand the number of times she had held an infant. Having experienced mothers like Lady Priscilla and the village women who shared their milk was a blessing.

The thought of her hostess brought another question to mind. Why had the lady felt the need to discuss marrying beneath one's social status with her? Tales of misalliances spread everywhere, even to isolated country estates like Layden Mote. The nobility who insisted that the bloodlines of the peerage be kept untainted refused to acknowledge those who disregarded Society's stringent rules.

Was the lady trying to reassure her, or remind her of the dangers of following her heart? Not dangers to her, but to Theo. The reputation of a gentleman with less standing than an earl, like Lady Priscilla's father, might not be equal to the gossip sure to ensue if he married so far below him. Such negativity could taint even the strongest of hearts and drive love from it.

Had the lady guessed the truth about her? Adelaide had tried to be careful about hiding her past, struggling to copy the ways of her betters. Maybe she had tried too hard, and it had become obvious to everyone.

Even Theo? He treated her with the same gentility he did Lady Priscilla. If they knew, why did they continue to act as if she was their equal?

Unable to sit while unsettling thoughts roiled through her, Adelaide stood. Her toe struck the baby's basket, sending it skittering across the floor. The basket hit a leg of the bed and tipped over, spilling everything in it.

"Bother," she murmured as she glanced at the cradle.

Lily did not stir.

Squatting to gather the blanket and the small clothes she had packed in the basket, Adelaide shook her head at her own reaction to a task she once would have done without complaint. She needed to return to her own world before she no longer fit there.

But if she left Mermaid Cottage, she faced being stalked by the man with the single hobnail in his boot and failing to find food for the baby. She could not risk that. Not yet.

If only Lady Norah and Lord Layden would come. . . .

She might as well wish for Lily to be able to eat with a fork and knife in the morning.

Keep busy, her mind urged her. *Keep busy so you don't have time to think about the "what ifs."*

Heeding her own advice, she sorted out the contents of the basket. Blanket, baby clothing, and . . .

Where was the book of poetry?

She touched the locket around her neck. It was there. She sighed in relief. Lady Norah had entrusted her daughter, her book of poetry, and the necklace to her. Adelaide intended to return all three to her.

But *where* was the book?

She glanced around the room, as if the book would appear because she willed it to. Drawing aside the blankets, she peeked under the raised bed.

Nothing.

Nor did she see the missing book by the dressing table or the chaise longue. Lying flat, she scanned the floor under the cupboard. She tried to put her fingers past the board along the bottom, but there was not enough room. If her fingers could not slip beneath it, neither could the book.

So there was no way the book had fallen out when she kicked the basket.

She stood. *Think!* Lady Norah must have had a reason for putting it into basket with her child. How Adelaide wished her lady had confided in her! Perhaps, as with the extra money, Lady Norah had forgotten in the chaos.

If the book was not in her bedroom, and half an hour of looking told her it was not, it had to be somewhere else. Checking again to make sure Lily slept, Adelaide slipped out and down the stairs. The ground floor was dark, and she guessed the family had retired for the night. She heard hushed voices. The servants were finishing the last of their chores before going to bed.

She went into the front parlor. She was glad the rain had ended, because a faint trail of moonlight allowed her to find a candle. Lighting it from a lamp in the entry hall, she began to search the room.

The book was not on the furniture, nor was it beneath the cushions. She did find two coins and a button. Using the moonlight as much as the candle, which she left on a table, she knelt and looked under the furniture. She saw nothing, not even a clump of dust.

"Adelaide, is that you?" asked Theo from behind her.

Looking over her shoulder, she saw him in the doorway. His boots glistened in the thin light as he stepped into the room. "Lose something?"

"Other than my mind?" She was relieved her voice did not sound as brittle as she felt.

"One seldom looks for their mind from such a position." He squatted in front of her. "Can I help you find what you've lost?"

For a moment, she hesitated. Lady Norah had hidden the book, which meant she wanted it kept a secret, but Adelaide needed Theo's help. "I lost a small book of poetry," she said, surprised how the truth eased the web of lies constricted tightly around her.

When he asked her to describe it, she did, letting him think the book belonged to her. She watched his shadowed face and wondered how many of her half-truths he believed.

"It's clear the book isn't here," she said, standing.

"I'm sorry it is lost. It may turn up soon."

She shook her head. "I *must* find it. I took the basket to church this afternoon. I need to look there."

"Adelaide, it is after dark," he argued. "You could walk right past the book and never see it."

"If I don't find it at the church, I'll search the road between here and there tomorrow. It's possible one of the children looked at the book while the others were practicing." She stepped around him. "It won't take long to check inside the church tonight."

He blocked the doorway. "You can't go out at night alone."

"I was hoping you would go with me."

"Better," he said with a grin. "I haven't been anyone's knight in shining armor in days."

"Your armor may get rusty if it starts raining again." His laugh followed her up the stairs as she went to get her pelisse and ask the housekeeper to check on the baby while Adelaide was out of the house.

Less than ten minutes later, Adelaide walked into the dark church. A single lamp burned low. Theo used its flame to light another lamp which he carried as they walked to the front of the church. She stopped by the pew where she had left the basket while she and Theo worked with the children.

He held up the lamp so the whole pew was awash with light. When she saw a small dark shape, her heart leaped with excitement. She sighed as she picked it up and discovered it was a child's glove.

It took longer than she had expected to search the church. There were too many places a small book could be. With each passing minute, she became more frantic. How was she going to explain to Lady Norah that she had lost it?

"I don't think it's here," Theo said, his mouth working to stifle a yawn. "Why don't we come back in the morning when we can see better?"

"I've got to find it!" She was not being reasonable. She knew that, but she had promised to take care of Lily and *everything* in the basket.

"Adelaide —"

"No!" She spun away from his outstretched hand. She did not want him trying to calm her. She had to find the book. Kneeling, she peered under the nearest pews.

"Adelaide, nobody will be here before dawn."

"You don't understand."

"Help me understand." He took her hand and brought her to her feet.

The world seemed to shift as they stood face-to-face, and then everything but the two of them melted away. He held her hand as if she were as fragile as Lily. His arm slid around her waist, and in his eyes, she saw the truth. The choice of what they did next was hers and hers alone. The longing to kiss her was in his eyes and his uneven breath, but, as when he asked to address her by her first name, he was letting her decide.

A hundred different reasons ran through her head, reminding her why she should put an end to this. A single reason urged her to stay. She might never have another chance to kiss this man who had found his way into her heart. Raising her arms, she curved them around his neck.

Slowly, tenderly, he drew her closer. Standing heart-to-heart, she felt her breathing match his. When she ran a finger along his cheek, she could feel his pulse race as fast as hers. His breath caught, and she wondered if her heart would burst with joy. Anticipation quivered along her spine, and she could no longer wait.

As she raised herself on tiptoe, he gasped when her breasts caressed his hard chest. She heard nothing else as she guided his mouth onto hers.

The kiss was everything she had hoped for . . . and so much more. The heat of his mouth seared hers, setting each inch alive as if her lips had been waiting for this moment. Deep inside, fire seared her, and she was aware of her body as she had never been before. His hands stroked her back, pressing her close enough so she could feel the thunder of his heartbeat.

The small voice in her mind shouted that kissing him was wrong, but she no longer cared. His lips rose from hers, and she groaned a wordless protest. It became a soft cry of delight when his mouth slid along her jaw, setting her skin alight. She tipped her head, and he trailed fiery kisses from her ear to the throbbing pulse on her neck. Her fingers clutched his uninjured shoulder as she fought not to be washed away by her own yearnings.

When his lips captured hers again, she surrendered herself to every bit of ecstasy in their touch. The kiss lasted an eternity and the briefest second she could imagine, because time had lost any meaning.

He cupped her face in his hands. The smile on his face matched the joy swirling through her. A tiny portion of her mind tried to remind her this happiness could not last. She ignored it as she leaned into another kiss. If the happiness was fleeting, as it must be, she was going to relish every bit of it while she could.

CHAPTER NINE

Adelaide wanted to skip down the stairs to breakfast or slide along the banister as if she were no older than Daphne. Being in Theo's arms last night had been a dream come to life, a dream she had not even dared to have before she met Theo. After breakfast, she and Theo would return to the church and search again for the missing poetry book. He had vowed to check beneath every bush and hedgerow along the way. She knew he would do just that.

She heard voices from the dining room. "Gone? He's gone?" asked Lady Priscilla in astonishment.

When Adelaide paused in the doorway, she saw the lady looking at Dr. Flanders with dismay. The vicar and his wife faced her, and her heart stopped.

What she saw in their eyes told her the truth.

Theo was gone? Impossible!

"He left?" she whispered. *Without saying good-bye after what we shared?*

Tears blinded her as her happiness collapsed into a bottomless well of pain. She had not guessed he had been kissing her good-bye. Had anything he said been honest? He had spoken about spending tomorrow — today! — with her. He had offered to help her find the book this morning. In addition, he had asked her if she would wait for him after the pageant practice at the church so she could offer her opinion about how he and Kingsley looked as the Hooden Horse.

"Have you checked the church?" Adelaide asked. Maybe he had already gone there to try to find the book.

"Yes," Lady Priscilla said, coming around the table. "I'm sorry, my dear."

Adelaide nodded, not trusting her voice. Did promises mean so little to Theo? Did *she* mean so little to him?

She forced her feet to carry her toward the door. "I need some time to think."

She did not get that time. Outside the house, a carriage came to a sudden stop. Through the window, she saw a man in an ebony cloak jump out.

Seconds later, he burst into the house. Mr. Hathaway! He was back.

209

Was Theo with him?

He pushed past her as if she were not there and strode into the dining room. Without a greeting, he said, "I need to speak to West. Is he here?"

"No." Lady Priscilla put a calming hand on Mr. Hathaway's arm. "He's gone."

"When?"

"Early this morning, we guess," Dr. Flanders said.

"Do you have any idea where he went?"

Lady Priscilla shook her head. "None. He left no note."

Mr. Hathaway whirled, sending his cape flapping behind him. "Miss Rowland? Surely he told *you.*"

"No." She could manage to utter nothing else. That Mr. Hathaway had suspected she and Theo were becoming friends — and more — did not surprise her. She doubted there was much Mr. Hathaway's sharp eyes failed to see.

She fought not to let her hot tears fall. Why did everyone leave without explanation? First the Laydens, now Theo. None of it made sense.

Mr. Hathaway slammed his fist against the dining room table, which trembled. "He must have given you some hint, Miss Rowland!"

"Maybe," she said, thinking about the conversation she had with Theo after they went to get the Christmas greenery, "he went to see your friend who has been sick."

"He told you?" He stared at her in disbelief as his voice dropped to almost a whisper. "About Lady Layden being ill?"

She had not imagined she could be shocked more, but she was. Groping for a chair, she clutched it before her knees failed her. It took every bit of her strength to ask, "You know Lady Norah?"

"It is clear *you* do." His cool mask dropped back into place.

They could keep skipping around the truth, or one of them could admit it. She chose the latter. "Beatrix's real name is Lily. She is the daughter of Lord and Lady Layden of Layden Mote in the northern lakes district."

Mr. Hathaway swore. He glanced at the vicar and Lady Priscilla and started to apologize, but Dr. Flanders waved it aside.

"Lord Layden?" asked the vicar. "I attended school with a Harold Layden years ago. He was a second son. Could we be talking about the same man?"

"Yes," Mr. Hathaway replied. "His older brother died before their father, so the title came to him instead." He affixed Adelaide

211

with his intense gaze again. "That you knew him, Lazarus, is the reason, I would wager, Miss Rowland was sent here. Lord Layden must have hoped she would turn to you for help if she needed it." A terse laugh shot out of him. "The person I've been looking for has been under your roof all along."

"I'll get Lily," Adelaide said.

Mr. Hathaway stretched out a long arm to keep her from walking out of the room. "I'm not talking about the baby. I'm taking about you, Miss Rowland. *You* must be the courier we've been waiting for."

"You're mistaken. I was instructed to bring Lily to Stonehall-on-Sea, nothing more."

"Come with me, Miss Rowland. I need to get you to Dover. Maybe you'll believe the Laydens, as I can see you don't believe me. What you carry must be protected at any cost, and we can't delay delivering it any longer."

Adelaide hesitated. Why should she believe Theo's associate? Both men could have been lying the whole time she had known them.

"Go, Adelaide." Priscilla gave her a bolstering smile. "I would trust Neville with my life. You can trust him, too. Go! We'll watch over Lily."

Adelaide saw many questions in the lady's eyes, but she also saw Lady Priscilla's utter faith in what she said.

"I'll go with you," she said. "Let me get my pelisse."

"And the baby's basket!" Mr. Hathaway called after her.

She paused with her foot on the first stair. "Why?"

"Layden may have put something important in there." Again, he was equivocating, evidently not wanting to reveal anything she might not already know.

"Do you mean the book of poetry?"

Relief flooded his face. "Yes. A small book. So you found it?"

"Yes, but it has disappeared. I don't know where it is. We searched the house and the church last night to find it, but it's gone."

His face grew ashen. "Then everything may be lost, Miss Rowland."

"I don't understand. What's going on?"

"I can't say, and please refrain from any more questions while we travel to Dover. All will become clear if this situation can be salvaged. If not, none of it matters." He put his head in his hands. "None of it."

Theo woke to a familiar headache. He had been struck on the skull before, and he recognized the dull thud of pain that accompanied the blow. Before opening his eyes, he tried to move his hands, then his feet. They were not bound, which surprised him. He had assumed whoever had sneaked up behind him and delivered the sharp blow would not want to give him a chance to flee.

His last memory was of wasting time with the framework of the Hooden Horse. He had cut the practice short, wanting to return to Mermaid Cottage and to Adelaide and her sweet kisses. It was time for him to tell her the truth.

Everything after that was lost in a fog of pain. How long had he been senseless? Seconds or hours? He suspected it was closer to the latter by the way his head throbbed. The blow had been ruthless.

He opened his eyes, not surprised he was in darkness. Pushing himself up to sit, he winced. He felt as if he had been dragged behind a runaway horse.

A light appeared, blinding him even though it was not strong. He blinked. It took several seconds, but when he could see, he did not believe his eyes.

Kingsley, the front half of the Hooden Horse, stood by the door. He held two pistols. When Kingsley motioned with one for Theo to come out, he did. Picking his

214

battles with care had kept him alive for the past five years. He had seen others die when they had not waited for the best moment to make a move. It was a lesson he had tried to impress on Hathaway. He hoped he had succeeded, because he might not see the young man again.

Theo thought having Kingsley as his captor was the biggest surprise, but he had been wrong. He stepped through the doorway and found himself in what looked like a dilapidated bedroom. At least, there was a bed along one wall. A man was lying on it, and a red-haired woman stood beside him, anxiety and fear in every inch of her pose. Beyond the bed, a banked fire burned, little more than embers, and offering scanty heat. The dim room stank of mildew.

"I don't believe introductions are necessary," said Kingsley with a laugh.

The woman looked over her shoulder and gasped while Theo swallowed one of his own, not wanting to give Kingsley the pleasure of hearing his shock. He had never expected to see this woman so disheveled and frightened. She usually was as steady as bedrock.

"Lady Layden," he said, keeping his voice calm, "I trust you are well."

"I am." She glanced at the bed. "But

Harold isn't. He needs a doctor, and *he* refuses to send for one."

Theo did not look at Kingsley as he crossed the room to appraise the man he had met a few times and respected. One glance was enough to see that Layden had been stabbed twice in the right side and was in a bad way.

"Send for a doctor," Theo ordered, facing the other man. "What good will it do you if he dies?"

Kingsley sneered, "The chess master doesn't leave the pieces unguarded until he's ready to make his final move."

"If the king dies," he replied, "the game can't be won."

"Did you think I'm after the king?" Kingsley laughed. "I'm after the pawn, the piece the king and queen abandoned, but the one that is key to winning the game."

"Tell us what you want in exchange for sending for a doctor."

"She knows what I want." He waved the gun toward Lady Layden. "She chose her pawn well. It took me days to discover the identity of her courier. Tell him, my lady!"

When she shook her head, he moved toward her. Theo stepped between them, but not before he heard the sound Adelaide had described to him. The sound of a single hobnail in the heel of a boot.

"Leave her alone!" Theo shouted. "I know the name of her courier."

Kingsley halted. "I thought you might after seeing you pretending to court Miss Rowland. Were you collecting information along with whatever else you could get from her?"

With a quick glance at Lady Layden, Theo shook his head to let her know Adelaide had come to no harm at his hands. His fingers itched to go around Kingsley's throat and tighten until the man choked out an apology for speaking so crudely about Adelaide.

No, he couldn't think of her now. He had to be the agent he was trained to be. Evaluate the situation and find a way out of it with the smallest amount of carnage possible.

He looked at Kingsley. He wondered which nation he worked for. France? Russia? America? Not that it mattered. He wanted the information he believed Adelaide had, and he was willing to let people die to get it.

The rattle of a carriage slowing came through the room's single window on the wall opposite the bed. When Kingsley glanced out and grinned, Theo took a step toward him. He halted as Kingsley re-aimed

217

the guns at him. Lady Layden moaned and covered her mouth with her hands. One look at her face, and Theo knew the worst was to come.

"Let me go first," Mr. Hathaway said as he assisted Adelaide from the carriage on a slovenly Dover street. "Just in case."

Ice clamped onto her heart, and she knew whatever was about to happen could be terrible. She had spent the long trip holding Lady Norah's locket to help herself believe everything would turn out well, that she would be able to return it to the lady soon. That hope had been dashed when they stopped at the elegant townhouse the Laydens had borrowed in Dover.

A note had been waiting for Mr. Hathaway. It told him to bring the courier with him to the street where the carriage was now parked. That request was followed by the threat that the Laydens were breathing . . . at least for now.

Mr. Hathaway opened the door and entered. She followed. When he went up a staircase, she hoped the rickety stairs would hold them. She held her pelisse away from the damp walls. He threw open a door at the top of the stairs.

A shout resounded from the room, followed by a thump. Rushing up the last few steps, she cried out when her arm was grasped. She was yanked into the room. Theo! What was he doing here? He shoved her behind him, but not before she saw the incredible sight of her lady standing by a bed. She cried out in horror when she saw a bloody Lord Layden lying on it and Mr. Hathaway, motionless on the floor.

Then she heard the sound that had haunted her nightmares. The click of the single hobnail. She stared in disbelief at Mr. Kingsley who held two pistols, aimed at her and Theo. What was happening?

"Welcome, Miss Rowland," her stalker said with a cruel smile. "I'll take it."

"Take what?"

"Don't play coy with me! I'll put a ball through your lady's head."

"I don't know what you want!" she cried.

"The locket. I should have seen earlier it was too fine for a housemaid." He shoved one pistol in his belt and held out his hand. "Give it to me."

Theo's shoulders had stiffened, but Adelaide's sagged as Kingsley ripped away her pretense. Now Theo knew what she was. A maid who had let him believe she was of a much higher class, so he would spend time with her.

219

She shoved the pain aside. Her masquerade no longer mattered. What mattered was saving lives. She stepped around Theo.

He cried, "No, Adelaide!"

She faced Kingsley, the man who had chased her across England.

Theo started to move, but Kingsley growled, "You were lucky last time I shot you, West. You won't be as lucky at this range."

Kingsley tore the locket off her neck. Adelaide yelped when the chain cut into her before breaking, but she aimed a warning glance at Theo. He must not try to halt Kingsley who kept one pistol aimed at her lady.

With a sneer, Kingsley pushed past them and toward the door as he shoved the locket under his coat. "You thought to fool me, Lady Layden, by giving your maid two items. I thought the one you hid with your child was what I sought." He pulled out the small poetry book. "I should have guessed it was useless when the baby's basket was left in plain sight in the parlor."

Adelaide understood immediately. When Kingsley had come to talk to Dr. Flanders ostensibly about the Hooden Horse, he must have searched the basket.

"It was there to confuse me." He tossed

220

the book toward the hearth. It fell short of the fire. The leather cover began slowly smoking. "Now that I have what I need, I bid you adieu. I trust you know better than to give chase."

He slammed the door shut, and the click of a lock was followed by the sounds of his boots on the stairs.

The minute the door was closed, Theo leaped to the window. When it refused to open, he pounded his fist against the wall in frustration. "He's getting away." He yanked at his boot to pull it off.

"Use Harold's," Lady Norah called, running across the room with it.

Theo took the boot and swung it at the glass. It shattered. He called down to the coachman to come up and unlock the door. Lady Norah knelt beside Mr. Hathaway, checking to see the extent of his injuries.

At the same time, Adelaide ran to the fireplace and plucked the book from the hot ashes. She burned two of her fingers, but not badly. The book might not have any value to Kingsley, but it was important enough to her lady that she sent it with Adelaide and Lily.

Stuffing it into the apron pocket beneath her pelisse, she rushed to the bed where Lord Layden was not moving. She heard sounds behind her that she guessed were Mr. Hathaway and Lady Norah coming to their feet. Glancing back, she saw the dark-haired man holding a hand to his head.

She turned her attention to Lord Layden. Someone had ripped his lawn shirt along his right side, and she was relieved to see that his wounds had not begun to fester.

"Is there any candle wax here?" The fire was the only light in the room.

"None." Lady Norah inched toward her. "Can you help him, Adelaide?"

"I can try, my lady, but I need —"

"This?" asked Theo, holding out a small jar. It was the salve she had mixed for him. When she stared at it in astonishment, he said, "I found that whenever my shoulder hurt, putting more of this on it helped."

"Thank you." She took the jar and asked for water and clean cloths.

The door burst open, and the coachman came in. The three men left to locate what Adelaide needed. More quickly than she had hoped, they returned with a bucket of water. She had them set it to boil over the fire while she and Lady Norah ripped fabric into strips. Even that shrill sound did not rouse Lord Layden.

As soon as the water had boiled and then cooled enough so she would not scald the wounded man, Adelaide cleaned the wound. She did not look up from her task when Mr. Hathaway sent his coachman to get help. She put a generous amount of the salve on the sliced skin of Lord Layden's side. Later, when she was sure the wounds had finished draining, she would sew the slits closed. For now, she made thick pads for bandages and held them in place by wrapping the rest of the fabric around him.

"Thank you, Adelaide," the lady said, wiping tears from her eyes. Fear stole any hints of color from her face as she whispered, "What about Lily?"

"She's safe in Stonehall-on-Sea. We waited there for you at Dr. Flanders's house. He's the vicar."

Lady Norah nodded. "I knew I could trust you to do as you promised. What I didn't know was how sick I would become on our way south. Because I was so ill, we came here to stay with friends until I recovered." She glanced at her husband. "If he'd sent his friend the vicar a message as I asked, we might have avoided this whole mess."

Adelaide cleaned her hands, then dried them on her apron. "I'm sorry about your locket, my lady." She reached into the pocket where she kept her herbs and pulled out two miniatures that she had found inside the locket. "I took these out."

Taking them, Lady Norah touched a fingertip to the small portraits of her husband and her baby daughter. "Thank you." She glanced at the hearth. "Where's the poetry book?"

"Here." Adelaide retrieved it from her pocket.

"Open it." The lady's smile strengthened as she looked from her to the men standing behind her.

Adelaide did and gasped. Mixed in with the lines of poetry was more writing in a paler ink. The words were written in Lord Layden's hand. She read only a few before Theo reached over and closed the cover. It was enough for her to realize the previously hidden writing contained confidential information about the ongoing hostilities between the British and the French.

He took the book from her without a word. She longed to say so many things to him, but would he listen, after she had lied over and over to him?

When he spoke, it was to Lady Norah. "How brilliant of you! You created an invisible ink activated by heat and gave Adelaide the locket as a diversion. Kingsley had what he sought, then threw it away."

As they continued to talk, making plans

to get Lord Layden to Mermaid Cottage where he should be safe while recovering, Adelaide stepped aside. Her place as a servant was to do her job and be unseen otherwise. She should not be part of a conversation between her lady and Theo. No, she needed to think of him as Mr. West again.

Mr. Hathaway hurried to the door with Mr. West. He left, but Mr. West stayed behind in the doorway a moment. His gaze found hers and held it. She saw a blizzard of emotions, each one stormier than the previous, in his eyes. He started to speak.

"Come on, West!" shouted Mr. Hathaway from the stairs. "We need to get that information to Whitehall before Kingsley learns he's been duped."

Mr. West said, "Go with the Laydens to Mermaid Cottage, Adelaide. You'll be safe there."

She nodded, though she wondered why he thought she would go anywhere else. Her place was with her lord and lady. His was with. . . . She did not know, but it was not with a housemaid. The fantasy of them being together was over.

Epilogue

"A little bit to the right. Perfect."

At Lady Priscilla's words, Adelaide looped the Christmas greenery over the drapery rod in the back parlor and climbed off the chair. They were decorating the house on the afternoon of Christmas Eve to have it ready for the Christmas Day party.

The lady and Dr. Flanders had welcomed her into their home. Neither had mentioned her deception. Instead, they hailed her as a heroine. Lady Cordelia, who had returned to Mermaid Cottage and was upstairs with her grand-niece, had complimented her on her bravery.

But everything had changed. Not just because she was a serving maid again. Her life had a hole in it without Theo — Mr. West in it.

"How about more greenery on the chimneypiece?" asked Lady Norah from the chair where she held a sleeping Lily. She seldom let go of the baby other than when Lily was nursing.

On the settee beside them, Lord Layden reclined. More than a week after they had brought him to Stonehall-on-Sea, he was still suffering from the after-effects of his wounds. The local doctor had warned him he would never be able to live such a rigorous life again. The Laydens had let the doctor believe Lord Layden was wounded in a fight, because they had to protect their secret lives.

Adelaide had not been astonished to learn Lady Norah and her husband served the Crown as she guessed Mr. Hathaway and Theo did. She was not sure exactly what they did, but guessed their work might explain the many strange visits and guests to Layden Mote. Lady Norah had explained only that their part in the espionage had been discovered, putting them, their child, and their work in jeopardy. With minutes to flee, they had devised a way to protect the information they had gathered and their child.

Once Lord Layden was well enough, they would return to Layden Mote and begin repairs, for it had been damaged by those who wanted to put an end to them and their work. For now, however, they were guests at

Mermaid Cottage. Adelaide had relinquished her room to her lady and offered to join the other maids in the attic. Lady Priscilla insisted she use a smaller room on the second floor to be close to her lady who needed help tending her husband's injuries.

Adelaide had been relieved to hear the man from Stonehall-on-Sea who was traditionally the head of the Hooden Horse was also recovering. After he took Kingsley in, believing his tale that he was a starving traveler, Kingsley had slowly poisoned him. The man had come close to dying, but was regaining his strength. It would not be in time to play his part tonight. She wondered what other men Dr. Flanders had found.

Upon their return from Dover, one day had flowed into the next. Adelaide found herself caught between two worlds, the one she had known as a servant and the one where she was a guest in the vicarage. She was happy to see Lily in her mother's arms and relieved when Lord Layden began to recover, but her heart ached at what she had lost.

Not what. Who.

"Adelaide, could you bring more of the greenery from the entry hall?" Lady Norah asked. "We'll need it for the other windows."

"Certainly, my lady." She curtsied.

Cold air struck her as she reached the entry hall. A footman was opening the door. She hurried to push the greenery aside before it could be stepped on.

"Let us help," said Mr. West.

Adelaide straightened at his familiar voice and saw him in the doorway with Mr. Hathaway. As they pulled off their gloves and hats and scarves, she dipped in another curtsy.

Mr. Hathaway gave his partner a curious smile, then clapped him on the right shoulder before following the footman toward the back of the house.

Mr. West stepped around the greenery and took her hand, bringing her to her feet. "Don't do that, Adelaide."

"You now know what I am."

"True, but you don't know what I am."

For a moment, her heart leaped with hope. Was he of the lower classes, too, in spite of his fine clothing and polished manners? Could he have been playing a role as she had?

"Miss Rowland, have you heard of Westenwald?"

She had. While serving tea, she had heard Lord Layden mention Westenwald, a German state beyond the border of France, many times. The rulers were distant relatives of King George and his family. Why was Mr. West mentioning it? She thought he was from Hanover. Or had he only mentioned Hanover to let her — and everyone else — assume it was his homeland?

He confirmed her thoughts when he clicked his heels together and dipped his head. "I am Theodore Christian Albert Maximilian of the principality of Westenwald."

She wanted to moan at the pain spearing her heart. That made Theo . . . a prince? She blanched as she thought how she had treated him with the same informality she had a country parson. She needed to beg his forgiveness, but how?

"Say something," he whispered as his gaze searched her face.

For what did he seek? She had no idea.

"I don't know what to say," she said.

He raised her hand and pressed his lips to it as he bowed over her fingers. The sweet fire he had awakened with his first kiss surged through her, and she knew no other man would make her feel like this.

Not ever.

Lifting his head, he looked into her eyes. "I love you, Adelaide. You know that, don't you?"

"What I know means nothing." She drew

her hand out of his.

"What you feel means everything to me. Do you love me?"

Yes, her heart begged her to answer, but Adelaide edged away to put some distance between them.

"What I feel doesn't matter," she said. "I mean, it doesn't matter, your majesty."

He frowned. "Why are you calling me that?"

"Because you're the prince of Westenwald, aren't you?"

"My father currently holds the title."

She hated how her heart began to beat rapidly again, believing they could have a future together. Whether he was a prince himself or not, nothing had changed. She was a servant, the daughter of a family in service for generations.

"You'll like my father, Adelaide, and my mother. They've been insistent I leave my work for our cousins here and serve Westenwald at home. I've resisted because I wasn't ready to end the adventures I was living." He ran his fingers along her cheek. "I want a new adventure now, an adventure with you. Tell me that you love me, Adelaide, and will return to Westenwald with me."

She shook her head. "My parents depend on me. They're elderly, and what I earn

231

feeds and shelters them."

"Bring them with us, if they wish to come. If not, I'll arrange for them to be provided for in comfort here." His gaze captured hers. "Please tell me that you love me, Adelaide, and will return to Westenwald with me."

If she agreed to his offer of a place in his bed as his mistress, she was destroying any future she would have in service. No household would hire her, considering her immoral. But she would be with Theo for as long as he wanted her. What should she say?

The answer was simple. "Yes," she whispered.

He grinned, grabbed her hand, and pulled her along the hallway. Everyone in the parlor froze as he shouted, "Hathaway, you lose the bet! She said yes."

Adelaide's face was as hot as the hearth. She had not expected Theo to announce in front of her now former employers that she had agreed to become his mistress. Especially not when a vicar and his wife were present.

"I'm happy to be wrong, but we're even, because you didn't think we'd capture Kingsley and his cronies before they escaped to France," Mr. Hathaway said, laughing.

"You did?" she asked, looking from him

to Theo in astonishment.

"Why else do you think I would delay coming for you?" Theo winked before adding, "Hathaway, as the winner of our bet, I claim the position of being the head of the Hooden Horse and give you its rear end."

"It'll be my pleasure. And may I say, you're already a blushing bride, your highness?" he asked with a half-bow to Adelaide.

"What?" she asked. "I'm not going to be — That is . . ."

Theo clasped her shoulders and brought her to face him. "Have you changed your mind, Adelaide? You don't want to be my bride?"

She stared at him in disbelief. He wanted to marry her? A housemaid?

"I didn't think you wanted to *marry* me. I am —"

"A serving maid, but you are also the woman I love. Let me make myself clear in front of these witnesses. Adelaide, I love you. Will you marry me?"

"Yes!" She caught a glimpse of broad smiles on Mr. Hathaway's and Lady Priscilla's faces and the astonishment on Lord and Lady Laydens' before Theo's lips found hers. She returned the kiss, thrilled that it would only be one of many they would share through the years to come.

At a soft cry from Lily, she started to pull away to help Lady Norah.

Her lady motioned with a warm smile for Adelaide to stay where she was. "My husband and I will always be grateful for your service, but you have a different life ahead of you."

Theo drew her to him. "I'm glad you like children."

"As you do. I saw you with them at pageant practice." Noticing the challenging twinkles in his eyes, she asked, "Shall we have a houseful?"

"How about a castle filled with them?" he asked, smiling.

She laughed and welcomed his lips on hers again.

■ ■ ■ ■

THROUGH THE EYES OF A CHILD

BY KAREN FRISCH

■ ■ ■ ■

To my friend Linda Lucas,
Wishing you happy endings always.

CHAPTER ONE

"It is unfortunate the axle broke just when your carriage was needed most," Edmund Hadleigh, Viscount Tyndale said shortly, "but as I told your father, I am perfectly agreeable to having you accompany me to Stephen and Letitia's Christmas gathering. Perhaps it will make the time pass more quickly for both of us."

Yet she knew it would not make the ride more pleasant for either of them. Annabelle Sedgwick gazed out the window miserably as Edmund took his seat beside her in the carriage. It was unfortunate the incident had occurred just as she was about to set off, but it was also just too coincidental. While Annabelle knew little about carriage construction, she knew her family well enough to wonder if they had a hand in damaging the axle to force her to travel with Edmund, instead of with her sister and her family. The hint of awkwardness in his tone suggested Edmund was not entirely comfortable with the arrangement either, but had been too polite to refuse. With Derbyshire still several hours away, she had no choice but to share his company in the barouche.

Annabelle fought to drown her resentment in her love for her sisters. They were her best friends, and she depended upon them for her very happiness. Yet once again, they had interfered with her plans. Beside her, Edmund remained silent, his gaze riveted on the snow-covered hills beyond the window. If he sat any farther away from her, she thought with resentment, he would risk tumbling out the door. He turned to her abruptly.

"I was sorry to hear of the death of your husband," he said, his tone stiff yet regretful. "He served with the Lines of Torres Vedras, did he not? Please accept my condolences."

He had broached the issue she dreaded most not fifteen minutes into their journey.

"Thank you. The loss was completely unexpected." She paused awkwardly. "Frankly, I am relieved my period of mourning has ended. I look forward to spending happier moments with my nieces and nephews at Christmas."

Edmund murmured his agreement before resuming his silence. A wave of relief mixed with humiliation flooded through her. He had acknowledged their separation while expressing his sympathy. Did he know her husband of three months had not died of enemy fire, but from the accidental discharge of his rifle while he had been cleaning it? If so, Edmund had chosen to spare her the humiliation she felt and perhaps deserved. But then, Edmund had always been considerate.

Was it selfishness on her part, Annabelle wondered, to want to enjoy Christmas this year? Her year of mourning had lasted longer than her three-month marriage to Randolph. Edmund's curt tone suggested he had not entirely forgiven her. Heat rising at the back of her neck, she tensed against the squabs. If Edmund had returned from the Peninsula after his first injury as he should have, they would have been married and had children by now. Far from being the betrayal he considered it, her marriage to Randolph had sprung from her desperation to start a family.

As the miles passed, he resumed casual conversation, inquiring about her parents. "I have always had great respect for them and enjoy your father's company especially," he admitted. "Will they attend Stephen and Letitia's house party this year?"

"Father does not celebrate Christmas. He has never recovered from the loss of Charles so close to the day." Annabelle saw little point in discussing a forbidden subject. "But my sisters and their families will attend."

A frisson of jealousy nagged at her. As the youngest of the four, she had been happy enough when Grace, the eldest, had married and welcomed baby Margaret into their lives. It was when Pamela, her second sister, had married while Edmund was at war and proceeded to have twins that Annabelle's patience had snapped. Only Beatrice, dear Beatrice, had hesitated to entertain the idea of courtship until Annabelle found herself with suitable prospects. With Edmund refusing to come home despite his injury, Annabelle had impulsively sought happiness elsewhere. She'd found it almost immediately with Randolph.

She had often complained to Randolph that patriotism had mattered more to Edmund than romance did. She never imagined Randolph would enlist and then perish. It was not until she was in mourning that she wondered if jealousy had made him determined to show her he was as brave as Edmund. In short, her marriage had been a disaster. But she would not tell Edmund that. He would undoubtedly think less of her than he already did.

Annabelle smoothed the rug over her lap slowly and deliberately, despite the jostling of the carriage. How was she to occupy the hours until they reached Lavendam Manor if that awkward exchange alone filled such a brief period? Of all people with whom she might have traveled to Derbyshire for her cousin's house party, Edmund was the least desirable. Yet they were forever destined to encounter each other at gatherings, for her cousin Letitia was married to Edmund's brother Stephen.

Since they were traveling together, she might as well take advantage of the opportunity to ease her worries about Edmund's physical health. From the corner of her eye, she saw he was as handsome as ever with those chestnut brown eyes and dark hair. While his features were not precisely symmetrical and his hairline receding slightly, it was his thoughtful manner and painstakingly chosen words that had commanded her adoration. Close friends knew his speech contained a truth that could not be debated.

Yet her family had feared his wounds might impair his ability to live a normal life.

The first injury, one that had severely damaged his leg, forced him to walk with a cane. The second had affected his vision, leaving him partially blinded in one eye. The description alone had made her flinch. But her emotional pain, she thought with a pang of guilt, hardly rivaled the agony he had endured in Spain. What had happened to the sense of humor that had always delighted her? He had not smiled, she realized, since they had set off.

While they had corresponded by letter initially, silence had been the only thing between them for more than two years. His gaze was focused on the stark landscape beyond his window. His eye injury must be severe, for he no longer drove the carriage as he always had but left it to his driver instead.

Even as she hoped the remainder of their journey would proceed uneventfully, he broke the silence. "Please forgive my tardy arrival," he muttered. "I had not traveled far before realizing I had forgotten the Christmas gifts and had to return home."

Her tone, when she spoke, sounded stiff even to herself. "It is hardly surprising on your first Christmas home. That alone is reason to celebrate."

"I suppose it is. At any rate, I am afraid

we shall have yet another delay," Edmund said vaguely. "The servants told me a messenger called with a letter from my superior officer. Apparently, I must collect the letter at the Foxwell Inn before going on to Lavendam Manor."

Annabelle could not repress the familiar surge of bitterness. "Again, the war," she blurted. "You have been home nearly eight months, and yet you are unable to leave it behind you."

While the twilight left his face partially shadowed, his voice was edged with resentment. "I have left it behind," he retorted. "Are you not satisfied the war left me with injuries so severe that those who greet me with respect whisper behind my back? Is that not punishment enough for leaving you for a cause to which England was compelled to give her all? I have never encountered a more selfish attitude."

How could he of all men have uttered such a hypocritical statement? Her fury nearly choked her. "You need only look within to find selfishness, my lord," she said coolly. "While you claimed you loved me, it was apparently not enough to bring you home to me."

When she fell silent, unable to find her voice, he continued, his tone bitter. "Christmas will be here and gone before you and I have settled our differences. Even though we cannot exchange words without bickering, circumstances have forced us to travel together, and we must make the best of it. It is time we focus on the future, not the past."

They would ride in silence then, Annabelle vowed. The lonely thud of horses' hooves and the muffled grinding of carriage wheels on packed snow were more welcome than the bitterness in his voice. At his feet lay a battered haversack that looked as if it had gone to war with him, the corners of envelopes protruding from the top. Perhaps he continued to correspond with soldiers in his unit. She smothered her hostility, remembering she would soon hear the excitement in her nieces' and nephews' voices and see the amazement in their eyes again.

The miles passed more quickly than expected. Shortly after dusk, they reached the inn where Edmund was to have his meeting.

"You might wish to warm yourself indoors while I retrieve my letter," he muttered, his tone colder than the wind-whipped snow that blew in her face when he opened the carriage door.

"I suppose this meeting will have less to

do with Christmas than with matters of war," she retorted, arranging her hood before taking the hand he extended to disembark.

"The matter was not discussed with my servants," he said as he handed her down. "It is confidential."

They were greeted at the door and shown into a private parlor where Annabelle seated herself on a sofa, fighting to repress her irritation. As darkness had already fallen, another delay meant they might be forced to spend the night. Edmund paced as they waited in silence. She could not help but notice how he had aged in the years they were apart. The changes made her heart contract. Was it really such a short time ago, she reflected with a pang of grief, he seemed so tall and proud? Now he walked with a limp, his back slightly hunched from wounds that necessitated the use of the cane. His presence still made her heart pound.

Annabelle knew from friends that the second injury had affected his vision severely enough to ensure his departure from Spain. Still, despite two injuries, he had not wished to return to England but was forced to acquiesce to pressure from his superiors. She turned away, unwilling to think about the changes war had brought about in him.

The aroma of a fresh pot of tea and a light repast set out for them by a waiter lifted her flagging spirits. Perhaps the meal would stave off her weariness. She approached the sideboard but had no chance to sample the tea or the covered dishes. At that moment, the door opened and a messenger in military dress entered the parlor. His expression was grave as he bowed politely to her. She saw Edmund's face alter. The soldier saluted him before they clasped hands.

"Private Ellis," Edmund exclaimed warmly. "I am glad to see you well. Better than when we last met."

The soft cries of an infant beyond the door made Annabelle wish she might offer assistance to the parents while Edmund had his meeting. How tedious travel must be for a child. She flushed with resentment at the slight irritation that crossed his face at the sound. The soldier invited her to be seated before turning back to Edmund.

"It is an honor to see you again, Captain. I apologize for delaying your supper, for surely you are hungry from traveling," he said soberly, "but there is a grave matter that must be addressed. I regret to inform you I am the bearer of sad tidings from the front."

Alarmed by his tone, Annabelle found her attention riveted abruptly. Though not of great height, the private seemed to dwarf Edmund, even though he stood as erect as possible.

"Do not spare me," Edmund said quietly.

"My superiors attempted to contact you, but the message apparently went astray." Private Ellis paused, his youthful features betraying his struggle to relay the news. "I regret to inform you, Captain, that Major Joseph Enderfield and Mrs. Enderfield have been killed in Spain."

Although she had never known the victims, Annabelle's heart skipped a beat. She watched Edmund freeze with shock, his pale expression contorted in disbelief.

"Surely it cannot be," he objected. "It must be a mistake. Not both."

"There was an ambush in the night. It came without warning," the messenger continued softly. "Major Enderfield and his wife did not suffer. Troops were lost as well, twenty men in all. The unit remains strong, although the loss is a blow from which it is difficult to recover."

"The loss is unimaginable," Edmund muttered, still absorbing the reality.

As Private Ellis revealed details of the attack, Annabelle heard little. Instead, she

249

watched the denial in Edmund's face crumble and soften to resignation. Alarm filled his eyes suddenly.

"Their child," he blurted before the messenger raised a reassuring hand.

"The child has been spared," Private Ellis assured him quickly.

Before he could continue, the cries of an infant resumed from the hallway. Annabelle turned as the door opened slowly. Heartwrenching sobs filled the parlor as a baby cradled in a blanket was carried into the room by a dark-eyed, dark-haired woman in peasant dress. Her guarded expression brightened with recognition when her gaze fell upon Edmund.

"Rosa," Edmund whispered, his voice breaking as he reached for her hand.

"*Capitán,*" she exclaimed, her eyes filling with tears even as she smiled with relief. "*Capitán, Jose es seguro.*"

"*Gracias a Dios.* Thank God Joseph is safe." The doubt in Edmund's face faded as a smile struggled to his lips. "And you are safe, Rosa. *Y que está a salvo.*"

Overwhelmed with emotion, Annabelle felt her own heart stir as he embraced the woman and child with slow, careful movements. Tears streamed down Rosa's cheeks.

"Our soldiers removed the baby from

250

harm's way at once," Private Ellis continued quietly, addressing Edmund. "Either the French soldiers did not see him and his nurse, or they chose to spare them."

Listening in shock and horror, Annabelle watched Edmund attempt to digest the news, his face contorted with pain. He turned back to the soldier, the despair in his eyes wrenching her heart.

"Joe Enderfield was my closest friend," he said quietly. "What is to become of Joseph now that his parents are gone?"

The soldier raised his chin slowly. His intense expression made Annabelle's heart thud.

"The child has been left to your care, Captain Hadleigh," he announced carefully, his steady gaze focused on Edmund. "Major Enderfield had composed a new will naming you guardian should any misfortune jointly befall him and his wife in wartime. It is an ironic stroke of foresight that such an eventuality has come to pass." He paused before his tone softened. "The colonel extends his deepest sympathies to you. He also expressed his confidence that you will assume these new duties with the same sense of responsibility he has come to expect from you."

Stunned by the turn of events, Annabelle

watched Edmund's face pale at the unexpected news.

"Of course I will raise their child, without hesitation. It is a duty I shall honor," he replied, his tone husky. "I understood Major Enderfield had only an elderly father left. I believe they had been estranged for many years."

"That is correct. Mrs. Enderfield was orphaned young and raised by an aunt who is now deceased."

"So Joseph has no one," Edmund reflected after a moment.

"He has you, sir." The private paused. "The child has been spared and, thanks to you, has a life awaiting him. For the immediate future, since he is just four months old, he will have Rosa to care for him. Of course, a child of his breeding would benefit from the attentions of a gentlewoman." He smiled faintly. "Let us hope misfortune shall lead to greater good in time."

Her heart pounding, Annabelle felt dazed. She could think of no one less prepared to inherit the daunting responsibility of an infant than Edmund.

Even as the thought crossed her mind, he stepped forward toward Rosa. The infant she held was quiet at present. Rosa smiled as Edmund paused before her, unsure how to proceed. As she extended her arms toward him, he reached out slowly for the child that had suddenly become his.

Of all messages that might have been delivered, Edmund thought as they followed the porter upstairs minutes later, this was the last he could have imagined. The child was accompanied by a letter from the major to be read at Edmund's discretion. Joseph also came with an inheritance and property, Private Ellis had informed him, and with journals of his father's that Edmund might wish to share with him one day.

Joe Enderfield, gone so soon. His best friend. The man who had saved his life. And his wife Eliza with him, the essence of kindness. How was he to manage after such a loss? Edmund had watched too many men suffer. He had wiped away their tears, cleaned their wounds, spoon-fed some back to health even.

He had held their hands as their eyes closed one last time. The brief passings had been merciful. But he could never have imagined this loss. Both parents, dead before they could watch their son outgrow childhood.

Until today, Edmund had known of Joseph only through his father's letters.

This baby, born in war, he vowed, would now live in peace. His thoughts refused to focus as he reflected on the extent of his new and unexpected responsibilities.

At least witnessing the results of his suffering had silenced Annabelle. Perhaps his criticism of her was undeserved. She could not comprehend all he had endured on the front lines, for he had spared her the reality. The crying of infants had always irritated him until he saw Rosa carry Joseph through the door. He had never felt so relieved.

As the porter led the way to their rooms, Annabelle walked several steps ahead.

"Su esposa?" Rosa asked him shyly, nodding at Annabelle with a curious smile.

She was not his wife, Edmund explained in Spanish, but rather an acquaintance of long standing. The situation would be easier if they were married, he thought, for young Joseph would have a mother's care and devotion. Having Rosa remain to nurse the baby was the best possible solution, for her own child had died soon after birth and her husband had perished in the war.

While they waited for rooms, they were made comfortable in a private parlor. Taking a chair opposite the sofa where the women sat, Edmund saw the tenderness in Annabelle's features as she watched Rosa, rocking Joseph quietly in her arms. Annabelle's enthusiasm had not changed in his absence. He had missed the sweetness and vulnerability she reserved for those closest to her. They were now evident in her eyes, as boldly blue as forget-me-nots. And he had not forgotten them. With her face bent affectionately over Joseph's, she was still as beautiful as she had been when he left, he thought reverently, if not more so.

His heart had skipped a beat when he saw her this evening for the first time in nearly four years. When she had married Randolph Sedgwick so unexpectedly after Edmund's first injury, his pride had suffered a blow worse than any the war had dealt him. How typical of Annabelle, he reflected, to be too impulsive to wait for his return so they could marry as he intended. They had not written each other since. Of course, even when she had begged him to return home after his first injury, Edmund had refused to leave his unit despite his shattered leg.

But then, she had not known the real reason he could not abandon the men, he reminded himself.

During their ride, he had expected to see the effervescent smile he had longed for, or to listen as she described the pain of widowhood. Since she had not, perhaps she found the subject too awkward. Knowing she had lost Randolph at war, Edmund refrained from mentioning his own experiences. Her unexpected marriage soon after his injury had hurt him more deeply than any other injustice life had handed him. He had hoped, believed even, that a reconciliation between them might be possible, even now.

Perhaps he had been mistaken.

She had not smiled once during the ride. An emotional distance separated them, smothering the impulsive woman he remembered. The lighthearted warmth and enthusiasm he had loved in her were absent. What had happened to the idealistic hopes they once shared?

If she truly believed he had not loved her enough to come home for her, he thought resentfully, nothing he said now would convince her. He resigned himself to the reality that what they had shared together was lost.

At last, she turned to him.

"To say this is a surprise would be an understatement," she said in a tone of reverence. "Your commanding officer must have had great trust in you to name you as guardian."

"Their first delivery was a stillbirth," Edmund admitted quietly, remembering the grief of that night. "I learned of Joseph's birth by letter. I had no idea Joe and Eliza would leave this life so soon after."

And now he must nurture their child, helping him navigate his way through life. Was it so difficult for Annabelle to believe he could be responsible for a child?

"How cruel this war is, to leave an infant without parents," she said, her tone bitter.

"It is the cost of a civilized society," Edmund replied shortly. "At any rate, I hope Stephen and Letitia will not be inconvenienced to have one extra at their gathering."

Annabelle flashed him a defensive look.

"Joseph is a mere infant," she retorted. "He shall be received with open arms and a great deal of love. You have been gone so long, you have forgotten what Christmas means."

"I understand perhaps better than you the true meaning of Christmas," he muttered, turning away. "During our trials in Spain, we had far fewer comforts."

She might have been more charitable, Edmund thought irritably, especially now. Christmas was perhaps the high point of the year during the war, yet the sting of being away from loved ones made it bittersweet. He reminded himself that she spoke from ignorance, with no comprehension of the hardships and dangers of military life.

"I merely meant that raising a child is a daunting prospect," Annabelle amended after a moment, her tone subdued, "especially when there is no mother present."

"Indeed," he agreed. "It is a matter of great consequence."

"The major and his wife knew you were not married, yet they left their son to you," she persisted. "Were there no relatives to care for the child?"

Edmund hesitated. Joe and Eliza Enderfield had heard him speak often of his love for Annabelle. Despite his own doubts, they had believed she would wait, ready to marry upon his return. How disappointed they would have been, he thought bleakly.

"We grew to know one another well in the time I spent with my unit," he admitted. "I suspect they wanted Joseph to be raised by someone who shared their values if something were to happen to them."

"They must have shared your enthusiasm for the military," she returned, her voice subdued, "if you still wished not to return home after suffering two major injuries a mere eight months apart."

At last, the hostility he had expected. His concern about their reunion had been warranted, for her disapproval had not diminished with time. How could she not be sympathetic, having lost her brother in the war? Refusing to remain mired in bitterness as she had, he changed the topic.

"How fares your father these days?" he inquired.

"Papa remains angry over Charles's death," she admitted, subdued. "How is he to feel otherwise, having lost his only son in battle? He has not attended Stephen and Letitia's house party in years. And Mother will not leave his side at Christmas."

Edmund digested the revelation soberly. How her life must have changed in his absence.

"Are not four living daughters of as much account as one lost son?" he ventured tenderly.

Annabelle shook her head. The tears that clouded her eyes stirred his soul to its core.

"He is grateful we are female," she muttered. "But no one can replace Charles. I wish Papa had come. Visiting our cousins would do him a great deal of good."

She kicked awkwardly at the haversack Edmund had set on the floor while they waited for their rooms to be ready, its strap entangled at her feet. "Remnants of the war?" she inquired, her tone crisp.

"Just a few things to share with Stephen," he muttered, snatching the bag up.

The slight movement awakened Joseph, who began to fuss in Rosa's arms. Smiling, she cooed affectionately at the child, rocking him tenderly until he grew quiet again.

"Joseph will need a committed parent, now that the war has robbed him of his family," Annabelle observed with a sigh. "War exacts a high price in grief."

"War is the cost of freedom," Edmund countered quietly. "The English will not accept a society ruled by a tyrant. Joseph might have been born in Spain, but he will grow to understand his father's commitment and sacrifice."

Was it sarcasm Edmund had detected in her tone? As soon as she continued, he realized he had been wrong.

"I believe you shall make a fine father," Annabelle resumed in a subdued tone, gazing at the infant in Rosa's arms. "Joseph is fortunate to have you. You understand the meaning of commitment. At any rate, it is too late an hour to debate our differences."

Must this gulf always remain between them? Frustrated, Edmund fell silent. The rooms would surely be ready shortly. He glanced down at Joseph.

"Here, let me hold this child," he said to

Rosa in Spanish. "He will need to grow accustomed to his new father."

Yet how was any child expected to adjust to such an unexpected change? Edmund himself had not fully adjusted to the idea of fatherhood. As Rosa stood and laid the child in his arms gently, Joseph gave a start. Edmund saw an expression of concern replace the calm that had been in his eyes a moment ago. Fussing gasps broke the stillness, growing in volume until they became a tiny wail.

Edmund suddenly felt more helpless than the infant in his arms. Why could he not remember holding his own nieces and nephews when they were this little? He realized with dismay they had been born while he was away.

When the wailing showed no sign of stopping, a look of sympathy spread across Rosa's face. As she reached tenderly for the baby, murmuring words of comfort in Spanish, Edmund relinquished Joseph with a sense of helplessness. A wave of relief swept over him as the child gradually succumbed to exhaustion, his cries lessening to soft murmurs as Rosa cradled his head on her shoulder and rubbed his back.

"Too much change," she murmured, shaking her head.

How, Edmund wondered, had Rosa been able to soothe Joseph so quickly when he would eventually be responsible for the child's care? As if that were not sufficient to distress him, he saw the porter returning at last, his face creased with a concern that did not bode well.

"I offer my humblest apologies for the delay," the porter said with embarrassment, his face flushed. "I believed we had two rooms left, but I fear we have but one."

His heart sinking, Edmund sighed in frustration. While he had not expected to board there overnight, they could travel no further. Rosa and Joseph were exhausted after their journey, and unfamiliar circumstances had left the child in need of rest. The impatience on Annabelle's face turned to concern when his wailing resumed.

"This problem is easily solved," Edmund announced diplomatically. "We will not trouble the child by traveling further tonight. I shall leave the room to Joseph and the ladies and board in the stable." He reassured the porter who protested in mortification. "You need not fret over my comfort. Having recently returned from the war, I will be comfortable enough in the hay."

Perhaps, he thought with irony, sleep would come more easily outdoors. Even with four in one room, no indiscretion could have been committed. Still, if Joseph decided to cry, no one in any upstairs room would be likely to sleep.

It was not yet Christmas Eve, and already there was no room at the inn. Perhaps he would have a better night's sleep outdoors. It would feel a bit like being with his unit again. Yet, twenty minutes later, when he found himself in the stable, curled in a cramped position on the seat of his carriage, he realized that slumber, if it came, would not be without a degree of discomfort. He would try the hay if the seat became too unbearable or the air too cold. It was far better that he ensure the comfort of Joseph and the women indoors. With Christmas less than a month away, the irony of the child's name was not lost on him.

It seemed as if Christmas Eve had come early, but not at all the way either he or the Biblical Joseph had envisioned it.

How ironic to be sleeping in a stable so near Christmas. It would be the first sacrifice of many, he supposed, that he would make for this unexpected child and heir, the last and most significant bond to the major who had befriended and advised him during the hardships of war. His closest friend. The new goal gave him tremendous comfort.

There was so little room to sleep in his carriage, only a small space in which to stretch out. He adjusted the haversack beneath his head, hoping it would soften the sensation of the door handle against his skull. Should he remove one of her letters to read again? He decided against it. Perhaps another night.

The blanket wrapped tightly about him did little to dispel the chill that penetrated the carriage. Yet the sacrifice was worth it. At the very heart of the season was love and good will, even if he had seen no sign of affection in Annabelle's treatment of him. She had been his first love.

There would never be another, he reflected, who would matter as deeply.

How, he wondered, had life gone so wrong? Even knowing her father's demeanor since her brother's death, Edmund had expected she would marry him upon his return. He had intended to save the proposal until then, when life would resume as happily as before. He had joined his regiment with optimism and faith, praying she would wait despite her impatience.

And then came the injury. While he became a hero by enabling Colborne's Light Division to attack and capture the fort at

Ciudad Rodrigo, the fall had shattered his leg and nearly killed him, leaving him with a permanent limp and a cane that made him appear old and weak. Still, his success had made him feel stronger than ever.

He had only heard from Annabelle twice since then. When he refused to take his superiors' advice to leave his unit and return home as she expected, she revoked the devotion she had promised, the love upon which his existence depended. Her second letter two months later contained a notice of her marriage to Randolph Sedgwick.

Did she even know of his second injury, he wondered, the one that left him with permanent damage to his vision? That was the breaking point, the event that made Joe Enderfield insist he consider his decision carefully.

Only the left eye was affected, Edmund reasoned, for he had been looking down the rifle through his right. He was not blind. While his sight was so severely damaged that images only inches before him remained unclear, limited vision was a small price to pay for freedom.

But perhaps, he thought abruptly, it had not been so small to Annabelle.

CHAPTER TWO

The sunlight would be more pleasant, Annabelle decided as the carriage set off the next morning, were it not so blinding. With Joseph asleep in Rosa's lap, the glare through the window forced her to pull the curtain. Too late, she realized, it had awakened the baby. He began to fuss steadily, his discomfort turning at last to pitiful crying.

Despite Rosa's efforts to comfort him, he cried continually until his wails were almost deafening to all but Edmund, maddeningly, who slept throughout the ride on the seat across from them. The sight made Rosa chuckle.

"*Capitán* is tired," she said sympathetically. "No sleep last night."

As Rosa sang tenderly to Joseph, Annabelle was content to listen. Edmund had been impressive, she mused, speaking fluent Spanish with the English private. She gave a self-conscious start. Had he spoken Spanish

266

during the exchange to spare her details of the massacre?

If so, he had been unexpectedly considerate.

Rosa continued to sing softly until Joseph nodded off, giving Annabelle hope that he might sleep at last. The quiet lasted mere seconds before it resumed in earnest, with extra vigor this time. She was startled when Rosa lifted the infant, extending her arms toward Annabelle.

"You hold?" she ventured with a shy smile.

Surprised by the gesture, Annabelle seized the opportunity to cuddle the child despite his insistent cry. She held her breath as Rosa laid Joseph carefully in her arms. His small form filled them perfectly. Accustomed to holding her sisters' children, Annabelle relished the chance to hold one who would not immediately cry for his mother. She eased back in her seat as Joseph settled into her arms, his cries ceasing as he stared up at her, his blue eyes holding her gaze.

"Ah, he like," Rosa exclaimed, her grin broadening.

Annabelle returned her smile. While he did not close his eyes, she watched the child's lids grow heavy until he could no longer fight the weariness that finally overtook him. His slumber, along with Edmund's, allowed the two women to enjoy the remainder of the ride in peace.

Edmund awoke only moments before the coach entered the drive at Lavendam Manor. Adjusting to his surroundings, he observed the baby in Annabelle's arms.

"Joseph appears content," he muttered. "Let us hope he remains that way."

Annabelle stared at him. Had the war caused him to forget the happiness a baby brought?

"The house will be filled with children," she reminded him shortly. "I am certain my cousin, as well as our nieces and nephews, will welcome him as one of their own."

Rosa shifted in her seat, preparing for the third time to take Joseph back into her lap but without success. He fussed loudly at each attempt to remove him from Annabelle's arms.

"You hold?" Rosa asked anxiously.

"I will," Annabelle agreed serenely, delighted that Joseph found comfort with her.

Their calm was shattered minutes later when the great oaken doors of Lavendam Manor were thrown open and her cousin emerged. Letitia Hadleigh's smile was as wide as her open arms. At once, Letitia caught her breath, her face transformed with delight at the infant in Annabelle's arms.

"Annabelle! I would hug you but for this sweet baby!" Letitia exclaimed, slipping an arm about her shoulders, her eyes on Joseph. "Boy or girl? And whose child is this?"

"It is good to see you, Letty," Annabelle replied, laughing as her cousin stared, wide-eyed. "He is a boy, and it is a long story. I shall let Edmund tell it."

Without waiting for her to finish, Letitia gave her a brief hug and ushered them inside, welcoming Rosa warmly and bestowing a warm embrace and kiss upon Edmund. Cradling Joseph in her arms, Annabelle saw her niece and nephews seated on the floor before the fire in animated conversation, toys spread out before them. Turning, Annabelle handed the sleeping baby to Rosa so she might embrace them.

She waited expectantly as Robin, Mary, and Geoffrey leapt to their feet when the front door closed, their eyes widening upon seeing the child as if Father Christmas himself had arrived. Instead of hugging her, they ran past, descending upon Rosa who laughed as they jostled each other for a glimpse of Joseph, all speaking at once.

"We didn't know you had a baby," exclaimed Robin, at ten, the elder of the two boys.

"His fingers are so little," Mary said enthusiastically, reaching for Joseph's hand.

"Is it a boy?" five-year-old Geoffrey asked, his tone hopeful.

Stephen, Letitia's husband and Edmund's brother, chuckled as he greeted Annabelle with an embrace and a brief kiss on the cheek. "Delighted to see you all safely arrived. I look forward to hearing the story behind our unexpected guest."

While the children cooed over Joseph, Stephen and Letitia listened as Edmund related the story quietly and briefly. The excitement turned to horrified dismay at learning the child's parents' fate.

"The baby was accompanied by a letter from Joe Enderfield," Edmund concluded quietly as Joseph squirmed restlessly in Rosa's arms, "and by Rosa, his nurse."

Letitia clucked with sympathy. "I know Joe was more of a friend to you than a superior officer. How dreadful for the poor child. You need not worry about clothing," she assured him, "for we have plenty."

Observing Joseph with intense curiosity, Robin and Geoffrey pushed closer, tumbling over the good-natured spaniels that were accustomed to unexpected movements from their young masters and mistress, welcoming their attention with wagging tails.

"We have a new cousin!" Mary, now seven, exclaimed gleefully. "And Aunt Annabelle is a new mommy!"

"What is your baby's name?" asked Geoffrey, polite but shy.

"His name is Joseph, but he is not my baby," Annabelle cautioned quickly.

"Yet what an appropriate name!" Letitia noted. "We already have Mary, and now we have Joseph."

"We can have our own nativity!" exclaimed Robin.

"If Joseph were laid in the manger, he would probably scream so loudly, I suspect we could not even hear ourselves caroling," Stephen said, laughing as Joseph fussed in Rosa's arms.

"Is this the real Joseph?" Geoffrey asked softly, wide-eyed as he looked up at Annabelle. How much he had grown, she thought.

"He is not the Joseph we read about in the Bible, but he is a real baby," Letitia explained, chuckling when the child lost interest and ran back to his toys. "Geoffrey is apparently more intrigued by his soldiers. Speaking of soldiers, Edmund, how delightful that you will be with us this year."

271

"I hope Joseph is no bother," Edmund apologized, entering her embrace.

"You could have brought us nothing better." Letitia bestowed a brief kiss upon his cheek that made him flush and smile. How handsome he was, Annabelle noted, when his face was touched with emotion. "Did you truly think bringing an orphaned child to your brother and his wife at Christmas would trouble us? I should be most upset if you did, and more upset if you had not brought him. A baby is the most wonderful present. Here, let us make him comfortable."

Miss Milbury, the children's nanny, stepped forward for a closer look. "Poor child, having endured so much misfortune," she murmured sympathetically. "How confused he must be with all the changes."

"He needs love and attention now," Letitia agreed.

"Soon, this little one will be running about with the rest. What jolly fun the children shall have with him," exclaimed Stephen, his eyes twinkling as he stepped forward to clasp Edmund's hand. "Good to see you again, Edmund, although you look rather pale at present."

"Becoming a father unexpectedly does that to one," Edmund replied.

"Why don't you lay Joseph in this cradle, Rosa? I had it brought downstairs for Mary's dolls. You must all be exhausted. Come, make yourself at ease," Letitia said, ushering Annabelle to a comfortably cushioned chair. "Here, sit. We will bring you what you need."

Settled in the wooden cradle, Joseph refused to close his heavy eyelids as the children crowded about him. After studying Joseph and whispering for some time, they looked up at Annabelle, their eyes wide.

"May we play with him after his nap, Aunt Annabelle?" Mary asked softly.

"Remember, he is very little yet," Letitia cautioned. "We cannot play with him as we would a doll. But if you are very careful, you might hold him in your lap when he awakens."

With simultaneous gasps of delight, Mary and Robin exchanged excited glances, hovering over the cradle with Geoffrey as their nanny chuckled. While Edmund spoke privately with Stephen across the room, Annabelle watched the children swarm about the cradle until Joseph was hidden beneath their collected heads. Joseph was the centerpiece, she thought in amusement. Even the spaniels sniffing about did not trouble him.

"Give him space," Letitia cautioned in her most motherly tone, "for he is little, and we are strangers to him yet. While he is much like a doll, imagine how Joseph sees us."

The children protested in dismay before they finally rose and scurried away.

"The children shall be talking about their new cousin for days," Letitia laughed.

Annabelle watched them return to their seats near the warmth of the fire before she gazed down at the cradle where Joseph fidgeted restlessly, his eyes opening. Perhaps this is how the baby Jesus had looked, she reflected. The thought sent shivers through her.

"I wonder what the world looks like through Joseph's eyes," Letitia mused.

"He has had such a hard beginning," Annabelle murmured. "We shall make this a Christmas full of love for him."

"He and Grace's Margaret shall be play-mates, for he is only a few months younger. And wait until Pamela arrives with Abby and Rose," Letitia confided, excitement in her tone. "The last time they were here, the twins spent the entire day ordering Mary about, remember? To think they are three years younger."

Annabelle laughed. "Yet Mary was most sporting about it."

"I was proud of her, even a bit surprised," Letitia confided, watching the children. "Christmas does not really begin until Grace and Pamela and their families are here. And Beatrice, of course. It will be so cozy this year with Edmund home at last. And it is only two weeks until Christmas." Seizing Annabelle's hand, she sighed pensively. "If only your parents would come, the whole family would be together."

Annabelle hesitated to tell her favorite cousin of her own reluctance to attend. She had not realized, until this moment, how deeply she had feared seeing Edmund again. Her bitter words to him during their journey rose in her memory like shadows from a nightmare, haunting her. How could she have accused Edmund of not loving her enough? He possessed such a generous nature and was always placing the comfort of others before his own. She fought the humiliation flowing through her as she realized her folly, born of impulsiveness.

Not only had she destroyed Edmund's hopes of marriage and a happy homecoming when he desperately needed to believe it while he was away fighting, she had destroyed her own opportunity to have what she wanted most from life — a husband and children. In the heat of the moment, she had ruined both of their lives by marrying a man whose temperament and desires were completely unsuited to hers. Worse, her own complaining about Edmund, the only man she had ever loved, had driven Randolph straight to his death even before battle, all while trying to prove to her that he was just as brave and heroic.

That effort alone was folly, for who could ever compete with Edmund for her heart?

And then the realization came to her — despite her every action to the contrary, a part of her still loved him. She had never stopped loving him. The truth dawned as if the snow-covered roof had released its weight on her all at once.

Yet even with Edmund, she had spoken in the heat of the moment, blurting out her frustrations without regard for the pain she caused him. Could he ever forgive her foolishness? Glancing at Edmund laughing casually with Stephen, she suspected her regret had come too late.

The magic they had shared was likely never to be rekindled. It had vanished over time, broken away bit by bit with her refusal to wait.

Perhaps, Annabelle thought when she and her cousin were alone in the parlor, a walk might clear her head. She had begun to feel smothered by her thoughts and restless from having ridden so long. As she stepped outdoors, the gleam of sunlight on snow hurt her eyes while it refreshed her. She set off on the old path Letitia had recommended, one that had obviously not been used for years, considering the amount of brush that had fallen alongside it and had not yet been cleared.

How had she come to believe she would never have children, she wondered as she meandered along the trail? Edmund had been on the verge of proposing before he left. His father had fought in the American Revolution, like her own. There was little question he would follow the honorable course.

She must do the same, she reminded herself. Yet what was honorable now? As she walked, the old landmarks began to look familiar. The gnarled tree with the branches that had seemed threatening when she was younger. The oak grove, its height towering above her. Even the small stable remained in place. It seemed little more than a shed now, with some of its boards loose and crooked. Her heart skipped a beat as memories overwhelmed her.

She had walked here many summers ago

with Edmund beside her. They had ventured into the privacy of the stable for their very first kiss. While he had been a complete gentleman, her heart had soared as it never had since.

It was the moment she knew they were destined to be together.

Her heart stirred at the memory. Many other kisses and embraces had followed during their walks along these paths. She recalled conversations they had shared, about where they would live, and what their children would look like, and how they would pass their time when they were old. The memories prompted an unwelcome melancholy. It all seemed so far in the past.

Now here she was again, at Christmastime, but Edmund was not with her the way she had dreamed he would be. They should have been married by now, surrounded by children of their own. She could still visualize the Christmas tree she had imagined, their children seated around its base, awed by its grandeur as she had always been. While there would be a tree this year, it saddened Annabelle to realize that the children of her imagination had disappeared from her earlier vision.

Before she had a chance to recover from her reverie, the sound of footsteps in the brush startled her. Someone was making his way along a trail that forked with hers. Turning, she came face to face with the person who owned her thoughts. Edmund's expression froze with uncertainty before he gave her a lopsided smile, aware of their closeness. The gravity in his features made her wonder if he had hoped to walk alone, just as she had.

"I was anticipating solitude on this trail," he confessed. "But if you are making your way through the woods back to the house, I would be happy to accompany you. Some of the branches have come down and the trail is precarious."

He must have managed to clear the brush, she mused, even while using his cane.

"Apparently you were as restless as I for exercise." Annabelle smiled. "If the walk is somewhat treacherous, I would appreciate your company."

They walked in silence, Edmund taking her arm as they were forced to step carefully over occasional fallen tree limbs. Did his heart stir as hers had, she wondered, to see the shed where they had shared their first kiss?

"This path appears to have been cleared a bit since we were last here," he noted, keeping his gaze on the frozen landscape as he held her arm securely, his other hand clutching his cane. "I remember it being overgrown at one point."

Between periods of awkward silence, he reduced the conversation to insignificant matters during their exchanges. As usual, she thought in dismay, he overlooked what mattered most. After all they had endured while apart, how could he ignore issues that had forced her to end their engagement? Perhaps she was merely impatient.

"Amazing how trees can stand so many years," he commented casually, "and still survive the fiercest storms."

Annabelle paused before turning to face him, checking her impulse to criticize him for refusing to address the heart of their differences. "After all our years apart, is that all you have to say?" she ventured softly.

He gazed at her in silence, his expression torn by conflicting emotions.

"I enjoy being with you in a spot we once loved so," he admitted quietly. "There were times I thought I might never share your company again. These woods bring me great solace after having been on the front lines."

"They bring back memories for me as well," she countered. Did he understand that her emotional pain, while not as deadly, had been as intense as a physical wound?

Deciding it was time to raise the matter that troubled her most, she addressed him gently. "You never explained to me why you did not return after your injury. You were nearly killed. You, who bravely climbed mountains with such confidence, suddenly had wounds that were so critical, your commanders recommended you come home. Yet you did not." The subject distressed her still. She paused, wishing he would answer so she need not continue. "You had already shown yourself to be a hero. What more had you to prove?"

He paused for some time, answering quietly at last. "My unit needed me desperately. They required my presence more than you did. I wanted to spare you the reality of the dangers we faced. I hoped you would love me enough to try to understand."

Annabelle's heart sank. No one needed to see that Edmund was safe more than she did, yet he'd refused to come home despite having almost died. Why did he hesitate to answer the question directly? She held her tongue. Impatience would not get the better of her again.

"How was I to understand," she countered, "when you were not here to tell me? You were my whole life."

"Clearly, I was not, since you found

another in the darkest moment of mine." The intensity in his gaze matched her own with exasperating tenacity.

Was it disappointment or blame she saw in his features? The need for honesty was clear in the demand in his eyes. How was she to explain why she had been unable to wait? The answer demanded a level of courage she could not muster. As a captain, he possessed more integrity than had ever been demanded of her. If she told him how desperately she had wanted children, would he understand? He might never forgive her for refusing to support his sense of patriotism.

"I felt your troops mattered more to you than I did," she faltered helplessly. "When you did not return as you promised, I turned elsewhere."

"No individual ever represents one's whole life. Our very existence relies upon many people. I hope one day you will learn that."

His tone was objective, Annabelle thought, but he might as well have pierced her heart with a sword. It was clear he considered her among those upon whom he could not rely. She tried to swallow the lump in her throat.

"You married another rather than wait for me to return," Edmund continued without emotion. "Apparently, disloyalty was preferable to loneliness. Did it never occur to you I was lonely as well?"

"I knew it too well," she managed to whisper.

While she remained frustrated, at least she had not lost her temper. She had proven that she could discuss their differences without becoming defensive and making remarks she would regret. For once, she had held her tongue.

How the tables had turned, she thought, now that Edmund had accepted the responsibility of an orphaned child. The fact that she had failed to recognize the depths of his heart filled her with dismay. Perhaps one day, they would be able to establish a relationship again. Then she remembered how she had allowed him to believe she remained loyal while waiting for his return, but turned to Randolph instead.

It was hard now to imagine she had accused him of not loving her enough to return. Had she not wanted children so desperately, she would never have spoken so. She regretted her harsh words, for traces of the deep love she had felt for him lingered in her heart.

But he might never forgive her.

While he must have dreamed of her love

during the lonely nights at war, she had given it to another. To Randolph, who had not a fraction of the integrity or character Edmund possessed.

They returned along the path in silence. Even if she had forgiven him, she realized with a sinking heart, it would be a long time before he would ever trust her again.

The children had won and lost snowball fights, gone sledding on the gentle hills surrounding Lavendam Manor, and, with Edmund's assistance, built a snow army consisting of half a dozen soldiers that afternoon before they finally returned indoors. Where, he wondered, did such energy come from? He was surprised when, after consuming great amounts of hot chocolate and apple tarts that would have been a veritable feast for soldiers following a battle, they returned outdoors accompanied by their mother and aunt. Exhausted by trying to keep up with them, Edmund was more than happy to retire to the study with his brother.

"Still having doubts about fatherhood?" Stephen inquired with a grin.

"I am relieved the women have taken charge," Edmund confessed. "So much noise and confusion."

"The energy of childhood is overwhelming." Chuckling, Stephen reached for a bottle of brandy on the sideboard. "But compared to war, it has not nearly the chaos or confusion. I am surprised you should not find it relaxing to join in their merriment. It is all rather exciting stuff to young ones, this business of winter and snow."

Edmund was more amused by the incongruous toy soldiers lined up on the Earl of Stavemorton's desk, undoubtedly left by his sons. Stephen laughed at his description of his makeshift bed at the Foxwell Inn's stable that allowed Joseph and the women to sleep in comfort.

"That is only one of many sacrifices you shall make, and willingly." Stephen grinned. "Do not doubt me when I tell you that having children requires change."

"It is more challenging without a wife or mother," Edmund admitted. "But there is Rosa."

Stephen looked at him doubtfully. "You will need more than a nurse. But there will be opportunities in the coming weeks. You were once friendly with Katherine Fortenberry, who is away visiting relatives. But Eloisa March will be here."

It would be a challenge, Edmund reflected, to peel away the war years separating him from his past. Katherine had been an acquaintance, Eloisa less so. Annabelle had been much more. He realized, with a sinking heart, that there would be nothing further between them, for she appeared to have little desire to resume what they once had. Despite her betrayal, Annabelle would have been ideal. He had been riveted by her letters describing her bond with their nieces and nephews.

Watching the children play together that afternoon, he had realized with apprehension that Joseph would be among them within a few years. For now, Rosa would stay on as nurse. But when her role was finished, she might wish to return to Spain, where she had family beyond the husband and son she had lost. He recalled she had once discussed the possibility of remaining with the Enderfields as a servant. Could she be more, he wondered? Having a mother would be far more critical to Joseph than having a nurse. She spoke only a bit of English, but she would learn more now that she was in England. Of course, she could not compare to Annabelle.

Being entrusted with a child, he suspected, would alter his life in ways he could not imagine. As if reading his mind, Stephen confirmed his reflections.

"Having a child is a tremendous responsibility, even more so when the child is not yours by birth." Stephen paused, resuming in a gentle but frank tone. "I remember you wrote me of your regret at being forced from the war before your time. You would likely have been killed had you stayed. And Joseph might have been orphaned or killed as well." He smiled bleakly. "You might not have realized it yet, but this is a marvelous inheritance."

Edmund fought his trepidation. The war had left him with injuries that had changed his life, making him feel old and infirm. And yet, a sense of guilt clung to him. He would have fought on and been with his unit the night so many of his comrades were lost. He could suddenly see the situation the way Annabelle had.

As if reading his mind, Stephen raised the very subject Edmund wished to avoid. "Have you raised the matter of your differences with Annabelle?"

Edmund shook his head pessimistically. "She continues to hold me responsible for relations ending between us, despite the fact that she chose to marry in my absence."

"Is she aware no one else in your brigade possessed your ability to climb mountains? You won the siege for Wellington because of our childhood summers in Geneva." Stephen gave him a meaningful stare. "You were sent on ahead of the troops because no one else could scale the wall of that redoubt with your speed. It allowed Colborne to take Ciudad Rodrigo from the French within minutes, and with ridiculously few casualties. You are a hero. Never think otherwise."

Edmund acknowledged his praise with a rueful grin of amusement. "If only the French had not cut the rope, my leg would still be useful."

"Yet I have never seen anyone so badly injured manage as capably." Stephen raised an eyebrow. "Afterward, you became even more essential to your commander as a master tactician. No other officer had your ability. You understood enemy strategies, analyzed intelligence, even knew their thinking. Why then did you not explain to Annabelle that you could not return because no one else possessed your skills?" he persisted. "Wellington would not have succeeded without you."

Unfortunately, Edmund was not skilled enough to be a tactician when it came to women. He had had no strategy for courting and keeping the woman he loved. Where matters of the heart were concerned, there had only ever been one. Even without a formal commitment, he had expected she would wait. While it had cut more than any wound, he realized that what he had viewed as treachery had merely been a desire for children. He shrugged.

"At the time, the assault on the fort was confidential, of course. And I resented her marriage. I was too proud to contact her afterward." He changed the subject, noting how Stephen's gaze remained riveted on the view. "Apparently you have not had enough snow to have tired of it."

"When children are young, your view of the season changes." Stephen chuckled before pausing thoughtfully. "It is noble and natural that your heart is still in the war. But mark my words, in time you shall come to love this child as if he had been born to you."

"Spending one night with the responsibility of a new child hardly gives one time to do more than rest in preparation for the decisions to follow," Edmund complained. He had barely held Joseph long enough for the child to recognize him. But there would be time for that on his return home.

"At any rate, sleighs await us tomorrow," Stephen continued.

"Sleighs?" Edmund attempted to hide his

dismay. The prospect of interacting with Annabelle appealed to him less than the prospect of sleeping outdoors at the inn yard again.

"And later, Letty's friend Eloisa March is expected along with Tom Skeffington. I believe you have met Skeptical Skeff."

Edmund seized the opportunity to confide in his brother. "Stephen, tell me Letitia has not intended this gathering as a matchmaking venture."

"Is it not possible relations might be restored between you and Annabelle?" Stephen's eyes creased with interest. "Now that she is a widow, she is free to marry again. Perhaps it is fated to be. Joseph seems to prefer her company over anyone else's."

Sadness filled Edmund as he remembered the conversation on their woodland walk. "Her attitude toward my commission differed greatly from mine," he admitted quietly. "The decisions she made in my absence appear to have closed the door to any possibility of a reconciliation."

"I am sorry. I hoped it might be otherwise." Stephen paused. "But you must admit the timing is a stroke of luck. Now that you have inherited the responsibility of fatherhood, the presence of marriageable women with whom you might socialize could prove a blessing."

Edmund sighed, attempting to hide his frustration. "While I suspect I have had more than enough blessings for one fortnight, I should like to add a good dose of brandy to that list."

"Allow me to oblige you." Stephen chuckled. "Perhaps what you need to restore your perspective is a charity of some sort."

Edmund fought to turn his grimace into a grin as Stephen reached for the decanter. His brother's assurance that they would have fun left Edmund doubtful. He could not erase from his mind the image of the children gathered about Joseph's basket as if he were the Christmas centerpiece.

"I am sincerely sorry to hear of the loss of Enderfield and his wife. What a terrible shock." Stephen paused. "I know you had great respect for him."

"Even knowing an ambush was always possible, it is difficult to imagine." No words could describe Edmund's sense of loss. The news had struck him with the force of a cannonball to the gut. "I cannot help but think had I been there, the unit would have had an extra watchman to intervene and perhaps lower the casualties."

"To wonder if you might have changed the outcome is folly," Stephen cautioned.

"Do not trouble yourself with such an unlikely possibility. Your service cost you the comfortable use of a leg and considerable use of an eye. That is sacrifice enough."

They had failed to notice Letitia in the doorway, hands on her hips, reproach in her face.

"Edmund, it is indeed folly to consider such a thing," she said softly. "It is true that gentlemen, particularly youngest sons, are destined for military service. But you did your duty, and your wounds were sufficient to send you home. What would Joseph's fate have been without you? Had you remained at the front, there would be no one to tell him of his parents' service in the war. You are here because you were meant to be."

Edmund shook his head. "I admit I find the adjustment unsettling. Perhaps I am overwhelmed at being back and having a child, and by the noise the children make."

"But it is such a happy noise," she exclaimed, taking a seat opposite him. "It is natural to feel overwhelmed after all you have endured. You have only been home half a year. We are fortunate to have little ones underfoot at the same time. This child coming to you now is a blessing. Childhood is a delight, and it lasts such a short time." She patted his hand, her eyes glistening. "Once you spend time with Joseph, you shall see why it passes all too quickly."

How, Edmund wondered, was one to stand that much joy amid the noise? In battle, there had been screams, cannon fire, and rifle shots, but most of the time, war was relatively quiet. The only noises were the whinnying of horses, the clanging of shovels, or the ringing of metal dishes. At night, he listened for enemies approaching.

He envied Letitia's confidence as commander of a brigade of children whose respect she maintained admirably. Would he ever reach that point? Since coming home, he had preferred the company of dogs to people, for he found their uncomplicated presence comforting. And horses, he had to remind himself, were meant for riding through the countryside rather than into battle.

Yet he had discovered, since arriving at Lavendam Manor, that despite the noisy mix, dogs preferred the company of children even when their paws were accidentally trod upon. The sympathetic hugs that followed made it worth the moment of pain.

"You have fulfilled your destiny, Edmund, and you are meant to serve in a different way now. You shall serve the memory of his parents by raising Joseph Enderfield

Hadleigh." Letitia must have seen the confusion in his expression, for she paused. "That will be his name, will it not? Did you consider that while holding him?"

Duly chastised, Edmund felt his heart sink. "I held him only briefly before returning him to Rosa."

A look of gentle reproach spread across Letitia's face. "Do you mean to tell me you have held your son only once? If he was not asleep, I would bring him to you right now. He is such a handsome boy with those big blue eyes."

Striking blue eyes like Major Enderfield's, and large like Annabelle's, he realized with a start. He managed a shaky smile as he gazed at Letitia apologetically.

"I have led troops into battle with less trepidation," he confessed. "Yet I feel inadequate to the task before me."

"It is natural to feel overwhelmed. It took Stephen time to adjust, and he expected children." Letitia spoke gently as she took his hand in hers. "This little boy will be toddling about and running before you can imagine it. We will be here to help with whatever you need."

The son of his best friend and revered commander deserved every ounce of devotion he had to give, Edmund resolved. No couple could provide a more exemplary example than his brother and his wife. As a new father, he could not hope to compare, but he would give his all in the attempt.

Yet how was he was to succeed at his new assignment, he wondered, without a mother for his child?

CHAPTER THREE

"The children shall have their rides this afternoon," Letitia told Annabelle as they waited outdoors for the sleighs to be brought 'round the next morning. "While we ride, Miss Milbury will watch them enlarge the snow fort Edmund started yesterday. Impressive, is it not?"

Who better to build it, Annabelle thought, than the former soldier whose heart remained with his regiment? Fighting a rare moment of melancholy, Annabelle took a closer look and saw how secure and well-crafted the snow fort was. Yesterday, while Edmund had taught the children strategies for winning snowball fights, she had noticed the care and time he put into it, its roof packed tightly so it would be less likely to fall in upon the children.

He had considered every aspect carefully, as he did all aspects of life. Waiting for the sleigh to arrive, she watched the children emerge from the fort and chase each another around in the snow, their nanny joining in as they squealed with delight under the sun's bright rays.

The children viewed their Uncle Edmund as a hero. To many, Annabelle realized, he was. Perhaps it was time that she appreciated his contribution. She saw no sign of him as she waited restlessly. Had yesterday's exchange troubled him so that he did not wish to share a sleigh with her today? Her heart sank at the idea.

"Of course, I hope matters can be resolved between you," Letitia confided diplomatically, "but should you seek company, Tom Skeffington and Eloisa March are due to arrive today. Tom is intelligent and well-read. And Eloisa is pleasant, so you need not feel you must spend all your time with Edmund."

Smiling gratefully, Annabelle turned to gaze at the frozen hills, bright with snow crystals. "I appreciate your thoughtfulness, but I suspect an English apology to the French is more likely than any romantic reconciliation between us."

"Be that as it may," Letitia replied, following her gaze, "the light on the snow is quite magical. Today's ride will take you up around the pond through the woods. I hope it makes up for the time Edmund has missed."

While they waited for Edmund and Stephen, the new guests arrived within fifteen minutes of each other. Thomas Skeffington expressed doubt as to the wisdom of embarking upon a sleigh ride after being so long in a carriage. The slender Miss March agreed, voicing her suspicion that the cold would be more irritating than refreshing. As they were shown indoors, it was decided they would ride together after resting, for at present, neither possessed the energy to engage in lively conversation.

"I suspect Eloisa is better suited to indoor activities, for her arms are as thin as the snowman's," Letitia confided in amusement, taking Annabelle's hand. "I hope I did not do wrong inviting her. But it is the season of hope, after all. Perhaps the presence of others will relieve the awkwardness, now that you and Edmund are no longer on the best of terms."

She herself had always been too headstrong, Annabelle thought abruptly, waiting impatiently for the fulfillment life would bring. She had wanted children and married another man, and ended up with neither. And now it might never be, for she was too impulsive to make anyone a suitable wife. Her last opportunity to have children had disappeared with Randolph's death. Yet she had made her choices and had to accept the consequences.

Her apprehension at the prospect of riding with Edmund had apparently been for nothing, she realized soon afterward. He appeared moments later with Stephen, both chuckling and in high spirits. As they approached over the rise of the hill, the cane was temporarily out of sight. The wind rippling through his dark hair stripped away the years between them, giving Edmund the appearance she remembered so well. The inherent strength in his features and his relaxed demeanor removed a weight from her shoulders.

After retrieving Geoffrey from the snow-bank into which he had tumbled, Letitia joined Stephen in the sleigh, waving as they set off. Their laughter lingered in the air, echoing even after the horses and riders had vanished from sight. In an awkward attempt to step into her own sleigh, Annabelle tripped on the hem of her cloak, bringing Edmund to her side to assist her as he climbed in beside her.

He had always intended well, she realized, treating everyone with the same chivalry and consideration. How had she ever thought him haughty? She saw no sign of it now, for a respectful silence hung between them like a third party once they were alone. Edmund muttered insignificant comments about the weather to which she murmured agreement.

"I understand you endured a great deal while I was away," he admitted abruptly. "I am not surprised to find you changed, although I confess it troubles me."

His candor surprised Annabelle. "You are not the cause, at least not entirely. It is what came afterward, with Randolph — to lose first my brother, and then my husband."

"I would not have left you so soon after marriage." Despite Edmund's soft tone, she heard the concern in his voice and waited for his explanation. "I do not regret leaving my country to do my duty. But I would not have taken the risk of leaving you a newly married widow."

"Married or unmarried, it did not matter." She tried to explain gently. "The risk of danger does not trouble you, for you are brave and have never suffered such a loss. After we lost Charles, Papa was never the same. I feared you would be next. I could not bear the thought of losing you. I understand if you feel differently, yet it is good to have you home."

"I did not die, despite your worrying. There were many men far braver than I who risked their lives as well." Taking a deep breath, he laughed awkwardly, his hands gripping the reins. "It is true I did not expect to be home so soon. Nor did I expect to be gone so long. I assumed we would have defeated the enemy by now. While I consider our army stronger than Bonaparte's, I suspect we underestimated the tenacity of the French. I never imagined that after my service was done, I would inherit the responsibility of nurturing and educating a child."

Annabelle turned to him, startled, noting his brown eyes focused on the path ahead. She looked for love in them but saw only caution. If love was there, it was disguised as a plea for help.

"I know you did not wish to return, despite being severely injured, and despite the recommendation of your superiors. But perhaps Joseph was the reason you were forced home by your injuries," she suggested delicately.

"While I was away, my greatest consolation was knowing that those at home were safe, especially you, and that you were happy in your new marriage," he conceded, flashing her a smile of reminiscence. "I suppose our lives have been generally satisfying, despite our occasional losses."

How could he feel so charitable, she wondered, having suffered so profoundly? Deep within her heart, she knew he had not been so deeply attached to the soldiers that he preferred their company to hers. Yet terror had overtaken her faith, and she had been able to wait no longer.

It felt, she realized abruptly, as if she had been expecting him to die before returning to her. She felt herself shaking as her old fears returned, joined by new ones that threatened tears.

To think Edmund believed she had been happily married. He could not know how it had hurt to watch her relationship crumble so soon after marriage, to hear Randolph declare that he was tired of competing with Edmund for her affections. That he would prove he was just as good a soldier if not better. She had not realized she had driven Randolph to war by comparing him to Edmund until it was too late. Her sense of guilt over his death was deeper than her love for him had been in life.

It was a private humiliation she would never share with Edmund. He might not want to be near her if he knew she had treated Randolph so thoughtlessly. Somehow, she had always known that Randolph's character had little substance compared with Edmund's quiet humility. His frank and gentle honesty startled her back to the present.

"Should there be any doubt in your mind, I want you to know I have forgiven you. I must ask your forgiveness as well," he announced abruptly, his tone more tender than it had been on their earlier walk. "I was wrong to blame you for marrying while I was away. I had no right to do so. Neither you nor I had any way of knowing the turns our lives would take. It is clear to me that you loved Randolph deeply and still mourn his loss. I respect your decision and hope you understand the need I felt to do my patriotic duty." He gave her a brief smile tinged with an apology. "It is not the way we planned it, but we are traveling separate paths that have taken us in unexpected directions. I hope you can forgive any hardships I have caused you. Now let us move forward without looking back, shall we?"

Stunned into silence, Annabelle could not catch her breath. What was she to say? To admit that Randolph had not been all she had believed would diminish both her deceased husband and herself in Edmund's eyes. She could not speak. She felt as if her heart had stopped.

Was there to be no reconciliation now? She would have given Edmund another chance if only he still loved her. But it was too late. He had moved on without her. He had not even mentioned the possibility of a more significant relationship between them. She swallowed the lump that had formed in her throat, attempting to pull her emotions under control.

"Do you think you might stop this sleigh?" she heard herself ask, her tone as frail as the emotions that threatened to break from her at any moment. "I am not feeling entirely well. I shall walk back to the house."

From the corner of her eye, she saw the alarm in Edmund's eyes as he assessed her intentions.

"Surely you do not mean to return on foot," he said at once, alarm in his voice. "The winds are so brisk, they would give you a severe chill before you had gone half-way."

"Then perhaps we can switch places so I might return with Letty," she insisted.

Annabelle's growing despair turned to relief as she glanced sideways in time to see the other sleigh making its way through the woods. In a matter of minutes, it would return to the open stretch of hills over which she and Edmund had just traveled.

"Please do not worry," she said abruptly. "As I am feeling a bit queasy, I suspect I merely require rest." She forced a shaky smile. "I hope you have a more pleasant ride with Stephen and the children."

What had she done, Annabelle wondered recklessly? Having confided her sense of loss to Letitia as much as she had been able to through tears, she was relieved when the sleigh reached Lavendam Manor at last. She managed to compose herself before they were greeted by the children, with Miss Milbury taking advantage of the sunshine to play with them out-of-doors.

"The children have been most creative," Letitia observed as they stepped from the sleigh.

Annabelle looked up, greeted by two snow families the children had created near the manger that would remain empty until Christmas Eve. She recognized Edmund at once, the tallest, clad in a muffler and top hat. The stick they used as a cane made her throat tighten. The children had wrapped a slightly shorter snow figure in the rose-colored shawl she had brought.

Her affection for the children with their kind intentions turned to heartbreak when she saw the tiny snow child wedged between the two adult figures. She managed to hide her tears as Mary, serious and owl-eyed, ran to greet her.

"Your baby misses you," she said in a confidential tone. "He is upstairs with Rosa. He was crying for you before we came outside."

"Thank you for telling me, Mary. I shall tend to him right away," Annabelle promised, patting her cheeks. "Perhaps we shall find time later to play that game you promised to teach me."

Annabelle hugged the children before they ran back to their fort. While Mary's revelation was perhaps the last thing she had wanted to hear, her words were oddly comforting.

"I appreciate your enthusiasm," Letitia interrupted, "for I suspect Eloisa has far less interest in children or fussing babies. Perhaps she will be able to occupy Edmund while you tend to Joseph. Holding him will make you feel better."

Annabelle struggled to smile as she watched her nephews, preoccupied now with strengthening their snow fort. Yet, she felt her own defenses falling. She barely managed to stifle a sob before her fears tumbled out. "I do not expect to marry Edmund," she admitted miserably. "It is satisfactory for all, for he does not wish to wed me either."

"Of course he wishes to marry you." The indignation on Letitia's face would have been comical, were it not for the anguish that left Annabelle numb. "Why would he not?"

"Why would he?" Annabelle countered in despair. "When he was at war, I feared he would never come home. Now that he has, we are both resigned to being apart. It would have been nice if we could have been together again, but it is not to be."

Letitia sighed. "But what of Joseph? He misses his mother so. You are the closest he has come since her death. Watch him closely when he is in your arms, for that is where he longs to be. It is as if he has chosen you for the role. If Rosa does not already think you are Joseph's future mother, she assumes you will be. Do you not recognize yourself and Edmund in these snow figures? Mary told me that they built Joseph upright, for they feared the dogs would trample him if he were lying down."

The effort the children had taken to build the snow families touched Annabelle's heart. She could not deny her growing attachment to Joseph. Yet how was she to become his mother when she had rejected his father?

"I am grateful you have my interests at heart, Letty," she told her cousin gently. "But Edmund and I have changed over time, and we are resigned to the way things are."

Letitia's objection gave way to capitulation. "Very well, Annabelle. I am sorry you feel as you do, but I understand. Perhaps he might find a match in Eloisa, if she proves a satisfactory choice for Joseph."

It was the result she desired least, Annabelle thought with a sinking heart. Yet it might be the best outcome for Joseph, even if it was not for her.

Edmund had watched Annabelle trudge through the snow behind their sleigh after her departure with a mixture of concern and bewilderment. He had watched as Stephen drew his sleigh up sharply at Annabelle's unexpected approach, listen to her concern, and kindly vacate his seat for her so that she might return with Letitia.

He reflected on the sheer irony of it in silence while returning with Stephen. While she seemed so fond of Joseph, it was Edmund himself she had not been able to forgive. Her only request had been that he come home after his nearly fatal injury.

While he had wished to, the request was one he had been unable to grant. She could not have known, nor did he wish her to, the desperation the troops had faced in Spain. She did not know the depth of his pain or the way he mourned the loss of men following his departure, especially Joe and Eliza. Had he still been in Spain, he might have known of the unexpected attack and been able to save them all.

Was it too late to recover the feelings they had once shared? Perhaps it was unfair to ask it of her. While Annabelle was as lovely as ever, she considered herself on the shelf. He had done that to her, he realized with guilt. For a brief moment, he resented the life he might have given her had he not gone to war.

How tragic that she had lost Randolph so soon after marriage. They had barely had time to grow accustomed to each other before her husband had perished abroad. The loss had made Annabelle a widow far too young, leaving an emptiness in her heart that could not be filled by anyone, not even Joseph.

Edmund's spirits fell so deeply that he did not know how to proceed. While he had not expected Annabelle to consider resuming the relations they had once shared, he had hoped.

While he was certainly able to provide for a child, it would be far better if Joseph had a woman's presence in his life. Annabelle would have been the logical choice. Her situation complicated matters, leaving him in a difficult position. Was there no way, he mused, to bring her back into his arms? While their past was behind them, surely the parts worth saving could be reclaimed if she were to agree to marry him. Yet under the circumstances, it seemed impossible.

One way or another, Joseph needed a mother. Fortunately, Letitia had invited others to her house party. Where romance was concerned, Edmund knew, he needed educating as much as a child.

It was ironic that he, the great strategist, knew no strategy for courting and keeping the only woman he had ever loved.

He barely knew Eloisa March, and had no common ground on which to begin a conversation. Letitia had been wise in realizing he would need a wife. Although he had no desire to court anyone but Annabelle, he would respect her wishes and turn his attention to Eloisa.

Upon his return, he discovered the children still playing outdoors with Letitia supervising. While Stephen returned indoors to greet Thomas Skeffington, Edmund remained outside, watching the children.

"I am sorry, Edmund." Letitia shook her head wistfully. "I suspect deep within, Annabelle regrets her behavior and wishes for your forgiveness."

"She has a most unusual way of displaying regret." Edmund managed a crooked smile. An optimist by nature, Letitia perhaps had more insight into her cousin than he did.

Would he ever be as good a parent, he wondered? Letitia marched the children along with the confidence of an experienced colonel. Joseph did not respond well when Edmund picked him up and fussed when he laid him down. Was it possible, he wondered uneasily, that young as he was, Joseph associated him with the war that had claimed his parents? The thought left him discouraged.

Yet Joseph appeared to enjoy the company of the other children and, of course, Annabelle's affectionate manner and maternal kindness. How, Edmund wondered, would he be able to keep up with a child? Even using his cane, it took him far longer to return to the house than anyone else. He watched Letitia's children lying in the snow while thrashing about, laughing and whooping with great hilarity.

"Does it not look like fun? They are making angels. Do you see their wings?" Letitia indicated the sweeping motion of their arms. "Joseph was here for a time. But when the wind picked up, Rosa took him indoors. Despite the children's protests, of course."

Edmund gave a start. The women had described Joseph as content, curious, and fascinated by new faces. They were so attentive to the baby that Joseph had barely been in Edmund's arms long enough to recognize his new father. It was indeed an act of grace, he thought reverently, that so young a child had the ability to adapt to a new individual thrust upon him as a parent.

Letitia smiled. "The children have grown quite fond of Joseph. It will be difficult to let him leave once the house party ends. You are most welcome to stay longer, you know. Indeed, I hope you will."

"Perhaps." Edmund watched the children uneasily, noting the vigor with which Robin, the older boy, leapt to his feet, shaking off snow. "Is it safe to let the older ones play with one so little?"

Letitia waved his concerns away with a dismissive gesture of her gloved hand. "They are most protective of him. He is one of them now. Next year, at this time, Joseph shall be toddling about with them, if not running."

The very idea set Edmund's nerves on edge. It was difficult to imagine such a drastic change in so small a child. He watched in surprise when a servant approached them, handing Letitia a letter that was to be opened at once.

"It is from my sister. John has called upon our parents," Letitia exclaimed, opening the letter and scanning it quickly. "Oh, happy news! John writes that by this time next year, she shall be Lady Laura Talbridge, Viscountess Chalbray. To no one's surprise! And with little over a week to go before Christmas. I am so happy for them. Of course he wishes to ask our father properly, yet he cannot think to surprise him, for Father has looked forward to this for some time."

Edmund murmured his congratulations, startled when Letitia stretched her arm about him, laying her head against his shoulder sympathetically.

"Dear, dear Edmund. Grief is natural after all you have endured," she confided quietly. "But over time, even grief passes into memory. In this season of hope, do not forget the things that matter most."

Edmund managed a smile despite feeling hollow inside.

"Thank you, Letty," he said, wishing his voice were not quite so husky. "Have I told you how wise Stephen was in selecting a wife?"

Letitia patted his arm before releasing it. "Grieve all you must. But when you are done, join us for hot chocolate and sledding."

That evening, having fulfilled Joseph's most basic needs, Rosa handed Joseph to Annabelle before bedtime, as she did each day. With snow falling beyond their window, Joseph gazed up at her, his eyes as alert as her own. What did he see, Annabelle wondered, when he looked at her? So much took place in the minds of even the youngest children that adults could only imagine. Edmund had said Eliza Enderfield had blue eyes and blond hair. Perhaps she reminded him of his mother. She felt a catch in her throat.

When, she wondered, had handing Joseph back to Rosa become so difficult? Initially, she had been relieved to relinquish him before she could become too attached. Now he smiled each time Annabelle came into view. She was so accustomed to his voice, she could distinguish his cries of hunger from those of weariness.

Joseph belonged where he was happiest, she reasoned. If the possibility of marrying Edmund no longer existed, it seemed unwise and unkind to let him believe she would be a permanent part of his life. Yet her heart sank at the thought of leaving him behind.

Letitia laughed when she saw Annabelle seated comfortably with Joseph in the rocking chair.

"As the children said, we are ready for Christmas now that we have Mary and Joseph," Letitia said affectionately. "Look how content he is."

Yet, while Joseph was indeed content in Annabelle's arms, she had resigned herself to handing him back to Rosa each night. She had never experienced the profound joy she felt whenever Joseph was returned to her. Was it possible she was jealous of Rosa?

She had begun to feel as if she really was Joseph's mother. Yet she knew there was no future in it.

Had Edmund bonded with him as she had? They needed time together as well, especially since Joseph might not have a mother for some time. Her throat went dry at the thought. She did not often see them together. She saw less of Edmund each day, she realized with sudden melancholy. The sight of him talking with Eloisa March late this afternoon had filled her with unexpected dread.

Perhaps, she thought as she put Joseph to bed that night, she should spend less time with him. She did not wish to have her heart broken by both of them.

Assuming the role of father was difficult enough, Edmund reflected. But finding a mother for his new son was harder than he would have believed. And he desperately needed to find one, for what was he to do with a baby by himself? Life as he knew it was supposed to resume upon his return. Yet, he had lost the opportunity to court Annabelle as he had intended. She had made her feelings clear. For him, their attachment had ended prematurely.

Perhaps the lost opportunity meant it was time to pursue Eloisa. His only opportunities to meet women were at the homes of friends. He should be grateful to Letitia for arranging the gathering.

But what did he know of romance? He remembered the nights he had yearned for Annabelle, believing she would wait forever. She was as naïve as the children playing in their snow fort. They did not hear the cries of men and hear their dying words delivered to their sweethearts.

Here, on his first Christmas home, at least he would have Joseph. It troubled him to find his anticipation mixed with regret. He had always imagined Christmas would be spent with Annabelle, surrounded by their children, collecting happy memories.

How would he manage on his own? He knew men who had been raised by a widowed father. Some were not polished. Affection in childhood might have made them more secure and optimistic. He would not let that happen to Joseph.

What, he wondered in sudden dismay, could he offer a child? With only one good leg, he would be unable to keep up. Soon enough, Joseph would be walking.

What would the world look like through Joseph's eyes then?

The only way he would achieve his goal was with assistance. The likeliest source of help was Rosa. Yet she might expect to return to Spain where she had cousins. Having grown comfortable in her presence, he sensed she felt the same. After reflection, he spoke with her that evening.

"I hope you will consider remaining in England," Edmund concluded in Spanish after explaining his wishes.

"Forever?" she asked after a pause.

"I would provide for you," he explained. "You would enjoy watching Joseph grow, would you not?"

Noting her broad smile, he relaxed, awaiting her acceptance. Her reply stunned him.

"I regret that I cannot. I love Joseph, but my family awaits my return," she said apologetically.

Desperation welled within Edmund as she informed him she expected to leave once Joseph was weaned. What was he to do? His physical limitations would never allow him to keep up with a young child. Any man with a cane, even a young one, would be at a disadvantage. He could not raise Joseph alone.

He needed a wife quickly. If Annabelle persisted in closing the door on their past, he would have to look elsewhere. Having been away so long, he knew few women. Laura Barclay, Letitia's sister, was spoken for by John Talbridge. Annabelle's sister Beatrice remained unattached, but that scenario would prove too awkward.

And there was Eloisa March, who had been too fatigued from her journey earlier to engage in substantial conversation.

Romance, he mused, had always seemed

more complicated than military strategies. He would rely on his wits. If one path was blocked, he must find another.

And since Rosa was unable to remain, and Annabelle unwilling, he had no choice but to pursue Eloisa. So why did his heart sink at the thought?

CHAPTER FOUR

There was still one matter he must address, Edmund acknowledged the following morning. The time had come to read Joe Enderfield's letter. He had had neither the heart nor the strength to read it until now. It was composed of three lengthy pages, written four months after Edmund had been sent home.

By the time he had finished, the catch in his throat made breathing difficult. Joe described his love for his wife and child, explaining that the differences between him and his father demanded he find a loving home for Joseph.

"Should I die in battle, this letter shall reach you after I am gone. Eliza and I believe our decision to bequeath Joseph's care to you is right and appropriate. You spoke of your Annabelle so lovingly, we believe Joseph could find no better home. You were not certain whether your love was meant to be, but I was. I suspect she will not have married in your absence. Try to view her perspective through loving eyes, for she cannot comprehend the conflict we have witnessed. I suspect there is enough understanding and forgiveness in your hearts to overlook your differences and find the happiness you deserve."

His eyes misty, Edmund laid aside the letter with an unsteady hand. It seemed an order from heaven. Yet how could his best friend have made such a decision without knowing whether he and Annabelle would be reunited? Joe's faith had been misplaced. Edmund rallied his strength, rising to the challenge as he would have in battle.

The commander for whom he had the greatest respect had entrusted him with life's most precious gift. Edmund had a home and title to bequeath to his new son and resources to ease his transition to being a parent.

Yet would he be able to satisfy Joe's wishes? That decision, he acknowledged, his heart pounding, was beyond his control.

Her well-meaning cousin, Annabelle realized with chagrin, had given her guests yet another opportunity to socialize and perhaps make a match. That morning, Letitia announced there would be a wreath-making party to decorate the guests' carriages. Laid out in the morning room were wreaths fashioned from yew boughs, with an assortment of bells and red velvet bows.

"There shall be surprises for each woman and man whose wreaths are judged to be most seasonal and most imaginative," Letitia concluded, beaming with joy.

Joseph became the centerpiece when Rosa laid his basket on the table temporarily. Kicking his legs, he gazed anxiously about until Annabelle appeared, giving her a smile of recognition that drew expressions of affection from the children.

"He always quiets for you," Letitia murmured, stroking Joseph's cheek with her finger.

"I am usually the last to hold him," Annabelle reasoned. "By that time, he is worn out."

It was true that Joseph wanted to be held constantly. Yet dared she give her heart to a child from whom she would soon part?

"You cannot deny he cries far less with you. He has chosen you," Letitia insisted meaningfully. "Here, we shall put him beside you where he will be content."

"Mama, may we take Joseph outside to the manger?" Mary begged, pulling on her mother's sleeve. "He can play Baby Jesus in our nativity on Christmas Eve."

"No, loves, we must wait for the proper time," Letitia advised gently, "for we do not want to occupy the manger until then, and only if the weather allows. Joseph is very little yet."

"Could we practice in the old stable, even though it is a long walk?" Mary pressed, following her distracted mother like a duckling, Annabelle thought in amusement.

While the servants finished arranging tables, the men gathered, Edmund among them, Annabelle noticed, conversing as arrangements were prepared. To distract herself, she entertained Robin, Mary, and Geoffrey by working with them on the smaller wreaths until they decided they had had enough and left to play upstairs.

Letitia did not notice Joseph's blanket slip to the floor as she placed the cradle beside the chair Annabelle was to occupy. From across the room, Annabelle saw Edmund approach alertly, struggling to retrieve it. Even with the use of a cane, he was unsteady on his feet, she realized in alarm. With Letitia's back to him, he stumbled as he bent over, his face contorted in pain. Retrieving the blanket unexpectedly, he presented it with a grin and final flourish to Letitia.

Annabelle's heart skipped a beat. Had she been the only one to witness the incident? Before she could react, Edmund had made his way back to his table.

What agonies had he endured on the front lines, she wondered with a pang of guilt, while composing heartfelt letters to her? She had answered them with complaints of loneliness.

How selfish she had been. Her misery so acute it turned her stomach, she felt suddenly queasy. Witnessing Edmund's limitations firsthand, she saw the pain he had never mentioned, too considerate to trouble others with his infirmity.

Physically challenged as he was, how could he raise a child alone? Simple acts she took for granted would be impossible for Edmund without help.

The shock left Annabelle defeated. She was unable to erase the painful image from her mind even as Letitia joined her. Turning to work on her wreath, Annabelle listened distractedly as Stephen discussed the purchase of horses in the spring with Thomas Skeffington. She could not help but notice that Eloisa, arriving late, had sat beside Edmund at the gentlemen's table.

"Perhaps she is merely reserved," Letitia

suggested quietly, following Annabelle's gaze.

Annabelle longed suddenly for the company of her sisters. Their lives, along with Letty's, focused on their children. Already, at two and twenty, Annabelle was at the age at which she should have children of her own. To think, she had once been filled with hope for all life had to offer, ready to embrace marriage and happiness.

Except she had not been able to wait. Not even for Edmund.

In all her life, she had never met anyone who compared with him. No one was as ideally suited. Edmund possessed the gift of patience even when she was at her most impulsive. Perhaps it was their differences that made them so well matched, she thought. Each possessed qualities the other lacked.

Had she lost her chance altogether, Annabelle wondered with a pang of grief? She was aware of Miss March laughing with Edmund as he assisted with her creative efforts at the opposite table. Already, she thought irritably, Edmund's spirits seemed to have lifted.

Seized with a sudden competitive desire, she vowed to make her wreath the most artistically decorated of those created this morning. She carefully chose plaid bows and other ornaments that would make hers outstanding. As she laid out her decorations to create a pleasing effect, Letitia turned to admire her creation.

"How lovely, Annabelle," she exclaimed. "Your carriage shall be charmingly decorated indeed if you decide to cross the border to Gretna Green."

"At this moment it hardly seems likely, does it?" Annabelle returned, her tone harsher than she intended. As she moved her feet, she accidentally jostled the basket, causing Joseph to fuss. His cries strengthened in volume until Letitia's look of concern told her any creative attempts had come to an end.

Lifting Joseph gently from his basket, Annabelle moved to the window seat, snuggling with him. She had done it again, she chastised herself, allowing her impulsive side to rule her better nature. While she was disappointed that her artistic efforts had ended, she was more troubled by the likelihood that Joseph would soon leave her life for good.

She watched Edmund discreetly assessing Eloisa at the far table. Annabelle had lost him first to war, now perhaps to another woman. Could she relinquish Joseph to someone who might not love him the way she did?

She must be charitable, she reminded herself, for Joseph needed a mother. Could he be happy with Eloisa? Earlier, through the window, she had seen Edmund and Eloisa walking through the gently falling snow. Her spirits plummeted at the memory.

She realized abruptly how desperately she still wanted to marry Edmund. For Joseph. For this. This instant motherhood, a bond of pure love, this sudden attachment.

But whom did she love? A suffocating panic seized her. It was most certainly love she felt, but did she love Joseph more than his father? Her priorities had changed.

If she truly loved Edmund, she had been shallow and foolish to have treated him so poorly.

She had often feared he would not return from the front. He must have endured unimaginable horrors while they were apart. He had undoubtedly protected her from the worst of it. How foolish she had been, she realized with a burst of humiliation, and so self-centered. Guilt, mixed with melancholy for all she had lost, consumed her despite the gaiety about her.

How dry and stiff Eloisa seemed, until a remark from Edmund transformed her face into a beguiling smile. Annabelle's heart tightened with jealousy. Miss March was a very real threat.

Annabelle snuggled closer to Joseph, content to linger with him even if it did break her heart to know that he and Edmund would return to Yorkshire without her. He would likely fuss the entire way. She felt compelled to hold him every time he cried, knowing how he must miss his mother. Could she bring herself to marry for motherhood only?

Would Edmund give her the opportunity?

Perhaps it was already too late. Eloisa was all smiles as Edmund tied bows on her wreath, having apparently abandoned his own.

Trying to be unobtrusive as he watched Annabelle, Edmund was puzzled. Had she moved to the window seat because she was offended by the attention he paid Eloisa, or was she simply tending to Joseph's needs? His attempt to remind her that Eloisa was also eligible failed the moment Thomas Skeffington joined them, he realized in dismay.

"I have never seen such clever creativity," Skeffington exclaimed from the opposite side of Eloisa, gazing at the miniature books that graced her wreath. "How imaginative to include reading in your design. I have little talent when it comes to such activities."

"It is simple. To make a book, you merely fold the paper in half." Eloisa demonstrated with a slip of red paper. "One might even write a title on the front, if one is so inclined. Anyone can do it — even you, my lord."

She exchanged a furtive glance with Skeffington before they laughed. Recognizing a rival for her affection, Edmund threw down his ribbon in frustration.

"How is one to succeed at such a traditionally feminine activity?" he muttered.

"Do not men have imaginations as well as women, Edmund?" Letitia scolded him mildly from the next table. "Come, borrow some ideas from Stephen."

"You shall need to take a greater interest in such things now that you are a father." Stephen chuckled sympathetically.

Studying his half-completed wreath, Edmund wished he might abandon his efforts altogether. He had intended to sit with his son until Annabelle had swept the child away as if he were her own, he observed irritably, apparently content in her solitude. He seemed doomed to succeed at nothing, for Miss March showed less interest in him than Annabelle had. Sharing a confidence with Skeffington, she had moved so close that Edmund might as well be sitting alone. And Skeff, he thought darkly, did not appear to be the least bit skeptical toward Miss March despite his nickname.

While Edmund had enjoyed Eloisa's company on a short walk yesterday, she claimed the chill penetrated her very bones. How was she to manage at his Yorkshire estate, he thought in exasperation, if she could not tolerate northern winters? Her glance at the children playing had ended with a critical assessment of their noise. And she had not once asked to hold Joseph after inquiring as to his age, nor had she attempted to engage him as any woman who loved children would. He could not picture her playing in the snow as Annabelle did.

But how could she, he mused, when the only woman Joseph wanted was Annabelle?

Annabelle was still lovely, yet far enough past her prime, he thought wistfully, to consider herself unworthy of a second chance at marriage. His heart twisted with a sense of responsibility. Only Annabelle had ever fully appreciated his disciplined nature and commitment to those he loved. She understood his sense of duty, if not to his country, then at least to his family. Their interpretation of love might have changed over time, but the heart's emotions were permanent. It was more than mere responsibility he felt for her, he realized abruptly.

It was love. Not only love, but passion. Yet how was he to convince her when she did not wish to hear it? She no longer believed it, he reminded himself.

Yet he had also changed, Edmund realized. He felt his heart stir each time Rosa handed Joseph to him. He had developed a new sense of commitment to his son. Joseph recognized him now. There was a look of security and comfort each time Joseph looked into his eyes.

What had happened to his expectations of settling into his dotage upon returning from Spain, he wondered? While he had not been prepared for fatherhood, the irony made him grin. The Enderfields had known of his acute disappointment at Annabelle's final letter. While they might have seen this legacy as a chance to reunite them, he thought cynically, they were to be disappointed.

Suddenly, to his surprise, Annabelle rose and made her way across the room, cradling a sleepy Joseph on her shoulder, shifting him rhythmically as she walked, until she paused beside Edmund. As he opened his mouth to speak, she put one finger to her lips.

"I shall put your son to bed," she whispered, smiling humorously at him as she carried Joseph from the room.

Edmund took a deep breath. Suddenly, for one moment, all seemed right with the world.

Despite their one light moment of the previous day, Annabelle paused awkwardly when she encountered Edmund leaving the morning room early the next day, the bulky haversack over his shoulder. Her heart pounded. In this joyous season, were his thoughts still mired in painful memories? He froze in place as their eyes met, his distraction replaced by a self-conscious awkwardness. As he attempted to stuff a letter into the haversack, it slipped from his hands and fell to the floor.

He muttered apologies as he bent to retrieve it. Catching a glimpse of the handwriting on the front, Annabelle caught her breath. The penmanship was her own.

"Is that — ? The letter," she said in confusion. "It is one I sent you."

Gazing into her eyes, Edmund did not reply. His stunned expression at having been discovered hit her as if a curtain had been pulled away, revealing a truth she had never imagined. Rather than being missives related to war, the bag bulged with letters she had written him. So many expressions of love, every one from her heart. Every word true.

"The letters in your bag. They are the ones I wrote. Why did you not tell me?" she demanded, staring at him in humiliation and dismay. "You kept them."

"Every one." A tentative, crooked smile spread across his face slowly, giving him a self-conscious charm. "What was there to tell? I enjoy reading how deeply you loved me." He hesitated, chuckling. "After you married, you see, it did not matter if I did not return. I had less to live for."

The past tense moved her heart until she feared it would break with shame and regret.

"How foolish I have been," she whispered, overwhelmed by the reality she had failed to recognize. Staring at the letter as if it were a treasure, she asked in a small voice, "May I read that one again?"

He handed it to her with a grin. "You may read them all if it will help to refresh your memory."

As he laid the bulky haversack on the floor beside her, she found her voice despite the humiliation that threatened to sink her. "How could you still love me after all I have done? Do you?"

His eyebrows rose with surprise above his tender gaze. "I never stopped loving you."

She was glad he had set the letters aside. He stepped toward her slowly, his gaze never leaving hers. Her heart began to pound. This was, she told herself, the chance she thought she would never have again. As he opened his arms slowly, she took a single step toward him, breathless, before she heard a door opening nearby. Before she could move, Stephen had entered the room, shattering the moment.

"Edmund is about to help me with the most important task a father has," Stephen announced, smiling broadly. "He has promised to help me select the finest tree in the forest for this year's Christmas. As it is already late, perhaps we should select it today and cut it tomorrow."

Annabelle stared at Edmund, dismayed yet giddy with possibilities. Could Stephen have chosen a worse moment to interrupt? Edmund grinned at her knowingly. For a moment, her heart refused to beat. She felt her face turn crimson with an inner warmth she had not felt in nearly a decade. The feeling of bliss remained when Edmund spoke at last.

"Perhaps you shall find these enlightening

reading. Let us continue this conversation upon my return," he suggested, his half smile suggesting he looked forward to speaking further.

A wave of relief as high as she had ever known washed over her. "Oh, yes, please," she whispered.

CHAPTER FIVE

His efforts at wreath-making and tree selection behind him, Edmund enjoyed an exceptional glass of elderberry wine with Stephen before the library fire the following afternoon. They reflected on a friend who still fought abroad.

"Timothy was fortunate to survive Albuera when many did not. At least he has not much longer to serve." Turning philosophical, Stephen glanced toward the window with its view of evergreens. "One must seek comfort somewhere. I find it in nature."

"Derbyshire is especially lovely at this time of year," Edmund agreed.

"Letty and I prefer it to London," Stephen admitted. "This is where the children belong in their youth. They will have time for drawing rooms when they are older."

The waning light and the strength of the wine combined with his uplifting conversation with Annabelle had changed Edmund's outlook. Annabelle had been content to sit with Joseph yesterday rather than design a wreath. His own would have been outstanding with her touch, for she possessed the ability to make life sparkle. Yet, at one point, her look of serenity had turned to a sadness so deep, he wondered what had troubled her. Could it be that she was thinking of Joseph's departure? She had loved children as long as he had known her. Clearly, she loved Joseph.

It was just as obvious that Joseph loved her.

He did not wish to separate them, for they seemed destined to be together. But how was he to convince Annabelle to marry him? Before he could even consider it, he had to find a way to forgive her. Not only had she failed to appreciate his military contributions, she had not waited for him as she promised. She was once everything he had wanted in a woman. While he still yearned for the life he had hoped to have with Annabelle, he wanted to be certain it was meant to be.

Could he swallow his pride for his son? Had he not gone to war, they would have had children of their own by now. In the time he had been gone, two of her sisters had married and had children. He had been far more effective on the front lines of battle, he realized with a start, than he had been at winning Annabelle. The giggles and shrieks of triumph beyond his window reached his ears. He wondered what had caused the sudden excitement.

There she was. Annabelle had gone outdoors with the children and was now engaged in a snowball fight with them. Gazing out upon snow so bright it hurt his eyes, he had a clear view of her mussed golden hair as her hood fell back, her disheveled cloak spotted with patches of snow that had found their target. The combination of the children's squeals and the lilt of her laughter had resulted from snowballs encountering her nose and hair. The combination of her blue eyes, red cheeks, and white snowflakes was patriotic and feminine at once. And enchanting. She had never looked lovelier. Or happier, he thought.

He remembered Eloisa's awkward return to the house after walking in snow, without so much as a smile for the children. Annabelle knew precisely how to handle them, how to comfort them when they were ill or unhappy.

Edmund realized he did not have a clue.

The merriment that filled him now was a joy he had never felt at war. Here, he realized abruptly, was his real life. A life that no longer revolved around strategies and tactics and forming square to give his soldiers the advantage of protection. Instead of defending an army, his duty would now be to provide every advantage this orphaned child would not have otherwise. He must learn to see the world through Joseph's eyes. His son would see a world filled with cousins who would prove the best playmates. A world with a father and mother.

If Annabelle would consent to marry him, that was. What was he to do when the one woman his son wanted as a mother might not want his father?

He gazed out the window again. Seeing the joy in her eyes that he remembered so well, he realized how deeply he loved Annabelle still. How much he wanted her.

He might have sacrificed part of their past, but he would not ruin their future. Joseph, he realized, had chosen the same woman for his mother that Edmund wanted for his wife.

Perhaps this was the moment, he thought, to begin the life that awaited him.

Dressed for the cold, Edmund headed outdoors soon afterward. Had Annabelle not noticed his approach behind the snowbank? He had a distinct advantage, for he could watch her unobtrusively. Her face was aglow with laughter at the joyous squeals from the children as she hid behind a hedge, a snowball in her mitten, while they huddled within their snow fort.

Reaching down, Edmund formed a snowball of his own. He was in perfect position to strike. If he threw it, would she respond in kind? Rising slightly behind the snowbank, he hurled the snowball directly at her. It found its mark against the side of her head, bringing down her golden ringlets and leaving her momentarily dazed.

Edmund jumped to his feet in alarm, fearing he had injured her.

"Is that any way to treat the lady you escorted here?" she demanded with mock indignation.

"Shall we call a truce?" Edmund approached slowly, his arms raised, his heart filled with hope. He had waited a long time to hear such happiness in her voice.

"You ought to be nicer to the woman who pacified your child while you kept company with that stuffy Miss March," Annabelle said slyly as he stopped. "Joseph requires your attention, after all."

He frowned. "Do you think I am not suited to be a father?"

"You are not accustomed to being a father," she amended. "That will change in time."

Her voice was still somewhat guarded, he thought as they strolled side by side, while the children waited for the next snowball to be hurled.

"Have you any doubt you shall make a fine father?" she asked.

From behind them, Geoffrey's small voice cut the frigid air. "I'm cold. I want to go back inside."

It was a stark reminder, Edmund thought, that his life was about to change forever.

He was pleasantly surprised when Annabelle turned and laid her hands on his shoulders. The warmth of her closeness ended abruptly when she wedged a snowball down the collar of his greatcoat, a spark of playfulness in her eyes.

"It is time the children returned indoors," she called over her shoulder, breaking into a run.

Watching her hair tumble down her back as the arrangement loosened, Edmund thought the cold had never felt more refreshing.

After Edmund's departure to cut down the tree he and Stephen had selected, Annabelle retreated to her room to continue reliving her earlier days, perusing one of her letters as if reading it for the first time. Perhaps she was, she mused, for although time had changed her, she recognized in her words emotions that had come from her heart. Every missive brought back the depth of love she had felt for Edmund. Their true emotions lay in their letters, she realized. Despite the grief they had caused each other, regardless of their emotional distance, that love still lived in her heart.

She was startled when her reverie was broken by the sounds of hurrying feet and panic in a woman's voice. Was it Letitia's, Annabelle thought with alarm? After a rapid knocking, her door was opened abruptly. Letitia's face was pale.

"I cannot find the children," she announced, her voice edged with panic. "I went to get them to help decorate. Miss Milbury believed they were playing in the nursery. Joseph is missing also. Apparently, they told Rosa he was with you."

"I have not seen Joseph or the children since early this morning." Annabelle's heart clenched with alarm. "Perhaps they hid in the back of the sleigh behind Stephen and Edmund."

Letitia shook her head miserably. "The

sleigh was empty to make room for the tree. The servants waved Stephen and Edmund off."

A thorough search of the house by everyone present revealed no sign of the four children. A careful inspection of the grounds where they were accustomed to playing gave no hint of their whereabouts, even when their names were shouted.

"They must have taken Joseph somewhere," Letitia blurted frantically. "Where could they have gone? It is already snowing lightly."

"Surely they must be indoors," Annabelle suggested, "somewhere we have overlooked."

"I will continue to look outdoors with the servants in places they would not ordinarily play," Letitia announced nervously. "If you could check the house again —"

Assuring her she would do so at once, Annabelle hugged Letitia in an attempt to reassure her before they embarked upon their separate quests. Her continued search of the home from top to bottom with the female staff yielded no clues. Overwhelmed by frustration, her heart pounding, Annabelle retreated to her room, dropping onto her bed in disbelief.

Wherever they were, she mused, Robin,

Mary, Geoffrey, and Joseph had to be together. The elder children had learned how to carry Joseph in a safe and responsible fashion. It was likely they had taken him somewhere without telling anyone. But where? She wracked her memory for recent conversations with them.

More than once, they had expressed the wish to practice the nativity scene using Joseph as the Christ child. The manger in the front yard had already been searched. If they were not there, where would they go?

And then she remembered something Mary had said during the wreath-making party. They must have decided to rehearse their nativity in the old stable, the same spot Annabelle had avoided the day she walked the old path with Edmund.

The spot where he had first kissed her. Why had she not thought of it earlier? Perhaps the adults had been too preoccupied with making wreaths to have heard Mary's request.

The parlor and surrounding rooms were empty when she hurried downstairs. The servants, she remembered, were all out searching with Letitia. Why wait for them to return when she knew where to look? There was no time to waste. Snow was falling steadily beyond the windows.

She scribbled a note saying she had gone after the children, before she set off, the wind and snow whipping against her face as she closed the door behind her.

"A more perfect tree I have never seen," Stephen complimented Edmund cheerfully, drawing the sleigh up before the doors of Lavendam Manor in the driving snow and wind. "You are well prepared for fatherhood as far as Christmas is concerned."

"I suspect we shall wait before attempting to bring the tree indoors," Edmund said doubtfully, the wind whistling as the snow increased in intensity.

"We shall do well to get ourselves indoors." Stephen chuckled. "The children will be disappointed, but the servants can brush the snow off easily enough before bringing it in."

Edmund's spirits were high as he and Stephen hastened toward the entrance. His first Christmas home from the war would contain more joy than he had ever expected. He looked forward to a bit of brandy to remove the chill once they were indoors.

And then, he thought, his heart soaring, he would resume his conversation with Annabelle precisely where they had left off.

His expectations were dashed as the front

door was flung open by Letitia, her expression frantic, her eyes brimming with tears.

"The children have disappeared," she blurted. "We cannot find them anywhere. When I came back from searching, I found a note from Annabelle, saying she had gone outdoors to look for them. She thinks she knows where they are, but she did not say where. She has been gone over an hour in this storm. I hope she is dressed appropriately. I fear she will freeze to death."

"Her note gave no clue where she was headed?" Edmund demanded, a knot tightening around his heart.

"No. She told no one." Letitia's eyes swam with misery. "Joseph is gone also."

"We will find them while you wait here," Stephen promised as he took her hands, the controlled anxiety in his expression signaling his concern to Edmund. "When the children return, they will need your reassurance after such a prank. In places we cannot reach by sleigh, I will walk."

Edmund made up his mind. "We shall go in separate directions to cover more ground, I on foot, you by sleigh," he announced abruptly.

Stephen glanced at him doubtfully. "Can you manage with a cane?"

Gripped with doubt, Edmund felt his love

for Annabelle conquer his apprehension.

"I shall use skis to cover more ground. We will return with them," Edmund promised Letitia.

But was he indeed capable with his physical limitations? Heading outdoors with Stephen, his heart pounded with fear. He hoped they would not be too late.

Where would Annabelle have gone, Edmund wondered fiercely as they headed in separate directions? He would search nearby while Stephen covered remote areas. It was likely Annabelle and the children had become stranded or trapped by the storm. He braced himself for a concentrated effort to find her, relieved when he discovered the ski poles could serve as two canes.

He remembered strategies he had used in war. Mentally, he reviewed every detail of Annabelle's life with which he was familiar. That she was impulsive was without question. Her bravery was one of the qualities he had loved most about her. He remembered challenging situations she had faced with formidable emotional strength. Even at war, he had tried to emulate her confidence.

She must have been convinced she knew where to find the children. Though she knew better than to venture out alone, her fear for the children obviously overrode her reason. But where were they? And how did she know where to look? Children were naturally curious, he reflected. If they had wanted to play in the snow, they would probably have remained close to the house. Since they had apparently not done so, they must have had a particular destination in mind. They knew the landscape and the structures on it. And when he found the children, he would find Annabelle.

There were several outbuildings on the property where they might have taken shelter if they had wandered far. Which had they chosen, he mused? He considered their interests. The greatest one to date had been the nativity they would present for their aunts and uncles and cousins. For that, they would need a stable.

His heart skipped a beat. He knew just where to find one, a good distance away where their deceit would not be discovered. Annabelle, too, knew the spot well.

Yet Stephen and the remainder of the staff had already gone out to search. Every sleigh was in use, Edmund thought, his heart sinking. He remembered how overgrown the path had been when he walked it with Annabelle. Today's snow was deepening by the moment.

Would the hike prove too overwhelming to accomplish on his own, he wondered? The ice beneath the snow was treacherous, and he had only ski poles for support.

He had no choice. Even if he was trapped with Annabelle and the children for hours, at least they would be together. The snow would stop eventually, and they would be able to venture out.

But first he must reach them.

If he could survive the war in Spain, he could survive this snowstorm. Even with his injuries. He would do it. He was still close enough to the house that he could return to tell Letitia his destination, for he was not as impulsive as Annabelle. At least Stephen and the servants would know where to find them when the snow finally ended and the drifts allowed a safe passage through.

Let her be impulsive, he thought. He intended to be nearby to rescue her whenever she needed it.

"It was nearly two hours later when I finally reached the stable," Edmund recounted to Stephen and Letitia late that evening.

"I was too far from the house to return when the storm blew in," Annabelle explained ruefully over a cup of hot chocolate.

349

She was sitting wrapped in a blanket and surrounded by the adults while the children recovered from their ordeal in slumber. "I had to find the children, knowing how frightened they must be. I was certain they had gone to the old stable." She shivered abruptly. "Being there made me wonder what the war must have been like if surviving this storm was so brutal."

Despite her mussed hair and disheveled appearance, she had never looked more beautiful, Edmund thought.

Stephen gazed at her skeptically. "The boards on that stable are worn thin now. You must have huddled together to stay warm."

"We gathered around Joseph to warm him," Annabelle replied with a small shudder. "We also stacked hay against the walls and doors to block the wind."

"But how did you know where they were?" Letitia asked solicitously, sliding her arm about Annabelle's shoulders. "You took a great chance straying so far."

Edmund's eyes locked knowingly with Annabelle's. "They spoke of the nativity so often, Annabelle realized that the old stable had to have been where they had taken Joseph." He smiled with amusement. "I never imagined I should see the real Mary and Joseph together, with a manger nearby."

The sight of the five faces that had greeted him was the most beautiful thing he had ever seen, Edmund thought, even though they were all filled with fear and one or two tear-streaked from terror. Joy and relief had ended their worries when he finally succeeded in opening the battered door. The wind had been fierce enough to make the children believe it might destroy their shelter while they waited for help.

"I will never understand how you managed to maneuver that distance through such deep drifts," Stephen admitted frankly, concern wrinkling his brow. "We could barely get through in sleighs, much less with skis."

Edmund grinned, his eyes meeting Annabelle's. In them, he saw the love he had yearned for during their years apart. "I suspect it had to do with the discussion we had, Stephen, about the responsibilities of fatherhood."

No one, he was certain, could imagine the slow clumsiness with which he had lumbered through deep snowdrifts on foot, using only his ski poles for support. His love for Annabelle had enabled him to do what he considered impossible. Rescuing her, he proved to himself that he was capable of looking after those he loved. Until today, he had been unsure. He prided himself on having informed Letitia of his destination. It had allowed the first sleigh that returned to the house to be sent to the old stable, ensuring that the five who were stranded would not freeze to death. It was delightfully entertaining to find that she'd changed into his breeches before heading out. He was both surprised and relieved she'd had the sense to realize she might need them.

And as the children ran around excitedly inside the stable, happy they would soon be home, Edmund had seized the opportunity to pull Annabelle close, encircling her waist as he lowered his lips to hers in the place they had shared their first kiss, ensuring it would not be their last.

They waited until Stephen and Letitia went upstairs before confiding their deepest fears to each other.

"You never told me why you did not come home when you nearly died," Annabelle said quietly when they were finally alone.

Edmund sighed, his face turning grim. "After we retreated into the Pyrenees, we found ourselves in imminent danger of an assault at one point." Alarm gripped her heart as he chose his words carefully, his voice dropping to a whisper, not taking his eyes from hers. "Having climbed there before my leg was broken, I was familiar with the region and knew a way to safety. If I had left the men to come home at that point, it would have been a death sentence for the whole company. And these were the men who had saved my life. How could I not be loyal?" He shook his head as if reliving the event. "I still knew the mountains well. By then, although I could no longer climb as I once had, I had become a competent tactician and knew my knowledge was still of value to my unit."

Annabelle felt her heart clench with pain. "I have been so selfish. Forgive me. I did not know."

"I did not wish you to." Edmund smiled bleakly at her. "Nor did I tell you that your letters were what saved me through the worst of war. The blackest moment was not when I was injured, but when I received your letter breaking it off, saying you had married. I had no future. It had been my only hope."

Annabelle stared at him in dismay. "How can you ever forgive me?" she whispered.

"We must learn to forgive each other. And I know an excellent way to start," he whispered, moving his lips toward hers.

CHAPTER SIX

Anxiously watching the snow falling beyond the windows on the afternoon of Christmas Eve, Annabelle prayed it would not affect travel for her sisters' families. Her private tradition had been to take a moment every Christmas Eve to reflect on the joys of the past year. This year, her thoughts were focused on Joseph, the most wonderful surprise of all.

She was surprised again in the early evening when Edmund made an unexpected announcement after nearly a dozen friends had arrived.

"It is my intention in the coming year," he declared as they gathered about the Christmas tree, "to create a foundation to help returning soldiers without means. It will include lodgings that injured men with no place to go could not afford otherwise. All of this shall be in exchange for work in the community or with participating landowners."

Edmund revealed details of his plan, including his intention to seek out officers who had returned to their normal lives in England, some of whom had already agreed to hire soldiers in need.

"Your endeavor has great promise," Stephen congratulated him once they were alone. "Yet you must not feel the need to fund this charity entirely on your own. Let me be the first to offer my support."

It was the first time in years that Annabelle had heard genuine optimism in Edmund's voice. The sound sent a surge of joy through her, warming her to the core. It was the same confidence Edmund had possessed before leaving for Spain. Perhaps, she mused, her heart brimming with hope, the project would restore his joy and lead to greater good.

The privacy and peace she had come to enjoy over her holiday ended when she looked out the window and saw a row of carriages approaching. Her sisters had arrived!

"Perhaps you might satisfy their curiosity by telling them we have resolved our differences and leave it at that," Edmund suggested with a grin, joining her at the window.

Letitia finally acknowledged that the whole family had conspired to bring Annabelle and Edmund together again, starting by sabotaging her carriage. While her reunion with Edmund had been worth the deception, Annabelle thought, her sisters should be filled with guilt for trying to manage her life. But instead of embracing her upon entering the house as she expected, they brushed past her, descending upon Edmund at the sight of the baby cradled in his arms. Even the children jostled each other for a glimpse of Joseph, all demanding an explanation at once.

"We certainly did not expect a baby," Pamela exclaimed.

"Do not tell me you found this child along the road," Beatrice said with a laugh.

"You mean that road I traveled without you?" Annabelle teased, giving her a dark look as Beatrice colored with embarrassment. "How could you, of all people, trick me like that?"

"Such a wee one," murmured Grace, her husband Martin holding nine-month-old Margaret.

"Look, Mama!" Geoffrey exclaimed. "Joseph is smiling. He must know it is Christmas!"

"He is waiting for his presents!" Mary

exclaimed, jumping up and down as she clapped her hands.

"Joseph is the present!" Robin corrected his younger sister in a tone of reverence.

Pamela's four-year-old twins inched closer to the baby, their father Peter beside them.

"What do you think he is thinking?" Rose asked curiously, studying Joseph's face.

"I think he is thinking about food," Abby, her twin, replied bluntly.

"Can we give him some of Cook's marzipan?" they begged their mother.

"Joseph is far too little to have marzipan yet," Pamela explained gently. "But I imagine he would be happy to have some milk."

Her sisters listened as Edmund quietly related Joseph's history to the children on a level they would understand with sorrow rather than fear. The joy Annabelle's sisters and their husbands had felt turned to horror at his parents' fate before their focus returned to the child.

"What a challenge it must be to adjust to a child so unexpectedly," Pamela exclaimed.

"Having a child is an adjustment. Inheriting one is complicated," Edmund admitted. "I confess that, while I was not ready to devote all my time to fatherhood initially, I am now."

Behind her, Annabelle heard the front

door open amid shouts of children hurling snowballs at each other. Letitia's admonition to aim carefully was followed by an enthusiastic greeting. Annabelle turned, her pulse quickening at the unexpected clamor of familiar voices.

"Aunt Margaret! Uncle Joseph!" she heard Letitia exclaim. "What a delightful surprise!"

Before Annabelle could convince herself the moment was real, her mother struggled through the revelers to grasp her in a snug embrace.

"Happy Christmas, my dearest," she proclaimed in a tone of deep affection.

"Mama, I am so happy to see you. And Papa!" she cried in disbelief, stunned to see her father, his greatcoat spotted with snow. "Young Robin has a fine aim with a snowball," her father announced, opening his arms to Annabelle.

"We did not expect you," she said awkwardly, reluctant to acknowledge his sudden change of heart for fear of embarrassing him. "I am so happy you have come."

"You know how reluctant your father is to travel at the holidays," their mother exclaimed, her amazement matching Annabelle's own. "I had almost convinced him to come, and then we received Edmund's note."

"But we invite you every year, Uncle," Letitia protested. "You are always welcome."

"You have never had the orphaned son of a war hero before," their father replied, one eyebrow arched. "Edmund is a hero as well. His service nearly cost him all. But he survived."

His voice husky, her father embraced Edmund for a long moment. Finally Annabelle spoke up, confused.

"Edmund's note?" she repeated, turning to him. "You invited my parents?"

Edmund grinned at her, his face ruggedly handsome in candlelight. "I wanted their blessing," he explained, suddenly self-conscious, "since you have not yet given me yours."

"Annabelle," her father demanded, turning to her, "what do you mean, refusing Edmund? He is the only man worthy of you. It appears your marriage to him is the only way I shall get my grandson. This child shares my name. I understand he favors you. Whether you see it or not, it was clearly meant to be." His tone softer now, he turned to Beatrice meaningfully. "And once you are wed, it shall be Beatrice's turn."

"He is counting the days, Annabelle, until

he is rid of us," Beatrice exclaimed as Annabelle felt her face reddening.

"Might I give you a piece of advice, if you will be so sensible as to consider it?" Annabelle asked confidentially. "I saw your reaction when you saw Frederick Albright this evening. It is rare to find such compatibility between two individuals. And he is taller than you, Bea. Think on it!"

"Perhaps you need not wait that long, my lord," Edmund suggested. "If my new endeavor becomes a great preoccupation for me, Joseph shall require someone to watch over him."

Annabelle stared at him, looking for clarification. While Edmund remained evasively silent, he could not keep from grinning as he took her hand in his.

"You have not given me your thoughts on my new venture," he reminded her casually.

"Your friends have been so supportive of your idea that I have not yet had the opportunity," she admitted, laughing with delight. "I think it is a marvelous idea. How like you to be so generous with your time and financial resources. Your efforts will help so many."

"Landowners shall be able to trade a room in the barn, even, for labor. It is economically simple. All it takes is an inquiry among friends."

Seeing the gentleness in his eyes, Annabelle hesitated. "We speak of charity toward others. Odd, when I have shown so little to you. I am ashamed for having treated you so poorly." She paused, shaking her head, speaking in a whisper when she resumed. "All those years we lost."

"We have many years ahead," Edmund assured her, laying his hand on her arm, speaking with the familiar humility and respect that characterized his every statement. "The blame for what happened is not all yours, Annabelle. I have to own my share of it. But another year is approaching. What better time to begin anew?" He shrugged, his eyes never leaving hers. Abruptly, he drew her aside and handed her a cloak. "Here, let us take this outside, for it is not the way I intended it."

"Are we to go outside in this snowfall?" she demanded as he ushered her outdoors.

He grinned. "Even your manner is a bit like that of Joseph's mother," he said, brushing snowflakes from her hair as they trudged through the snow.

Annabelle paused. "You did say I look a bit like her."

"I believe it is more than that." Edmund smiled gently, turning to her with a shrug.

"My son has made his choice clear. Who am I to deny him? Our future lies in the form of a baby."

Annabelle stared, her heart beating too quickly to interrupt.

"Somehow, all that has happened was meant to bring us to this point. This child was not meant for me alone, but for you also," he continued. "You see, although you never met his parents, I spoke of you so often, they felt they knew you."

Her heart pounding, she listened as he told her of the letter from Major Enderfield, his tone humble.

"I was one of the fortunate to be given a second chance," he said softly. She stiffened as Edmund took her mittened hands in his. With snow falling softly about them, he lowered himself to one knee, his eyes gazing up into hers. Annabelle felt her breathing stop.

"I am about to do what I should have done long ago. I must ask, Annabelle, before you change your mind." He paused, his face anxious. "I am prepared and ready to embrace parenthood with all of its traditions. I know you love Joseph. But do you love me enough to marry me? Will you be my wife? The mother of my children?"

Her heart was so full for a moment she

could not speak.

"Am I to have a husband and a child at once?" she asked in an awed whisper. From the corner of her eye, she was aware of the draperies being drawn back inside the house, revealing faces in the windows. "Yes. Oh, yes, Edmund. I have wanted to tell you, but I was afraid you would think I was marrying you for Joseph."

"I would not have minded," he said, sincerity in his tone.

"But children — more than one?" She felt her eyes mist over, her words coming out in a whisper. "I hope there is time. Joseph might be an only child."

Edmund sighed knowingly. "Letitia said that was a matter of concern to you. She told me she has entered her fourth decade, and Geoffrey is only five years old. There is hope."

"If Joseph ever has a sister, perhaps she should be named Patience. It is what I have learned the hard way." She paused, shaking her head. "It is no irony, I suppose, that my father has come to our Christmas the same year Joseph has."

Staring into her eyes, he broke into helpless laughter. "After all the losses I have suffered, I will not blind myself to all I have gained. The irony is that I had to come home from war to be rescued," he said softly. "I needed you. Life did not begin for me until now."

He gazed up at the slowly falling snowflakes, gesturing heavenward.

"Has this not been wonderfully joyful, being surrounded by so much love? Surely our two hearts together can hold love enough for more."

Annabelle stared at him. He had offered her the greatest gift she could have wished for.

"It is my sincerest wish," she whispered, her lips meeting his in the twilight.

■ ■ ■ ■ ■

BABY'S FIRST CHRISTMAS

BY SHARON SOBEL

■ ■ ■ ■

*For
Michael Nash
With Love on His Most Special Birthday*

*For Keeping the Traditions and Joy of
Our Family's History Alive,
His Cousins are Most Grateful.*

CHAPTER ONE

"Is this your fine plan for Christmas?" Liliana Hampshire scolded as she pulled off her brother's spectacles, little minding that the earpiece caught the knot of his cravat. "Do you intend to spend the season drawing your boring maps for the Foreign Office? I am sure no one reads them."

Josiah Hampshire, the Earl of Kingston, frowned as he looked up at his younger sister and groped distractedly for his desk blotter. "I provide very valuable information, for which those concerned with the sovereignty of our nation are extremely indebted."

"I am sure they are," Liliana responded. "But surely no one shall be reading them over mulled cider and ale on Christmas Eve."

"And they are not boring," Josiah added, deftly removing his spectacles and reaching for another pair from his collection in the drawer of his desk. He was accustomed to replacing fragile possessions, for Liliana always was a bit too exuberant. He supposed it had something to do with living with him, and her efforts to liven things up. "But as it turns out, I am writing personal letters to several of my friends. They are not boring either."

"Wishing them the best of the season, I suppose?" she asked softly, but her sarcasm was dry enough to empty a well. "Ha."

"I see nothing amusing in my words."

"Truly, Josey? Truly?" Her voice rose to a squeak. "You do not have any friends!"

"I most certainly do," he argued, though he could not think of one. He was far too busy on matters of state to maintain any friendships, and accompanied his sister to dinners and balls only when absolutely necessary.

"Oh, please!" she muttered under her breath, and stalked from the room.

He watched her depart, catching his breath for only a moment when her swinging arms threatened to knock his precious Venetian paperweight off a table. She had every right to be frustrated, for she was young and witty, and there was not much society to speak of in their small community. She was stuck living with him at

King's Stone, a lovely estate far from anything that mattered, except for the place itself. Ages and ages ago, an ancient king had been crowned on the site, on a great outcropping that had never quite been identified. Their father had devoted much of his life attempting to identify the stone and thus elevate his position, but he never managed to surpass the title to which he had been born. It was not the only great disappointment in his life.

But while a quiet existence at King's Stone suited Josiah just fine, it recently occurred to him that Liliana might be less than content.

After she disappeared through the open door, he heard her raised voice in the foyer, and the rather more soothing tones of Mrs. Grimm, the housekeeper.

Reluctantly, he rose and set his new spectacles on his nose as he walked to the door. Emerging from his sanctuary, he met the accusing glances of the two women.

"Do you have plans for our Christmas?" he asked his sister. He supposed he could mollify her by inviting some of the neighbors to join them for Christmas Day. The vicar was a pleasant enough fellow, though his wife had opinions about everything. "Shall we host a dinner?"

Liliana crossed her arms over her chest. "Mrs. Grimm shall be in Yorkshire, you may recall, visiting her daughter. Mrs. Ellis is prepared to come up from the village to prepare our meals, but I do not intend to ask the good woman to cook a goose and plum pies."

Josiah waited expectantly, knowing more was coming, undoubtedly something that would not particularly please him. Mrs. Grimm murmured her excuses and scurried from the room. Liliana looked like she was silently rehearsing her proposal, which did not make him feel any better. He thought about the map he had abandoned minutes before, and the next project he promised to complete for Lord Dailey at the Home Office. Unfortunately, he had the sinking feeling that his valuable work would somehow be deferred into the new year.

"Do you recall my old friend Marianne Westlyme, who accompanied Cousin Isabelle and me to Bath?" Liliana asked sweetly. Too sweetly, he thought.

"She, who later married Lashton? I seem to remember escorting you to London for the wedding, surprised that the man finally decided to become domesticated," Josiah said. He knew other things about Lashton, but decided not to share them with his sister, who surely was too innocent to even imagine them.

"And I was surprised you were actually acquainted with the horrible man," his sister said tartly. "As a matter of fact, he did not become so very domestic, after all. He was killed in a duel November last, skewered by a cuckolded husband."

Josiah swallowed. Perhaps his sister was not quite so innocent, after all.

"Lady Lashton has invited us to spend the Christmas holiday with her at Parkside House, her London home. I wish to go, but will not leave you alone to spend the week hunched over your desk. You must come with me."

"But I enjoy . . . ," Josiah protested. The thought of being surrounded by strangers in a strange house, making idle conversation and doing nothing of any use, was odious to him. But he did not mind London so much, and perhaps he could spend his afternoons reviewing several assignments at the Home Office. Besides, it would make his sister very, very happy. The visit could even be his Christmas gift to her, instead of the warm woolen socks he planned.

He took a deep breath. "Very well. But I hope there will not be too many guests at Parkside House."

"You will not be bothered by other people, my dear Josey. Our cousin Isabelle will be in attendance; you recall she is Marianne's second cousin as well." Liliana suddenly brightened, as if the sense of adventure had just come upon her. "And there is the baby, of course. Lord Lashton, for all his dangerous liaisons, left my friend with a darling little boy."

"Oh, dear God," Josiah said, already regretting his decision.

Liliana raised one brow. "Yes, I imagine He had something to do with it, for my dear friend would have been bereft without little Gabriel. Certainly, she would have had to return to her parents' home, as the Lashton properties would have gone to her husband's younger brother, if not for the infant earl. And she now has a person who is dear to her, whom she loves and he loves her. It is truly a blessing."

Josiah looked down at the thick Flemish rug on which they both stood, feeling humbled. He, who always had everything he desired, could only guess at the uncertainty in the lives of others. In some ways, his younger sister was more astute than he.

"Do you have any objections to little babies, Josey? As incomprehensible as it may seem, you were one yourself, thirty years ago. And unless you wish for King's Stone to pass to our American cousin — who will likely invite all his countrymen here and destroy the place — you should consider making a few babies yourself."

She was right, of course. Mr. William Harcourt of Boston was not likely to be very interested in the noble history of the property he would stand to inherit. But it was not the time to be burdened with such thoughts.

"I should have to marry first," he said, though that was a burdensome thought as well. He again considered his father, a man who embraced all the traditions and history of the Hampshire family, including the rather extraordinary belief that true love came with the brilliance of a thunderbolt, and always at first sight. And so it had been with his father.

Unfortunately, the lady upon whom he had fixed his greatest hopes had rejected him, and so he settled on another. Josiah and Liliana's mother was beautiful and worthy of enduring love, but their father was never able to recover from his first grand passion.

"Indeed," said Liliana. Returning with a rush to the present, Josiah looked up at her and saw that she regarded him with her arms crossed and her expression severe. "And that means you shall have to meet a woman and actually talk to her. Perhaps bring her flowers. Propose marriage. Show up in a church at an appointed time. I don't know how you will manage."

"Neither do I," Josiah said honestly. He suspected that the last week of December in a widow's home would neither present the season nor the place for thunderbolts, and so he was prepared to mollify his sister. "But I imagine London might be a place to start."

Marianne Westlyme, Countess of Lashton, hummed as she stepped into the nursery. Although the generations of children who grew up in Parkside House were always relegated to rooms on the upper floor, Marianne had set up her nursery in the room recently vacated by her beloved husband. After all, Gabriel now held his father's title and no one else would be bedded in the vast bedchamber for many, many years, for she had no thoughts of marrying any time in the future. Already knowing too well how suddenly she could sustain a grievous loss, she wanted her child close to her.

"My lady, you are cheerful this morning," said Mrs. Bell, Gabriel's elderly nurse. She sat with him in a large rocking chair, and

Gabriel held out his tiny arms to his mother. "It is good to see you thus, for the spirit of the season must be upon you."

Marianne picked up her child, and tickled him under his chin.

"It is better than that," she said to Mrs. Bell. "Do you recall me speaking of my dear friend Liliana Hampshire? She has agreed to visit and spend Christmas with us here. I have not seen her since my marriage, and she has never met my little darling boy."

"It is best to share the holidays with friends and family. You shall have a lovely time together."

Marianne paused. "I have little enough of either, Mrs. Bell. My parents are in the far north, and the roads are full of hazards in the winter. My mother writes that they already have a foot of snow on the ground. But my friend Miss Hampshire will arrive next week, and Cousin Isabelle soon thereafter."

"Poor Gabriel," Mrs. Bell said with a laugh. "Our little man will be adored by a bevy of ladies and will scarcely have time for his morning nap."

"There will, alas, be another attending," said Marianne quietly. "Miss Hampshire will be accompanied by her brother, the Earl of Kingston."

Mrs. Bell had the audacity to clap her hands. "Well then, our little boy will have to share the attention of the ladies. A single gentleman, did you say?"

"I did not say," Marianne said, "though, indeed he is."

"How splendid," Mrs. Bell continued, "No wonder you are happy."

Marianne shook her head. "I cannot imagine a gentleman less likely to contribute good cheer to our little party. Unlike his sister, he is stern and silent, interested in little more than his books and his maps and his work for the Home Office. Liliana tells me he is highly regarded as a military strategist. I can no more envision the man dancing a Christmas jig than the prince knitting a shawl."

Mrs. Bell smiled. "And yet, who knows what talents lie hidden beneath a man's exterior? The prince may have very nimble fingers . . ."

"Oh, I am sure he has."

". . . and your earl may be a fine singer, a keen dancer, a teller of riddles, a master of charades. He may teach you all how to skate on the pond, or help decorate the halls. He may wish to hold our little boy and amuse him all day."

"I think the spirit of the season has bewitched you, Mrs. Bell. I have no such hopes for the Earl of Kingston, and daresay we will hardly see him during the days they are with us. He will have us believe he has much more important things to do than amuse several ladies and a baby all day."

Mrs. Bell ought to have understood, for Marianne and she were usually in perfect rapport. And yet, the older woman looked as if she was about to argue. After a few moments, she seemed to relent. She looked up from the rocker and Marianne put Gabriel back into her arms.

"Indeed, you are correct, my lady. Perhaps the gentleman will wish to spend his days amusing just you, instead. It would be a splendid way to end a sad year."

"I have better hopes for the prince to present me with a knitted shawl for Christmas, Mrs. Bell. The Earl of Kingston has no interest in me, and I certainly have no interest in him. He comes only to be with his sister, and she interests me a great deal," Marianne said, though she tried to recall what the gentleman looked like. Dark, thick hair, she thought. And rather tall, if a little stooped from spending so many hours at his desk. She remembered spectacles that seemed to pinch the bridge of his nose. He was quite the opposite of her late husband.

"The brother is not at all the type to engage me."

Marianne's final words to Mrs. Bell continued to haunt her for several days, as she gave orders for her staff to prepare for their Christmas guests. It was not so much that she pondered the suitability of Liliana's brother as a suitor, but that she gave a great deal of thought to the man whom she somehow believed was her "type." Her husband had been clever and handsome, and managed to captivate any audience with his bright eyes and his amusing speech. He had seduced his way through society with words and deeds, and Marianne had fallen victim to his charm within minutes of their meeting. She'd absolutely adored him, certain he was the one man she would ever love.

Foolishly, she believed a man of his nature, once married, would begin to cut a narrower swath through society and spend time with his bride.

But within weeks of their marriage, she suspected her bed was simply the last he visited on any particular evening, and within months, his affairs were confirmed. Within a year, he was dead at the hand of an angry husband. And now she had been a widow longer than she had been a wife.

She, who had exhibited such poor judgment in choosing a husband, bestowing all her love on a man who did not love her in return, could hardly identify what kind of man would be her type.

These sobering thoughts were with her as she decided to discard her widow's weeds, and have several new dresses made for the season. She did not imagine she would impress Kingston, but perhaps it was time to impress herself.

Now, as she looked critically in the looking glass, noting that her lines were curvier than they had been before she married and how the elegant blue of her dress suited her very well, she heard carriage wheels crunch in the icy layer of snow on the circular drive in front of the house. Liliana had been rather vague about the time of their arrival, but she'd posted a more specific hour after her brother advised her on the precise details of her journey. In the lines of her letter, Marianne could read affectionate exasperation. It was a tone with which Marianne would probably become familiar over the next weeks.

She glanced to the window and confirmed the arrival of a rather elegant carriage, of a style that was no longer entirely fashionable. She then berated herself for even thinking such a thing, for the Kingstons were country folk, and such things could not matter outside of London.

Truly, they should not matter inside of London either. But they did.

Coaxing her lips into a cheerful smile, Marianne left the comfort of her chamber and prepared herself to meet her guests.

But any illusions she had about making a grand entrance were dashed when Liliana spotted her descending the staircase, and dashed up to greet her.

"Marianne! My darling girl! It is a wonder to see you again!" she cried and flung her arms around her. Marianne groped behind her to grasp the railing and support them both. "I thought we would never get here, for the roads are covered with snow!"

"And yet you have arrived precisely when you said you would," Marianne said and sneezed as she inhaled the scent of wood smoke on Liliana's garments.

"That is because my brother calculated our progress based on the amount of snow on the ground. It seems absurd, but it appears to have been effective." Liliana loosened her hold.

"Your brother?"

Just then, the Earl of Kingston walked into

the hall below them, carrying his own bag. His damp black hair glimmered in the candlelight, and his broad shoulders were covered with a mantle of fresh snow. Pausing in the center of the hall, he slipped off his spectacles, and wiped them with a linen he pulled from his breast pocket. Blinking, he looked around him, until his eyes settled on Marianne's face, several inches above him.

"Your brother," Marianne said, looking down on him.

"Oh, yes," Liliana said, remembering her manners. "Marianne, Countess of Lashton, please meet my brother Josiah, Earl of Kingston. I call him Josey."

"Well, I shall not," Marianne said.

Kingston bowed deeply, and melting snow fell off his broad shoulders. "My lady. Thank you for your generous hospitality. It is a pleasure to be here this Christmas." He glanced at his sister, as if awaiting her approbation.

Good heavens, Marianne thought. Did Liliana make him come against his will?

She reached for her friend's hand, and together they descended the stairs. Kingston grew taller and taller and as they came close, she noticed his eyes were quite as dark as his hair. She felt she could lose herself in his gaze, until he replaced his spectacles and a glass wall came up between them.

"It is a pleasure to have you both join me. It will be a rather quiet affair, I fear, for we will only have Cousin Isabelle to join us. And Gabriel, of course."

"The angel?" he asked, and she hoped he was attempting to be a wit.

"He is certainly that to me," Marianne said. "He is my little boy, and just beginning to say his first words."

"Oh, truly?" Liliana cried. "What could be more adorable? What does he say?"

Marianne looked at Kingston and saw he was already bored with this conversation, and was looking about at the fine statuary that lined the circumference of the room.

"He says 'Mama,' of course. And 'spoon,' 'fish,' and 'cat.' There does not seem to be a pattern to his words, but it is so much fun to see what interests him."

"Is that not wonderful, Josey?" Liliana asked.

"Yes, it most certainly is. I would say it is from the school of Michelangelo."

Marianne followed his gaze to a marble faun. "You are rather astute, my lord. It most certainly is that, done by an unknown artist, and not the master himself."

384

He turned to look down at her, and it seemed they remained as frozen in time as the little faun, until Liliana cleared her throat.

"Well, I am so glad that is settled," she said. "I was much concerned about its provenance."

Marianne laughed out loud, marveling at how good it felt to be able to do so. "You ought to be more concerned about my hospitality, for here you both are, still in your travel clothes. Please follow my maid to your rooms, which are both on the family floor. For, indeed, you are like family to me."

"I shall not be long, Marianne," said Liliana. "I wish to renew our acquaintance before Cousin Isabelle arrives. After that, we shall hardly get a word in between us."

"You are undoubtedly right about that, because I suspect she gets out more in society than we do, though she is twice our age," Marianne said, wondering what gossip Cousin Isabelle might have heard about her own nephew. She looked up at him. "Please join us in the parlor, my lord. We shall become better acquainted."

"Yes, please do," said Liliana, and there seemed to be a challenge in her words.

"I fear you will find me poor company. I

am not able to renew an old acquaintance, and should have very little to recommend me for a new one," he said.

Marianne glanced at Liliana, who merely rolled her eyes.

"Well then," said Marianne, "since you are uncomfortable joining our conversation, perhaps I shall deliver Gabriel into your care. You gentlemen should have much to talk about, though I must warn you that he is a man of few words."

Liliana caught Marianne's elbow and started to pull her away, toward the stairs. "That seems very apt," she said, "for my dear brother remarked on very little other than the topography of England during all the hours of our journey. He is also a man of few words."

Chapter Two

Josiah looked about the well-appointed room to which a young maid had led him and his valet, and decided it would do quite well for the duration of this visit. His valet was much more interested in the maid, but Josiah was pleased with the large writing desk, the window that opened to the park below, and the fireplace somewhat closer to the area in which he would write and read, than to the large bed. Indeed, he assessed the comfort of the desk chair before he sat on the mattress.

It would do quite well, if he could manage to apply himself to his work.

"Shall I lay out your dinner jacket, my lord?" Donovan asked. "Will the gentlemen meet in the parlor before then?"

"There are no other gentlemen," Josiah said. "And I am not certain the ladies are at all interested in an old scholar and his valet."

His words were tossed casually in the

warm room, precisely the sort of dismissive remark Josiah repeated through the years. But somehow, in an unnervingly short time, something had changed. Moments ago, Lady Lashton's attention had been all for Liliana, and she was no more than polite to him. But when she looked up at him, her large eyes unblinking in the warm candlelight, he was struck by something entirely unexpected and rather remarkable.

She might not be at all interested in him, but he suddenly wished nothing more than to be in her company and hear her voice again.

Donovan did not seem to sense anything amiss and went about his business with unusual efficiency, undoubtedly looking forward to tea in the kitchen with that pretty maid. The weeks ahead might prove a cheerful diversion for the man, so far removed from their rather ordinary existence at King's Stone. It was just as well. Josiah shrugged off thoughts of Lady Lashton, reminding himself that he was perfectly comfortable with his life as it was, and intending to just carry on as usual while in London. He had already arranged several important meetings at Whitehall, and had completed maps based on current reports to deliver in person to Lord Dailey. Perhaps he would also take a brisk walk to the library, or enjoy an evening at the opera. He had brought a trunk full of books and papers with him, and should be able to fully engage in his work.

"Before you dash off to persuade the cook to prepare your favorite pie, I should like to change out of these dusty garments, and set out my writing instruments on the desk," he reminded Donovan. "Then you can leave me in peace." If such a thing were now possible.

"With your permission, I should like to see something of town," Donovan said. "I hear the Tower is worth a glance."

"More than a glance, I should think. But you need not rush out, for we have many days here. You may go off to view one prison, and I shall remain here in mine. We shall both be happy."

Donovan, who knew him as well as anyone, had no answer. After the man had helped his employer dress, Josiah waved him off to enjoy himself while he busied himself arranging his desk to his specific preferences. There was enough room for his books and for a large blotter. He carefully placed several pairs of spectacles in a shallow drawer. While he debated the placement of his inkwell, Donovan slipped out of the room.

All was perfect, or at least as perfect as a situation could be if one was not at home. Or in the proximity of a very compelling lady.

Josiah stared out on the park, noting the traffic of riders and carriages, often blocking the path of others as friends paused to greet each other. In the distance, a lake was frozen to pale blue, and small figures endured the cold to skate upon it. The bare trees were stark black slashes against the darkening sky. The prospect was Elysian, nearly as peaceful as his landscape at King's Stone.

He sharpened the point of his pen and dipped it into the inkwell, newly filled. He had several important letters to write, two of which he might deliver in person to the recipients. Composing several lines in his head, he set the pen to the paper.

And then a baby started to cry.

His gaze returned to the window, looking to regain his composure while he waited for the wailing to stop. But he could not help but hear someone scurrying around, another person running down the hall, and the sound of women's voices. And still the crying continued. Josiah tapped his fingers impatiently on the desk, until he realized he was stamping a smudge of ink on a leaf of paper. He thought he heard his sister's voice. And then another he already recognized as belonging to Lady Lashton. It was, honey-smooth, a bit deeper than that of most women, and deliberate in enunciation. It was very soothing voice.

Apparently, the recalcitrant child thought so as well. The wailing subsided to an intermittent cry, to a whimper, and then — absurdly — to a giggle. The women started to giggle as well, and made all sorts of ridiculous sounds. The baby laughed louder.

Josiah sat at his desk, shoulders slumped, hands in his lap. The cries of an infant, and the seductive voice of a woman.

How had he imagined he might do any work at Parkside House?

Within an hour of her dear friend's arrival at Parkside House, Marianne was reminded of why she loved Liliana. The intimacy of their conversations, the intuitive understanding of what the other meant in very few words, the moments of pure joy, were all reminiscent of the wonderful journey they had made with Lady Isabelle Delaroy when they had both been nineteen and truly innocent. Only six years had passed, but so

391

much had changed for her in those years.

She remained in London society, while Liliana lived in the country. She had been introduced to many eligible gentlemen, some interested in her family wealth, and some interested in her. But she made the sad mistake of passionately loving a man who seemed somewhat diffident, an air she mistook for honorable behavior. And so she married Marcus Westlyme, and discovered that diffidence was actually indifference. Their marriage was over nearly as soon as it begun, though she continued to adore him. She thought things would change when she happily told him she was with child. He did not seem quite so happy. And then he foolishly got himself killed by showing up drunk to a duel, and never met his heir. Gabriel was born into his father's title, but did not share his name. Marcus once told Marianne that there were already too many Marcuses, though she did not appreciate the intent of that remark until she learned of his many infidelities.

"Society in the country is so limited," Liliana said. "But I truly am not complaining. I enjoy many things."

Marianne shifted Gabriel to a more comfortable position and he continued to amuse himself with a ball. It was already twilight, and Mrs. Bell would soon take him to his bed. But for now, they all sat congenially in the parlor — or nearly all, for Lord Kingston did not join them.

"I do not go out in society very much, but since my year of mourning has just ended, I suppose I ought. It will never again be as it was, dancing and being courted by eligible young men. Being a widow with a child is something else altogether. I feel rather old."

"I imagine it gives you more freedom to do as you like. I, on the other hand, am the same age and have never been married. So I have neither freedom nor youth," Liliana said. "I have a brother."

Marianne laughed, and Gabriel twisted in her lap to look up at her. "Is he interested in marriage?"

"In mine, or his own?" Liliana asked. "I doubt he ever thinks about either."

Marianne laughed again, but realized her friend was not amused. "A fine pair we are. You do not have the opportunity to go out in society, and I do not have the inclination. What say you to a longer stay here at Parkside House? We might soldier on together, and attend dinner parties and such. And if we find ourselves bored — which is most likely — we will at least have each other." Marianne's words were heartfelt, spontaneous, composed even as they were uttered.

Liliana's expression of surprise was gradually nudged into a smile. "I should like that very much. But what of my brother?"

Marianne was about to retort that he could take care of himself, when the man himself sauntered into the room. He bowed and seated himself beside Marianne before he asked, "What of her brother?"

"I propose to steal her from you, and bring her to parties and balls. We shall make a big splash in society and break men's hearts." As she teased, and came precariously close to flirting, Marianne watched Gabriel reach out to Kingston. It was rather extraordinary, because the baby was usually afraid of strangers.

"That sounds rather brutal. Can you not merely enchant rather than actually kill them?" he asked and smiled. Or nearly so. That seemed extraordinary as well.

Gabriel waved his arms, stretching his whole body in an effort to touch Kingston.

"If they die, it will be with a smile on their face," Marianne said. For a moment, she wondered what it would be like to enchant the man beside her. "Your sister and I are compassionate ladies, after all."

"Marianne is teasing you, Josey."

Kingston turned to his sister. "Do you

mean you are not truly compassionate?"

She scowled at him. "We will not break anyone's heart. We will just enjoy ourselves, as we did so many years ago. Cousin Isabelle will accompany us."

Marianne watched the repartee between brother and sister, the closeness that comes with knowing everything about the other. She had no idea what their mutual cousin would say to this sudden change of plans, but perhaps it did not matter. Cousin Isabelle was of a certain age, and quite capable of serving as chaperone.

Kingston did not answer, but held out his hand to Gabriel, tentatively, curiously. Gabriel lunged forward, almost falling from Marianne's lap, and closed his fist over Kingston's forefinger. Wordlessly, Marianne shifted her little boy closer to him, and he nearly fell into Kingston's arms. Man and boy settled back into their chair, Gabriel exploring the pair of very large hands, and Kingston seemingly fascinated with being the object of fascination.

"Well, may I stay in London after Christmas?" Liliana asked, a bit impatiently.

"As you wish," Kingston responded, not looking up.

Marianne's eyes met Liliana's and they each shrugged in some confusion. They did not quite understand what was happening, but it seemed to be all for the best.

Some hours later, after Lady Lashton made rather a big show of bidding her son a good night, and after a dinner as simple as it was delicious, Josiah retired with the two ladies to a small room near the dining room. He looked around at the mirrored rooms and dainty French furnishings, and realized this was where ladies went when men retired to a game room or some place with an abundance of alcohol and New World cigars. Since they would not send him off by himself, he was permitted to enter their sanctuary.

"You seem very comfortable with a child in your lap, Lord Kingston," Marianne said. "Have you had much opportunity to be with children?"

Liliana snickered into her tea cup.

"I have had no opportunity at all, Lady Lashton. The last child I held was my sister, who squirmed out of my five-year-old arms and fell on her head. You can see the result of that sorry episode."

He could see Marianne was amused and wondered how he managed that. Being in her company nearly rendered him speechless. But in the best of circumstances, he was as inexperienced in talking to ladies as he was in holding babies, and certainly was never known as a wit.

"In that case, I should not trust you with my little boy, my lord," she said lightly. "But then, you seem to be the first person he seems truly drawn to. He most definitely wants to be with you."

"Perhaps I remind him of his father," Josiah said, a little embarrassed. In rethinking his words, he was even more so.

"That would be a fine feat, since Lord Lashton died months before his son was born," Marianne said with clear regret, her deep voice choking up. "No, my son will never know his father."

"I wonder if he already senses the loss," he said softly.

When Marianne did not answer, he glanced up and studied her face. Her cheeks were damp with tears and she seemed humbled by a great sadness. What little he knew of her story was reported to him by Liliana, but his sister could know nothing of her friend's heart. No one could know such a thing.

And yet he imagined Marianne's loneliness and disappointed hopes and humiliation. It was presumptuous of him, but he was angered by the man who could abuse her so.

She sniffed and thrust back her shoulders, showing both her defiance and her excellent figure. Josiah kept his gaze fixed on her face, no matter how tempting it was to look elsewhere.

"I shall endeavor to compensate for the absence of his father. While most people would regard a child born into privilege and wealth as having a blessed life, I know there are things he shall miss. My late husband's brother has no particular affection for my son who, after all, deprived him of a great estate and title. I, myself, do not have a brother, and my father lives very far away."

"Do you not look to marry again, Marianne?" Liliana broke in. Josiah had quite forgotten she was in the room.

"It is too soon to look, or to marry, Liliana. And if I ever do, I will have to consider the desires of two people."

"Do you mean Gabriel and yourself?" Liliana asked.

Marianne did not answer, though her lips parted and closed, as if she thought better of her words.

"It is no matter, dear. It is none of my business, after all," Liliana said quickly.

"No, it is quite all right. As the two of you

are here to share this sacred time of year and the prayers for the new one, I might as well be honest. I did mean Gabriel and myself, but now I realize that I must also consider the desires of any man I marry. I thought Lashton loved me, but he did not. I ought to have recognized that, but I was a fool." It was an appalling admission, but uttered with a great deal of dignity. "Cousin Isabelle is arriving in a few days, and she will drag everything out from under the rug. So you may as well hear my confession first."

"It is an awful thing," Liliana murmured.

"My marriage, do you mean? It did not seem that way to me at first, but I do my best to only remember the good in it. And the very best thing is that the love I once had gave me Gabriel."

Josiah said nothing. But he realized Lord Lashton had been a bigger fool than he ever thought possible.

Liliana and Marianne set out the next day to enjoy the crisp winter day and to purchase gifts in some of the best shops. Liliana was unaccustomed to the array of wares that London merchants offered, and Marianne had scarcely indulged in any pleasures for a year, so the day promised to be a great adventure. They hoped Kingston would be willing to join them, of course, but he demurred, saying he was far too busy to be frivolously shopping and that they would have a better time without his company. He retreated to his chamber soon after their breakfast.

This is what Marianne imagined when she invited Liliana to join her for Christmas, and yet she could not help but wonder what Kingston was doing, if he was comfortable, if he regretted not joining them on Jermyn Street. He was a bit of a quiz, seemingly severe and uninterested in idle conversation. And yet, she glimpsed a part of him that was warmer, kinder, a burning coal that might flare when stoked.

"I shall purchase that for Gabriel," Liliana said, pointing to a metal figure in a shop window. It was a soldier, painted in the bright red uniform of the militia.

"He will promptly stuff it into his mouth and cut his cheek on the rifle," Marianne said, though it was a very fine model. "You need not purchase anything for him, for he is just a baby."

"Oh nonsense," Liliana said, pulling her into the shop. "You shall put it on a shelf in the nursery and when he asks for it, you will tell him that his dear Aunt Liliana purchased it. And I shall give him a gift of one every Christmas until he has a veritable army. Let this be the first recruit."

"It is lovely and generous of you," Marianne said. "And you are not his aunt."

"Of course, but would it not be great fun if I were?" Liliana murmured. Marianne was not sure she heard the words properly and was, in any case, speechless.

Marianne was exhausted when they returned to Parkside House, but promptly went up the stairs to the nursery. Hearing no sounds from within, she opened the door quietly, as she assumed Gabriel slept. But the room was quite empty, and his little bed neatly made up. She stepped back into the hall, listening to the sounds of her home, alert to the chirpy baby sounds that had become her only source of pleasure. She heard nothing.

She passed Liliana going up the stairs as she ran down, and waved off her surprised expression. She further surprised her own staff with her entrance into their dining hall. But Mrs. Rains, the housekeeper, had not seen Mrs. Bell and Gabriel, nor had two of the maids. Kingston's valet had only seen the maids, which was not surprising.

Where was her child?

Sensibly, Marianne knew she had no reason to be concerned, for she absolutely trusted Mrs. Bell. The answer was probably so obvious as to be self-evident. But she had never faced a moment of such fear, even when she heard her husband had been killed. She pressed a hand on her thumping heart and closed her eyes, trying to shut out visions of terrible accidents and criminal behavior.

Nine out of ten women would retreat to their bed, calling for a cup of tea to calm their nerves.

Instead, Marianne stumbled to her husband's library, where every volume offered refuge. She pushed open the heavy oak door, surprised to feel the warmth of a fire in this room so little used since Marcus's death.

"And here is your Mama," Kingston said calmly. He sat by the fire, with books stacked on the tables beside him, and Gabriel on his lap.

"Good heavens!" Marianne gasped. "I thought I would never see him again!"

Kingston looked at her in surprise. "Surely it is not so drastic as all that. He and I decided to spend the afternoon together."

"How did that come about?" Marianne asked, her hand at her heart, trying to sound as if she had not just run from Marathon to Athens. She reached for her son, who glanced back at Kingston with an expression that looked like regret, and took him into her arms.

"Why, his Mrs. Bell wished to make some purchases for Christmas, and everyone seemed busy, so I offered to entertain him for the while. I confess, I was rather entertaining. Or, at least, little Lord Lashton thought so."

Marianne studied him warily. He must know he had not answered the question. She understood that Mrs. Bell could choose an opportunity to slip outside during the day; the poor woman hardly left the house. But with a house full of servants — not all of them so busy, despite the season — how had this responsibility fallen on her solemn guest? One who was not that comfortable with little children?

"You said you had much business to which to attend," she accused him, though of what she could hardy say.

"I completed what I needed to do," he said, reasonably.

"You said you were unaccustomed to babies," she argued.

"I decided I might enjoy them, after all," he shrugged, quite matter-of-factly.

"I have a house full of servants."

"But only two lords. We gentlemen must stick together," Kingston said, and wiggled his fingers in the air.

Gabriel thought this was uproarious and stretched his arms out to his fellow gentleman.

"I see the two of you are of a similar mind and wit," Marianne said.

"Joe," Gabriel said, quite clearly.

Josiah Hampton, Earl of Kingston, smiled like an idiot.

"Good heavens," Marianne said for the second time in five minutes, but this time it was an expression of exasperation. She handed her son back to his buddy. "He has just said your name. Or something like. You may both be earls, but it is disrespectful."

"Not at all, Lady Lashton. It suits me just fine," said Kingston. He turned Gabriel in his lap to face him, and tapped him on the nose. Gabriel laughed so hard, he nearly fell off Kingston's lap.

"Joe?" she asked, incredulously. This whole episode was ridiculous.

"Yes?" he answered, surely knowing that was not the answer to her question.

"Even your sister does not call you Joe," she argued.

"Well, then, young Gabriel can be the

first. I rather like it." As did Gabriel, apparently, who proceeded to pronounce it another five times.

In spite of her reservations, in spite of her fears, and in spite of the revelation that her son seemed to prefer to be with a stranger rather than with his mother, Marianne could not help but laugh.

By the following morning, the gaiety of the previous afternoon seemed a distant memory. Kingston remained in the library while Marianne brought Gabriel to the nursery, and he did not emerge until just before the dinner hour. While Liliana related every detail of the shopping excursion over roasted beef and scallops, Kingston looked distracted and barely spoke. Marianne wondered if he regretted their companionable episode in the library, but his sister just rambled on, indifferent to his silence.

His quiet demeanor had the appearance of spilling over into breakfast, when Marianne decided to liven up both the conversation and the room. "Last Christmas, I hardly had the heart to celebrate," she admitted. "My husband was only recently dead, and I despaired of bringing a fatherless child into the world."

"Yes, of course," Liliana murmured. "It

was an awful time for you."

Kingston said nothing, of course. He removed his spectacles and slipped them into his breast pocket. His dark gaze met Marianne's.

"But while we rode through the park yesterday, I noticed a large cluster of mistletoe on a juniper tree," Marianne continued, studying him.

"Oh, let us ask one of the servants to bring us some! We can wrap it about the candles and over the mantels," said Liliana. "And hang a small spray on yonder doorframe, as our mother used to do at King's Stone. It will be very festive!"

"Do you refer to *Viscum Album,* that parasitic plant that suffocates its host?" Kingston asked, sensibly enough. "Also referred to as mistle twig?"

"Yes, I suppose I do," said Marianne, leaning toward him and wondering how this man could manage to make botany sound so seductive. "I am not proposing to plant it in my garden, only to bring some greenery into the house. If it is as evil a species as you suggest, would we not be helping that poor juniper in the park? Mistletoe cannot do much harm on our table."

"Unless one eats it, of course. It is not poisonous to birds, but can make a person

406

rather ill."

"Then I shall advise Mrs. Rains to leave it out of the stew," Marianne said. "And I shall ask one of the men to prune some switches and bring it to us. I daresay it would do rather nicely on the gates of Parkside House as well."

"Yes, it will, especially if it snows," said Liliana. "But do not forget to leave a sprig for the doorframe."

Marianne and Kingston turned to her, but said nothing.

The servants made short work of procuring the Christmas greenery, surely happy to be restoring some gaiety to a household that had been in mourning for over a year. Following Marianne's direction, they arranged mistletoe and fir branches on the iron railing that surrounded the house, and still had many boughs for use within. Though Marianne could have delegated this project as well, she decided to do it herself, with Liliana as her willing assistant. Mrs. Bell sat with Gabriel in a rocker, offering advice, and admiring it all.

Kingston retreated to his chamber after breakfast, claiming to be busy with his own Christmas preparations, and they did not see him all afternoon.

"The decorations are quite wonderful," Liliana said. "I wonder why I did not think of doing something like it in all these years."

Marianne looked down from where she stood on a sturdy chair. "Perhaps it is because your brother is so solemn and proper that he would not bring something as frivolous as tree boughs into King's Stone. You might get sap on your silver."

Liliana nodded. "Yes, there is that. But our father was of a similar disposition, while our mother pushed against his natural resistance and always tried to be cheerful and generous." She began to say something else and seemed to think better of it. And then, she offered simply, "Theirs was not a happy marriage."

Marianne sighed, thinking of her own.

"But you must not think Josey is truly like our father, for all his serious ways. He would not, intentionally, inflict pain on anyone."

"And my son seems to approve of him," Marianne murmured, and went back to her task of draping greenery. In truth, she approved of him as well, for all his staid and stuffy ways. He was clever and amusing and instinctively knew how to handle a tiny child. And it was impossible to ignore his vital presence, for when he pocketed his spectacles and straightened his frequently stooped shoulders, he was rather splendid. Handsome and tall, with his dramatically dark hair and eyes, he was a man who commanded attention in every way.

He was not like Marcus, who had inflicted pain on the one who loved him most. Most importantly, Kingston seemed like a man she could trust.

"Oh, mercy!" Mrs. Bell cried out, breaking Marianne out of her reverie. She forgot she was standing on a chair and turned so quickly, she almost fell off. Liliana had already rushed to Mrs. Bell's side, and retrieved Gabriel just as he retched all over Mrs. Bell's apron.

"What is it?" Marianne cried out, and jumped off the chair.

"It is his luncheon," Mrs. Bell sobbed. The poor woman was now covered in it.

"And something green," Liliana whispered. "I think it is . . ."

"Not mistletoe, surely," Marianne said urgently. "Mrs. Bell what has he been eating?"

The horror on the woman's face told the story before she did.

"I was holding a small switch of it, and he grabbed it from me. I pulled it away as soon as I realized what was amiss, but he must have eaten some of it."

Marianne took Gabriel from Liliana's arms. "Please find your brother. Mrs. Bell, fetch one of the men and send him to Dr. Farquar's office at once. We must act quickly."

She pulled her son close, and held his head down, so he could bring up the poisonous leaves. Seized with the same fears that nearly stole her reason the day before, she could only bargain with God that Gabriel be spared.

Suddenly, he was out of her hands, as Kingston seized him and started slapping the baby's back. More of the wretched mess spilled onto the rug, and then Gabriel started to cry. Kingston handed him back to Marianne, who held him close and soothed him. But then he went still.

She started to sob. "I have lost him."

Kingston shook his head. "He is asleep. This little episode has exhausted him, poor chap. He will learn to never sample greenery that is not served on a plate before him."

Marianne knew she was beyond rational thought, but cried, "How can I keep him safe? There is so much for him to learn and not enough I can do to protect him! He is all I have."

She would surely have gone on and on but that she felt strong arms wrap around

Gabriel and herself and hold them both close. Kingston took long and deep breaths, until she closed her eyes and followed his lead. He smelled of wood smoke and spice, and his hair brushed against her forehead like gentling feathers.

"The doctor . . . ," Liliana cried behind her, before faltering, ". . . is here."

Kingston did not release Marianne at once, and when he did so, it seemed he did so with reluctance. She looked up into his face, but could not read his thoughts in his expression or in the depths of his dark eyes.

"My lady," Dr. Farquar said softly, and pulled Gabriel from her arms. She watched as he gently laid the sleeping baby on the couch and kneeled at his side.

Standing close to her, Kingston murmured, "You have others to help and protect you."

Unable to look at him Marianne studied the floor, where she saw Kingston's spectacles, crushed and mangled by someone's shoes.

Gabriel was not the only one exhausted by the afternoon's misadventure. Marianne reported that he awakened briefly to study his surroundings, push away the bowl of porridge that Mrs. Bell offered to him, and

411

promptly returned to sleep.

Over dinner, Josiah sat with his two companions, and they poked listlessly at their meals. His hostess said little and Liliana nothing at all. While this circumstance would have ordinarily pleased him, the air was fraught with tension. His beautiful hostess, at his left, had not recovered from her fear and — perhaps — her guilt, while his equally beautiful sister, across from him, looked pensive. He did not yet know how she had interpreted the intimate scene she had burst upon, or if the subject would ever come up between them.

He was not sure about it himself, other than to admit he was prompted by more than decency to offer Marianne comfort, and that he could not remember feeling so needed as he had in that moment. But he knew there was more, some great sense of wholeness he'd experienced as he had embraced this woman and her child.

He also knew what all the great writers had written of love and how the rules had been carefully spelled out by Andreas Capellanus, so many centuries ago.

Love is a certain inborn suffering derived from the sight of and excessive meditation upon the beauty of the opposite sex, which causes each one to wish for, above all things, the embraces of the other. . . .

The old boy certainly knew what he was about, for Josiah could think of little else but Marianne. He was grateful he remembered to bring several pairs of spectacles, the better to see her. He had managed almost no writing since his arrival at Parkside House, and he could scarce concentrate on his maps for his associates at Whitehall. He found himself pausing as he passed the closed door of her bedchamber, and looking for the chance to verbally spar with her. She owned many charms to seduce him, as any desirable woman might, but one surprised him most of all.

Last night, he had dreamed about teaching a little boy to angle.

He wanted her most desperately. But he also wanted to be Gabriel's father. It was a most unexpected sentiment, for he had schooled himself so carefully through the years to resist any notion of love at first sight.

"May I be forgiven if I do not join you for coffee this evening?" Liliana asked. "I have never felt so weary in my life."

"I hope it is not due to our clever repartee here at the dinner table," said Marianne, a spark of wit breaking the general silence.

"I think I am so unaccustomed to excite-

413

ment, my nerves can scarcely bear it." Liliana trifled with her silver spoon. "Gabriel gave us a terrible fright today."

Josiah knew the truth of it. But he also understood how fear had led them to another sort of excitement. "I imagine a household in which young children live is full of adventures we old folk can hardly imagine."

"Lord Kingston," Marianne said, smiling. She seemed to have recovered from her ordeal with her spirit intact. "I hardly think that the three of us qualify as 'old folk' and the adventures of our past are not so very far away. Did you never get into mischief when you were a boy?"

Liliana laughed out loud, and Kingston dreaded a recitation of his youthful exploits. But his sister was rather discreet, if not actually complimentary. "Of course my brother would do nothing to displease our parents," she said to Marianne. "He could do no wrong."

"It is as I suspected then," said Marianne, studying him.

Josiah shifted in his seat, uncomfortable with being the object of their humor. He wished Liliana would plead a migraine and run from the table.

When she finally stood, he wondered if he

had said the words aloud.

"On that note, I shall bid you both a good evening," she said. "I believe my cure is nothing more than sound sleep."

Kingston stood as she came around the table, and kissed her on the cheek. Her face was cool and she seemed quite satisfied with herself.

He would wager a guess on why that was so.

"Would you like to join me in the library, Lord Kingston?" Marianne asked, as soon as the door closed behind Liliana. "We can enjoy our coffee surrounded by the society of the wise and wordy."

"I only desire your society tonight, Lady Lashton, so I hope the philosophers and poets are not too disappointed." Josiah did not say if she but asked, he would join her in the stable, or any other place she desired.

"But whatever shall we talk about?" she asked as she stood to join him and lent him her elbow. Other ladies were likely to begin a flirtation with those words, but Josiah rather thought Marianne meant them.

"I can begin by telling you that I was not the paragon my sister would have you believe. Our parents certainly did not think so. I recall I once constructed wings made of wax and leaves and jumped off the roof of the stable," he said. He folded his arm through hers and brought her closer to his side.

"Oh, not truly!" she said. "Did you injure yourself?"

"More my dignity than my person. My father thought it very clever of me, but my mother was quite prepared to lock me in my bedchamber until I was old enough to go to Cambridge."

"That certainly would have kept you safe," Marianne added with a smile.

They walked into the library, and he led her toward the glowing fireplace. She sat on a well-cushioned chair and gestured for him to sit close by.

"I am not so certain of that. When I was twelve years, I experimented with a lens near the window and set the draperies on fire."

"Oh, dear heavens!" she cried, but he saw that she was laughing. "And is this what I can expect in the years ahead?"

"From me?" he asked, surprised. A moment later, he realized his foolish mistake, the utter presumption of his words.

Marianne was equally surprised. Shaking her head, she said, "Why, how could it be so, Lord Kingston? I meant of my son, of course."

One of the maids came through the door with a vast tray of desserts, quite enough to satisfy five people. Josiah had no appetite for any of it.

"Of course," he said quickly. "And did you ever get into mischief as a child, Lady Lashton?"

"Oh, certainly. But nothing more daring than running in the field without my slippers, or spilling ink on one of my father's precious books." She served him a cup of coffee, but neglected to ask if he preferred sugar or cream. "I suppose the riskiest thing I ever did was marry Lord Lashton."

He accepted the cup, but was no more interested in it than was she. "But you must have known something of his reputation, Lady Lashton. Forgive me if I am too presumptuous."

"Lord Kingston, I daresay everyone in London understands the situation. But I truly loved him and honestly believed that he loved me."

"As we are being honest with each other, I will confess that my mother loved my father, but I do not believe he was truly capable of loving her in return. He spent years of his life mourning the loss of his first true love."

"She must have been very young when she

died," she said.

"She did not die," he quickly corrected her. "She would not have him. It is mourning of a different sort."

"But mourning, just the same." She sighed.

"But I suspect you are stronger than my father, Lady Lashton. I am sorry to hear of any man's death, but your husband will not define your character, nor that of your son."

"That is very kind of you to say so, Lord Kingston," said Marianne. She picked up a biscuit, and dropped it onto a plate.

They sat together in peaceful silence, watching the glowing coals in the fireplace. At least, Josiah hoped he gave the intention of doing so, for he was actually watching Marianne. Her nose was as elegant as the rest of her features, fine-boned, but not particularly delicate. He saw now how much Gabriel favored her and supposed it must be a comfort that the child did not daily remind her of the man who disappointed her.

"We were interrupted in our decorating this afternoon," she said suddenly. "The boughs are rather crooked, and the poor mistletoe looks like it will topple with the slightest gust of wind."

"They are rather sturdy things, you know.

418

Once they grasp hold of a branch, it is doomed, for it embraces it for the rest of its life," he said, knowing of what he spoke.

"It does not sound like such a bad thing," Marianne murmured, and turned toward him.

Perhaps he did not know.

"Ah, if you wish, Lady Lashton, I should be happy to help you finish the day's work. Our cousin Isabelle arrives tomorrow, and I recall she is a bit of a perfectionist."

"You recall correctly, my lord. Though I would say she is not so much of a perfectionist as merely someone who always wishes to have her own way."

Josiah stood. "I will affix the mistletoe, if that would make both of you happy." He retrieved a plain wooden chair from the perimeter of the room and brought it to the doorframe. Stepping upon it, he caught the dangling little sprig and wove it through the wire loop Marianne had prepared earlier. It soon was perfectly secure, but so small a piece, he wondered if anyone would notice it.

"It looks lovely," Marianne said, standing just beneath him. He had not heard her approach. She looked up at him, and he was able to admire her pale neck and shoulders. Her gown dipped just suggestively enough to reveal a birthmark on one of her breasts.

He stepped down off the chair. "I was thinking the very thing," he said.

"Lord Kingston," she said, not shying away from his gaze. "I am speaking of the little parasitic plant of which you are so censorious."

"And I am speaking of you."

And then, because there was nothing he wished to do more, and because the damned parasitic mistletoe was an invitation for such mischief, he caught her by her lovely shoulders, pulled her toward him, and kissed her.

She was soft and yielding, with none of the shyness he had met on those few occasions when he had yielded to such temptation in the past. Her lips were warm and tasted vaguely of nutmeg. Her hands wandered to his neck and face, and pulled him even closer. For all the proper layers of clothing they wore, he could feel her heart dancing beneath them.

"Josiah," she said, her voice a caress. "Joe."

He was not Joe, and the name certainly did not sound as sweet.

"No one calls me Joe," he said.

"Except for my son. If he likes it, then so do I."

"Do I have no say in the matter?"

"Will you not allow me to decide my own

preference?"

Josiah hesitated, not sure what she suggested. He considered himself a very logical person, but just three days in this woman's society had managed to challenge all reason. "Because you are my hostess, do you mean?"

"No, because I . . ." She stopped suddenly, and pulled away. Her pale breasts and shoulders were aflame and she tapped her heart, as if willing it to slow.

"Because it is Christmas, and you must grant me what I wish," she finished. He knew it was not what she intended to say.

"Do I not get my wishes as well?" he asked.

She looked a bit worried. "What are they, my lord?"

"Let us start with the easiest, my lady. If you would call me Joe or Josiah, you must be Marianne."

He saw the relief on her face.

"That is perfectly reasonable. I hoped you would not wish to call me Mary," she said, and smiled.

He looked into her face, and knew he was hopelessly, utterly gone.

CHAPTER THREE

Lady Isabelle Delaroy fell into the hallway of Parkside House on a gust of wind and snow. Though assisted by one of the servants, she nearly slipped on the damp marble floor, but caught herself up quite quickly. Always dignified, always self-sufficient, she was probably the only woman Marianne's mother had trusted sufficiently to escort her darling child on a journey to Bath all those years ago. That the Earl of Kingston's younger sister was also a member of the party was an additional advantage, for that ancient family of King's Stone was well known for its sobriety and good sense.

As Marianne rushed toward her cousin, the years passed away like the melting snowflakes on Isabelle's bonnet, for she remembered the fascination and delights of that wonderful trip. She had been a different person then, utterly naïve, and holding the highest expectations. That they were not to be truly realized could not have been known, and the time they spent in Bath remained a youthful threshold through which she had happily passed into adulthood.

Cousin Isabelle looked just as she had then. There were a few more gray hairs, perhaps, but nothing that did anything to diminish her beauty.

"My dear cousin," Marianne said, as she clutched Isabelle in her arms and warmed her. "I have looked forward to this for so long."

Cousin Isabelle took a playful tap at Marianne's cheek. "It is not so very long. Was I not here the very night of Gabriel's birth?"

"Indeed you were, and it could not have been more appreciated. I was in great need then, and would not have wanted to be alone." Marianne remembered the dark and uncertain night with perfect clarity, wondering if she would live, wondering if her child would survive, imagining bringing a fatherless child into the rough world.

"But, hush. We need not talk of these things now. It is Christmas, after all, and I see everything has changed."

Marianne had no idea what had changed,

other than months of devoted attention to Gabriel, but knew it was not the moment to pursue the conversation. Isabelle had traveled far and was undoubtedly in need of rest and warmth. She shed her damp outer garments and danced a little pirouette in the round hall.

"Oh, but it is good to be here!" she cried. "And to have you and Liliana both!"

"And Lord Kingston, of course," Marianne added. "This will not quite be the lady's society with which we lived quite comfortably in Bath. There will be a gentleman with us at all times."

Isabelle stopped suddenly. "And that changes everything."

Marianne knew the truth of it. In the days leading up to the arrival of her visitors, she had only anticipated the company of Isabelle and Liliana. She had yearned for it. But now, after last night, she somehow only thought about Kingston, and what they should say and how they should behave.

Where was he?

"In some ways, I suppose it has," she said softly.

"And so I see," said Isabelle, looking directly into her face.

Marianne took her cousin's elbow and led her toward the parlor. "I cannot imagine what you see. I am a hostess happy to welcome people into my home, grateful to have been delivered of a child in the spring, and just as grateful to have been delivered of a year of mourning."

"It was very hard on you, I suppose," Isabelle said, following along.

Marianne shrugged. "But of course. How could it have been otherwise? My Lord Lashton left me with no illusions about my life, his love for me, or his expectations for the birth of an heir. Back in the days we enjoyed in Bath, none of us would have imagined such a sad scenario."

"But I pray that now that your period of mourning has passed, you can begin to imagine again, my dear."

Marianne knew that Isabelle studied her for any sign, any indication, that there was some reason for hope. But how could she deliver what she did not yet know? She only knew there was a man in her house who engaged her as no man had ever done before. And yet they hardly knew each other. She could not yet imagine that her happiness might be bound up in his.

"You are making too much of this, Cousin Isabelle. It is only that it is Christmas. How can one not get caught up in the gaiety of the splendid season?"

Isabelle looked up at the mistletoe as they passed under it and moved into the parlor.

"I hope you are making some use of that little weed," she murmured.

"That is precisely what Josiah would . . ." Marianne began, startled. "I mean to say, Lord Kingston has already informed us superstitious females that it is a parasitic plant and hardly deserves a place of honor in our revelries. We have hung it from nearly all the doorframes on the first story."

"That sounds like the man I remember, just like his father. I daresay he also has much to reveal on the maps of military history and zoological oddities. How odd he agreed to accompany Liliana to our little hen's party."

"I am sure she coaxed him until she got her way," Marianne said, leading Isabelle to the hearth. "And he does not seem to resent it. As a matter of fact, for all his stiff ways, he is having a rather good time with little Gabriel, and it surprises me."

"Tell me more about his stiff ways," Isabelle said, very casually.

Marianne froze. Here was the part she had managed to forget in the years since their adventure in Bath. Isabelle did not mince words about things men did or what they wanted. Her idea of a suitable education for

426

her young cousins was not simply to lead them through the ancient Roman statuary, remarking on intriguing body parts. She told them precisely how they were used.

"He reads a great deal, and often retires to his bedchamber to prepare strategic information for the men at Whitehall. That is all I know, but it seems rather important."

"Does he go alone?"

"To Whitehall?"

"To his bedchamber."

This was quite enough. "I do not imagine he retrieves Gabriel from the nursery before he prepares maps of the North American continent."

The door opened behind them. Liliana ran through, scarcely able to contain her excitement, and Kingston followed, quite capable of containing his.

"Cousin Isabelle?" Liliana cried. "When did you arrive? Why were we not informed?"

"You have missed no gossip," Isabelle assured her. "I only commented on the cold and the snow, and the mistletoe. Kingston, are you here as well? What brought you down to London in this cold climate?"

Kingston smiled and straightened his back as he approached her. Marianne thought he gained two inches on his already commanding height. "The same thing that brought you out, dear cousin," he said. "The promise of good food, warm parlors, and excellent companionship."

"And yet, here you are in the company of ladies. I am sure you prefer your atlas to our society," Isabelle said playfully.

"Even bears prefer to wander from their caves on occasion, my dear. I cannot contemplate more delightful company than appears here." He took Isabelle's hand and deeply bowed. "But I must remind you that there is another gentleman present. Or there will be, after his morning nap."

"I have not seen Lord Lashton since his birth," Isabelle murmured. "But surely he is not so precocious as to provide you with the sort of conversation you desire."

She sat upon one of the sofas and her younger cousins settled around her. She patted down her elegant skirts and proceeded to hold court.

"On the contrary," said Josiah. "I am delighted with his conversation; the little chap already knows my name."

"How extraordinary," Isabelle said, her eyes on Marianne.

"Gabriel knows several words, cousin," Marianne added. "But he does seem drawn to Lord Kingston."

"I cannot imagine why," Isabelle said.

Marianne tried to discern if her cousin was being clever or censorious. What drove her to say such things? But Kingston did not seem to mind. "But, of course, you may teach him many things, so perhaps he looks to you for instruction."

This seemed to bother Kingston.

"I cannot . . . I will not presume to step in for another man. The boy does not have a father, but there are others who claim a far closer relationship," he said. "I am a mere acquaintance, present for a brief week or so of his young life."

"And yet, that could count for a good deal," Isabelle said. "But have a care, Kingston. Do not do to the boy as your father did to you."

The lady was in rare form. But then, Marianne reconsidered, this was actually customary form. And what had been utterly liberating and even reckless to a girl of nineteen would naturally seem somewhat outlandish to a widow of twenty-five. Still, Marianne had no desire to see any of her guests insulted. And Isabelle, for whatever reason, was critical of both Kingston and his father.

"A man can only do his best, Cousin Isabelle. None of us can hope for much more than that," Kingston said. "Did you have a pleasant ride into town?"

His words should have closed down Isabelle's campaign, and nearly did, but for the fact that the older woman always needed to have the last word.

"A driver can only do his best, Kingston," she said. "He is but a man, so my expectations do not run very high."

"I insist you tell me what happened in there," said Marianne, following Kingston's path to the small conservatory in the back of the house. She reached out her hand to him, but withdrew it nearly at once.

He turned soon enough to see her gesture and reached out to her. His hand was cool, and she decided he was not nearly as upset with the episode as was she.

"Do you mean last night?" he said, glancing toward the parlor. "I took a great liberty, and demanded something of you that you would not wish to give so readily. But I intended no disrespect nor to make you uncomfortable. I was only motivated by a great desire to bring you close and allow you to understand how much I admire you."

Not expecting this rather starched-up explanation for a moment of passion, Marianne could only gape at him. He did indeed look most sincere. But he looked much better than that, and she was tempted to come into the circle of his arms and see if the reality of another kiss was as keen as the memory.

Mindful of the moment, however, she closed her lips.

"I have already forgotten last night," she said primly. "I am speaking of our little interview with our mutual cousin."

"Oh, yes. There is that as well." His hand suddenly grew warm. "There is some family history, you understand. You are Isabelle's cousin as well, but quite down a different line, and may not be aware of the subtleties of our relationship." He pulled her into the winter sunshine of the conservatory, where ripe oranges and lemons burdened the thin branches of trees harbored for the season. "My father and Isabelle were to be married. The familial relationship was sufficiently distant, and, by all reports, it was truly a love match. Or so it seemed."

"Then Isabelle was jilted? I wonder how she can bear to be with you and Liliana, the children who might have been hers."

"I daresay she is up to the task," Kingston said. "But she was not jilted by my father. She walked away from him. I have sometimes wondered if her attention — particu-

431

larly toward my motherless sister — has been a form of atonement for the pain she caused him."

"But why?" Marianne asked, sitting down on a delicate iron bench and tapping the seat next to hers. Kingston promptly sat beside her, careful to leave a space between them.

"Why atonement? She may believe she roughed him up pretty badly. We are accustomed to gossip about vulnerable females, left to bear the scars when a lover changes his mind and looks elsewhere for greener pastures. But, though loathe to admit it, men are equally vulnerable and feel just as keenly the effect of a love that is scorned. My father never quite recovered from her rejection, and proved incapable of giving my mother the love she deserved."

She knew the truth of it. Though she was not en rapport with many men, she knew that a love denied was just as sad in the stables as it was in the parlor.

" 'If love diminishes, it quickly fails and rarely revives.' "

"What is that?" Marianne asked, pulled out of her reverie. "I have heard those words before."

"In the schoolroom, if not in the world, perhaps. Andreas Capellanus wrote those words in the twelfth century," Kingston said. "I scarcely realized I said them aloud."

"And yet they hold true. Isabelle must have passed her affections to another, and yet I know she never married."

"I do not know if she ever transferred her affections," Kingston said. "But she did not jilt my father for another beau. I believe she only had a complaint with him."

"I see," Marianne said slowly, vaguely wondering if her own husband's infidelities could rise to the level of a complaint.

"I suspect you do not, Marianne. Though I only have his perspective on the matter, she did not distrust him nor find him hideous nor dislike the way his valet tied his cravat. Rather, she resented his studious nature and the time he spent in his library. She argued that his interests would interfere with her pleasures."

Marianne reached out to once again take his hand in hers. He was much warmer now, but then so was the room in which they sat, and the subject they discussed. And he called her by her name, which was precisely what he'd promised the night before.

"It is much the same with you," she said softly.

He looked surprised at this pronouncement. "Our cousin has influenced you, then? You must think me a frightful bore, but I prefer to believe I am not so bad as all that." He slipped his spectacles off his nose.

"Isabelle and I may find pleasures in different things, Josiah," she said. His name sounded awkward on her lips, but she thought it held an inherent dignity and it suited him. "I do not consider a gentlemen possessed of intelligence and the spirit of inquiry to be at all boring."

He laughed, but not with any humor. "Then you are a rare woman, indeed."

They studied each other for several moments, she wondering what he saw in her, but acutely aware of what she saw in him. His dark eyes were very much the window to his soul, hinting at great depths. His straight hair seemed casually tossed with a spray falling on his forehead, but a man as deliberate as he surely expected it to look just so. And his lips, slightly apart, said nothing while revealing everything. She could hardly resist him.

Without the advantage of the mistletoe hanging above their heads, she closed the small space between them and kissed him.

He tasted of cinnamon and spice of the breakfast room, and the cold fresh air of the street. When his arm came around her and drew her closer, she knew what it was to be fully embraced, entirely bound to a person. She would have done anything he wished at the moment, no matter where they sat in her busy household.

"I could not have asked for a finer dessert, my dear Marianne," he said at last, his lips on her forehead. "I came to Parkside House expecting to savor the sweets of the Christmas season, but never imagined you would be among them."

"No more than I," she murmured. "And yet, I am not all that satisfied being compared to a savory syllabub. Can a man of your talents not offer a better metaphor?"

"One need not look to metaphors when a mother named Marianne is in possession of a splendid little son."

"Gabriel was born in the spring," she whispered.

"But I have met him, and you, for Christmas, and so it will always be."

"Please do not speak to me of 'always.' "

"It is the only wish I have, for now."

"We have only just met."

"And yet I have known you forever."

Marianne smiled and shook her head, recognizing the hopeful flirtatious steps of courtship. She looked around their warm sanctuary, noting she could soon expect sweet oranges with her tea, and moss roses on her dressing table.

"Next spring, the gardeners will bring in their wagons and remove these plants to the gardens, where they shall thrive in the sun and heat of summer. They will grow stronger and taller, and little remember the vicissitudes of winter. They only know to go on."

"But we know better," Josiah said.

Josiah surprised even himself by the events of the past day. He had come to London for no greater purpose than satisfying his sister, and yet found himself scarcely seeing to her enjoyment, nor wondering what she did. Instead, he'd found a lady and her clever little baby, both beautiful and compelling, both artlessly drawing him into their circle. This was the great thunderbolt, the passionate tradition that seemed to strike the men of his family. His father's sad experience made him believe it was something to fear and possibly avoid.

But here it was, most unexpectedly. And it was extraordinary.

"We must be off to make some purchases," said Liliana insistently. They sat at the breakfast table, and Josiah thought he would be perfectly content to remain seated here for hours. "It is but five days before Christmas and I still do not have all the gifts I require. Marianne, I know you will take us to all the best shops."

"I suppose I shall, but I have completed my shopping. I confess I started crafting little gifts for everyone once I realized my intent to invite you all here for the holiday."

"That is all well and good for those who can sketch and embroider and knit, but for those of us who lack any talents in those areas, our handcrafted gifts are not all that appreciated. I cannot imagine who would wish to receive an embroidered handkerchief from me. Marianne, you would not be able to tell if it was initialed with an 'M' or an 'N,' " said Isabelle. "But the maids would find it useful as a rag, I suppose."

Marianne's laughter filled the room. "And yet, I consider you a lady of many talents."

"Needlework is not one of them," Isabelle grumbled. "I intend to deplete my purse on Oxford Street."

"Then I shall happily assist you," said Marianne. "While widows must shop as well as any woman, I simply have not gone out into society this past year. It shall be a great treat."

"And what of you, Cousin Josiah?" Isabelle asked. "Will you accompany us?"

He would have accompanied Marianne anywhere, but the prospect of shopping with three ladies was daunting. "Would my presence not defeat the purpose of this expedition?" he asked. "Do I presume too much to imagine I may be the recipient of a few of those purchases? I daresay you will all do very well without me."

"Have you already decided on gifts, Josiah?" Liliana asked pointedly. "You cannot be without them, for it is much more noble to give than to receive. And you do not have Marianne's excuse of being able to make anything."

"You can understand why I always thought boys should be tutored in needlework," Isabelle said.

It was Liliana's turn to laugh. "I am sure they will be, when girls are taught Greek and Latin, and how to use a sextant."

"Gentlemen learn some handiwork skills, of course. Some are great painters or musicians, but a man can whittle little figures or write some lines of verse," Josiah said, feeling a need to defend all mankind.

"And yet you have none of those skills, brother," said Liliana, still very much amused.

"I am sure Lord Kingston has other talents," Marianna interceded.

Josiah looked across the table at her, and thought she looked remarkably refreshed, despite their late evening the night before.

"So I have been told," he said softly.

His words silenced the conversation for several moments.

"Well then, it is settled," said Isabelle, always impatient with silence. "We three ladies will venture out on a shopping expedition, while you attempt to carve a crèche and all the attendant animals for our dinner table. Would you like to borrow my knife?" She held out her butter knife which he accepted with some ceremony.

"I will do my best," he said.

"It is indeed settled," Liliana said. "Will young Gabriel come with us?"

"Leave him with Cousin Josiah, dear Marianne," Isabelle said. "Perhaps he will learn some of the manly arts from his older relation."

"We are only distantly related, you recall," Josiah murmured. He ran the blunt knife blade along the tablecloth, creating a crease that looked something like a map of the undulating course of the Thames.

For several hours that afternoon, Marianne was unburdened by the cares that she had borne like an unyielding weight for over a year. She already knew that many young widows were plagued by financial hardships, but that had never been her concern. She was left with more than sufficient funds to live in the style to which she had become accustomed at Parkside House. She was only left without a husband.

As such, some ladies no longer considered her welcome in their society, particularly because of the nature of Lashton's scandalous death. Some, aware of her somewhat liberated status as a widow, chose not to have her around their husbands and married brothers. But whatever their reasons, no one invited her out for a walk in the park, or an excursion to the shops.

"This is rather cunning," said Liliana. She held out her hands for Isabelle and Marianne to see what she found.

"It is a rock," Isabelle said scornfully. "And one without the distinction of being a diamond or a ruby. You can save yourself several pounds and retrieve one from the banks of the Serpentine, my dear. This is without value."

"It is a fossil," Marianne said, pointing to the spiraling pattern of an ancient shell. "It is the sort one might find along the beach at Eastbourne. I recently saw sketches of particularly notable specimens."

Isabelle looked at her two young cousins and shook her head in mock despair. Then again, perhaps it was real despair. "And for this, I brought the two of you to Bath that summer years ago? Did you not learn anything of the social graces?"

Marianne glanced at Liliana, who could hardly contain her laughter.

"As I recall, you instructed us on the subject of how to please a gentleman, dear cousin. I do not know whom Liliana has in mind to surprise with this trophy on Christmas morning, but I should not be surprised to learn it is her brother. He would prize this above rubies."

Isabelle flicked her fingernails dismissively against the rock. "You seem to know much about that gentleman," she said, "and yet I thought you were hardly acquainted."

"We are not, and I do not know very much. But he is a bit of a naturalist, and Liliana's discovery of this fossil in this odd curiosity shop just confirms what I already believe."

"Josey will appreciate this more than a knitted scarf or warm stockings," Liliana said.

"Oh dear," Marianne said. "I knitted a scarf."

"I am not surprised," Liliana laughed, "for what can be more impersonal than a scarf? But he will surely appreciate it on his long walks through the King's Stone property, keeping him warm while he pokes around in burrows and overturns rocks."

"Like this one," Isabelle said, picking up Liliana's treasure. She placed it in her basket, and then her gaze returned to Marianne. "But knowing him as you do now, what would you have made for the man?"

"That hardly seems a fair question, since I have no idea what he already possesses. But I might have made him a fine felt case for his spectacles."

"That would prove even more useless than a rock, my dear, for he wears his spectacles all the time," Isabelle scoffed.

Marianne knew she was being tested somehow, and decided her companions would believe what they wished to believe, no matter what she said.

"No, that is not quite correct. He removes them when he feels at his ease, I suspect, and certainly when close scrutiny of print is not required," Marianne said. "In watching him in those rare moments, it seems to me that his spectacles allow him a barrier against the intrusions of others, against the trivialities of our everyday lives, which do not interest him all that much. Perhaps, if he had a case in which to protect his spectacles, he would venture out from behind that barrier more often."

"Perhaps he finds other temptations, as well," Isabelle said. "Well, I daresay we might find a nice little leather case somewhere about this shop."

Liliana nodded approvingly. "Oh, yes. Would you like to purchase one for Josey?"

"I shall, for Marianne makes a most compelling argument," Isabelle said. "And you, my crafty cousin, can give your knitted scarf to another, and present Kingston with a rock as well. They are certainly available in abundance. He will either be delighted, or simply appalled. I suspect the latter." She glanced around the shop.

"I have already made the scarf," Marianne said. "You may present it to him if you like."

"You may use it to wrap up your rock. But Kingston requires something for his spectacles. I shall purchase it myself, if you will not." Isabelle glanced around the shop and picked up a small hoop. "And here is a perfect gift for little Gabriel. Or it shall be, once he manages to take his first steps."

"Or run," said Marianne, remembered her own games with a hoop when she was a child.

"But it is always wise to start slowly," Isabelle argued. "Move at a pace with which you are comfortable, and then proceed to run with it."

By the time they returned to Parkside House, her companions had drifted off to sleep in their warm carriage, and Marianne was convinced that her cousin was just as inclined to be as dictatorial as ever. She parsed each of Isabelle's sentences, groping for some meaning, some direction, and walked into her house believing that Isabelle regretted her long-ago rejection of a good and worthy man, a man who had loved her. Perhaps in realizing her error, she wished for her younger cousins to learn something from her experience. She did not profess to have high expectations of any man, and yet Marianne sensed that her words might be hiding a deeper pain.

Marianne knew something about that. Having been burned so cruelly by Lashton, did she still have any interest in a beau? How much would such a man complicate her life, and that of her little son? Was she not perfectly satisfied being a young widow, able to dictate the calendar of her days and do as she wished?

But if there was such a man to dissuade her out of her own satisfaction, what would he look like? Oh, certainly, one could have nothing to complain about Kingston's appearance, with his dramatic contrast of fair skin and dark hair, and his commanding presence. But she was rather more concerned with how he would look in her house, at her table each night, in her bedroom.

She sucked in her breath, distracted with the thought.

"Are you well?" Liliana asked. She blinked into the dim light.

"Of course. I am only looking at the sky and wondering if we are to have more snowfall."

Liliana blinked again. "If we are snowed in, then we shall be very cozy and comfortable in your lovely home, Marianne. It shall not be much of a deprivation."

Marianne reached the same conclusion. To be snowbound with such a one as Kingston would not be a deprivation at all. It would be divine.

Together, the three women entered the house, the servants following with all their purchases. Marianne heard one of the men jokingly ask another if a particular package had rocks in it, and she stifled a laugh. Indeed it did, for the fossil was not the only natural specimen they'd found in the shops. Liliana and Isabelle could hardly wait to retire, and Marianne waved them upstairs, simply content to be home.

Gradually, the sound of Parkside House settled around her, and she realized there were unaccustomed noises coming from the parlor. It took a moment to recognize them for what they were, and she proceeded in their direction.

Suddenly, it occurred to her that while she was still attempting to visualize Kingston in her life and home, she was already accustomed to the sound of him.

"What on earth!" Marianne said as she opened the door. Her infant son sat on the rug, wrapped in a roll of paper, holding a chalk marker. Above him, Josiah — though he seemed more like Joe at the moment — was pointing out something in a large book. Both his jacket and his spectacles were off, and one sleeve was rolled up nearly to his elbow.

In the corner, near the fire, Mrs. Bell snored loudly in her chair.

"That is precisely the point, Lady Lashton," said Josiah. He glanced at the sleeping Mrs. Bell and amended his comment, "Marianne."

"A baby should not be holding anything with a point, Josiah," she admonished him, though Gabriel looked quite content. There was a line of dark chalk across his forehead and his little white shirt looked like he had played in a dustbin. But he appeared happier than she had ever seen him.

"The only damage he might do is to his garments. Mrs. Bell did not seem so very concerned."

"Yes, I can see that," Marianne frowned. "At the moment, Mrs. Bell would not seem to be concerned if the house burned down around us."

"I should wake her if such a thing happened," he reassured her.

But she was not reassured.

"Gabriel is a baby, Josiah. He needs direction, guidance, not a free hand with a stick of carbon. Next, I will find scribblings on the nursery walls, or paint spilled across my rugs."

"That might not be such a bad thing," Josiah mused.

"This, coming from a man who prefers the safety of his chamber to the rigors of Oxford Street? Shall I raise my child to be a bohemian free spirit?"

Josiah thought about that for several moments, while Marianne wondered what had come over him. Was he not usually the most staid and proper of all men? Did he not say he would eschew socializing in favor of retreating to his books and papers in his chamber?

But did he not kiss her?

Indeed, he had not seemed very proper then. His assault on her senses had been unexpected and quite delightful.

"This is not quite what it seems, Marianne," he said at last.

She looked up, startled, thinking he referred to their brief intimacies.

"What is that, Josiah?"

Now it was his turn to look surprised. "Why, our little endeavor here in your parlor. I have been giving Gabriel some instruction, as I assured Mrs. Bell I would."

"The dear woman must be more easily convinced than I," Marianne said, wondering how and why her orderly little life was suddenly falling into disarray. Even her growing belief that Josiah cared for her might be shaky. Because it suddenly seemed possible that Josiah might want her son more than he wanted her.

"We are making maps," Josiah uttered, as some great pronouncement.

The thought was too absurd. "Maps? Maps? Gabriel has scarcely been beyond Mayfair. He would not know the Thames from his bath water. What might he learn of maps?"

"One could only hope," Josiah said. "He might learn a good deal. Perhaps I will set him on a course to become a great cartographer. I shall introduce him to important men at Whitehall someday."

This was outside of enough. Marianne looked behind her, and settled in a deep chair. Gabriel started to crawl toward her, ripping through the paper that was entwined about his little body.

"I would be happy enough to see him take his first steps," she said, holding out her arms, and pulling Gabriel into her lap. At once, she saw a streak of charcoal on her pink dress. "But to what end? Why start so soon, especially as you may never see him again?"

She knew she was distracted, and she knew she would have liked for Josiah to welcome her into his arms as she just did Gabriel. But she did not think she imagined the brief expression of pain on Josiah's face.

"I gave the matter some thought," he said, recovering quickly. "After our breakfast conversation of crafting our own gifts, I realized I had very few skills in that direction. I do not whittle, I am not a blacksmith, and I certainly do not possess any knitting ability. But I have some skill with a compass, and I do know how to make a map. I thought it might make a fine offering for Christmas, and I thought Gabriel might make one, as well."

There was something beneath his words, something he was trying to tell her. He looked more concerned than triumphant, more intent than one would be over creating a simple sketch of lines and places.

"Is it best to give it to one who is lost?" she asked, simply, though realizing she was opening herself up to vulnerability.

"I suppose it would be a gift, in that case. But a map is also a tribute when something is found, particularly something one never knew existed in the first place."

"One must venture far to such a place. To the New World or to Australia. I understand Lord Merriam has found a small island in the Atlantic Ocean."

"One may travel far, but not necessarily by ship," he said solemnly, and took her hand. He studied her palm and ran a warm finger over her lifeline.

"Are you also a fortune teller, Josiah?" she asked, quietly. Lulled by her tone, Gabriel settled against her breast and closed his eyes.

"Would that I were," he said. He caressed her palm in a series of circles and then traced the thin blue lines at her wrist. Pushing up the wide woolen sleeve of her gown, he slowly burned a path up the length of her forearm to the crook of her elbow and pressed against her pulse with two fingers. "I would then know where this path would lead."

Marianne's heart thumped along at a breathless pace. "Where would you like it to lead?" she asked.

"To your heart," he said, in a voice that did not sound like his at all.

Marianne's eyes never left his face. Shifting Gabriel against her, she reached out to take his hand and brought it to her breast. Her garments were thick and warm, but seemed to not exist at all. His touch was both familiar and achingly wonderful.

He felt it as well; that much was certain. Slowly, so close that she saw double, his head dipped toward her, and his lips parted.

"Oh, heavens, what am I about?' Mrs. Bell cried out from her corner. "And where is my little boy?"

Josiah straightened and took a step backward. "Your little boy has drifted off to sleep, Mrs. Bell. He is quite safe in his mother's arms."

"And here I am with Christmas greens strewn about me, quite forgetting myself. And what are we to do with this paper?

451

Forgive me, my lady!"

Marianne cleared her throat. She felt as if she hadn't spoken in a week. "There is no harm done, Mrs. Bell, and I know how exhausting one little boy can be." She glanced up at Josiah. "Big boys, as well."

Josiah studied her for a moment, and she could read the amusement in his eyes. Yes, she was quite prepared to be exhausted.

Mrs. Bell scrambled to her feet. "I must clean this at once!"

"Leave it be, Mrs. Bell," said Josiah. "I intend to go through it all and salvage what I want."

"May I not help?"

Marianne wished nothing more than for Mrs. Bell to leave them. "Do take Gabriel, Mrs. Bell. That is all that is required. He may very well sleep into the evening, but if he awakens, he most desperately requires a bath."

"So do you, my lady, if I may be so bold to say so." Mrs. Bell spoke with the familiarity of being an intimate in the family. She peered at Marianne curiously. "The little master has left his imprint on your beautiful face and all the way up your arm."

Marianne glanced at Josiah as she lifted her awkward bundle into his nurse's arms. Mrs. Bell happily cooed over her charge and whisked him out of the room.

"I cannot put these charcoal smudges to Gabriel's credit, Josiah. Your hands are just as chalked as his, and covered a good deal more territory."

"I would have wished to cover more, but for Mrs. Bell's presence. But, as she says, an imprint has already been made."

"Would a cartographer say that you have staked a claim?" she asked coolly, reminding herself how she had been burned before. Doubts suddenly overcame her.

"A cartographer might, but I would argue that I would never venture where I am not wanted." He caught her hand and pulled her to her feet. Together, they stood in the rustling papers and discarded Christmas garlands.

"This is too soon, Josiah. I would lie to you if I said I am not tempted to some indiscretion, but it is just over a year since Marcus's death. I am not simply a widow, but a mother of a young lord. My behavior necessarily affects his reputation as well."

"I would not wish harm on either of you, for I have come to care too much about what happens. You are indeed a young widow. But he is also a fine little fellow in his own right, a boy any man would want for his son."

Marianne hastily brushed tears from her eyes.

"And yet his own father was not overly concerned to live to see his birth. He certainly anticipated it, and made it clear a boy should not be named Marcus, for he already knew too many little boys with that name." Marianne wondered if she ought to say more, such as how many of those boys resembled her late husband.

Josiah looked perplexed. "But as to that, there surely are as many Gabriels as there are Marcuses in the world."

Marianne reached up to cup his jaw, rubbing her thumb gently against the rough skin. He really was the dearest man, and in a surprising way, somewhat of an innocent.

She cleared her throat. "I believe he referred to his other sons, largely unacknowledged, born to women he had no intention of ever seeing again. A man of honor would have staked a claim, but I now know that my husband was not — and had no intention of being — a man of honor."

"I see," he said quietly.

"We thus have evidence of one not caring enough. But you have just spoken of caring too much. Is such a thing possible?"

"I do not truly know, Marianne, for I am, most unexpectedly, traveling without a map to guide me. I shall need a compass." He smiled and leaned closer.

She reached behind his neck and guided his lips toward hers. She would be his compass, and anything else she desired.

"Marianne Westlyme is my very best friend, Josey," Liliana said, rather sternly.

Josiah looked up from his papers, wondering why Liliana thought it necessary to make this pronouncement. "I can certainly see why this is so, as she is a lady of wit and intelligence, capable of finding pleasure in many things."

"That is precisely the reason why I must speak to you," Liliana continued.

"Ought we not find pleasure in this season? Surely there is nothing inappropriate about it."

"There is nothing inappropriate at all. It is only that you are not one to usually find pleasure in charades and gift giving and culinary treats only prepared this time of year. I suspect that but for the snow occasionally interfering with a trip to the Royal Society or British Museum, you pay no heed to Christmas at all," Liliana said.

"That is not altogether true, my dear. Did we not roast chestnuts last year?"

"Yes, we did, but in February. A few weeks

after that, you gave me a pair of pearl earrings."

Josiah did not doubt she was correct, but
preferred not to look entirely foolish.

"I believe they were for your birthday, and
just delivered a bit early in the season."

"Oh, yes, I suppose that is possible, even
though my birthday is in August," she said,
and put her hands on her hips. He knew a
challenge when he saw one. "What, then,
did you give me for Christmas?"

He did not know, and wondered if he
could resurrect the memory. "What did you
give me?" he asked.

"A marble globe from Florence. It sits on
your desk at King's Stone," she answered
quickly.

"Ah yes, I have been meaning to discuss
that with you. It is not a very exacting study.
All of the Iberian Peninsula seems to be one
country, which might bring joy to Bonaparte, but it is sure to make the Portuguese
upset."

Liliana glowered at him for a moment. "It
is intended to be a paperweight, not a
navigational device. And, in any case, you
have not answered my question. If the earrings were for my birthday, then I believe
you did not give me anything at all for
Christmas."

Josiah had a feeling she was right, and since he could remember none of it, that feeling would have to stand as the truth. But he still did not understand why this should be an issue just now, and why it mattered. Those were very nice earrings, he recalled, purchased from a jeweler in York.

"For all you accuse me of being indifferent to Christmas, I do know that it is often said that it is better to give a gift than receive one," he added.

"Yes, that is precisely the trouble," said Liliana and waited for him to puzzle it out.

He could not.

"What is the trouble?" he asked. He might not have articulated the words before, but they already echoed in his head.

Liliana gave a great sigh, and dropped into a nearby chair. Her expression was one of pure exasperation and he was quite familiar with it.

"Marianne is my best friend. Though we have not seen each other as often as I would like, we are frequent correspondents and understand each other very well." She picked up a leaf of paper from his desk and examined the little patterns he had sketched there. "She has endured much this past year."

"And seems to have emerged the stronger for it."

"That is a platitude comparable to the justification of not giving one a gift, dear brother. One does not need a scoundrel of a husband to develop strength of character." She dropped the paper onto the desk. "I do not believe pain is a necessary trial, and yet my good friend has experienced it in abundance."

Josiah nodded, thinking of Lord Lashton's cavalier attitude toward his wife and unborn son. The pain that man had inflicted was unnecessary and, as such, particularly cruel. Having now been struck by the thunderbolt himself, he understood that — and the disappointed hopes of his own father — all too keenly.

"I would not have her endure more," Liliana continued.

"This seems a rather perambulating way to remind me to purchase Christmas presents," Josiah said.

"There is more, Josey. You know there is. I sense it as acutely as I smell the candle wax in this room." She leaned forward, so close that he could sniff her lavender cologne above the aroma of the candles. "You are trifling with her affections. She has not gone out in society very much all this year, and

458

you are surely the first gentleman to be a visitor at Parkside House in some time. When I asked you to accompany me, I wanted nothing more than for you to have company for Christmas, and I fully expected you to spend all your waking and sleeping hours in your chamber, as is your habit. I did not expect you to join us for every meal, and play with Gabriel, and entertain us each evening."

"Shall I return to my old habits, then?" he asked, thinking his own sister thought him an old drudge.

She narrowed her eyes. "No, I rather like this new Josiah, no matter how unexpected he is. But if you are only exerting this effort in the spirit of the season, I am cautioning you to have a care near Marianne Westlyme. She is apt to take this attention most seriously and then will once again be pitied for a woman of foolish hopes."

So that was it. Because she was so long accustomed to his indifference to society and only his occasional association with ladies, Liliana could not believe him a credible suitor.

"What if I tell you that I think your dear friend the most excellent lady of my acquaintance. I have no intentions of trifling with her now, or in the future. Indeed, I am even making her a Christmas gift," he declared.

Liliana nearly slipped off her chair. "Are you indeed telling me that, brother?"

He caught her arm to hold her steady. "I am."

They studied each other for several moments and he thought how very much she looked like their mother. Liliana should have had a whole string of suitors by now, but for his own reluctance to bring her out in society. He must remedy that oversight.

"Then I will not torment you if you do not create or purchase a Christmas gift for me this season, Josey. For the prospect of my only brother and my best friend finding joy with each other is better than any gift I can imagine."

CHAPTER FOUR

"I would have liked to have had a child," murmured Isabelle. "A little girl, of course, and one who shared my features. A talented singer and a fair watercolorist. I would have been quite content."

Marianne caught Gabriel before he slipped off her lap, and laughed. "A baby is just as likely to look like his or her father, and one has little say in the matter. No matter one's hopes, one cannot request a little boy or girl, or insist on a child's talents. We take what God gives us and are grateful."

"Therein lies the problem. One requires a husband for the business, but it seems a great injustice if the child resembles him. After all, the mother has carried the burden."

Marianne reflected that her cousin sounded very much like someone who had never loved nor particularly cared for anyone other than herself. A little girl in her

461

own image would have been the true realization of her self-adoration. Briefly,
Marianne wondered if that long-ago adventure in Bath had not come from simple
generosity, but of Isabelle's desire to assess
how much her young cousins could be
molded in her style. Envisioning herself in
Isabelle's favorite yellow gown, Marianne
shook her head to dispel the picture.

"But what if you love the father of your
child, Isabelle?" she responded. "You must
have been happy with what you saw in him,
so why would you not be delighted with his
miniature?"

"I did love a man once, and he told me he
loved me most passionately in return. But
he had a good many interests that did not
involve me, and I become somewhat jealous
when his attentions strayed elsewhere. I
rejected him before we reached the altar,
left him bruised and in pain, but never
found the man to match him." Isabelle
sighed. "I have spent years trying to convince myself that I made the right choice,
and now it is certainly too late for me to
change the path of my life. The men I am
apt to meet are settled in their ways and
only desire a lady to serve their needs. I
confess it is only a real child I would wish
for, not a full-grown one who demands my

attention and tells me what I ought to do."

Marianne thought the description suited her late husband rather well. Marcus had been terribly irresponsible, neglecting nearly all his obligations, but that did not stop him from advising her on matters ranging from housekeeping to what theater productions were most edifying. Truly, now that she thought about it, he was rather boorish.

He had been rather handsome, however.

"But you seem to have a greater talent for loving. I would not have thought so when I brought you to Bath and you rebuffed the attentions of at least three gentlemen," Isabelle mused. "You were the envy of the other girls."

Marianne looked up in surprise. "I do not recall attracting any particular notice, either from the young ladies or gentlemen."

"You may have been as oblivious to attention as is Liliana's brother."

Marianne knew that any bit of information she imparted, any observation at all, would be caught by Isabelle like a large ball and she would run with it. And yet it seemed profoundly ungenerous to withhold something that would — she believed — give her cousin some pleasure and allow her to take all the credit for arranging it. An announcement was certainly premature, but it would not be untoward to suggest that she and Josiah had come to an understanding of friendship. In any case, their companions could hardly miss it. Isabelle seemed to already sense it on the morning of her arrival, before Marianne came to believe it herself.

But what did Isabelle sense? It was not unusual for two people in close circumstances to become friends. But it was more than that, certainly. Marianne could think of little else but the man who was a guest in her home, and this went beyond any friendship she ever experienced. Indeed, it went beyond any feelings she had for her late husband. And yet, she believed she had loved Marcus, in her fashion.

And as for Josiah, one did not fall in love with a man in a matter of days. It was the stuff of theater, of comedy more than tragedy. And yet, Romeo and Juliet had experienced a lifetime of love and marriage and death in the space of a week.

"Lord Kingston is not as oblivious as one may think," Marianne hinted, hoping that would be enough, for now.

"Do you mean, Kingston is not entirely dedicated to his maps and little chunks of rock?" Isabelle asked, feigning amazement.

Marianne was not prepared to concede all

that much. "One can be absolutely devoted to one's work, and still find time for diversions."

"You are wiser than I was at your age." Isabelle nodded. "And yet, one wishes to be a good deal more to a man than a diversion. The question is: would you be happy accepting something less than the entire man?"

It was an honest question, and deserved an honest answer.

"A woman ought to be happy to have captured the affections of a man of many pursuits and facets," Marianne responded.

"Were you happy with Lashton?" Isabelle asked.

"For a time. You must know I married him most willingly. I thought I loved him," said Marianne. "But it is one thing to love a man whose interests are bookish, and quite another to love a man whose interests are entirely of the flesh. And not necessarily the flesh of his own wife."

Isabelle remained silent for some time. For the first time, Marianne wondered what her cousin's life had been like after rejecting Josiah's father, if she'd had other lovers, if she'd had offers of marriage. Now that her pale skin was wrinkled and her eyes no longer sparkled, did she dream of the children who would have cared for her in her old age?

Marianne looked down at Gabriel, now sleeping peacefully in her arms. When did innocence and hope give way to resigned acceptance and the wistful acknowledgement of what might have been?

"You are a more generous woman than I, dear Marianne. And one blessed with the opportunity of a second chance."

Marianne could not pretend she did not know what Isabelle meant. "Very few people would say that a widow of twenty-five with an infant born after his father's death is living a blessed life."

"But I am. You will not be a widow forever."

"I may never marry again."

"But you might. Indeed, I predict you shall," said Isabelle. "My great love was not as devoted to his papers and books as I believed, for it did not take him very long to settle on another wife. She was a sweet lady, a kind and tolerant one, who took him for all his passions."

"She was your cousin, I believe. They married and had two children."

"Of course. And I see in the son the strengths of the father, and know he is the sum of many, many parts. He is a splendid man, but I am far too old for him." Isabelle sighed, and leaned forward to pat Gabriel on his head. "But you are not, my dear Marianne."

"You would approve the connection, then?" Marianne asked.

Isabelle laughed. "Do you need my approval? Of course you do not. You are a widow of independent means, and can do whatever you please. But I confess I would very much enjoy the connection. It will be quite convenient to have several of my cousins under one roof. I shall save considerably on christening gifts if two cousins share one child."

"Is that it, then?" Marianne asked, confirming what she already knew about Isabelle's self-interest. And yet, she now understood that there was a good deal more to her cousin's sensibility than was often revealed. Nevertheless, she could already imagine Isabelle telling people that her cousins had entered into a marriage of convenience — her own convenience, of course.

Neither of them said anything for some minutes, and the only sound in the room was that of Gabriel's regular breathing. Marianne guessed that, as always, Isabelle would have the last word on the matter.

"Of course it is not all, my dear girl," Isabelle said at last. "I feel that you have a second chance at joy, at a love that will endure. You will have a man who deserves you, for he does everything with passion and commitment."

Marianne did not know whether she should laugh or cry. "I think there are few who would say that Lord Kingston is a man of passion. Indeed, his reputation suggests quite the opposite."

Isabelle rose to her feet, as if her chair could no longer hold her. "Then those people would be quite wrong. Passion is not reserved for those who are quick to challenge others to a duel, or who run off in the middle of the night to Gretna. Passion can burn deeply and remain alight for an eternity. I made the error when I was young and stupid, and I have suffered because of it. You are still young, but not at all stupid, and know the truth of it." Isabelle walked to the window, and tossed aside the heavy drapery to look out into the darkening day. "Do you find him a passionate man?"

Marianne blushed like a girl in her first season. She would be as honest with Isabelle as Isabelle had been with her. "Yes. I know he is. And even worse, I am a more passionate woman when I am with him."

Isabelle came toward her. "That is not worse, Marianne. That is ever so much better."

Josiah breathed in deeply, wondering why King's Stone was never blessed with the sweet aroma that invaded every room of Parkside House. Within the walls of both homes there were undercurrents of smoke, to be sure, and his own cook had as generous a hand at cinnamon and nutmeg as did Marianne's. But there was something else, something fresh and clean, and quite unexpected in a house in one of the busiest cities in the world.

It made him think of the Christmases he'd enjoyed as a boy, when his parents opened the great house to the whole neighborhood, and friends and family reveled until all hours of the night. He remembered sitting in the musicians' gallery, his legs dangling through the banister, watching the guests at the King's Stone annual ball. No one ever seemed to notice him there and he was able to spy with some impunity, noting lovers exchanging stolen kisses and passing small gifts to each other.

Now he knew that he, too, was in love.

A week ago, he would have laughed off such a thought, believing the grand tradition of loving at first sight a legend fostered by his disappointed father to justify his behavior toward Josiah's mother. He, himself, had never before succumbed to such a raw emotion, and doubted he ever would. And yet here he was, absolutely enamored of a lady he scarcely knew, and a little boy who was not his.

His eyes alighted on the blasted parasitic mistletoe, remembering the kiss that seemed to set his future in motion. The little cluster of leaves was framed by long boughs of fir and holly that spread across the parlor to the mantel, over the modest landscape paintings, and to the line of windows. It was the greenery, he suddenly realized. For all that King's Stone was surrounded by forest and neatly cultivated trees and shrubs, rarely were their fresh leaves brought within in recent years. He wondered when he and Liliana had ended that holiday ritual. Undoubtedly, when they had ended all the others.

He did not know he missed the sweet scent of greenery until he came to Parkside House.

But he also did not know he missed the heart-thumping passion of love until he came there, either.

"Josiah? May I interrupt you?" called

Marianne, before she entered the room. And then, when he did not answer, she stepped within. "Ah, I see you are contemplating something very seriously."

Indeed he was.

He looked down at the papers before him, and wondered why he had thought a consideration of the flora of the Leeward Islands to be more worthy of his time than an afternoon in Marianne's company.

"Have you ever thought to bring knotweed into the house?" he asked, artlessly. "The Japanese mix it with their tea leaves, and it has a fine aroma."

"I have some growing in the garden and it threatens to overgrow its way into the hall. Are you about to tell me how odious a plant it truly is, nearly as vile as the mistletoe?" she asked.

He thought, perhaps, one of the reasons he loved her was because she never missed a heartbeat in picking up a conversation, no matter how irrelevant it was to the present circumstances.

"I do not recall calling the mistletoe vile," he argued, guessing that she would recall it perfectly. "In fact, I have rather come to like it."

"Is that so?" she asked. He knew her well enough to know this was an invitation, of sorts. "And what has made you revise your sentiments?"

Josiah stood, and smoothed down his tweed trousers before he approached her. "I believe you already know the answer to that."

She remained where she was, close to the door and the insidious little plant that dangled above it. Yet, he only saw her. Until the moment when their lips met and he saw nothing at all.

The clean and alluring scent of Marianne was also lacking from King's Stone, from his own parlor and from his bed, and he wondered how quickly he might remedy that situation. She would bring all that was fresh and good to his quiet estate and make his house a home. She would be his wife. He brought his arms around her and held her close, embracing all that she was and all that he loved.

But her hands were restless, and set out on a path to explore the features of his face, his hair, and his neck, while tugging blindly at his cravat. Soon they were pressed against his chest, as light and soft as mourning doves.

"Tell me more about the knotweed," she said. Or, at least, he thought she said that. Her warm tongue licked the skin over his collarbone, revealed by his loosened cravat. "And about the flora of Japan and why it seems to thrive in our rainy, smoky climate."

Josiah gasped, reveling in her powers of temptation, by which the allures of her body heightened a conversation that no other lovers would find seductive. Even in his distracted state, he knew she was the one woman for him.

"I prefer to speak of the fauna of England, and their particular mating habits," he said, and then pulled her gently away, so that his lips could find hers. She opened to him and edged one leg between his.

"How do they begin?" she asked, after getting the reaction from him that she sought. Josiah reminded himself that she was a lady of some experience, and was enjoying that experience as much as he was.

He answered her by demonstrating some possibilities, all of which seemed to appeal rather strongly to her, and had him wondering how quickly he might manage to deliver her to his chamber.

Suddenly, she pulled away. "Thank you for illuminating that for me, Lord Kingston," she said, a bit too loudly.

He reached for his cravat, wondering what on earth she was talking about.

She turned to the right. "Your brother has

just rearranged the mistletoe, Liliana, though we know he finds it an odious little parasite. One of the maids must have put it in disarray while dusting."

"Indeed," said Liliana. "Josey is not always predictable in his likes and dislikes. Did the maid also take a broom to your silk tie, dear brother? It seems to be in disarray."

Liliana grinned like a servant who was tipped a guinea instead of a shilling, and immediately disarmed any argument he could possibly make.

"Is it?" he said softly. "I shall find Donovan at once." He started to walk from the room.

"Did Marianne tell you about the guests this evening?"

"We never reached that point in our discussion," Marianne said, and shrugged.

"Undoubtedly," said Liliana. "You were far too busy with the mistletoe to mention it. As it turns out, the Wheldons are in town. Marianne and I met their daughter years ago in Bath, and we shall renew the relationship tonight."

"Are they also Isabelle's cousins?" he asked, already dreading an evening of frivolous conversation, when he'd prefer to do nothing but spend time with Marianne.

"Not even Isabelle can have so many

familial connections. But I recall the Wheldons have much musical talent and they have promised to entertain us," Liliana said.

"They are also quite accomplished at charades," added Marianne. "It seems to be just the thing to add to our pleasure in this last night before Christmas Eve."

"I am sure we could have thought of one or two other things," Josiah said, before turning and walking into the hall. He was certain both ladies knew precisely what he meant.

At the time Marianne extended the invitation to the talented Wheldons, she was certain the family would provide a congenial evening of entertainment. Aside from a few Christmas carols in halting German, sung by Isabelle as she remembered hearing them from Princess Caroline, there had been very little singing in the house. And other than trying to understand what Gabriel meant when he cried or fussed, there were few charades. But the Wheldons' concert went on a bit longer than was cheerfully tolerable, and by the time it was over, she was too exhausted to play anything at all. Nevertheless, the dinner went fairly well and everything remained cordial.

But Marianne could think of little else but

the taste of Josiah's skin, and the way her leg had been held tight between his.

Indeed, the happiest moment of the night was when Anne Wheldon uttered a great dramatic sigh and announced it was time to return to Edgware Road. Marianne's protests were polite but not insistent and she was delighted to wave them off in advance of an approaching snowstorm. Otherwise, they might have been singing all through the night.

And now, in the silence and solitude of her room, came the second happiest moment. She need not do anything but dream about her lover. A year ago, only recently widowed, and soon to be a mother, she could not imagine feeling the sweet aching pangs of pleasure again, the heat that came unbidden when she awoke in the midst of a dark night. She believed she had known love with Marcus, but after her great disillusionment with him, she doubted she would ever lose herself in such a manner again.

But here she was, undeniably and passionately in love. It was unexpected. It was impossible. It was divine. She studied herself in her looking glass, wondering if something had changed in her appearance from last week to this, and if others recognized something that she did not. And indeed, there was something: she did not see Gabriel's mother so much as she saw someone who might be Josiah's wife. She could only hope Josiah saw the same thing, for he had been spending as much time with her little boy, playing with paper and chalk, as he had spent with her.

She was startled out of her reverie by the sound of a scratch at her door, so soft she thought it might be one of the house cats trying to get in. Indeed, one of the tabbies might prove to be a good companion on this cold night and she started toward the door. But before she got there, it opened with a boldness no cat ever managed.

"Josiah!" Marianne said, sounding more surprised than she truly was. She knew why he was here, and she wanted him. "Have you lost your way? Do you require a map?" She smiled.

He studied her for a few moments, and she regretted her teasing words. It was not quite an appropriate welcome for someone who took every word uttered by another so seriously. He looked like a man who had been wrestling with a problem, which did nothing to diminish his attraction. In fact, with his hair mussed and the dark shadow of a beard shading his jaw, he also looked like a man who had spent more hours in the field than in his study.

He took a step toward her, and closed the door behind him.

"I believe I have, at long last, found my way. And it is not a map I require," he said.

"Come to me," Marianne murmured, but in fact, it was she who walked into his open arms.

She was home at last, warm, protected and loved. Josiah held her as if some great storm was raging within the walls, instead of without, and his hands glanced over her shoulders and her arms and her back, as if reassuring himself that she was still with him. She was, entirely, and the sensation was powerful enough to make her knees grow weak.

"Come to my bed," she said. "I want you there with me."

Josiah's knees proved to be steadier than hers, for he promptly scooped her up in his arms. Her bed was no more than ten feet from where they stood, but it seemed to take forever to get there. He set her carefully down on the counterpane, and hesitated only a moment before he pulled off his jacket and leaned over her supine body.

She set to work on his cravat, a task with which she was comfortably familiar. He pulled her gown off her shoulders, a sensation with which she was not. But suddenly, her arms were free and thus capable of bringing him down beside her.

He was a large man, but as careful in his lovemaking as he seemed to be in everything else. He waited on her responses, on her willingness to ascend the same crests as he. But once he understood that she was as ready a partner as any woman could be, he dared to risk everything. And to her, he was everything, for it had been too long since she had been able to give herself entirely over to another person.

The snow and wind relentlessly stormed the streets of London, but they were nothing to the passions aroused in one lady's bedchamber, between her and her lover.

Marianne awoke to the sounds of bustling activity in her house, beyond the door. Icy rain now battered against the window and the bare branches of an ancient oak brushed against the sill. The fire had died down and her face and lower legs were chilled in the cold air. But when she reached to cover herself with her eiderdown quilt, she realized most of her body was beneath something a good deal heavier.

She turned her head into a warm shoulder that smelled faintly of sandalwood and more of Josiah.

She had not forgotten him, or their love-making. She was only uncertain if it had been a dream. But here he was beside her, his body entwined with hers, and his warm breath caressing her loosened hair. And the reality was even better than a dream, for his naked body, all muscle and firm flesh, looked better than even she could have imagined.

And she had imagined a good deal over recent days. Even as she did so, she tried to compare him with Marcus and wondered if she was being disloyal to one man and expecting too much of the other. But last night's passion did much to resolve that.

For several years, she had given everything to Marcus, for which she had been rewarded with a most wonderful child. She held on to Marcus's memory for Gabriel's sake and was willing to overlook the ways in which her husband had treated her most unkindly. But now, she considered that her remaining obligation was to raise Marcus's heir and never speak against the father to the son. That, she would gladly do.

But she was a woman as well as a mother, and deserved to live a joyous life with a man she loved. She need not have worried about expecting too much of Josiah, for he exceeded every measure. She trusted him. She admired him. She desired him.

"Is it already morning?" he whispered. She glanced up and met his gaze. His eyes were reddened and heavily lidded and she was heartened to realize he was as unaccustomed to late nights as she. Yes, he was a man to be trusted. "Why are you grinning? Have you never seen a man who looks like he's been in a shipwreck?"

"Is that what you would call it?" she said, and her smile broadened. "How very romantic. Well, I must look like a fair partner for you this morning. Is there seaweed in my hair?"

"There is indeed something. Hmm . . . it appears to be my cufflink. Well, no matter; you look beautiful." He shifted his arm and her head fell onto his chest. "I had hoped we might continue where we left off a few hours ago, but I believe it is already morning."

"It is not just any morning, for it is the dawn of Christmas Eve," she said, rubbing her hand over the hair on his chest.

"It would not be just any morning, even if it were dreary February." He paused and waited until footsteps outside the door passed. "But there will probably be much celebrating if we are discovered like this.

Our cousin will want a wedding by tomorrow."

"Because she is that anxious for us to marry?"

"Because she would consider it singularly efficient if she could combine Christmas and a wedding in one visit to London. And one visit to a church."

"Yes, there is that," Marianne agreed and nodded. He was not as soft as her pillow. "But all the better if you can manage to escape before Deirdre brings in my chocolate and biscuits. I need some shred of dignity before all the neighborhood hears the news from my servants."

"And a lady who dines on chocolate for breakfast deserves her dignity," he said, rubbing his hand over his eyes.

Marianne laughed. "Why, it is not all that unusual. What do you eat for breakfast?"

He stopped shaking the pillow and looked at her through splayed fingers.

"Do you not know what you eat for breakfast? You have been dining on herring and spiced sausage while at Parkside House," she added.

"Yes, but I suppose those are treats for Christmas. I am accustomed to oatmeal and cheese and an occasional serving of kippers. That will do for me," he said.

"You are a man of simple tastes."

"I am a man of very fine tastes, if our current situation is any indicator."

Marianne turned on him, prepared to challenge him on the use of the work "situation," when someone knocked softly at the door. Suddenly anxious, she slipped out from under her warm lover, and threw a cashmere coat over her naked body. She did not usually greet her servants at the door, but this was not a usual morning.

"Deirdre! Have I vastly overslept the start of Christmas Eve? What is the hour?"

Deirdre glanced over Marianne's shoulder, and then dropped her eyes to her toes. "It is very early, but Mrs. Bell asked me to wake you. The young master is feverish and crying for you."

Marianne grasped the door frame, certain she did not have the hardiness to endure the constant trials of childhood illness. And why should she, when every cough, every flush of fever, had the potential to take Gabriel from her forever?

"Wait here. I will get my slippers," she said.

"Do you need help, my lady?" Dierdre asked.

"No," Marianne said a bit too quickly, and closed the door.

"Is all well?" Josiah asked, turning on his side.

"All is not well," she cried, hurriedly pulling on the knitted shoes. "Gabriel is ill again, and is feverish. I do not think it is the mistletoe, as we have kept it away from him. Perhaps we should have kept it away from us. But you must go. I do not know how long I will be with him."

Josiah said nothing as Marianne reconsidered her words and how unkind they sounded. But this was not the time to explain them, to put some stops on an affair that was glorious but moving too quickly. At this anxious moment, her first loyalties were to a little boy, not the very big one lying in her bed. "I must go," she whispered.

"So you must," he said, and it sounded very much like a valediction.

CHAPTER FIVE

Josiah was both bothered and bemused to discover the odd places where his garments had spent the night. Confident that his stockings would appear in the general vicinity of each other, he nevertheless spent some time finding the match to the one stocking tangled in the bedclothes. He had discovered it dangling from the lampshade. Truly, it had been quite a night.

He knew what he must do this Christmas Eve morn, what a gentleman was required to do, but certainly what a man in love was compelled to do. Perhaps it would be best to run to Marianne's side to be with her as she cared for her baby. But there were practical considerations as well, and he guessed the shops would close early this day.

He had a Christmas gift for her, tidily wrapped in brown paper and tied with string in which he had inserted a sprig of mistletoe. Of course, she already expressed her disdain of the poor green flora, but he rather thought she'd enjoy his gift. After all, she had made it clear that handcrafted gifts were most appreciated. He did not know how to knit or paint flowers on china plates, but he was most skilled in another sort of craft.

He smiled as he slipped from the room, thinking that he had demonstrated some skills last night that he hardly knew he possessed. In fact, he had scarcely been tempted to demonstrate them before he came to Parkside House. Yes, he had an urgent mission this morning.

He was halfway to his chamber before he saw another person. One of the men dashed past him with a blanket in his arms, looking a bit frantic. The man stared at Josiah as if he had no idea how this person came to be in the house; it was not until Josiah arrived at his chamber and its small looking glass that he realized his buttons were awry and his ascot had gone missing.

"Did you lose your way in the storm, my lord?" Donovan asked, stepping out of the small dressing room. "You might have had need of one of your own maps."

Josiah started to unbutton his shirt. Having put himself together, it was time to undo his rough efforts at respectability.

"I found my way in this storm, Donovan," he said, as the man pulled off his jacket. "And no map was needed."

The throbbing migraine that threatened to paralyze Marianne on this blessed morning gradually diminished, along with Gabriel's fever. Her child's flushed face was now a healthy pink, and he slept easily in her arms. She rocked them both in the fine chair in the nursery, only once nipping the cat's tail under its wooden arc.

"Whatever do you suppose was the matter, Mrs. Bell?" she asked, unable to keep the last hint of fear from her voice. "Could it have been the porridge? He did not seem to mind drinking his warm milk just a while ago."

"The milk would have been soothing for him. It takes some of them that way, my lady."

"What way?" Marianne asked, tired and confused.

The nurse smiled, which did a great deal to reassure her mistress. "Put your finger in the lad's mouth, right in the center."

Marianne slipped her second finger between Gabriel's lips, and he began sucking contentedly. "Oh! I think there may be a bone or a pip there."

The nurse shook her head.

"Then whatever can it . . . oh." The happy truth dawned as slowly as had the late December day. "How very lovely. Gabriel has his first tooth for his first Christmas."

"It takes some babes with pain and fever. If he is a lucky lad, this first one will be the worst of it."

"Dear God. I hope so," said Marianne, and gently pulled away her finger. Gabriel yawned, and went back to sleep. "I do not know how I will survive the worry if this is to happen each time a little tooth appears."

Mrs. Bell lifted Gabriel from Marianne's arms. "Our mothers all survived it, somehow. Since the beginning of time, I should think."

Marianne might have argued that not every mother lived to see her babies mature, and not every father even lived to see his child born. But it was Christmas, and the day promised to usher in weeks of joy. And for the first time in a while, she had someone to share it with.

"Do you know where I might find your brother?" Marianne asked, walking in on Liliana and Isabelle. They sat in the parlor, close to the fire, and seemed to be twisting yarn between their fingers.

Her two guests exchanged a look, revealing nothing. "He must be somewhere about," Isabelle replied nonchalantly. "Perhaps he went for a walk."

Marianne glanced out the window, where the snow continued to fall at a prodigious pace.

"Oh, yes," Liliana said, sounding as if she had rehearsed the words. "He said he was going to the bookstore."

"On a day such as this?" Marianne asked. "I am sure the bookseller is warm at home with his own family."

"My dear friend," Liliana said, pulling a little yarn flower from her thumb. "When my brother is in pursuit of a book, he is capable of dragging the poor man out of his bed and demanding he open the shop."

Marianne winced, thinking she had been quite ready to pull Liliana's brother out of bed this very morning.

"You are blushing, Marianne," Isabelle said. "I hope it is not because of an indelicate reference to a man in his bed."

Marianne thought her face would now catch fire. "Not at all, Cousin Isabelle. You recall I am a widow." She walked to a chair in the corner of the room, far from the hearth. "Did he have a message for me?"

"The bookseller or my brother?' Liliana asked.

Marianne said nothing, but gazed steadily at her friend.

"Neither of them had a message," Liliana said, staring right back. "Do you need him for something?"

Oh yes I do. "I only wished to tell him that Gabriel is quite well, and his discomfort is nothing worse than the appearance of his first tooth," Marianne said. Then, seeing how obtuse her friends were prepared to be, "I speak of Gabriel, not of Josiah. And certainly not of the bookseller."

Liliana and Isabelle shared a glance.

"I thought Josiah might have been concerned because we awoke to the news of Gabriel's fever this morning." She regretted those words at once, and with good reason.

"You woke up together?" Isabelle asked.

Marianne cleared her throat. "Gabriel was crying quite loudly. I am surprised that neither of you heard him, but am grateful you did not. I would not want to be a poor hostess."

"You are proving to be an excellent hostess, Marianne," said Liliana. "The week is far more delightful than even I could have wished."

And Marianne knew why that was so.

490

"But Josiah said nothing?"

"Only that he had several errands," murmured Isabelle, and she and Liliana set about making their little flowers.

Marianne settled into the chair by the window and felt the chill emanating from the glass. Both her image in the glass and the chill were reflective of her own state.

Why had Josiah escaped the house on this, of all days? He knew how distressed she was to hear about Gabriel's fever; why had he not remained with her? Should he not have left her a note, informing her of his itinerary, so he could be reached if she needed him? What if Gabriel had been truly ill? How could she allow herself to trust a man, after being treated so unkindly by one she also thought she loved? Marcus had worn his indifference — even contempt — of her like a banner, and she thought she had learned her lesson. But it appeared her judgment was severely faulty and had not served her again. Once again, she loved a man who thought more of his own needs than of hers. She briefly wondered what was worse: a man who preferred other women to his wife, or a man who preferred his books?

The best that could be said is that few illegitimate babies were made in a bookstore.

Marianne pulled her shawl closer. She

really should move to another spot in the room, but she was in the mood to feel perfectly miserable. It was Christmas Eve day, and all of London was settling in for a festive respite, while she was still a sad widow with a fatherless child.

"It is very difficult to plan a wedding dinner this time of year," said Isabelle.

Marianne looked up at her. "Do you know someone who is to be married, cousin?"

"I believe I do, and should very much like to remain in town for the event. I prefer St. Martin-in-the-Fields above all of London's churches."

"But if the weather is a concern of yours, the location may not be congenial," Marianne contended. "There are many lovely local churches, of course."

"I like St. Paul's and should like to be married there," said Liliana.

"Oh!" said Marianne with forced cheerfulness. "We are contemplating your nuptials, then. And who is the groom?"

"There is none," said Liliana grumpily. "I never get to meet eligible gentlemen. My only hope doing so would be is if my brother decides to spend more time in town. But he already has an excellent tenant for the Kingston townhouse."

"Perhaps he shall live in another fine

home someday," said Isabelle. "And I shall be the first to ask for an invitation to visit."

Marianne sighed. Her friends' comments were as transparent as the glass on the window, or as transparent as it would be, if the snow had not obscured everything past her iron gate. The occasional carriage passed on Park Street, but no one approached the steps to her home. No one trudged along in the snow piled on the street.

"You can both visit me here any time you wish," Marianne said.

She watched them both bobble their heads in happy anticipation.

Josiah patted the breast pocket of his longcoat for the tenth time since he left Oxford Street, reassuring himself that his purchase was safe. He was quite lucky to have found it, for the item was being held for another, who decided not to make the purchase. His own choices, however, were now clearer than ever, and he had served himself well by going out this day.

But it was a most miserable day, cold and wet, and the streets slippery enough for even a careful fellow to take quite a tumble. He nearly did while he was once again checking the proof of his purchase, and decided he would ruin his whole intent if he allowed it to fall from his pocket and be swept up by a footpad who noticed how protective he was as he walked through the streets.

He paused and looked around him. Truly, he doubted even a footpad would venture out on a day like this.

Sliding in his water-stained Hessians, he made it to Park Street without incident. The steps had not been cleared for him, but then, the servants must be quite busy this day. And yet, he had a passing thought that his return to the house did not seem expected or welcomed.

This odd sense was confirmed once he was indoors. The butler did indeed appear to extricate him from his frozen coat, and his sister took that moment to pass through the hall.

"Ah, it is you, Josey," she said.

"Did you not expect to see me again?" he asked and grinned.

"I did, but the same might not be true for everyone," she said and walked away, as if her words would not matter.

He went into the parlor and found it empty. He next wandered into the game room, which he suspected had been Marcus Westlyme's sanctuary; it was deserted, as it usually was. Trying his luck, he ventured into the dining room, and he had the place to himself. Luncheon was a light affair, and one of the maids explained that the ladies were engaged in other things this day. He therefore ate alone, wondering if everyone else had embarked for the country without advising him of that fact.

Unless something happened to Gabriel? His blood went cold at the thought.

But he soon settled back in his chair, knowing he would have been told of such a thing as soon as he arrived. Nevertheless, his appetite was gone.

Deciding to spend the afternoon hours in the sanctuary of his chamber where, at least, he could converse with himself, he returned to the hall and the grand staircase. Marianne suddenly appeared from behind the great ascending wall, using a door that surely would only be used by servants.

"Lord Kingston," she said formally. Certainly far too formally for someone who had shared her bed with him the night before.

"Lady Lashton," he responded in kind. "I hope little Lord Lashton has recovered. I should not be surprised to hear he has sprouted his first tooth."

She was visibly startled, and perhaps a bit distrustful. "How did you hear of it?"

He smiled. "I did not. But I recall reading

495

about the development of children, and it seemed to me that the lad was at an age to expect such an outcome. Books are useful for many things, you realize."

"I do." She did not answer his smile. "And some people certainly prefer them."

He stood silently, not sure what she intended by her words.

"Please excuse me, Lord Kingston. I have much to do this day. We will have dinner earlier than usual, for I would like to have my son with me for his first Christmas Eve. It will not be as formal an affair as you might be accustomed, for there will only be the few of us in attendance." She glanced over his shoulder, suggesting she had a most dire need to be in the dining room.

"It has been many years since I enjoyed a formal dinner on Christmas Eve," he said, trying to reclaim her attention. "And perhaps I should not even say 'enjoy,' for I much prefer intimate family affairs."

She turned back to him. "Then you should be most satisfied, my lord. For your sister and our cousin will be at your side."

He wondered if now might be a good moment, an opportunity for him to say what he had been rehearsing all day, along with his prayer that what he asked of her would be accepted with joy and celebration. But something was wrong, and he did not know how to ask what it might be. He loved her and if he'd had any doubts of her affection for him, they had been most gloriously allayed last night. In the light of day, truths were often revealed, but he knew it had not been a dream.

"I am happy for it," he said. "For, at present, they are all I have of family."

"Well, then. I am pleased to have done the service of bringing you together, my lord," said Marianne. "Now please excuse me, for I like to have a hand in the plum pudding."

"Not literally, of course," he said, and forced a laugh.

She was quite serious. "Oh, yes. If I ever find myself destitute, I might be able to manage very well by hiring myself out as a cook. I have talents in that direction."

"You are a woman of many talents, Marianne," he whispered.

But it was the wrong thing to say; he saw resentment flicker across her face even as she turned away again.

Something was most definitely wrong. But he would be damned if he knew what it was.

She had lost him; that much was certain. But perhaps she had not ever had him, after all. Even worse, perhaps she did not want him either. By this day's events, he did not seem so very different from Marcus, for having had his moment of triumph, he was happy enough to abandon her and seek his enjoyment elsewhere. For Josiah, pleasures were to be found in a book.

"You have indeed had your hand in the plum pudding," Josiah said.

Marianne looked up from her place at the head of the table and met his eyes over the candlelight. He looked very elegant in a deep maroon jacket and a cravat so elaborately tied that it would confound any of her efforts to undo it. But, of course, she would not have the opportunity to do so.

It was Christmas Eve, however, and she would be a poor hostess if she spent the hours in a blue mood. And so she held up her right hand like a badge of honor, revealing the dark stains on her fingers.

"I should be lucky to remove these stains by Twelfth Night," she said cheerfully.

"Ah, I wish you had warned me," said Liliana, "for I have been invited to a winter ball. I shall be sure to wear gloves, lest they take one look at my hands and send me down to the servants' quarters." She held up her stained fingers as well.

Isabelle said nothing but waved her own

hand even as she forked her fish with the other.

Josiah looked from one lady to the next, clearly bemused. "I regret I was not invited to the baking party, for a man might learn a good deal from a bevy of talented ladies," he said. "Gabriel and I could have managed . . ."

"To make a mess of it?" Liliana teased.

Josiah made an attempt to look chagrined. ". . . to eat it all before it managed to find its way out of the kitchen."

"Then it is just as well," Marianne said. "For we would not be able to reap the rewards of our hard work."

Isabelle nodded. "It is great fun, but it is indeed hard work. I shall never again criticize my cook. And never quite look at a pudding the same way again."

They all laughed, and settled back into eating their Christmas dinner. Gabriel was quite happy to throw his food onto the fine Axminster rug and ignore the efforts of his mother and her servants to make a fine little gentleman of him. For his first Christmas, he was determined to be nothing more than a fine little baby.

When they had all had their fill, Marianne invited her guests to the parlor for coffee and chocolate, and reminded them that it was the custom of the house for the exchange of gifts to come this evening. Josiah promptly stood and came to her side to lift Gabriel from his high chair.

"My son has had quite enough for one night, Lord Kingston," she said. "His nurse will bring him to the nursery, and he will receive his gifts in the morn."

"But he and I have some gifts to bestow this night, for we have been planning this for over a week. We will not be long."

Gabriel reached up to Josiah, and wrapped his sticky fingers around his neck as he was lifted into Josiah's arms. The man held him comfortably on his hip, as if he was quite accustomed to the care of children.

"We will not be long," he said. "And will meet you under the mistletoe."

Josiah must have seen the expression of surprise on her face and amended his words. "We shall meet you in the parlor."

Fifteen minutes later, they were all assembled in the warm room, sitting companionably around the fire. Josiah set Gabriel on the rug alongside a tube of paper wrapped with red ribbon. The baby seemed perfectly content banging the tube against the leg of a chair, and chewing on the ribbon, occasionally looking up at Josiah for approbation.

"Please open my gift first," Liliana said, handing a flat package to Marianne.

Marianne carefully untied the package, and in a few moments, Gabriel had paper with which to play, and she had a delicately painted landscape of the pump room at Bath.

"I painted it before we came," Liliana said. "The three ladies near the window are intended to be the three of us, as we were years ago."

"How perfectly charming," Marianne said, as she handed her gifts to the others. She was a tad embarrassed now to present a box of fossils to Josiah. Rocks though they might be, they now seemed rather personal.

Josiah accepted his gift with obvious pleasure, and showed it off to Gabriel. Gabriel, however, was more interested in the wrapping paper.

"I have been impressed with the many talents of my cousins," said Isabelle, "so I have purchased gifts that might inspire some other talents. Liliana, here are several volumes of books from the authoress Jane Austen. I should so like a novelist in the family. And for you, Josiah, a case for your spectacles. I hope you are encouraged to wear them less often, and spend fewer hours at your desk." Isabelle handed him her package as if she were delivering an edict.

Josiah, in turn, presented Isabelle with a silver mirror, and his sister with a silk reticule. "I did not embroider it," he added quickly.

"And here is a red ball for Gabriel, and a new pen for my brother," said Liliana. "Though after this week, I believe they each might have a better time with the other's gift."

There was an awkward silence, during which only Gabriel expressed his delight with the growing pile of paper in which he might crawl. Finally, Josiah cleared his throat.

"Gabriel has something for the ladies, as well," he said, and handed them each a small tube of paper. Surprised, they each opened their gift to reveal scribbles on parchment. "He is learning how to make maps," Josiah explained. "We have not quite perfected the art."

Josiah interrupted their laughter by scooping the larger tube from Gabriel's side, and handing it to Marianne.

"I, however, have been practicing for years," he said. "Though Gabriel had a hand in it, as well."

Marianne accepted his gift, smiling even though she felt tears welling in her eyes.

That he would spend his time occupied with Gabriel, imagining he taught him some skill, and enlisting his help, belied all her thoughts of resentment and abandonment. She did not know why he had walked away from her this morning, but his manner suggested he intended to walk back to her.

She untied the ribbon and unrolled the tube.

It was a map. The little scrawls on the perimeter indeed looked like her son's handiwork, replete with tiny fingerprints and spills. But the larger image included markings clearly delineated streams and ponds, hills and valleys. The great meandering Thames was as clear as the Channel, and here and there were tiny sketched buildings, including one great edifice set in a wooded park.

"It is quite lovely, Josiah," she said, hesitating. Her dark blue eyes met his brown ones. "But I do not understand what it is."

He looked away to his sister and their cousin, as if he was not that happy to have an audience.

"It is a map," he said.

"Of course, I know that," she scoffed. "But of what? There is the river, and I suspect you have drawn in Hyde Park. Oh, yes, that appears to be Parkside House. You have gotten the initials in the gate with splendid accuracy. But why? Where does this road lead?"

He turned back to her, and tried to give them some small degree of privacy by turning his back on the others.

"It leads to me, to King's Stone. It illustrates the journey between you and me, with its highs and lows, bridges and barriers, until we find our way home. Will you travel it with me?" he asked.

She had no words, and even if she had, she was not certain she could speak them. She just gazed at him, with her lips slightly parted, and nodded her assent.

"What is it? What are you doing?" Isabelle demanded.

Josiah stepped aside, leaving Marianne feeling quite exposed. He smiled at Isabelle and Liliana. "I have made a map for Marianne, to find her way to King's Stone."

Isabelle gave a hoot of delight. "Well, at least that is settled," she said.

But it was not. At least, not quite.

Some time later, when they had all had their fill of chocolate, and the paper had all been scooped up off the parlor floor, Marianne sat with Gabriel sleeping in her arms, and Josiah close to her side. Liliana was already engrossed in her new book, and Isabella snored softly in her chair.

Josiah ran a gentle finger over the pert line of Gabriel's nose and paused at the tiny indentation at the apex of his lips.

"I should like a fine little boy like him," he mused. "But would have no regrets if I should be presented with a daughter, or even a dozen daughters."

Marianne laughed softly. "You would have a very exhausted wife. But I hope that someday you may get your wish."

He shifted in his seat. "I am an impatient man, and wish that someday would be now." He moved forward. "I would like for Gabriel to be mine. Yours and mine."

She knew what he was asking, and had wanted to hear such words from his lips. But something remained between them, something which she could not quite release.

"If you are so fond of him, why did you leave us this morning when you knew he was so ill? Why did you seek solace at the bookseller instead of with us?"

"The bookseller? Did I ever say so? No, I had an errand of a different sort, one that needed to be accomplished before Christmas Eve." He fumbled in his pocket, and withdrew a small box. "I prayed his ailment was nothing worse than a new tooth, but if

I seemed indifferent, it is only because I was thinking more of his mother."

He handed her the box and took the sleeping baby from her arms. "I have also found some rocks that I hope will give you pleasure."

Her hands trembling, Marianne opened the box, and pulled a glittering bracelet from black velvet folds. She held it up to the light.

"Name the gems," he said.

Dutifully, she placed a finger on each of the beautifully cut stones: "Amethyst, diamond, opal, ruby, emerald, diamond. They are beautiful, Josiah."

"And they spell?" he asked, as if an impatient tutor.

"They spell?" she questioned, and then, "Oh! A-d-o-r-e-d. Oh, Josiah."

"I adore you, Marianne, and I adore your little boy. I intend to love you both for all my years, if only you — the two of you — will have me."

"There is nothing else I wish for Christmas, or all eternity." All her foolish doubts were gone. "We are yours, Josiah."

He leaned toward her, and with the sleeping baby between them, they kissed.

EPILOGUE

Christmas, 1821

"The little chap deserves a more impressive name than 'Josiah,' " Josiah argued, lifting his new son from his wife's weary arms. Marianne sat in a cushioned chair, delighted to leave her bed, but not yet ready to greet guests who would soon be arriving to spend the holiday with them at King's Stone. She was happy to hand over the bawling newborn, who seemed to find peace in his father's arms.

But then, she knew how he felt.

"I think it is a very fine name," she said. "It suits his father, and I see a bit of a resemblance about the jaw and his eyes."

"What do you say, Gabe?" Josiah asked, looking down at his oldest son. He leaned forward so that the boy could better see his new brother. "Do you think the lad looks like a little Josiah?"

"Joe?" Gabriel asked, having never quite

507

given up the name by which he once knew his father.

"Yes, Joe will suit," Josiah agreed.

"But I prefer he not be 'Josey,' " Marianne said with determination.

"You will have to take that up with my sister," Josiah said, and looked to the window.

Liliana had spent the better part of the year with Isabelle at her estate in Surrey. Today, they were due to arrive with a young man about whom Liliana seemed most serious. Even more remarkable, another gentleman was to soon arrive, one who was already introduced to them as Isabelle's beau.

"It has been a most extraordinary year." Marianne said, knowing precisely what her husband was thinking.

"I could not have asked for a better one, nor a better gift." He rocked the baby gently in his arms.

"A new baby, of course," Marianne agreed.

"A new family," he corrected. "The map was drawn before I even recognized it, for it led me directly to you."

"And I, set adrift to find my own way, only awaited your arrival."

"So I did, and so you did, and now the

four of us have found our way home for Christmas. There can be no better end to the year."

If indeed there was, Lady Kingston could not imagine it.

ABOUT THE AUTHORS

Since her first romance novel came out in 1984, **Virginia Brown** has written over 50 novels. Many of her books have been nominated for *Romantic Times'* Reviewer's Choice, Career Achievement Award for Love and Laughter, Career Achievement Award for Adventure, EPIC eBook nomination for Historical Romance, and she received the *RT* Career Achievement Award for Historical Adventure, as well as the EPIC eBook Award for Mainstream Fiction. Her works have regularly appeared on national bestseller lists. She lives near her children in North Mississippi, surrounded by a menagerie of beloved dogs and cats while she writes. You may reach her at her website: virginiabrownbooks.com

Jo Ann Ferguson has been creating characters and stories for as long as she can remember. She sold her first book in 1987.

Since then, she has sold over 100 titles and has become a best-selling and award-winning author. She writes romance, mystery, and paranormal under a variety of pen names. Her books have been translated into nearly a dozen languages and are sold on every continent except Antarctica. You can reach her at her website: joannferguson.com or by email: jo@joannferguson.com.

Karen Frisch writes Regency romances for ImaJinn Books. She is the winner of the 2007 Writer's Digest Popular Fiction Awards, Mystery/Crime Category. An amateur genealogist, she also has two nonfiction genealogy books in print on tracing family history and identifying old family photographs. While tracing her family history as a teenager, she discovered she is a cousin of Edgar Allan Poe (removed by six generations). A lifelong resident of New England where she lives with her husband, two daughters, and two dogs, she is also a portrait artist. Follow Karen on her website at http://KarenFrisch.weebly.com.

Sharon Sobel is the author of eight historical and two contemporary romance novels, and served as Secretary and Chapter Liaison of Romance Writers of America. She has a PhD in English Language and Literature from Brandeis University and is an English professor at a Connecticut college, where she co-chaired the Connecticut Writers' Conference for five years. An eighteenth-century New England farmhouse, where Sharon and her husband raised their three children, has provided inspiration for either the period or the setting for all of her books.